The
LOVEDAY
VENDETTA

Kate Tremayne

The
LOVEDAY VENDETTA

headline

First published in 2010
by HEADLINE PUBLISHING GROUP

1

Cataloguing in Publication Data is available from the British Library

ISBN 978 0 7553 4768 1

Typeset in Bembo by Avon DataSet Ltd,
Bidford-on-Avon, Warwickshire

Printed in the UK by CPI Mackays, Chatham, ME5 8TD

Headline's policy is to use papers that are natural, renewable and recyclable
products and made from wood grown in sustainable forests. The logging and manufacturing
processes are expected to conform to the environmental
regulations of the country of origin.

HEADLINE PUBLISHING GROUP
An Hachette UK Company
338 Euston Road
London NW1 3BH

www.headline.co.uk
www.hachette.co.uk

None of my work would be possible without the love, support and understanding of my wonderful husband Chris

In loving memory of John Frost, a dearly missed brother

Acknowledgements

To my wonderful agent Teresa Chris who is forever an inspiration.

And my heartfelt thanks to the team at Headline for your encouragement and support and for being a joy to work with: Jane Morpeth, Sherise Hobbs, Celine Kelly, Jane Selley.

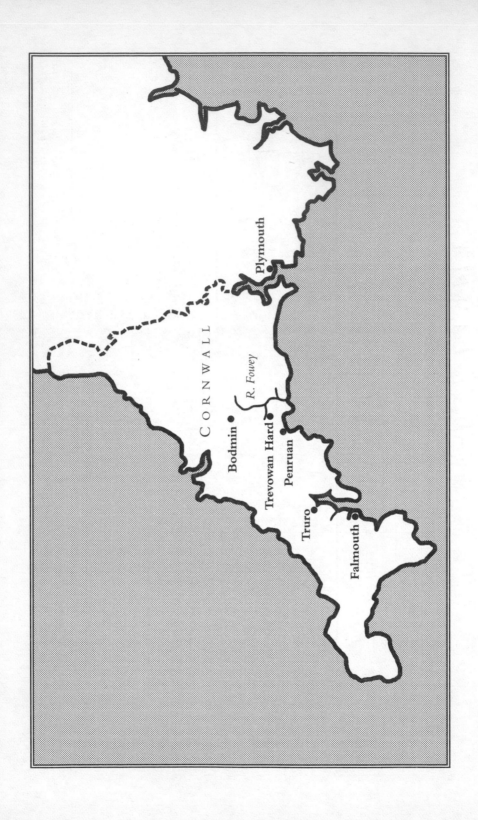

C O R N W A L L

Plymouth

R. Fowey

Bodmin

Trevowan Hard

Penruan

Truro

Falmouth

The Loveday Family

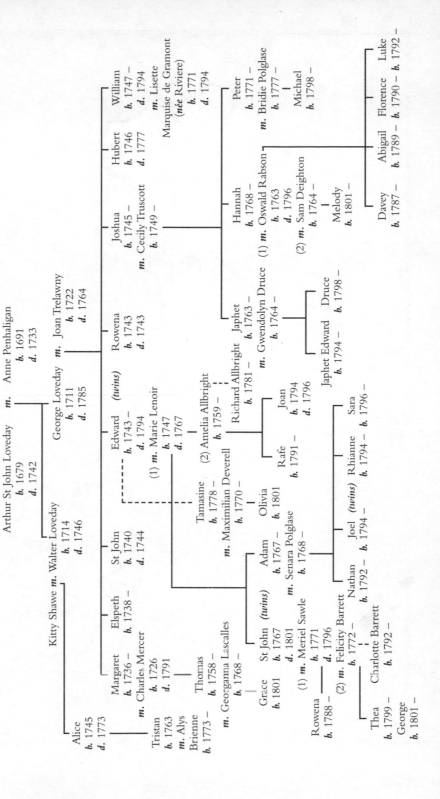

Prologue

The house was in darkness as the youth crept along the panelled corridor. He was careful to avoid stepping on any floorboard that would creak and betray his presence. Through the lattice window at the end of the upstairs passage the pale moonlight gave little illumination to his progress. Tonight, for the first time in his twelve years, his heart raced with a deep dark fear as he ventured through the familiar rooms of the home where he had been born. A home that had become a prison and a place of terror.

With every sense straining for any sound of danger, he kept looking back over his shoulder. The landing was deserted, but he was unable to shake the feeling that he was being watched or followed. His skin prickled like the time he had fallen into a nettle patch. To bolster his courage, he bit his lip so hard that he tasted blood, and every step aggravated the pain of bruised muscles and lacerated flesh. He pushed on through the discomfort, which had become an all too familiar companion at the end of every school term.

The sound of weeping was louder now. It had disturbed his sleep for nights, but locked within his bedchamber he had been powerless to investigate.

Tonight his gaoler had been careless, the smell of brandy heavy on his breath. Although the bamboo cane had cut more viciously into the boy's tender flesh, his punishment had been shorter, his attacker struggling for breath after his exertions. Yet his spent energy did not diminish the man's anger. He had continued to rage, the words barely coherent, and demonic in their frustrated fury.

'Curse you. Curse you all. You lie, but I shall break you. I shall break you both. One of you will talk soon. The treasure exists. It will be mine.' With a final vicious swipe at the boy, his stepfather

1

stumbled out of the room and slammed the door, making the linen-fold panelling on the walls shudder.

Alexander had crawled to his bed, burying his face in his pillow to muffle the sounds of his sobbing. That was when the distant weeping had penetrated his misery. There were also sounds of a door somewhere above him being hammered upon by angry fists, and screams demanding release.

He had hobbled stiffly to the door of his own room, wrenching its latch in frustration, expecting to find it locked. To his surprise, it had clicked open. In his rage, his stepfather had not locked it properly. On the landing Alexander hesitated, hearing the irate voice of Eugene Carforth bellowing orders downstairs. His hatred for his stepfather scoured his tortured body. One day that monster would pay for his evil. Then the outer door was slammed. Moments later a horse whinnied in pain, its hooves pounding as it was whipped to a gallop.

With the fear of discovery diminished, his courage became stronger. Carforth had ridden out. There was not a moment to lose. If Alexander's escape was discovered, his punishment would be even more severe the next day. He did not care. This was the first time he'd had a chance to visit his mother since his return from boarding school last week.

On the floor above him, the door was no longer being beaten, but the hysterical cries of a woman continued. 'Let me out! You can't make me do this.'

He recognised the voice of his stepfather's sister Arabella. He had not realised that she had returned from her visit to Spanish relatives. What had she done to displease the fiend who had brought terror to a once loving home? If he remained undiscovered he would try and speak to her later. For now his fears were all for his mother.

When he entered her bedchamber, he was greeted by soft weeping. He called softly to her, then held his breath, terrified at what he might find. The last time he had seen his mother, she had been lying unconscious at the foot of the stairs, his stepfather at the top, staring down at her, his hand still outstretched. The next day Alexander had been sent away to school.

A single candle on the bedside table lit the room. Even this dim light could not hide the shocking change in the woman on the bed. At least she was still alive. Every day of the last months he had feared to learn that she was dead. He thanked God that she had survived. But it appeared only just. The face on the lace-edged pillow was pale as the first fall of winter snow. The fair hair woven into a single plait draped across her breast had lost its thickness and lustre. At her side, leaning forward from a high-backed wooden chair, an olive-skinned maid was crying.

'Mama,' whispered Alexander.

The weeping stopped abruptly. The maid raised her head. 'Master Alexander!' She wiped her eyes and sniffed.

From the bed, a fragile hand was held towards him, and a weak voice crackled, 'My son. My beloved boy.' Then, as he turned from closing the door, his mother's stare travelled beyond him. Her lips trembled. 'It is not safe. He will come.'

'He is drunk and has ridden out,' Alexander replied, unable to keep the disgust from his voice.

The maid sneered. Josephina had served them devotedly for years, joining their household shortly after his mother was widowed. 'He will have gone to his whore. May they both be consumed by the flames of hell.'

His mother ignored the outburst. She beckoned her son closer and his hand was gripped and drawn to touch her sunken cheeks. The delicate beauty was gone, reduced to a skull mask. The trembling lips attempted a weak smile; only the orbs within the darkly hollowed eyes showed any of the animation he remembered: they burned with a love no suffering could erase. Her voice, although frail, was urgent. 'You must escape. Get away before it is too late.'

'I will not leave you, Mama.'

'I am not long for this earth.' The words trailed into a groan, and she drew up her knees as a pain ripped through her stomach, her face stippled with sweat. 'I am poisoned.'

Dread choked his voice. 'Josephina must summon a physician. Tell me where that monster has hidden Papa's sword. I will defend you, Mama. I will not let him near you. You shall not die.' He tossed a defiant stare at the portly maid. 'Go, Josephina.'

A fresh bout of weeping destroyed the maid's composure. 'It is too late. Do you think I have not tried?' She held up a bandaged hand. 'He thrust this into the fire when he found me trying to leave the house last month.'

'You know his evil, dear Alexander.' His mother entreated him with her eyes. 'I thought I would not see you again. You must flee. He must not kill you as he murdered your brother.'

He thought her illness had made her delirious. 'Howard died when his pony threw him, Mama. He broke his neck.'

'That is what he would have us believe. As he tried to kill me . . . and make it look like an accident . . . when he pushed me on the stairs. I survived . . . but my injuries put me at his mercy.' Her words were slow, the effort to speak making her gasp for breath.

Josephina explained. 'Honey was the sweetest and gentlest of mares. Why would she bolt? It was not in her nature. Thorns had been put under her saddle. Peters, the groom, told me. He went missing the next day and was found hanging from a tree in the woods. It was no suicide. He had a wife and child he loved. They were turned out of their cottage into the workhouse.'

Shock widened Alexander's eyes and fear ripped through him. 'I knew nothing of this.'

His mother held his hand tighter. 'I wanted to spare you. Your return from school must have been frightening for you. Has he harmed you?'

He hesitated. If his mother was sick unto death, he did not want to worry her. He loved her so much. A beating or two was nothing to endure if he could save her from unnecessary concern. She needed her strength to get well. She could not die. Must not die. She was still a young woman, only a few years more than one score and ten.

'I have been locked in my room for some misdemeanour,' he replied. 'Mr Carforth will not let me see you or talk with the servants. He was too enraged to lock the door properly after giving me a lecture tonight. I heard him go out.'

'You are a good and brave boy.' Mama stroked his cheek, her touch soft as a butterfly. 'I cannot rest knowing that you are in danger.' The effort to talk clearly tired her, and she closed her eyes. A tear seeped from beneath her lashes to trail across her ashen cheek, and then her hand fell to her side.

'How can I leave you when you are so ill?' he protested, reaching to take her hand in his. He willed his strength to flow into her body. 'I will fetch the doctor myself. I will tell him what you have told me. Carforth will be arrested.'

Mama shook her head weakly, and Josephina's voice trembled as she answered in her stead. 'He will not allow the doctor into the house. He will say you are a wilful, naughty boy who tells lies. It will be your word against his.'

Alexander held back from saying that the whip marks and bruises on his body would prove he was not lying. He would fetch the physician.

The pressure of his mother's fingers increased upon his hand. 'It is too late to save me.' Every word was laboured. 'Save yourself. Free Arabella from her room. She will take you away.' Her eyes closed and she struggled for breath.

Josephina cut in. 'Your mama must rest. You must do as she says, young master.'

'The doctor will make Mama well again,' he protested.

'You must go.' His mother opened her eyes, summoning the last of her strength in her desperation to convince him. 'I will die in peace if you are safe. Go far away. Kiss me and go. You must survive . . . Avenge your brother's death. This estate is yours.'

He threw his arms around her and kissed her cheek. 'I will first get the doctor. Mama . . . Carforth spoke of a hidden treasure.'

'He will not find it.' Her voice was so low he could barely hear the words. 'Your papa died before he could reclaim it.' Her speech had exhausted her and her face twisted in pain.

'What treasure is this, Mama?'

She did not answer. Josephina was fussing over her, pressing a glass of liquid to her lips, her voice harsh with insistence. 'If you know, you must tell him, madam. Is it not his right? Lean forward, boy, to catch her words.'

Alexander strained towards the prone figure, and tears flooded his cheeks. What did he care about any treasure? Mama's life was all that mattered. 'Do not die, Mama.'

Even as he pleaded, he felt her body grow still, her eyes staring sightlessly with their final entreaty.

Josephina remained turned away from him as she closed her mistress's eyes. 'Go now. It is your only chance. With your brother and mama dead, you are your father's heir. That fiend wants the estate and your wealth for himself. Do not let her death be in vain.'

He struggled in his grief to make sense of his mother's revelations. He stared at Josephina. 'What is this treasure?'

The maid shrugged as she straightened the bedclothes. 'A family myth, no more. Too many have died because of it. Go. Do as your mama says.'

An enraged scream from the upper bedrooms penetrated the grief cloying his mind. He demanded, 'Why is Arabella locked away? I thought she was in Spain living with an aunt.'

'He ordered her return. Like you, she has been locked in her room, in the north tower.'

'Why?'

Josephina dabbed at her red-rimmed eyes. 'She refuses to marry the man chosen for her by that devil. She loves another. A handsome man but without title or fortune. Your stepfather would starve her into submission.' The maid scurried around the bed and grabbed his arms, propelling him towards the door. 'Go now. There is little time. That harlot will keep your stepfather occupied until morning. Free Miss Arabella. I have packed the chests for just such an eventuality. Harte will drive you. I'll tell him to hitch up the horses.'

Alexander pulled back from the servant and stared disconsolately at his mother's corpse. He could not take in that she was dead.

Josephina shoved him roughly, hissing, 'It was her wish. Go. And in the future make sure that that devil pays for all the suffering he has caused that saintly woman.'

'What of you?' He paused long enough to ask. 'He will be furious. You will suffer.'

'I cannot leave your mama until she has been laid to rest. If he kills me, I shall die happy to be with her.'

'No, Josephina. Mama would not—'

She cut across his protest. 'I must stay to give you and Miss Arabella time to get far away. Tell Harte the baggage and chests are behind a screen in your mama's morning room. I smuggled a note to Arabella telling her to keep a travelling case packed with clothes and her jewellery, and to be prepared should the opportunity come to escape. There is a pouch of money in the baggage. It will pay for your passage abroad.'

Alexander sped towards the north tower, still too shocked to question the preparations Josephina had made. He assumed that his mother must have known for weeks that she was dying and had provided for his needs to escape the clutches of her husband. He

6

could do nothing to help her now, but he could save Arabella, who had always been like an elder sister to him, until she had been sent to finishing school and then to her aunt in Spain, where she was supposed to attract a wealthy grandee and marry. They must escape, and when he was a man he would exact his revenge on the tyrant who had tricked his beautiful mother into marriage and murdered his brother.

He reached Arabella's room. After a cry of surprise and an excited embrace, which he endured whilst he explained Josephina's plan, he was relieved when Arabella dragged a valise from inside a large wooden coffer.

'I am packed.' She was frantic in her haste. 'He will kill me if I do not obey him. I regret not being able to pay my proper respects to your mama. She was very kind and dear to me, but we must hurry. I do not trust Eugene. I will not be his pawn to riches. We go now.'

Alexander remembered little of their wild flight to the coast over the next four days. He was feverish from the brutality of his beating and the shock of his mother's death. Vaguely he recalled that they stopped only briefly when it was necessary to change horses and procure food. Arabella refused to get out of the coach, certain that her brother would pay an army of brigands to have them followed and captured.

The bumping and jolting was relentless as they avoided the main toll roads. Pain and fever blurred the journey. Even night did not stop their progress. Then, without warning, there was a violent collision. The coach swayed precariously, the door flew open. Arabella screamed and Alexander was pitched into nothingness.

When his senses returned, it was daylight. Strangers hovered over him. Every part of him felt as if he had been tortured. The pain was relentless. Terror gripped him. He did not know why.

Voices demanded his name. Where was he from? The fear was all-consuming. There was nothing but that swamping sense of horror. The certainty that death was stalking him. He welcomed the black tunnel that gave him peace.

Yet the voices did not stop their demands. The tunnel receded. He was dimly aware that he was in a room, in a soft bed, with a woman bending over him.

'Who are you? You have nothing to fear.'

But terror ravaged his feverish brain. Names eluded him. Places had no images or memories. His past was a blank. Only the shadowy world of pain, fear and unknown atrocities filtered into his mind.

Chapter One

May Day Eve 1805

Dearest Papa,

Why did you leave me? Was my love not enough? Was I too like Mama and you could not look at me and not see her betrayal? What could I have done to stop you taking your life? I, who loved you, thought you infallible; but others, older and wiser than myself should have seen your pain. They betrayed you and I cannot forgive them.

Oh, Papa, I need you so much. Everyone is against me. They do not look at me and see Rowena; they see Meriel. I am cursed with my mother's looks but it is not her blood that burns through my veins. It is yours, which drives me to prove that I am a Loveday – that my wildness is the heritage of men who would be conquerors, who rule their lives as they ruled the sea as buccaneers. Why will others not see beneath the image of my mother to the heart of Rowena?

I was so angry when you died, Papa. I hated everyone. What had they done to save you? They sent me away to school so that they did not have to trouble themselves over me. Only you would have understood. Only you truly loved me. Why did you forsake me, Papa?

When will this pain of missing you end? How can I show you that I am a worthy child of your blood?

Your devoted daughter,
Rowena

The handwriting with its extravagant flourishes and twirls ran together where Rowena's tears had fallen on the paper. This was the only way she could release her pain. The only way she could try and find an answer. The only way she could pretend that her father was still close to her and be proud that she could redeem the honour of their name.

She closed her eyes, willing answers to come to her. She had found a rare moment when she was alone and her stepmama and the children were visiting Aunt Cecily at the village rectory. She had declined to join them and had been accused of sulking when she had locked herself in the room she shared with her younger stepsister Charlotte, refusing anyone admittance.

The paper crinkled in her hand as tension ripped through her and the silence lengthened. No answers whispered in her ear. She was again forsaken. Following the ritual she always performed at these times, she touched the corner of the paper to the candle flame and watched it devour the words wrenched from her heart. At the last moment before her fingers were burned, she dropped the paper into a bronze bowl and stared at it until the flames died down and only ashes remained. She ground these to a fine dust with a wooden pestle, and then, opening the window, allowed them to drift on the breeze. With them went her simple prayer that they would travel through the ether to the afterlife, the words conveyed to her father. It was important that he should understand and not judge her.

No one else would witness the depths of her turmoil. Her pride would not allow her torment to be known. The words were the essence of her soul, her conscience, her way to make sense of all she had lost and to prove that she was not her mother's spawn; she was her father's daughter.

The next morning the shrill piping of whistles growing louder awoke Rowena with a start. She threw back the bed covers and cursed herself for oversleeping. The seeding had been completed in the fields and a day of merriment lay ahead. She had not intended to miss a moment of the May Day celebrations, which heralded the beginning of summer.

She ran to the window of Reskelly Cottage, threw it open and leaned out, the better to view the men and boys parading along the central street of Trewenna village. They were blowing cow horns or the pipes they had whittled from sycamore twigs. The sun was nestling in the treetops, where young leaves were covering the branches. Rowena squinted her eyes against the brightness of a cloudless morning, the growing heat rapidly dispersing the diamond droplets of dew as the shadows receded.

The village maids had joined the men. Earlier they had foraged in the wood for rowan and birch branches and hung them over the doors of their cottages to ward off evil. They had also woven mayflowers into garlands around their hair, and their laughter carried on the breeze.

At the head of the procession was a man dressed in a flowing cloak and robes. He wore a grotesque mask in the shape of a horse's head, his antics enticing the villagers to play louder and dance more wildly. Later the jack-in-the-green would join them and the real merriment of the day would begin, with wrestling and the men showing off their strength in a tug-of-war.

Rowena breathed in the scents of the dew on the grass and bread baking for the first meal of the day. She hugged herself to contain her excitement. May Day was her favourite time of year, and her pulses raced to be part of the revelry.

In the centre of the village green on the far side of the duck pond a maypole had been erected. The tree had been cut down yesterday from her Uncle Adam's land at Boscabel and decorated with a wreath of flowers at its top and coloured ribbons given by his wife Senara. Later there would be dancing, and with that thought, Rowena's lovely face twisted into a scowl. Not that she would be allowed to join in such common revelry, for her family considered her too old at seventeen for such unladylike antics. Her frustration burned more fiercely. Womanhood brought too many restrictions, when the music throbbed through her veins and set her feet tapping to its rhythm. At least in the afternoon there would be country dances, and no decree of convention would stop her enjoying herself then.

Rebellion deepened her scowl. She suspected that Adam's daughters would be permitted to dance around the maypole. Rowena hated the restraints now placed upon her, but she was wise enough to acknowledge the importance of safeguarding her reputation if she was to marry well. Her mother had been the daughter of Reuben Sawle, innkeeper and smuggler of Penruan. She may have married St John Loveday, but the scandal surrounding her later life, when she eloped with a wealthy lover, was still the butt of gossip in the county. Rowena had no intention of being tarred with the same brush. She had enjoyed the luxuries that had been provided by her father, and as a Loveday she was accepted among the polite society of Cornwall. She was determined to win the heart of a man of wealth and high social standing, but above all she would demand that her husband adored her. She did not want a life devoid of love.

Sharing a house with her stepmother and her half-brothers and sisters curbed the independence she craved; worse, women with no sense of adventure ruled it. After her father's gambling had lost the ancestral home at Trevowan, Grandmama Amelia had purchased Reskelly Cottage. Although Adam had ensured that the family wanted for little, Rowena resented the loss of Trevowan. And with a vengeance she hated the new cousin who had usurped them from the family estate. He was the one most to blame for her father's death. Tristan Loveday had plotted St John's downfall.

At least for the present Rowena was spared Amelia Loveday's censure and recriminations. She was in Bodmin visiting her daughter-in-law and two grandchildren. With mutiny still churning her mind, Rowena continued to watch the procession through the village. Behind her she was aware that Charlotte had stirred and risen sleepily from her bed, rubbing her eyes as she joined Rowena at the window.

The whining voice grated. 'Come inside, Rowena. Mama will be furious if she catches you hanging out of the window, and you still in your nightgown.'

'She may have locked the doors so that I could not join the village girls, but she cannot stop me observing their merrymaking.' Rowena continued to lean out of the window, the light breeze blowing her unbound blond curls around her face.

The window was at the side of the house, and she had a clear view of the double row of cottages, the church, rectory and village green. Her attention was drawn to a young man from the village, who had turned away from his companions and disappeared between two cottages. He emerged in the back lane that led down to the stone clapper bridge that forded the stream running past the garden of Reskelly Cottage. Rowena saw him from the corner of her eye and deliberately ignored his presence.

Jory Wibbley, one of the many Wibbleys inhabiting the local hamlets and villages, thought too much of himself. He was handsome enough for a labourer, and had an eye for the prettiest milkmaids and serving wenches. A year or so ago Rowena would have practised her wiles on him, but no longer. It was time he learned to pay due respect to his betters.

Jory had abandoned his sycamore flute and with his thumbs hooked over the waistband of his breeches was sauntering in her direction. When he began to whistle, imitating a skylark, Rowena giggled contemptuously.

'Listen to that coxcomb. He thinks he can summon any woman that way. I for one will not be skylarking in the hay with the likes of him.'

'Is that Jory?' Charlotte peered short-sightedly and dug Rowena in the ribs to press her face up against the windowpane. 'He is so handsome. He was exceedingly smitten with you not so long ago, and you were not so hoity-toity then with your company. I saw you walking back from the meadow with him last summer.'

Rowena had a fragile tolerance towards her thirteen-year-old stepsister, who was a timid, annoying sneak in her opinion. 'Little snoop, always prying. You saw nothing. He waylaid me, nothing more. Nothing happened, and if you tell lies to your mama, you'll regret it.' Charlotte's tattle-tales had earned Rowena more lectures and punishments than she cared to remember.

Tears glittered on Charlotte's cheeks. 'I would not tell Mama. You know I would not. You are mean and horrid.' She backed away from her stepsister, who often frightened her. Rowena was everything Charlotte dreamed of being but would never achieve.

As the sound of Jory's whistling became louder, Rowena flounced from the window and picked up a hairbrush to draw it through her tangled locks. 'Shut the window, Lottie. And you would do well to remember that I pay back with interest any who act against me. I am half Sawle as well as Loveday. And the Sawles ruled these parts with terror for decades, tossing their enemies' bodies into the sea.'

At the younger girl's horrified expression, she laughed. Charlotte was such an easy target to tease; there was very little pleasure in it. 'I am joking. You are such a goose, Lottie,' she placated. 'Your silly tears have made your cheeks and eyes puffy and quite ruined your looks. Hurry and dress. We will go down to the meadow and bathe our faces in the May dew, which will clear any blemishes from our complexions. Felicity cannot find fault with so simple a tradition, and we will remain in sight of the cottage.'

'You want to see Jory. I am not falling for your old ways and tricks.' Charlotte poked out her tongue.

'Charlotte, that is most unbecoming of a gentlewoman.' Felicity paused in the doorway, her expression stormy. She was in her nightgown and robe and her pale hair was in a single plait. 'Why can you two not be more forbearing of each other? Rowena, you have been back from the ladies' seminary less than a week and already you are encouraging Charlotte to act the hoyden. I despair that you learned nothing of the ways of refinement and ladylike deportment.'

'Your pardon, Mama,' Charlotte simpered.

Rowena remained silent, absorbed in untangling her hair.

Felicity regarded the older of the girls. Rowena posed, a picture of sweet innocence. Only there was little blamelessness in that young madam. Why must she be so provoking and lead dear Charlotte astray? 'And you would do well to remember all you have been taught whilst away, Rowena. Or you will be locked in your room until after the festivities.'

Rowena paused in her brushing and stood up to perform an insolent curtsey. 'I am no longer a child.'

Felicity sucked in her lips. 'No, clearly you are an ill-mannered young woman. And what are you doing up at this ungodly hour? Your loud voices have woken Thea and George.' To confirm this, George could be heard grizzling in the nursery. 'Since you are both awake, you will take charge of your sister and brother and keep them amused.'

'But it is May Day. The villagers are celebrating.' Rowena's eyes flashed with defiance. She resented being treated as an unpaid nurserymaid to her half-brother and sister.

Whilst Felicity continued her lecture, detailing all the disappointments Rowena had heaped upon her, the young woman blanked out her complaining voice. Thea at six was a snivelling crybaby and the image of her stepmother. At least at four George's tantrums showed a spark of spirit. He was constantly tripping over the long skirts Felicity still insisted that he was dressed in. He loved nothing better than to escape the nursery and explore, and was angered at being hampered by his clothing. During the heat of the day yesterday Rowena had removed them and he had laughed as he played on the edge of the stream at the bottom of the garden, slipping and sliding over the rocks. Felicity had been hysterical when she discovered them, screaming that he could have drowned. As if Rowena would have allowed harm to come to the mischievous lad. He had the spirit of a Loveday and Felicity wanted to crush it out of him. It was time George was in breeches and allowed to be a proper boy. Rowena did not want a milksop for a brother.

Felicity droned on, her words as irritating as a dripping water pump. 'And you may watch the dancing at an appropriate time when your chores and family responsibilities are done.'

'Cousins Abigail and Florence are coming into the village early,' Rowena announced. 'I arranged to meet them.'

'Then you can take Thea and Charlotte with you.' Felicity held up her hand when Rowena would have protested. 'Another word of insubordination and you will not be joining any dancing or feasting today. Now I suggest you get dressed and honour your duties.' She returned to her bedchamber.

Rowena dressed swiftly and twisted her hair into a chignon, leaving a long curling tress hanging to her shoulders on each side of her face. Charlotte dressed in a petulant silence.

'The least Felicity could permit is to allow us to bathe our faces in the morning dew.' Rowena snatched up the hazel circlet she had woven the previous evening. She would pick wild flowers to adorn it. As she flounced out of the room, she called over her shoulder to her sister. 'Are you coming, or playing the martyr here?'

'I do not wish to upset Mama,' Charlotte replied. 'We did wake George. I will tend to him.'

'No, the revellers woke him. Do as you wish.' Rowena ran lightly down the stairs and out of the back door before Felicity could see her.

Jory was leaning against a rowan tree by the stream. Angered at Felicity's demands, Rowena dismissed her earlier plan to ignore him. As she walked purposefully towards the stream, there was a sharp rapping behind her on an upstairs window. She did not bother to heed it. The fresh scents of the dew on the sun-dappled grass and the abundance of wild flowers in the meadows and hedgerows summoned the sensual and wild side of her nature.

Under the shade of the rowan Jory was grinning, his expression too assured, a lock of hair flopping attractively over his brow. With hair the colour of ripened corn, dark brows and piercing blue eyes, he was the most handsome young man in the five local villages.

When they had first moved to the cottage from Trevowan, it had excited Rowena to flirt with the older boy. By winning his attention she had shown the village girls that she was more beautiful than any of them. Her world may have been torn apart by her father's death, but her beauty and spirit had its own special power that made her feel less vulnerable.

When she noticed the mud on the knees of Jory's breeches and the careless way his shirt had been tucked into his waistband, she was less assured. How many maids had he stolen kisses from already this day? And more than kissing went on among the villagers revelling in the wood on May eve.

The transient pleasure of flirting with Jory was not worth the risk of banishment from the May Day celebrations. Rowena veered away from him towards the bank of the stream and stooped to run her hands through the dew and press her palms to her hot cheeks. A low interwoven fence marked the boundary of the cottage garden and the common land down to the river.

'A woman like you needs no aid to her beauty,' Jory said, and with a confident laugh leapt the barrier between them with an assurance that annoyed her.

Rowena kept her back to him and sauntered to where May blossom covered the hedgerow. She broke off three sprigs of flowers and spying some early bluebells also gathered these. As she rose, she felt his hand upon her waist.

She turned abruptly, her eyes dangerously narrowed. 'Take your hands from me.' She glared coldly at the grime ingrained beneath his nails. There was stubble on his jaw, and his movements were ungainly and his speech and manners uncouth. However had she once thought him attractive?

'Sweetheart, you know I am mad with adoration for you.'

'And every other foolish maid who falls for your false words.' She twisted away from him. 'You are trespassing.'

'High and mighty, bain't you, for a tavern-keeper's grand-daughter,' he sneered. 'Your ma were no better than she should be. Like mother like daughter, they say.'

She spun on the ball of her foot and slapped him so hard on the cheek that her palm stung. When he grabbed her wrist and would have jerked her towards him, she warned, 'I may be the granddaughter of an innkeeper, but I am also the granddaughter of

Edward Loveday, and you work as a labourer for his son. Captain Adam Loveday will have your hide and throw your family out of their home if you lay a hand on me. Release me at once.'

He dropped her wrist, his handsome face darkening with a scowl. It increased her anger. 'You may have forgotten your place,' she said in the clipped, cultured voice of authority that her years at the finishing school had instilled in her. 'I do not. I am a Loveday, and since you so crudely sought to remind me, my mother bequeathed me her Sawle blood. Neither family is known for forgiving those who act against them.'

She swept her skirts aside so that they would not be soiled by his touch and with her head tipped high walked regally back to Reskelly Cottage. Anger burned through her at Jory's assumption that she was no better than her mother. It was a bitter reminder how she was still viewed by those outside her family. It was also a timely warning. This morning she had discarded the years of etiquette and training to savour the wild calling of her blood. Such unruliness must be controlled. She had no intention of making the same mistakes as her mother. Meriel Sawle had been a scheming fortune-huntress who had seduced St John Loveday into marriage, but even then she had not been content. She had cuckolded him seeking higher riches, and would have died in the gutter if Adam Loveday had not shown compassion when she returned to Cornwall close to death.

Rowena had inherited her mother's beauty and St John's recklessness but had learned from her parents' downfall the destructive power of self-interest. The keen wit, pride and judgement of Edward Loveday also dominated her blood. She might not wish to bow to convention, but she had a healthy regard for respectability and the need to protect her reputation. She had the ambition to rise high and the determination to curb the spirited nature that could stop her achieving her dreams.

'I forbade you to leave the cottage.' Felicity confronted her as soon as she entered their home.

'I went only as far as the stream to pick wild flowers so that Charlotte and I can make garlands for our hair. I am now yours to command, dear Mama.'

'As ever, you have to do things your way and in your time,' Felicity fretted. 'Who was that you were talking to? It looked like Jory Wibbley. Have you no care for your reputation?'

17

'I have more regard for my good name than you give me credit for.' The retort was out before she could stop it, and she chewed her lip in mortification. 'Your pardon, why does no one have any faith in me? I have no intention of bringing shame to our name.' She walked away, calling to Charlotte, 'Once we have tended to George and Thea, I have the flowers for our hair.'

Felicity gasped at such an astonishing capitulation. Then her eyes narrowed. Rowena was a calculating minx, and too quick-witted for her own good. How could she trust this young force of nature? There had been too many wilful incidents in the past when a thwarted desire had revealed the wanton abandon that could make Rowena an outcast amongst society.

Chapter Two

Later that morning Rowena was holding court. It was how she liked to occupy herself most. Her years at the ladies' seminary had taught her deportment and social graces; her pale gold hair, hourglass curves and classical beauty effortlessly drew the attention she craved. A natural wit and vivid imagination ensured she kept her doting acolytes enslaved with stories and dramas of her own devising.

She was seated on the wooden seat in the centre of Trewenna village. Charlotte and a dozen village maidens and youths were spread around her. There was a blast of horns and pipes and a haywain decorated with hawthorn flowers and pulled by the two shire horses from the Loveday shipyard came into view. It was filled with the wives and families of the shipwrights. The men sang a shanty as they walked behind. Many carried stone flagons of ale and from their weaving step were already merry from their celebrations. The maids and youths shouted in excitement as they leapt from the wain and ran to gather around the maypole. A fiddler struck up a tune and they jostled in friendly rivalry with the villagers to claim a ribbon of their own as the dance began.

Behind the shipyard workers rode Captain Adam Loveday and his wife Senara. Their two daughters Rhianne and Sara also rode their ponies, but their sons were at boarding school and would not be home for some weeks. Not far behind them was a farm cart holding the servants and their families from Uncle Adam's estate at Boscabel. In their procession two men carried a cooked suckling pig impaled upon its spit. A small fire pit had been lit on the green, which would keep the hog warm until the feast was served.

As Adam and his family rode towards the rectory to join his uncle and cousins, Charlotte leapt to her feet to run after Rhianne. Senara waved to Rowena, who left her admirers, their adoration having served its purpose. Her stories had kept them enthralled and made it obvious that she had no interest in Jory, who since she had joined the revellers had been flirting with Willa Keppel, the crowned May Queen.

Now on her best behaviour, Rowena curtseyed to her aunt and uncle as they dismounted. Their servants were alighting, the men carrying two barrels of small ale to be stacked in the shade and broached later when the feasting began. Their cook Winnie Fraddon was instructing the maids to mount the suckling pig on its spit over the glowing fire pit. The smell of its roasted skin was a delicious appetiser for the meal later that day.

A shouted greeting from the other end of the village announced the arrival of Rowena's cousins Abigail and Florence as they swerved around the revellers and trotted briskly towards her. They had all been at the same seminary together, and Rowena preferred their company to the too-good-to-be-true Charlotte. In their wake rode their older brother Davey, their four-year-old half-sister Melody on her Shetland pony, and their mother, Rowena's favourite aunt, Hannah. Their ten-year-old brother Luke and Hannah's husband's ward Charlie were away at school.

Davey Rabson was now eighteen and had been eager to take on his responsibilities as heir to his father's farm. When Aunt Hannah was widowed, she ran the farm herself for several years until she married Sam Deighton, who was the guardian of his nephew Lord Eastley. With her new husband in charge of Lord Eastley's large estate in Devon, Hannah had made the difficult compromise of putting the farm in the care of a manager for most of the year while she and her family took up residence in Devon. They had returned to Cornwall as often as possible in the intervening years. Now she would stay here until Davey settled into his new life.

As Florence jumped from her mare, she could barely contain her excitement. 'I have been looking forward to this day for weeks. I love May Day. It is such a shame that the younger boys have to miss it.'

'Enjoy the peace while you can,' Rowena laughed. 'For the most part they are noisy, unholy terrors.' She smiled indulgently at her cousin, two years younger than herself. With her dark Loveday looks inherited from Hannah, Florence was the prettier of the sisters.

Abigail had the same dark colouring but the fuller features and heavy-lidded eyes of her father.

Aunt Hannah alighted gracefully. Rowena cast an envious eye over the mare she had ridden. The proud Arabian blood showed in the high carriage of her head and sleek muscles of her body. This was one of the mares raised by Hannah's older brother, Japhet Loveday, on his stud farm.

'Have Japhet and Gwen arrived yet, Rowena?' Hannah lifted Melody from her mount and set her on the ground. Immediately her daughter ran into the rectory calling for her grandmama.

'Uncle Japhet and Aunt Gwen are with your parents.' She dipped a respectful curtsey.

As Hannah impatiently peeled off her riding gloves, she added, 'How beautiful you look, my dear. That sprig muslin gown suits you. Make sure you do not break any hearts today.' She winked.

That was why Rowena adored Hannah. She had the irrepressible Loveday spirit, refusing to be bound by convention. During her widowhood she had confronted smugglers who had dared to use her land to hide their contraband. Despite now having borne five children, she was far from matronly, remaining an established beauty, with a sharp wit, charm and courage. And she was still as slim as she had been when she had been crowned Queen of the May before her first marriage.

Rowena asked, 'Aunt Hannah, may Abigail and Florence stay and watch the maypole dancing with me?'

'Give them a few minutes to greet their grandfather and grandmother and they will join you.' Hannah raised a dark brow and there was a glint of warning in her expressive eyes. 'I trust you have no intention of joining the villagers. That would be unseemly. There will be dancing enough for you and my daughters later.'

'Yes, Aunt Hannah,' Rowena replied with a demure smile, which broadened as Hannah entered the rectory. Florence was the first to reappear.

'I thought we would never get here,' she announced. 'Davey would not leave the farm until the morning chores were done and Mama insisted that we help him.'

'I would have thought Aunt Hannah would have higher hopes for you than learning farming ways to catch a husband,' Rowena taunted.

'She was happy as a farmer's wife,' Florence defended. 'She married my papa for love. After his death we would have lost the farm if she had not ensured the servants ran it smoothly. You cannot supervise that which you are ignorant of.'

'I meant no ridicule upon Aunt Hannah,' Rowena corrected but could not resist further teasing. 'Your mother is no shrinking violet. She would meet life head on in any circumstances. She even took on the smuggler Harry Sawle and won. Few men crossed my brutal uncle with impunity. Aunt Hannah is like no woman I have ever met.' Her admiration was sincere. 'Whether a parson's daughter, a farmer's wife or now the custodian mistress of Lord Eastley's estate until Sam's nephew comes of age, she is the personification of grace, dignity and pride. She is a true Loveday. She came to love Sam and would have married him even had he been no more than her overseer and not the grandson of a lord. We should all be so fortunate to find such love and wealth.'

'With your beauty, you will have no trouble marrying the man of your choice, Rowena,' Florence praised.

'Then she had better choose with discrimination,' Abigail taunted as she approached them.

The laughing figures of Rhianne and Sara ran to join in the start of a new dance and were each handed a ribbon. The three older cousins affected expressions of mild interest as they watched them weaving through their companions around the maypole. Yet beneath their elegant muslin skirts their feet tapped the rhythm of the steps.

'Look, the men are preparing for the tug-of-war between Trewenna and Trevowan Hard,' Abigail observed. 'After that there will be the wrestling. Will it be considered immodest of us to watch, or should we join our family?'

'Our uncles are coming out of the rectory. I shall stay until they tell us otherwise,' Rowena announced, daring the others to defy her. 'As in the days of jousting, we should support the workers of the shipyard against their rivals. It would have been more entertaining if it was still the fashion for a lady to give her champion a favour to wear in her honour, would it not?'

Abigail shifted uncomfortably but Florence giggled in alliance. 'And who would you choose as your champion, Rowena?' she mocked. 'Jory Wibbley?'

'Indeed not,' Rowena responded tartly. Another group of revellers had arrived and she was surprised to recognise several of the tenants from the estate at Trevowan. With them rode Tristan Loveday and his wife Lady Alys.

'What are they doing here? They must know that they are not welcome,' she bristled.

She stared across to where her two uncles were walking from the rectory and saw both their faces darken. Her eyes narrowed, glinting with venom. 'I hope they send that intruder off with his tail between his legs. The man is not fit for decent company.'

'Cousin Tristan is master of Trevowan, Rowena,' Abigail said with sad reasoning. 'Nothing can change that.'

'He is a thief and a murderer.' Rowena's hands clenched into fists. 'He stole our home and ruined Papa. My father would still be alive if not for him.'

Abigail put her hand over her cousin's fingers. 'What you cannot change you must accept. Tristan is still our kin.'

Rowena angrily shook off her touch. Her face was ashen and her body was trembling with hatred. 'If you side with him then you are no longer my friend. I hate him.'

'This is not about you, Rowena,' Abigail rebuked. 'It is about family loyalty. Mama says that whatever you feel in private is not for public gossip. If Uncle Adam and Uncle Japhet can be civil to him, then so must you.'

'My first loyalty is to Papa's memory,' Rowena defended fiercely. She glared across at the newcomers and was disconcerted to see that Tristan Loveday and Lady Alys had not come alone. Mr Bruce Trevanion and his younger brother, Wilbur, accompanied them. Wilbur bowed to Rowena and smiled broadly.

'I thought you would be pleased to see the doting Wilbur Trevanion.' Florence grinned.

A flush tinted Rowena's cheeks but her chin tilted in defiance. 'Not at the expense of suffering the presence of that viper Tristan. Uncle Adam should have run him through and had done with it.'

'That is not his way,' Abigail cautioned. Her own cheeks stained to poppy as her stare fastened upon the younger of the Trevanion brothers. 'Tristan broke no laws.'

Rowena continued to glare at her uncles, who had acknowledged Tristan with a terse bow of their heads but made no attempt to approach him. They also nodded to the servants and workers in the tied cottages of Trevowan who had served them during Adam's father's day. They would not place those who made their living at Trevowan in a position where they felt uneasy. A fragile truce existed between the cousins. They did not mix socially, but to the world they presented a united front, no matter the enmity that lay just below the surface.

There was another exception to their censure. The Lady Alys walked sedately to her husband's kin and there was reverence in both Japhet's and Adam's bow and greeting.

'It is a pleasant day for the festivities.' Lady Alys allowed her voice to carry to the curious villagers awaiting a reaction from the Lovedays. 'How much more entertaining for us all that the men of Trewenna, Trevowan and the shipyard now pit their strengths in contest than when just Trewenna and Trevowan joined in sport.'

'Lady Alys, as ever your presence brightens even the sunshine on this occasion,' Adam returned, and with cavalier aplomb raised her hand to brush it with his lips.

From a discreet distance, in a mocking rejoinder, Tristan swept his hat from his head and bowed to Rowena and her cousins. Florence giggled but Rowena deliberately turned her back.

Abigail mocked, 'Your histrionics are lost on him, Rowena. Tristan is too engrossed in talking with Bruce Trevanion to have noted your slight.'

Rowena ignored her gibe, intent now upon eavesdropping on Adam and Japhet's conversation as they strode to where the tug-of-war teams were gathered.

Adam ground out, 'Damned knave has ingratiated himself with the local gentry, and especially so with our newest Member of Parliament.'

'He is doing what each of us would have done in the circumstances,' Japhet replied. 'He married well and is using it to his advantage.'

As they passed out of hearing, the women emerged from the rectory and had no reservations in greeting Lady Alys warmly. Since Adam and Japhet had saved the life of the Lady Alys in France before she had married Tristan, her ladyship had refused to take sides against them and had been determined to build bridges between the three families through the women.

'Our men remain wary as fighting cocks,' Gwendolyn sighed. 'At least their truce stands in public. Much of that is owed to you, my lady.'

'Male pride and family stubbornness,' Lady Alys replied with a smile. 'In France they put aside their hostilities when we were all under scrutiny by Napoleon's Minister of Police for our work for the British government. They overcame their hostilities then for the good of England, and I cannot forget that Adam and Japhet also saved Tristan after he was attacked by my benefactor when he betrayed our cause.'

Senara added, 'Fate brought you all together in your work for our country and your desire to bring old enemies to justice. An almost unholy bond, but it did prove that despite our husbands' rivalry, they would all rally together in times of danger.'

Lady Alys sighed. 'A pity they cannot put the difficulties of the past behind them. I lost my own family in the political upheaval in France. A united family is the background of society and can overcome all adversaries. This erosion within does no one any credit.'

'I agree,' Gwendolyn stated. 'But family loyalty aside, there is still stubbornness and pride that drives our men. We can but continue our role as peacemakers.'

Wilbur Trevanion cut through the revellers towards Rowena with the unerring speed of an arrow. Florence tweaked Rowena's gown, getting her to turn round. 'Here comes your adoring beau. He looks as though he has lost none of his ardour. Will we be celebrating your betrothal before the end of summer?'

'Mayhap I would cast a wider net than Wilbur Trevanion,' Rowena parried. She did not mean to reveal her true intentions to anyone. To set your cap at a man who then spurned your affections would be the ultimate humiliation. Her tone was flippant. 'He is a younger son. Though he is handsome enough to turn many a maid's head.'

'If you do not want him you should not encourage him,' Abigail snapped.

'Ah, has the dashing Wilbur found favour in your heart?' Rowena eyed her shrewdly.

'He is handsome and charming. All you want is for every man to fawn at your feet. It is mean, Rowena.' Abigail returned with a betraying heat.

'Jealousy ill becomes you,' Rowena replied and turned her most dazzling smile upon Wilbur Trevanion as she skimmed a brief curtsey. He was one of the county's most eligible men.

Wilbur blushed, his smooth cheeks and finely accented features boyishly attractive. Yet he was no boy, but a young man of one-and-twenty, who had stolen a kiss or three from Rowena. His build was tall and muscular from his rugby-playing days at school. The thick curl of his honey-brown hair flopped over amber eyes that were ringed with scandalously long lashes. A woman would have to possess a stony heart indeed not to be affected by the handsome looks and accomplished charm of the brother of Bruce Trevanion, squire of Polruggan Manor.

Wilbur bowed to the three cousins but his gaze barely noticed the younger two as it fixed upon Rowena. Florence glanced anxiously at her sister, aware that Abigail was infatuated with their neighbour. There was a bleak hopelessness in Abigail's eyes that saddened her.

Chapter Three

Felicity had finally emerged from Reskelly Cottage. Charlotte ran ahead clutching George's hand as they headed towards their cousins. Felicity did not approve of the May Day celebrations. She attended out of duty, as the rest of her late husband's family would be gathered in the village. Her displeasure rose at seeing Wilbur Trevanion flirting with Rowena. She also cast an anxious glance across to the dancers and the rowdy men preparing for the tug-of-war. Adam and Japhet were laughing and conversing with the villagers. What were they thinking, allowing the girls to be unattended, especially on a day like this, when men were in their cups? May Day was the bawdiest of festivals, linked as it was with the old rites of fertility. They should be more diligent than ever protecting their offspring, for far too many women found themselves disgraced and were hurriedly married before harvest time.

When she noticed the men of Trevowan lining up for the first contest of strength, her discomfort increased. Their presence was a reminder of all she had lost and the humiliation she was now forced to endure. Upon spying Lady Alys chatting with Senara and Gwendolyn, the pain twisted deeper into her heart. If Lady Alys attended, then that scoundrel Tristan would not be far away. Felicity faltered. That was too much for her to tolerate.

She shuddered as she heard the despised cousin shouting encouragement to his workers as they took hold of the rope against the men of Trewenna and braced themselves for the first pull.

She was further mortified to discover that Bruce Trevanion was with Tristan's party. Was there to be no reprieve from the shame heaped upon her this day? She had thought he was her friend, and since he knew how she felt about the usurper of Trevowan, she felt

27

betrayed by his choice of company. There was a time when she had begun to hope that Bruce Trevanion would be more than a friend and neighbour. Yet as the months had slipped by after St John's death, she feared that she had been mistaken in his intentions. Even so, she dared to hope that his feelings were deeper than friendship. He regularly brought his daughter Tegen to play with Thea, and did not such a young child need a mother? Bruce had been a widower for some years. His name had never been linked with another woman, though many had speculated upon his intentions towards Felicity.

He had been elected to parliament shortly after he moved into Polruggan Manor, and was away from Cornwall for several months of the year. There must be many accomplished and beautiful women in London to claim his attention, and who would want a widow with three children of her own?

To Felicity's dismay, her vision blurred with tears. She brushed them angrily away. Both her marriages had been unhappy; both husbands had been self-centred and her love had quickly faded. The first had been a drunk, the second an obsessive gambler. Neither had provided her with an income that could furnish all her needs and those of her children. If Amelia had not given her a home, her circumstances would have been severely straitened.

Despite her resolution to be brave and show nothing of the turmoil and insecurities that still confounded her, her courage failed and she turned and hurried back to the cottage. She could not face the shame of the reminders Tristan's presence here raised. She would never acknowledge or receive him for the infamy he had levelled upon herself and St John. She alone of the Loveday women had cut Lady Alys's attempts at reconciliation. Whenever Tristan appeared, the gossips loved to resurrect old scandals.

The solid oak of the cottage door was a blessed barrier against spying eyes, and she leaned against it momentarily. Outside, the banging of drums and blowing of horns was broken by the cheers of the men shouting support for the teams now contesting. A deafening roar became a chant of victory for Trevowan. As ever, the rivalry was intense.

'Enjoy your victory. It will be short-lived,' shouted Ben Mumford, the master shipwright at the yard. 'You'll not fare so well against us.'

Felicity covered her face with her hands. Always there was rivalry between the men of the old estate and those of the shipyard. Each had to prove that their master was the champion.

'Men and their battles,' she groaned. 'What does it serve but to inflate their sense of self-importance and bring misery to their women?'

The next shout was to proclaim the victory of the shipyard over the estate. The shrill blasts on the horns and whistles set her head throbbing. She groped for the smelling salts in her reticule and inhaled deeply. The acrid aroma made her eyes water and her nose sting, and as it hit the back of her throat, she coughed.

There was a lull outside, then the villagers began to chant for Trewenna as they took their places against the yard. Safe inside the cottage, Felicity slumped into a chair. The years had not lessened the pain of her humiliation at losing her home; her son denied his birthright by deceit and trickery. She wiped away a traitorous tear. For the sake of her children she must be strong. She had always known she was not as resilient as the other Loveday women, but she certainly did not want them to see her weakness and vulnerability. She had tried so hard to be more like Amelia, her stepmother-in-law, whose own sensibilities struggled to accept the scandal and the lack of convention that infected the Loveday family. But Amelia was less beholden to her kin and was financially independent. Their neighbours also respected her, as she had been the wife of the estimable Edward Loveday, unlike Felicity herself, who had married the wastrel who had brought them close to ruin.

Felicity stiffened her spine. She despised self-pity. Tears were an indulgence that solved nothing and she certainly did not want others to witness them and regard them as a further weakness. Drawing several calming breaths, she dabbed at her eyes and rose to regard her reflection in the elegant Venetian mirror above the mantel. Her blond hair was thick and abundant, but widowhood had created lines around her eyes and mouth, thus marring the fragile beauty of her younger years. Yet even modesty did not prevent her accepting that for a woman in her early thirties, her features were still attractive and her figure trim. The swollen redness of her eyes made her frown. She must bathe them before she faced the villagers. At least when she ventured forth again she was prepared for the embarrassment that she must overcome.

A rap at the door made her start, and she hastily wiped a stray tear from her cheek. When the door opened and Bruce Trevanion filled the portal, calling her name, her heart jolted. Instinctively she bent her head to hide the ravages of her tears.

'Mr Trevanion, I thought your duties in the House kept you in London until the summer recess? This is an unexpected pleasure.' She was flustered that he had not waited for the door to be opened for him. Was that not a sign of the high regard in which he placed their acquaintance?

'Your pardon, I seem to have intruded at an inopportune time, Mrs Loveday. You are overset.' His voice deepened with concern.

'No, not at all. The wind blew some grit into my eye. It has gone now.'

'Would you then allow me the pleasure of escorting you to the celebrations? Tegen is with Charlotte and her cousins.'

Felicity's heart gave a traitorous leap. For him to so publicly act as her escort would set tongues wagging concerning his intentions. Had he missed her during the long months in London? People would already have noted that he had called at the cottage.

'That would be most acceptable, Mr Trevanion.' She was grateful at his consideration. It would be easier to face the villagers with him at her side. She gathered up her gloves and allowed him to place her pelisse over her shoulders.

When his hands did not linger upon her shoulders, she was unexpectedly disappointed. Just a second or two would have been reassuring after so long apart. Though except for today entering her house unannounced, he had always acted the perfect gentleman.

At the door she hesitated, saying with some anxiety, 'I saw you arrive with Tristan Loveday and Lady Alys. I have no wish to join their company. Perhaps it would be better if we did not socialise today.'

'I met your late husband's cousin on the road. It would have been impolite not to travel with him. I would hate to think that my acquaintanceship with him sours our friendship. Too many estates are won or lost through misfortune. I prefer to be on good terms with all my neighbours. Tristan Loveday broke no laws.'

She suspected a gentle reprimand within his words and became defensive. 'I however cannot forgive him, and ask only that you respect my sensibilities.'

'I understand your distress, Mrs Loveday. Your family have been remarkably restrained in their acceptance.'

It was enough to reassure her, and she conceded, 'Enough scandal has been caused without us adding to it.'

He offered his arm and she accepted it. She had suffered too many restrictions at the hands of Tristan Loveday and had no intention of allowing him to blight her friendship with Bruce Trevanion. The heat of Mr Trevanion's body penetrated the fine muslin of her gown and beneath her fingers the muscles of his arm were strong and supportive. Her heart was beating beneath her corset with suffocating intensity. The warmth of his smile lifted her spirits. Surely it was not foolishness to hope that friendship was the very least he intended for their future.

In his company she presented a smiling face to the village, though the flow of beer had made the shipwrights and the Trevowan servants argumentative. The tug-of-war match would have descended into a brawl had not Adam hastily intervened. The servants on the old estate resented the ease with which the shipwrights had beaten them.

'This is a friendly competition,' Adam warned Isaac Nance, the estate manager. 'If you wanted a fight you should have taken on the fishermen at Penruan, who are also old adversaries. It is the parish where you worship, just as we attend Trewenna church.'

'Estate has always competed against the shipyard.' Isaac's son Dick squared up to Jim Mumford, the cousin of the yard's master shipwright.

'But in friendly rivalry.' Adam stood between the two opponents. 'Our women are present. I will not have them witness old scores being settled in such a brutal manner. If this conduct continues, I shall ensure none of my men take part.'

'It were just a bit of harmless fun.' Isaac Nance put his hand on his son's chest to restrain him.

Adam dropped his voice. 'We all know it was more than that. If anyone wants to make a fight personal, take it elsewhere.'

Felicity had been holding her breath throughout the confrontation and did not relax until the tug-of-war was over. Then the wrestling began and she made her excuses to join the women. 'You will enjoy your sport the more in the company of your male friends. Thank you for escorting me to the green. I shall keep an eye on Tegen for you. She is happy with Charlotte.'

Trevanion tipped his hat in salute to her. 'Your company is always a pleasure, dear lady.'

Felicity paused before walking away, and glanced towards Rowena and the crowd gathered around her. 'I am not so sure that your brother Wilbur should spend so long with Rowena. It would not do to cause unnecessary gossip. He has been with her for the last hour.'

'There are other neighbours he has neglected. I will remind him.'

The men gradually broke into their different groups, and their women who had no wish for a time of merriment to descend into a drunken brawl pulled their partners away to join in the country dancing. In the shade of the trees trestle tables were being put up and plates of food prepared by the villagers were being laid upon it. Winnie Fraddon gave orders for the food brought from Boscabel to be shared. There were several large cakes and delicacies, which the children were eager to devour. The men had gathered on the far side of the green, and with Reverend Joshua Loveday, Japhet, Adam and Tristan in attendance until the end of the wrestling, no further disturbances marred the pleasure of the afternoon.

The smell of the roasted suckling pig being carved soon had lines forming to enjoy the fare. The ale and cider kegs were drained and several of the men were sleeping off their excess whilst Mo Merrin kept the dancers on their feet with the music from his fiddle.

Abigail watched Rowena flirting with Davey and Wilbur and whispered harshly to her sister, 'When will Wilbur realise that she has no interest in him? He follows her around like a lost puppy. Jory Wibbley has tried twice to gain her attention and she will have none of him either.'

'Jory would never be considered an apt suitor,' Florence replied. 'Rowena likes Wilbur.'

'She will break his heart,' Abigail returned. 'It is all a game to her.'

Wilbur had been trying for an hour to get Rowena alone. Finally he succeeded when Hannah called Abigail to join the women and children who were eating seated on a quilt spread under the shade of a tree. Felicity was beckoning to Rowena, but she had chosen to disregard the summons.

'What have I done to offend you, Rowena?' he implored. 'I thought we were friends.'

'We are. But many of my relatives are here today. And you should be mixing with *your* kin. People are watching us with too much curiosity.'

'Why are you suddenly cold towards me?'

'Is that what you think? Oh Wilbur, it is not you. It is Felicity. Do you not see how she watches my every move? She is waiting for me to act inappropriately. It is her fault I was banished from my family and sent away.'

'You were with Abi and Flo,' he reminded her sharply. 'Was that such a hardship?'

Her expression darkened, her eyes shot through with amber lights of fire. 'I like you, Wilbur, but you make it difficult for me. You must stop following me. You are too obvious. I will not risk my reputation.'

'But I worship you.' He grinned, refusing to take her seriously, and reached for her hands, holding them tightly. His touch sent a warning heat through her body. She stiffened and angrily shrugged out of his grasp.

'This is exactly what I mean. You treat me like a hoyden. I will not tolerate it.' Her indignation was whipped to cover her embarrassment. She did like Wilbur. He was one of the most handsome young men of her acquaintance. Her heart had an uncanny way of dancing a quadrille when he was near her, but that was because he was outrageous in his compliments. His attention made her aware of the effect she could have on men, and it was invigorating. It was also dangerous. 'I promised Mama that I would look after George. I have been neglectful in my duty.' She hurried away.

Felicity was displeased that Rowena was deliberately ignoring her siblings. Yet while Cecily was sympathetic to her complaints, Hannah and Senara dismissed them, insisting that it was a time when the older children should enjoy themselves. Unconvinced, she continued to monitor her stepdaughter. Wilbur Trevanion had stuck to her side like a burr and the villagers were beginning to gossip. Even now, when Rowena had left him, he was wearing his heart on his sleeve as he stared forlornly after her.

She remained uneasy when Rowena joined Hannah, who was mending Melody's garland as her daughter sat on her lap. Thea and

George were with her. There was no reprimand from Hannah. Rowena clapped her hands and sang to make the children laugh. At least her stepdaughter was being dutiful now.

Felicity turned her attention to another person who had not been so diligent in his attendance on her as she would have wished. Bruce Trevanion was laughing and clearly enjoying a conversation with Japhet and Adam. As though he had read her thoughts, he detached himself from Japhet and came over to the women. He smiled and bowed to them graciously. 'Dear ladies, your pardon, but I have to take my leave now.'

'So soon?' Senara objected.

'I have a prior engagement with the Rashleighs in Fowey.' He allowed his eyes to hold Felicity's for a long moment, and she was certain there was regret in their shadows.

She took encouragement from that. Now that he had returned from London, there would be many days when they could further their friendship. That crumb of comfort did not last beyond her spying him leaving with Tristan and Lady Alys. Was the hated interloper inveigling his way into the company of the most prominent members of their community by his friendship with Trevanion? Was that what Bruce had meant when he had questioned her antagonism towards Adam's cousin?

Frustration swirled through her and she blinked rapidly to dispel the sting of tears. Had Tristan not heaped enough humiliation upon her that her friendship with Bruce Trevanion was also to be tested?

Her spine stiffened. She could feel the speculation of too many eyes upon her. The gossips would be feeding off more juicy tidbits than just suckling pig after this day was over.

Chapter Four

The summer term dragged endlessly for Bryn Loveday. Impatience had burned fiercely in him for weeks as at first shadowy images, and then more distinct faces and places emerged through the veil that had hidden the memories of his childhood from him for so long. Ever since he had been in a coach accident and had been found unconscious by the Lovedays, his name, home, background and family had been lost to him. The coachman and the young woman who had been accompanying him had died in the accident. Adam Loveday had given him a home but despite extensive enquiries had been unable to discover his identity. All Bryn was aware of about those early years was a feeling of loss and an abiding sense of fear.

There had been times when a voice or figure triggered recollections from the past. The sight of a man beating a servant had conjured a single name, Carforth, but the fear that had swamped him with the memory had left him too terrified to reveal it to his guardian. Though his years with the Lovedays and their children had been happy, there was a certainty that haunted him that the night of the accident, he and the woman had been fleeing for their lives. That there was only danger behind them and that all those who had loved him were no longer alive.

He had written the incident down in a diary that he kept hidden. Over the years, if a name or a face was revealed to him, or even some item, event or feeling, he noted them down or drew sketches. Yet until a few weeks ago, nothing had opened a door on his memories. Then the name Willow Vale echoed through his dreams. He kept visualising a turreted dwelling surrounding by trees. There was also the name Josephina, and a misty image of a short, bustling middle-aged woman bending over a canopied bed and crying. The woman she tended was beautiful as an angel, and each time he recalled her face, a warm spread of longing heated his body, followed by a pervading chill of loss. He was certain that this woman was his mother and that she had been dying. He suspected that both his parents were dead, and also any close relatives. That was the only explanation he could think of why no one had answered Captain Loveday's notices in the news-sheets or instigated a search of their own for a missing boy.

Fragments of new information whirled through his mind as he struggled to remember any facts from his childhood. The images of Willow Vale were the most persistent. It was as though it was calling to him. A large house with many rooms and surrounded by gently sloping hills was conjured in his mind, and also a vast barren stretch of land that had to be crossed. Terrain where herds of deer rutted in the valleys. Was it a moor? he wondered. Not Bodmin, which he knew so well from his years in Cornwall, or Dartmoor, which he had visited last year when they had journeyed to Dorset to visit his guardian's half-sister. But there was wildness and a sense of isolation about the landscape.

He had pulled out maps from the school library and instinct had convinced him his home had been near or within Exmoor. He was certain it had not been near the sea, for he had no recollection of its distant roar or the wind carrying the scents of seaweed or salt. The mystery was his constant companion and the need to solve the riddle of his childhood too persistent to deny. He was no longer a boy but a young man attending his last year at school. There still remained an uncertainty about his age, but although Captain Loveday had thought when he had first found him that he was about ten, in the last three years he had grown to over six feet and prominent stubble coated his jaw every morning. During his last break in the school year, Senara had considered that he was nearer in years to seventeen than fifteen. He had stayed on at school with the younger Loveday boys, expanding his learning. He intended to enter Cambridge, and if he had to earn his living, wanted to take up the law.

But the urgency to complete the puzzle and discover his past and identity would not give him peace, and his customary caution deserted him. Adam Loveday had trained him together with his own sons in the gentlemanly arts of fencing and pugilism and he was an excellent shot. The fear that had haunted his childhood no longer daunted him. He would face without qualms any challenges in order to secure his future. The mystery of his past could no longer be ignored. It must be resolved. He was determined that whatever evil and sinister intentions had been the instigator of his childhood terrors, and also whoever was responsible, would answer to him and pay the consequences for those actions.

He had decided that he needed to be certain that his hunches had been right. That Willow Vale existed. If he could find his old home, he was convinced that his memory would return. Once the decision was made, he could not wait until the end of the term.

Bryn spent the evening writing a difficult letter to his guardian, promising that he intended only to visit the place where he believed he had once lived and learn about the family who had resided there. He expected to return to Boscabel by the time Nathan and Joel arrived for the summer. He packed a portmanteau with enough clothes for his journey and beside his sleeping friend left a note to Nathan Loveday asking to have his school chest transported with their luggage, and the letter to Captain Loveday explaining his quest.

When studying the maps of the West Country he had carefully planned his route, and he left the school at first light before the masters or servants were about their business. He had saved enough money from the generous allowance given him by Adam to pay for his food and lodgings and the hire of a horse for his travels.

As the door of the school closed behind him, excitement sent his pulses racing. Finally he would learn the truth of the wild flight across England that had taken the life of the woman who had travelled with him and stripped him of his identity. His dress, speech, education and manners at that time had been those of cultured youth. But was he from a family of means or was he a pauper? Yet that was not what drove him. It was time for the truth to be uncovered, and no matter what he unearthed, this adventure would shape his destiny.

For an hour he walked along country lanes to the main highway. The dawn chorus had sounded like a fanfare heralding the start of moulding his future. Twice deer bounded across the track ahead of him, and a fox broke cover and jumped a dry-stone wall, carrying a chicken raided from a farmyard. Then a low rumbling behind him made him turn his head. A farmer dozed over the reins of a chestnut plough-horse that pulled a cart with a half-dozen squealing piglets being taken to market.

Bryn stood against the wall to give the cart room to pass.

'Good day to you, farmer,' he said as the horse drew level.

The bewhiskered driver in a clean smock and with a red kerchief around his neck started awake and grunted. 'Good day, young sir. What brings you on the road at this time of morning?'

'I was hoping to get a ride into town. My horse went lame yesterday, it strained a tendon.'

'Then climb up, young sir. That be if you don't mind riding with the company of pigs.'

'Thank you.' Bryn grinned, climbing up to the driving board. 'Your pigs look fine to me, healthy and ready for fattening.'

'These be the runts, but there's many a goodwife be happy to fed them up for the winter. Who you be visiting in town?'

'Family,' he said easily, but hoped the man was not too inquisitive. 'They will loan me a mare for my return journey and a groom to accompany me.'

The farmer eyed him shrewdly. 'Thought you had the look and voice of a gentleman. Pleased to be of service to you, young sir. Happen you might mention Farmer Hopkirk to them if'n they be needing any pork for their table.'

'Usually we breed our own.' Bryn hoped to avoid further prying.

'Happen you would.' Hopkirk sounded disgruntled and lapsed into silence. Fortunately he was a man who did not find talking a courtesy or a necessity. For the most part he dozed, his horse so familiar with the road to market that he needed no guidance.

Once in town, Bryn hired a hack to ride to continue his journey. Taunton sounded familiar to him, and he decided to start his search from there. An overnight stay in the town revealed that he recognised the castle, a church and the streets. As he walked through the town in the fading daylight, shivers of anticipation sent tingles across his flesh. He paused by the river, his vision misting at the mixture of the darkening shadows of ships and the splattering of reflected lights from riverside buildings rippling on the waves. Appearing in his mind was the ghostly presence of a young boy enticing a family of swans and cygnets closer to the bank with the crumbs from a dried crust stored days ago in a jacket pocket. He could hear the laughter echoing in his mind and the impatient command from a tall man demanding they return at once to the inn before dark overtook them.

He swallowed against a sudden drying of his throat. He knew now that he had been here with another boy, older than him . . . a brother . . . Howard . . . The memory focused more sharply. His heart leapt. Howard was his older brother and the man with them was his father. Clearly he could recall the time when they had hurried back to the inn. The same inn where he had taken rooms this day.

Bryn let out a harsh breath. More veils were lifting. He had an elder brother. But what had become of him? He rubbed his temple, the recollection fading.

Once back at the inn, he was shaken to discover that he did not remember its interior from that time. He could not have been very old, yet his lack of recollection unsettled him. What if his imagination was conjuring people and places because that was what he wanted to believe? The taproom was noisy, jarring with his mood, and he went straight to the solitude of his chamber. He sank on to the bed with his head in his hands, willing himself to remember more. It was hopeless, and as a town clock struck midnight, he drifted into a restless sleep.

His dreams were vivid, like the pages of a book flicking open to reveal sketches from a previous life. He was transported into a coach travelling with his mother, father and brother. They were passing through Taunton, and the landscape changed to open countryside scattered with villages until they reached a desolate moor with hidden valleys and in the distance the twin towers of a welcoming home.

He woke with a start, desperate to hold those visions close, but as dawn brightened the interior of the bedchamber they vanished like mist in sunlight. One certainty remained: his home was on Exmoor.

Next day he allowed his instinct to guide him out to the countryside, continuing north-west. From what he could remember, he believed Willow Vale was another day's ride. It took three days, after several wrong turnings, to come to a familiar village. There was only one inn, but the natural stone structure with its tumbledown barn was eerily familiar. His heartbeat quickened. He was nearing his destination. A finger of sweat traced each notch of his spine.

Excitement mingled with fear. What would he find? He reminded himself to remain cautious. His identity must not be discovered until he was ready to disclose it.

The inn had only three customers: two youngish farmhands looking for work and a middle-aged pedlar whose red-veined nose showed his indulgence in ale. The bearded innkeeper was refilling a quart tankard in his hand.

Bryn sat close to the customers but at a separate table. 'I'll have a pint of your best beer, innkeeper, and have you a room for the night?'

A tankard was banged down on the table. The thickset landlord smelled of rancid fat and onions; the jerkin strained over his broad gut was splattered with grease. 'Room be free at top of stairs. There be rabbit stew if you want it.'

The pedlar waved a finger in a negative gesture at Bryn, who noticed that the traveller had a plate of bread, cheese and a chunk of ham before him. 'I'll have the cheese and ham,' he replied.

'A wise choice,' the pedlar grunted as the landlord ambled away. 'Unless you wish to spend all tomorrow in the jakes. New to these parts, sir? Looking for work?'

'Travelling through,' Bryn evaded. 'Do you know the district well, sir? Who owns the land here about?'

'Why you want to know that?' The landlord slapped down a dented tin plate in front of Bryn, his tone suspicious.

'I would not want to trespass.' Bryn grinned, feeling the need to lay a false trail. The menacing figure of Carforth had haunted his thoughts since his arrival in Taunton, and this could be an inn frequented by the man or his henchmen. 'I inadvertently took the wrong track yesterday and ended up on some estate. The irate gamekeeper threatened to blow my head off with his gun. It is not an experience I care to repeat.'

The landlord grunted and shuffled away.

'The gamekeeper must have been blind or drunk. A fine-looking gentleman like yourself should not be mistaken for a poacher or trespasser.' The pedlar sniffed, then gulped down most of his tankard. 'But then folk in the country be more wary of strangers. If you don't want trouble, best to steer clear of the moor. Any manner of peculiar incidents can bring a stranger to misadventure there.'

Bryn feigned shock. 'You mean outlaws and highwaymen?'

'There's been people venture on the moor who bain't been heard of again.' The pedlar nodded sagely and finished his drink.

'Let me buy you another, sir,' Bryn offered and raised his voice. 'A quart of your best, landlord.'

'Thank you most kindly, sir. Name is Monkford. Would you care to join me?'

Bryn moved tables, hoping that he could learn more of the area from the pedlar if they struck up an acquaintanceship. Monkford drank two more quarts purchased by Bryn and related all he knew of the farms and estates in the area, mostly stressing who were the most generous when it came to buying his wares.

'Is the moor as bad as the landlord says?' Bryn finally brought the conversation in a direction he hoped would benefit him.

Monkford was effusive in his tales of murders, outlaws and marauding gypsies, requiring Bryn to refill his tankard another twice as he became more confiding in the folklore and legends of the moor. When his companion did not mention Willow Vale, he probed further, hoping that he did not sound too eager for information.

'Moors by their very desolate landscape are always dangerous, are they not, but are not some of the tales exaggerated to keep strangers away?'

'I wouldn't cross it alone unarmed.' Monkford grimaced. 'I've been robbed myself more than once and almost left for dead. Usually now I keep to the villages and towns.'

'I would have thought you would be a welcome visitor to the houses of gentry. There must be several hereabouts,' Bryn persisted.

Monkford sighed and rubbed a hand across his face. 'There was a time when I first came this way a good living could be made. There were three fine estates and the ladies of the houses eager for news. I used to sell a lot of lace in those days; now it's mostly ribbons and gee-gaws.'

'Were these grand houses close by?' Bryn gestured to the landlord to bring more beer.

'One just before the moor.' Monkford was slurring his words and having trouble concentrating. When the landlord refilled his tankard, he nodded appreciatively. 'I shall visit there tomorrow. Another is further to the west, but that road be too dangerous to travel alone and the squire's wife now be old and there are no daughters to be interested in my wares. The other is ten mile or so.' His expression

41

darkened. 'That be a place it be well to stay far away from. It be accursed.'

Every hair on Bryn's body prickled with foreboding. 'Accursed? Surely you exaggerate, sir?'

'The devil took root in that place,' the landlord growled as he refilled Bryn's tankard. 'And no good came to anyone who stuck their noses into what went on there. Though there be stories that would make your flesh crawl.'

Bryn swallowed against a sick dread of foreboding. 'What is the name of this place to be so avoided? I will take care not to pass anywhere near it.'

The landlord raised a hand in the sign to ward off the devil. 'It were a decent place once, but you would be right to stay well clear of Willow Vale.' He lumbered away to bar the outer door.

It was dark outside and the tallow candle stubs lit by the landlord were smoking and guttering, giving a feeble light. The farm workers had left for their cottages and could be heard singing as they weaved their way home.

'Can any place be as bad as he says?' Bryn pursued in a conspiratorial whisper.

Monkford eyed him blearily. 'It be cursed indeed and all but abandoned and ruined. Once they were a proud family. Then the widow remarried and it all went bad. Stay clear of it.' His eyes closed and his chin drooped on to his chest, and a loud snore ended the conversation.

Bryn would be on his way at first light. As he trod wearily up the stairs to his room, he clamped down the sickening feeling of fear that threatened to unman him. Tomorrow he would face his demons, and before falling asleep he prayed for the strength to overcome them.

That night in his dreams he rode the night mare. There was no loving family. He relived his last night at Willow Vale and all the horrors that had led to his wild flight.

Chapter Five

Exmoor was vaster, wilder and more isolated than Bryn remembered. The hills were gentler than the rugged tors of Cornwall and streams frequently meandered across the lanes. Like all moors, heather and gorse covered the slopes and wild ponies and the occasional deer wandered freely.

As he entered a valley that looked vaguely familiar, he encountered two milkmaids driving their cows back to their field for grazing. He pulled his horse to the side of the lane, waiting for the cattle to pass. As the two women drew level with him, he raised his hat in greeting. Both of them giggled and eyed him boldly.

'Good day to you, fine sir.' One more provocative than her companion ran the tip of her tongue over her full lips. 'Not seen you in these parts afore. Handsome man like yourself is not a face I'd forget.'

He grinned, enjoying her flirting, but was embarrassed when a warm flush reddened his cheeks. 'I am looking for the Willow Vale estate. Am I travelling in the right direction?'

Their faces paled at mention of his destination, and the older one said, darkly, ' 'Ee don' want go anywhere near there. It be haunted for sure.' There was real fear in the woman's eyes.

He laughed uneasily, brushing it aside. 'All old houses are said to have their ghosts. I've never seen one yet.'

'Turn back now, sir,' the milkmaid implored. 'They say that place be cursed.'

'What nonsense is this?'

The younger woman was pushing at the rumps of two cows that had stopped to chew on some wayside grass. 'We got our work to do, Bette. Can't have the cows wandering off.'

'Bain't nonsense, sir,' Bette said, glancing nervously over her shoulder. 'What be your interest in the place?' Her pretty face had hardened with suspicion, all coquetry vanishing. 'It bain't about the trouble there, be it? Those men who rebelled be long gone.'

'What trouble was this?' Bryn demanded, the foreboding that had been with him all day growing more alarming.

'Folk hereabout want nothing to do with those monsters. If you've an ounce of decency, neither will you.' She slapped a cow to urge it forward, clearly not willing to be drawn further, and hurried to join her companion.

'What happened there?' Bryn shouted after them. Already unsettled by his dream the previous night, his years of horrific nightmares of beatings and shouted abuse set his nerves screaming, telling him to escape and wait until his guardian could accompany him.

He stamped down his fear. He had come too far and got too close to turn tail and run. Willow Vale was his land. He would not be frightened from it by nightmares, or exaggerated gossip.

When the young women kept their heads down and pushed impatiently at the cows to hasten their pace, he turned his mount and cut across their path, his voice sharp with authority. 'What happened?'

'I couldn't say.' Bette did not look at him.

The other milkmaid had opened a gate and the cows were now jostling Bryn's mount to get past him and enter the meadow. It took him some moments to bring the horse back under control, and by the time he did, the two women were on the far side of the field.

He decided against pursuing them. If their information came from gossip, then it was unlikely to be accurate. The sense of optimism that had started with him on this quest had now vanished, and an increasing dread pumped through his veins at each mile he travelled closer to his old home. Since his memory had started to return, he had realised that Carforth was a formidable adversary, but he was no longer a weakling child to be bullied. He had right on his side and his blood ran hotly demanding justice.

He paused at each track leading off the main route across the moor. None felt familiar, so he continued on his way. Finally he recognised an ancient oak split by lightning, whose shape had frightened him as a child. He remembered that he and Howard had taunted each other as to who could climb the highest. He could not suppress a grin. After the earlier morbid memories, it was good to recall happier days. The tree marked the border of his land. It was white as a phantom, with its bark long rotted from its trunk. He hoped it was not an omen to what lay ahead.

Further on he entered a hazel wood where the trees were dense. None had been coppiced in recent years and ivy held many of them in its stranglehold. Through neglect little light penetrated the overhead canopy, and the bark and stones beneath were thick with moss. It smelt of damp and decay. Again his unease increased, his emotions swirling in fear and turmoil at what he would discover once he came upon the house and hamlet.

The image of the cluster of houses and the friendly faces of his father's tenants came vividly to mind. He had forgotten the hamlet. He frowned. By now should he not be smelling woodsmoke from the cooking fires?

On the far side of the wood the overgrown lane went no further than a clapper bridge over a ford. The floodgates of his memory were opening fast with each fresh landmark. He and his brother Howard had often played here as children. But something about the scene before him was wrong . . .

With growing trepidation he urged his gelding through the water. Was this not where nine houses should exist? Shock made him pull his mount to an abrupt halt. The wattle-and-daub thatched cottages had been razed to the ground. From the scorch marks on the stonework that remained standing, it was clear they had been destroyed by fire. Brambles and tall grasses had invaded the old cottage gardens.

A feral cat with a dead rat in its mouth ran across his path and darted into the bracken. What disaster had struck here? And what had happened to the people who had worked on Willow Vale land? Anger heated his blood and blasted the fear that had been on the point of unmanning him.

It was not the only catastrophe he was to discover. The fire of rage within him turned to a white-hot furnace. The surrounding fields were filled with yellow ragwort that would have poisoned any livestock. Yet the greatest blow of all was when the house came into view. Or what was left of it. Only the north wing remained. The rest was a fire-blackened ruin without a roof, with paneless windows and tumbledown walls. All the flooring had burned and an upper-storey stone fireplace with carved cherubs without their heads stood guard over charred timbers. Brambles were growing through the lower mullions and molehills made the once immaculate lawns of the gardens look as though a drunken ploughman had tilled the ground.

An iron fist clamped around his heart and his throat clogged with impotent rage. He was appalled to discover so much destruction. There was nothing here that made him feel this had once been his home. The grounds were a wilderness and again unrecognisable. Another barb of despair fractured his heart. It was as though every part of all that was good and beautiful from those hazy childhood memories had been rent asunder. His hopes for his future were brutally desecrated.

What answers could he possibly find here? What had he even expected? Carforth would have ensured that no servants remained from his mother's time. An icy thorn scratched along his spine and he shuddered. Someone had just walked over his grave. Or perhaps someone from the grave was beckoning to him. He glanced through the trees to the tall church tower on the edge of the manor land.

The parish records would reveal what had happened here. He turned his mount in the direction of the church, his vision blurred by misery. As he skirted the churchyard wall with its overhanging yew trees, he rubbed his eyes and found his face was wet with tears. But the cemetery was as neglected as the estate. He dismounted and tethered the gelding to the broken lychgate. Many of the gravestones were lost amongst thigh-high grass, others tilted as though performing a macabre dance. The door to the ancient place of worship was barred and locked. Some of the panes in the leaded and stained glass were broken, looking as though they had been used as target practice for slingshots. Inside was the Bryant tomb, where his mother's body would have been interred. He could not even pay his respects to her. That wound cut deepest of all. In its wake, fury tore through him. This was his land; he would not be denied access.

He prowled round the perimeter of the church and discovered a panel in the chancel door that had been smashed by an axe, the splintered wood weathered by years of storms and wind. He climbed through the aperture. He had not believed he could be more shocked than by the sights he had previously witnessed. Yet clearly nothing here had been regarded as sacred. The flagstones were covered with rotting leaves that had blown inside over several years. The pews erected by his grandfather had been destroyed, scorch marks on the limewashed walls testament to the fires their wood had provided. Pottery shards and mildewed sacking, their innards of stuffed straw long rotted from the time they had served as mattresses, indicated that the church must for a time have provided a sanctuary for the homeless villagers. Darker stains on the walls had him reeling back in horror. They were splatterings of long-dried blood. Murder had been done here. Nothing else could explain the number of bloodstains, or the pitted marks where bullets had slammed into the walls.

He covered his mouth with his hand as nausea rose to his gullet. He swallowed it down with difficulty, and stumbled towards the carved marble tombs with the effigies of his grandfather and grandmother and that of his father. Their faces had been battered in a frenzy of destruction, the features unrecognisable. Was Carforth capable of such defilement? If so, it was another crime he must answer for.

Bryn ran his hands over the figure of his grandfather, who was holding a small Celtic cross, a replica of which he remembered had been in his father's study. His fingers played over the carved ring on the effigy's little finger. It was a ring he had seen his mother wearing on her index finger until her marriage to Carforth. Another heirloom lost to the avarice of the evil that had sought to obliterate everything his family had achieved.

But why so much destruction? The house, although far from palatial, was a large and comfortable manor. But Bryn's heritage had meant nothing to Carforth. Unable to acquire the estate legally, Carforth had made sure that his stepson would never benefit from the riches that he himself had been denied. But at least Bryn still had the land. He forced himself to focus on that. Carforth could not take that part of his inheritance. With keen wits and hard work, fortunes could be remade and properties rebuilt. His stepfather would not break his spirit or destroy everything his family had achieved.

He knelt at his father's tomb. The image smashed except for the same image of a Celtic Cross between his hands. He prayed for strength and guidance. There was no marble effigy of his mother, and when he examined the tomb, not even an inscription of her name beside that of his older brother. How could Carforth show her so little respect? Bryn could only assume that his mother had been laid to rest in the family crypt beneath the tomb.

His finger traced his father's name. Howard Alexander Bryant. The last piece of his forgotten past blasted his mind like a fanfare. His name was Alexander Bryant.

With a heavy heart he left the church. Trying to piece together something of the events that had ravaged the village and his home, he studied the gravestones as yet unmarred by the growth of lichen. A splash of colour drew his eye to a group of stone tablets where the grass was shorter and a bunch of dying wild flowers had been laid on the ground. He read the lettering on the stone: 1801. The year he and Arabella had fled this accursed place.

Here lie the remains of Iggy Avershaw and his wife Eve, their children Abe, 7, Jeb, 5 and baby Annie. Struck down by evil but assured of a place in heaven.

The words chilled him. How many other innocents had suffered at the hands of that demon?

He searched for Josephina's grave, but there was no headstone. What had become of the faithful servant? Had she escaped Carforth's vengeance? No wonder the country folk regarded the place as haunted and cursed. There was no one left except ghosts demanding retribution.

Desolation swept through him. He had come here to find answers to his past. Instead he had found desecration and a sinister mystery, which boded ill concerning his family and those who had relied upon them. He was swamped with guilt. Should he have tried harder to trace his family and home before now? Would he have been able to prevent whatever disaster Carforth had wreaked here? There was no doubt in his mind that his stepfather was the cause of the destruction. How many lives and livelihoods had been lost because of his own unwillingness to face his past? Did that not make him responsible?

As though felled by a slingshot, he sank down upon his knees in the churchyard and held his head in his hands. Remorse smote him. What price his neglect – his cowardice? He wept for those he believed he had betrayed.

The sun was low in the sky when he emerged from his torpor, resolved to seek justice and avenge those who had suffered when it was his family's responsibility to protect them. Reparation must be made or he would never feel worthy to carry the Bryant name with pride.

He staggered to his feet and stared up at the church, dedicated to St Michael. Then he drew the dagger from his belt and raised it aloft, its handle forming the sign of the cross. 'I swear before God and St Michael that I will right the wrongs done to our vassals and bring to justice whoever is responsible. So help me God.'

He closed his eyes, focusing upon his vow. The archangel St Michael had led the good angels in the battle against Lucifer and his followers. Bryn prayed now for the strength to rid the world of the devil who had invaded Willow Vale and defiled all that had been decent here.

Too late he heard the footfall behind him, and before he could turn to confront the intruder, pain flared through his skull and he receded into darkness.

Chapter Six

'So where by all that's holy has Bryn gone?' Adam Loveday waved the crumpled parchment written by his ward at his two sons. They were in his book-lined study at Boscabel and were standing with their heads bowed before him in front of his desk.

'You just said he had gone to find his home.' The younger boy, Joel, was scowling with disappointment. His thick black hair fell in natural curls to his shoulders. He had the looks of a dark fallen angel yet there certainly was little in him that was cherubic. He was hot-headed and impetuous, with no concept of danger in his energetic games. 'He should have taken us with him on an adventure of such magnitude.'

'This is not an adventure, Joel.' Adam fought to control his anger. He regarded Nathan, who was looking mortified. His lighter colouring and green eyes were very like his mother's, and he usually had her common sense and caring nature. 'Why did you not read the letter when Bryn left school telling no one of his plans?'

'It was addressed to you, Papa.' Nathan reddened. 'It would not have been right.'

'In extreme cases you have to use your instincts and not do what is right. If you had told the principal of his plans they would have sent someone after him.'

'But it does not say where he is going,' Nathan protested.

'A young gentleman on the road would have been seen.' Adam could not control his exasperation at their foolishness. 'We could have learned his direction and how he was travelling. Someone would probably have given him a lift and spoken to him. Even if he had to walk to the nearest town he would have passed other travellers. That was over a week ago. His trail will not be so easy to discover now.'

50

'Are you going to find him, Papa?' Nathan shifted from one foot to the other in his distress. 'Bryn spoke once of having discussed his past with you. I assumed you would know where he was heading. He said he would return to Boscabel by the time we arrived. He will be here soon. Bryn never lies.'

'Unless he has been prevented from returning,' Adam informed them bleakly. 'We knew there was a risk to his safety from his past. That he had been severely beaten as a child and that his nightmares confirmed our fears. That no notices had been posted in any of the news-sheets about his absence did not bode well. He could have walked into danger. He should never have set off alone. I would have done everything in my power to ensure no harm came to him and that we discovered the truth of his birth and childhood.'

'I'm sorry, Papa, but Bryn had been acting strangely all term,' Nathan said. 'And he towered above everyone in his class. He acted more like a man than a youth. He had even started to shave. I do not believe he is as young as we had thought.'

Adam sighed. He too had had those suspicions. 'But he is not experienced in the ways of the world. Or the dangers that lie in wait for an innocent on the highways.'

'Or adventures.' Joel's eyes were bright with excitement. 'You would have done the same, Papa. Bryn is brave like you. You fought battles in the navy when you were his age.'

'As a midshipman I was taught the skills to help me to survive, and there were a hundred other men on board who would have looked to my back in times of danger. This madness of Bryn's is not the same. And I hope you will think seriously about my warning, young man. Life is not about the glory you see in adventures. It is about responsibility and duty.'

'Was it not Bryn's duty to discover his past?' Joel stubbornly jutted his lower lip. He had picked up a wooden sailing ship from Adam's desk that his father had carved and was pushing it over the smooth surface.

'It was his duty to obey his tutors and guardian. He is not yet of age and I am responsible for his safety.' Adam dragged his hand through his long hair caught back in a black ribbon.

Nathan was standing to attention, his head bowed. 'Papa, I did inform our house master that Bryn had gone and taken some of his clothes with him. A search was made for him as far as the town. Do you really think that he could be in danger from those who beat him as a child?'

Noting the fear and despondency in his older son's eyes, Adam wanted to reassure him. Nathan was caring and thoughtful of others and he did not want him blaming himself if anything happened to Bryn. Yet because he had withheld information, Bryn's life could be in danger.

'I would be concerned for any young man unused to the ways of the world being taken advantage of, attacked and robbed, or finding himself out of his depth in any given situation. If he has not arrived here by tomorrow, I will set out to try and trace his journey.'

'Can I come with you, Papa?' Joel stopped playing with the ship and looked about to burst with excitement to be part of this escapade.

'Your mama would be distraught if I were to drag you or Nathan away from her when you have just arrived here. And I need to know that you will both be here to protect her in my absence.'

'Uncle Japhet will do that,' Joel pouted.

'Your uncle may wish to join me. And you also have your two sisters eager to spend time with you.'

'I don't want to be bothered with girls.' Joel scowled. 'They are boring and burst into tears over nothing.'

Adam bit back a laugh. 'Then do not taunt or tease them. And a man must always be deferential to the fairer and weaker sex. You pushed Sara into a stream on your last visit home. I will not tolerate such behaviour.'

'She would not play pirates with me. Nate and Bryn had gone off to Tor Farm to visit our cousins and you would not let me go with them.'

'Because the previous day you had terrified young Cissy Brown by chasing her wearing a sheet over your head and pretending to be a ghost,' Adam reminded Joel.

'Bah, Cissy's a halfwit. Anyone would know I was not a ghost.' Joel rarely admitted that he was in the wrong. 'Besides, she's a servant's brat.'

Adam was no longer amused at his son's irreverence. 'She was five and had nightmares for a week over that thoughtless prank. You must have regard for the children of servants.'

Nathan grabbed his brother by the arm and pulled him to the

door before he said something else that would get him into trouble.

Senara entered Adam's study as the boys ran past her. She moved into her husband's arms. 'What possessed Bryn to act so thoughtlessly?' Adam asked her. 'He must know we would be worried.'

'He is a young man and needs to know his background. If his memory has returned, he must have wanted to give us some positive news. He has lived with us for years and nothing has been uncovered about his family or his home.'

'But to do this alone . . .!' Adam groaned, absently stroking his wife's hair. 'He could be walking straight into danger if his nightmares are anything to go by.'

'Perhaps he needs to face his fears. They are his family. He is a sensible lad,' she reassured.

Adam stared at a deep groove in his father's old desk that had been brought from Trevowan. 'I cannot leave him to face peril alone. But where would I start to look for him?'

'What would you have done at his age in his circumstances?' Still within his embrace, Senara leant against the desk, her gaze concerned and searching.

'I would have been impatient to know the truth,' he acknowledged ruefully.

Senara put her hand on his arm. 'Yet you would know enough not to take unnecessary risks. Perhaps Bryn needs to find out if he has remembered his old home correctly, and discover anything he can about what is happening there now. I am sure he would not doing anything foolish.'

He covered her hand with his own and stared deep into her eyes. 'Do you think he is safe? What does your intuition tell you? It has rarely failed you in the past.'

She momentarily closed her eyes and drew a shallow breath. When she opened them, her gaze was shadowed. At Adam's frown, their depths darkened. 'I do not see everything, nor am I infallible. I love Bryn as though he was my own and have a mother's worry for him that he has acted recklessly in this matter.' Her voice changed. 'There is danger. His past cannot be escaped; neither can the consequences of it be avoided. Not for a man of honour. But this venture must be important to him.' She hesitated, choosing her words carefully. 'It is something he has to do for himself.'

'Not at the cost of his life.' Adam held her tighter. 'I will give him one more day. If he has not returned by tomorrow, I will—'

'Do what?' Senara interrupted with unusual heat. 'Set out on a wild-goose chase? Bryn could be anywhere. It is over a week since he left the school. His trail will have gone cold. You could even pass him a mile from a crossroads and miss him completely if he was on his way home.'

'And if I did nothing and we never heard from him again . . .?' He let his question hang ominously in the air. 'How could I live with that? What sort of a guardian would that make me?'

She kissed him with pride and no little foreboding. 'You will do what you feel and know is right.'

Bryn stirred. Red-hot pincers immediately snapped around his ankles and arms and he could not stop a grunt of pain. The sound was muffled. He opened his eyes, or did he? Obsidian darkness cloaked his vision. The pain gripping his body made him shake his head to clear his wits. Agony enshrouded his paralysed figure. His head pounded with greater intensity. A fragment of sanity penetrated the mists cloying his thoughts. He was not paralysed; his arms and legs were tightly bound. A gag leeched the moisture from his mouth and he felt his throat would close from the raw burning of thirst.

He dragged in air through his nostrils, his senses slowly returning. What had happened? Where was he? He could not remember. Fear clenched his heart. Not again. His memory could not fail for a second time. What is my name? he questioned desperately. Bryn; no, Alexander. No, it was Bryn Loveday. It was Alexander Bryant. He was Bryn and Alexander. He gasped in relief. He had come to Willow Vale to learn the truth. Images, fleet as swallows, darted through his mind. This time he had not forgotten.

But where was he? He had been in the cemetery of the church. Someone had hit him – knocked him out. He tested his limbs. The ropes held him tight. He was lying on a cold stone floor and the place smelt damp and musty. He could not tell if it was day or night.

There was a scraping sound and light speared into the room as a door above him was dragged open. A row of stone steps led down to the floor where he was trussed like a sacrificial lamb. That was not an image he wanted to retain. He did not move or cry out. He could gain an advantage if whoever approached thought he was still unconscious. Through his lashes he regarded the short bow-legged figure shuffling down the stairs. The man was carrying a plate of food and a thick woodcutter's knife.

He put the wooden plate down on the bottom step and stood over Bryn, the knife raised ready to attack. A horn cup was balanced on the plate beside a wedge of bread, and a skewer held half a cooked rabbit.

' 'Ee astir?' demanded a voice like splintering glass. A worn boot prodded Bryn's shoulder.

Bryn did not move, his mind racing to find a way of overcoming his gaoler and escape.

'If 'ee still be out cold I won't waste the food. I'll eat it meself. Or I could undo the gag.'

The smell of the rabbit made Bryn's stomach gurgle with hunger. He had a healthy appetite, and his light-headed feeling and weakness could be from lack of food. He needed strength to restore his wits and escape. He opened his eyes.

'Thought you were faking it.' The knife pointed menacingly at Bryn's throat. 'Don't 'ee move and I'll undo the gag.'

The overpowering smell of the midden wafted from the gaoler's body as he bent to untie the gag. Bryn almost choked on the stench as he gasped for air.

'Who are 'ee? 'Ee don't look like no thief or poacher.'

'I am Br—' He licked his cracked lips, his wits clogged from lack of water. He had nearly said Bryant, but after seeing the ruins of his home, he had no idea who was foe and who was friend. 'I am Bryn,' he croaked finally. 'Please . . . some water.'

Whilst the man thrust the rim of the horn cup against Bryn's mouth, he tried to make out his gaoler's features, but the light was behind him. He gulped down the liquid, some of it spilling over his chin and shirt.

'Bryn who?' the man snapped, rheumy eyes studying him closely. There was more belligerence than intelligence in his gaze.

'And who are you?' Bryn demanded with all the authority he could muster.

The gaoler's eyes narrowed with uncertainty at the sound of the cultured voice. Bryn continued in his challenge. 'Whose land is this that you attack innocent travellers? I demand to see your master.'

'Bain't no master,' sneered the man.

'The property must belong to someone.'

'All dead and gone. Or that be what they like folks to think.'

None of this made sense to Bryn. Unless Carforth was dead. A glimmer of hope was instantly doused. Someone had been responsible for the razing of the hamlet. That the manor was also burned sent shivers of alarm through him. What had the man meant? Carforth was a devious monster. He could have caused whatever tragedy had befallen here. Was his assailant his stepfather's henchman? If he was, Bryn dared not reveal his true name. Was it even safe to call himself Loveday? Carforth had wanted him dead, or at least out of the way, so that he could plunder the land and riches of his birthright.

'Do you intend to cut my bonds so that I can eat? If your attack was to rob me, you must have discovered I have little of value about my person.'

'I bain't no thief. You were trespassing.' The man shuffled away, his manner furtive. 'There be a reward for catching a poacher.'

A sorry tale and a lie, Bryn reasoned.

'I am no poacher. There are laws to protect the innocent from abduction and attack,' he bluffed. 'If you release me at once, I will not press charges. It must be clear to you that I am a gentleman.'

'I've seen rogues dressed in finery aping their betters. Why should I believe you?' The words rang ominously in the room.

His eyes now accustomed to the dark, Bryn noted the water seeping down earthen walls. He had been put underground. Whether it was the ice store or a cellar, he could not tell. Refusing to show his growing fear, he shouted, 'Release me!'

The gaoler shuffled away.

'At least untie my hands so I can eat. I need more water.'

The man halted and sat down on the bottom step. 'Not until you tell me who you are and why you are here.'

Chapter Seven

Dearest Papa,

Nothing has changed. The family patronise me or treat me like a child. Felicity regards me as an unpaid companion for Charlotte or nurserymaid for Thea and George. You'd be proud of George, Papa. He wants to explore everything, but Felicity would turn him into a milksop.

You know I adore you, Papa, but why did you marry Felicity? She is so prim, so fearful of what the neighbours will think of anything we say or do. Of course, nothing I do is ever right. I wish she were more like Aunt Hannah or Senara; they understand the spirit that drives us. It is as though Felicity is waiting for me to act the hoyden so that I can be punished. It makes me want to act as she so pre-judges me. Then the moment I behave unlike a lady I regret it. But I will never admit it. Excuses are for weak people. Amelia and Felicity care nothing for how I feel. And always they watch me. A misspoken comment or impulsive act and they exchange sly glances – a knowing look declaring that they condemn me as being just like my mother.

It is even worse when they condemn you, Papa. Their heavy sighs lead to snide comments about the economies they now endure and how life is difficult. We are hardly paupers! They saw your gambling as weakness. You lived life to the full – like Uncle Adam and Uncle Japhet. No one condemns them for abandoning their families to seek adventure.

I do miss Trevowan. I miss the freedom I once had. But I miss you more, Papa. Any sacrifice would have been better than losing you.

Her sharp senses detected a nearby movement. She was in the cemetery of Penruan church, sitting by the Loveday vault. Here she had hoped to be alone. She broke off from composing the letter to St John and hid the pencil stub and paper in her reticule, then sat perfectly still, hoping she would not be noticed. She did not want an intruder disturbing the privacy of this moment. This was a weekly ritual she did not wish interrupted. By her feet was a bouquet of carnations and roses that she had sneaked into the grounds of Trevowan to steal. She reckoned Tristan owed her father that small tribute at least. They were after all flowers planted during her grandfather's time. She did not care if she was seen. The servants and gardeners would never betray her, and if she were caught, then it would please her to have an excuse to tell Tristan Loveday exactly what she thought of him.

'So this is why the flowers at Trevowan never seem to flourish.' There was amusement in the sharp tone of the voice. 'I suspected it was you. A visit to the Dower House would have been welcome.'

Rowena turned a steady gaze upon her great-aunt, the oldest living Loveday. Although only three years short of her three score years and ten, Aunt Elspeth remained a formidable woman and one none of her family crossed lightly. She leaned heavily on her walking cane, but her slender body was straight as a pikestaff. In her free hand she carried a bunch of lilies. Rowena held her formidable aunt's stare with defiance.

'Aunt Elspeth, will my secret be safe with you?'

Elspeth limped to the stone bench by the side of the marble vault and sat beside her niece. Why spoil the young woman's act of rebellion by telling her that Tristan had known for months that she took flowers from Trevowan and had told the servants to act as though they had not seen her?

She held the lilies out to Rowena. 'Be so kind as to lay them by the tomb.'

Elspeth murmured a prayer as her great-niece placed the flowers. Sadness weighed heavily within her, and she missed the closeness of her loved ones around her: those both living and deceased. To hide the rawness of her emotion, she looked over the tops of the headstones to the headland beyond the harbour. It was filled with fishing sloops returning with their catch. The shouts of the fishwives grew louder on the quay as they gathered to gut the fish before hanging them in the drying sheds. The quiet of the morning was also broken by the squawking of gulls and terns lining up on the roofs of the cottages to scavenge the dropped entrails. She hoped the catch had been successful. Too many had provided scant nourishment for their families through the winter. With the war with France seeming never-ending, the fishermen were unable to sail far from the safety of their harbour for fear of being fired on by enemy ships. The other lucrative trade that was carried on clandestinely to supplement their income had also been severely interrupted – and that was the smuggling that had been so profitable before the war. A trade few admitted to any involvement within, although most families, including the Lovedays, had reaped the benefits in times past.

Rowena was gathering up her possessions preparing to leave. Elspeth studied her. Her great-niece was seething with a barely contained anger. 'Stay awhile, my dear. I see you so rarely these days.'

'It was your choice to live with the enemy, Aunt.'

Momentarily taken aback that one so young had the spirit to challenge her, Elspeth felt a stab of pride. The young woman reminded her of herself at that age. Elspeth had hated being constrained by convention. The resemblance mellowed her reply. 'I refused to be driven from my birthplace. Is that so wrong?'

'But how can you bear living on his charity and forbearance?' The youthful voice quivered at the force of her emotion.

'An unmarried women without a fortune of her own has few rights in society,' Elspeth sternly reminded her great-niece. 'Has not my role in life been to suffer the charity and forbearance of my father, my brother and my nephew before accepting the protection of my cousin, albeit twice removed or some such degree? Tristan has generously provided that I may end my days in the home of my ancestors and my birth.' She held up a hand when she saw that Rowena was about to interrupt. She was enjoying the verbal sparring and was intrigued to discover whether Rowena would continue with her stand, or crumble as others had before her. 'Pray, let me finish. Tristan Loveday, you and I all carry the blood of my grandfather, Arthur St John Loveday. I can accept Tristan living at Trevowan rather than strangers. With no disrespect to your dear papa's memory, St John gambled your inheritance away. Tristan saved it for the family.'

'By trickery and deceit,' Rowena flared, her slender body bristling with outrage.

'Or sharp wits and family pride. It depends how you view such actions,' Elspeth observed. 'I can understand your pain and resentment. I would ask you to consider my position and do not expect you to judge me.'

That momentarily took the wind out of Rowena's sails and Elspeth patted the seat beside her. 'Smooth down your feathers, my dear. Keep me company for a while.'

When Rowena hesitated, she chuckled. 'Stubborn like your father. He never liked being told what to do. None of us do, if truth be told. I would take pleasure in a moment of your time, young miss. That is, if you have no previous engagement to return to at Reskelly Cottage.'

'Only to play nursemaid to Thea and George.' Rebellion sharpened Rowena's tone, and with a twitch of her skirts that conveyed months of pent-up anguish, she sat on the edge of the seat.

Studying the stubborn tilt of her chin and the taut frustration and resentment of the clenched hands, Elspeth asked, 'Do you also visit your grandmother when you come to Penruan?'

When she felt Rowena stiffen, she added, 'Sal Sawle is an honest woman, unlike her husband and son.'

'Unlike my mother, do you not mean?' Rowena retorted, making no attempt to hide the anger blazing in her eyes.

'Do not put words into my mouth. I have never shirked from speaking my mind, so do not insult me now. Sal is a good woman. As for Meriel, she had her faults and would have needed an exceptional man to tame her.'

Rowena stared fixedly at the tomb carved with the Loveday name. A tense silence stretched between them. 'Even Papa would not allow her to be buried here. Would I also be so tainted if I died unwed?'

That note of vulnerability and uncertainty struck at Elspeth's heart. 'No one disputes your Loveday blood, my dear. You take these things too seriously. There are times when I see myself in you.'

Rowena's gasp made her laugh. 'That surprises you. Why do our young kinfolk think they are the first who ever wanted to rebel against convention and propriety? Any woman of spirit who would retain her good name must guard against indiscretion. It can be galling for those of us who are not mealy-mouthed puppets without an original thought in their head. There is within us the same blood craving excitement and adventure that drives our menfolk. Yet to

60

give into it we would be reviled and despised, while they are praised for their bravery and exploits.'

'Then we can be but half alive,' Rowena groaned. 'Not every woman wants to be shackled to a brood of squawling babies. Why does marriage have to be the answer to our role in life?'

Elspeth laughed. 'What is your definition of happiness?'

'No one has troubled to ask me so fundamental a question.' The tension left the young woman's face as she gave her answer careful consideration. 'Is it so wrong to want fulfilment, or not have every thought or move dictated by a man?'

'That sounds like an impossible paradise.' Elspeth had a twinkle in her eye as she regarded her kin with a deepening empathy. 'To find happiness we must learn to compromise and adapt whilst being true to ourselves, our honour and our goals.'

'And have you achieved fulfilment and happiness, Aunt? Have you not burned for more excitement in your life?' There was no disrespect in the question, only a desperate need for understanding.

'I may appear to you to be a staid old spinster, but I have had my moments,' Elspeth counselled. 'When I did not find love, I forsook marriage. I had a role bringing up your father and Adam when my brother was widowed. For twenty years I was the mistress at Trevowan – the home I adored. And I had my horses. They became my passion.' Although Elspeth's expression remained stern, her voice softened with reminiscence. 'Neither was I denied excitement. How could I not be involved in covering up some of the scandals that besieged our family? I took pride in my resourcefulness, and the fact that I would defend to the death any kin if they called upon my help. My brother Edward instilled in us the importance of family loyalty. It was our greatest strength in adversity.'

'I agree about family loyalty,' Rowena stared at the marble tomb, 'but how can I forgive the unforgivable? No matter how you paint Tristan's story, you cannot escape the truth that Papa would be alive if not for him.'

'Do not allow love to blind you, my dear. St John paid the price for his failings. He loved you, Rowena, you must never doubt that, but he could not face the dishonour he had brought upon us by his actions. No one is invincible. Even our menfolk need to compromise and adapt or face the consequences.'

Rowena stood up. 'I am not like you Aunt Elspeth. You betray my father's memory by living at Trevowan.' She showed no remorse at such a disrespectful outburst. Her chin tilted resolutely.

'You have the courage to speak your mind. Do not forget the wisdom of first considering the repercussions. And do not allow your father's death to distort your loyalty or honour. Compromise and adapt. It is all I ask of you.'

Rowena had listened to enough of her aunt's censure. As far as she was concerned Elspeth was a hypocrite. The old woman might preach the noble concept of compromise and adapt, but in truth she had betrayed the family by putting her own desire to die in the house where she was born before family loyalty. Tristan was no better than an interloper and thief who had deliberately set out to destroy St John. How dare Elspeth say they were alike? Rowena had no intention of ending her days as a dissembler and supplicant to suit her own ends.

Elspeth gave a wry laugh. 'Rebellion burns in your eyes. You wear your emotions too easily upon your sleeve. Did the ladies' seminary teach you nothing?'

'They preached the subservience of women,' Rowena flared. 'How we must curtsey to the superiority of men and surrender our will and our rights to their keeping. Your present example hardly conforms to the wishes of the Loveday men who are your closest kin, Aunt Elspeth. Adam considers you have sided with the enemy.'

'Your uncle is allowing his hot blood and his grief for your father to rule his emotions. He may not like what he sees as my defection, but he acknowledges that I show the outside world that our family is still united.'

'With respect, Aunt,' Rowena could barely keep her voice civil as her anger consumed her, 'you give respectability to Tristan. Our cousin is a blackguard.'

'Who is a Loveday none the less,' Elspeth snapped.

'I am not listening to this. Where is your respect for my father?' Rowena turned to flounce away.

'Come back here. Sit down and listen. You may learn a valuable lesson that will serve you well.'

Outrage at her aunt's duplicity brought her striding back to the older woman. Elspeth's scathing tongue did not intimidate her. Not when she considered that right was on her side.

Elspeth held her niece's glare and fired another salvo before the young woman spoke. 'Before you favour me with your opinion of my treachery, pray consider this. Whose reputation apart from your own would you not wish to be dishonoured?'

'Papa's.' She did not hesitate.

'And do you agree that losing Trevowan has been a great blow to our family pride?'

'Papa was not to blame.' Rowena clenched her fists. 'Tristan cheated him. Adam should call him out.'

'However much you love St John, you must realise that he chose to gamble away his inheritance.' Elspeth kept her voice low and reasonable. 'Now stop spitting feathers and sit down and listen.'

Rowena stayed to hear her aunt's words but continued to pace back and forwards in front of the Loveday vault.

'A duel between Adam and Tristan would solve nothing, except who was the better swordsman, or the better shot with a pistol. Family honour would not be restored; it would be brought into further disrepute. In this Adam has allowed good sense to override his hot blood. By appearing to accept Tristan, gossip is quelled, your father's death is accepted as an accident, and the good name of the family is not destroyed.'

The danger signs of anger and rebellion remained set within Rowena's features. Elspeth sighed. 'We all mourn the loss of St John. In that grief we want to hit out in anger. That anger can destroy us. It blinds us to reason. Our first instincts are to retaliate often without fully considering the consequences. In your anger you strike at those who love you most, Rowena.'

When the girl opened her mouth to protest, Elspeth cut off her words with another volley of her own. 'You quarrel continually with Felicity. You resent any words of advice given by your elders.'

'Felicity and Amelia never have a good word to say about Papa, or me. I can do nothing right in their eyes.' Her voice throbbed with pain and she stared into the distance, refusing to meet Elspeth's eyes.

'They may criticise your father as a wastrel to each other, but they never disparage him to any outside the family. Do you not think that Felicity feels any less angry and resentful than you do? She has lost a husband. A husband who left her sadly ill-provided to bring up four children as befits their station.' When Rowena would have interrupted, Elspeth again cut across her protest but did not raise her voice. 'You see her as stifling your love of life and freedom by her petty constraints, do you not? You do not make it easy for her. You show her scant respect, nor do you help her in her struggles to maintain a decent lifestyle for you and your brother and sisters. Wherever Felicity goes, the manner of your father's death follows her. She deals with her grief and anger with dignity. And you would be wise to follow her example.'

'I think not,' Rowena scoffed, her slender body stiff with indignation. 'I could never understand what my father saw in her. She is prim, and terrified of what others think of her. When did the Lovedays allow convention to govern their lives?'

'You view many of your kin's actions through the romanticised eyes of a child, my dear.'

Her great-niece spun on her toes and flounced away, declaring, 'No one knows what I feel, neither do they care.'

'Do not walk away from me,' Elspeth barked. 'Retaliation and rebellion bring further dissension. Stop fighting those who have only your best interests at heart.'

Rowena marched back with battle gleaming in her eyes. Elspeth admired her spirit. It made her own blood quicken in remembrance of what it was like to be young and believe that the whole world was at your feet. Sadly Rowena had yet to learn that by being a woman she would be forever fettered by propriety or face disgrace.

'My dear, truly we are not against you.' Elspeth gripped the top of her walking cane and studied Rowena without recrimination. 'You are intelligent. Use your wit to charm people around to your way of thinking. Use sweetness to beguile your enemies, and compromise and adapt.'

'You mock me, Aunt.' Rowena remained defensive. 'You say we are alike. Yet when did you ever sweeten your tongue? Even Adam has felt the lash of your denunciation.'

Elspeth could not contain a cackle and her eyes showed a rare light of mischief. 'My years have earned me the right to speak as I find. Not so when I was your age. George Loveday could be harsh and brutal. I had far less freedom than you. I learned to channel my resentment and weigh every word carefully. A reputation is fragile as a butterfly's wing battering against a windowpane. Its frantic attempt to find freedom destroys its ability to fly, and exhausted it soon withers and dies.'

'I am sure you are well meaning in your advice, Aunt Elspeth.'

Rowena did not hide her resentment. 'I would respect it more if you had shown your disapproval of Tristan by ostracising him, rather than accepting his bribe to live in comfort.'

She expected a blistering set-down; instead Elspeth gave a low chuckle, but her eyes were sombre. 'A great wrong was done to Tristan by my father. Indeed by all our family. I was no less hot-headed and condemning. Unjustly so. This is my way of righting my father's wrongs and an act of dishonour.' She shrugged. 'Sweetness does not come easily to me, but I know its benefits. I have compromised and adapted to uphold what I believe to be the honour of our family. Leave me, child, so that I can pay my respects, but you would be wise to heed my words.'

Rowena burned with the impotence of her anger. No one ever got the better of Elspeth, so there was no point in arguing with the harridan. She walked away at a furious pace, but found it impossible to dismiss her great-aunt's words. The meeting had been unexpected and rather bizarre. No one in the family had been immune from Elspeth's scathing tongue, but today her words had held more of a warning than a lecture. Perhaps on reflection age was mellowing the old girl. And not before time!

With a defiant toss of her hair over her shoulder, Rowena banished Elspeth from her thoughts as she approached Blackthorn Cottage. It was set back on the edge of the fishing village and required a steep climb up the sloping hill. She had no intention of snubbing her Sawle kin. Grandma Sal was always delighted to see her, and she liked the deference the old woman showed in her company. Unlike Elspeth, who always criticised. And Rowena was extremely fond of her young cousin Zach, the son of Clem Sawle and Keziah. When her uncle first married his wife, Keziah had insisted that he leave the smuggling trade and live respectably as a fisherman. They had bought this cottage away from the bad reputation of the inn run by Clem's father and his brutal son Harry, leader of the smugglers in their area. Sal had been a drudge to their manipulation. When her husband died, and the Dolphin was under the tyranny of her son, her health had declined from years of overwork and worry, and Keziah had insisted that she move in with them. Later, after Harry had been arrested for the murders and vengeance he had committed upon those who had defied him, and been hanged, Clem and his wife had taken over the inn and restored its reputation for fine ale, food and bedding, and travellers and the military now frequented it.

Entering the open back door of the cottage, Rowena called out a greeting to Sal. Her grandmother was in the kitchen, sitting in a rocking chair by the fire, a red shawl draped across her knees. She was now well fed and looked prosperous. A large mobcap covered her hair and an enamelled brooch pinned the edges of her wide lace collar. Her liver-spotted hands were folded over her lap and her double chin rested on her bosom.

Sal had been dozing and at the sound of Rowena's voice jerked awake. 'Kezzie, be that you?'

'It's me, Grandma.'

Sal straightened, sliding the shawl from her legs and brushing down her black skirt and white apron. She peered across the room. 'Be that you, Meriel, or Rose? Come closer. Not seen you for the longest time.'

Rowena smiled. Sal was hard of hearing; her sight was now poor and she often became confused over names.

'It's Rowena. Your granddaughter.'

Sal flashed a toothless smile. 'There's my lovely, come to see her old gran. You get more beautiful every day, my dear.'

Rowena kissed her creased and weathered cheek. 'I brought you a jar of honey from Amelia's bees and a pot of balm prepared by Aunt Senara to rub on your aching joints. Are you alone this morning? I thought Zach was back from school in Truro.'

'Zach has gone with his pa into Fowey. Clem had business to attend upon. Kezzie be out in the buttery supervising the making of her goat's cheese.'

'I do not know why she does not sell those smelly beasts now that the Dolphin is doing so well.'

Sal sniffed. 'She's always been a bit odd about them critters. Says the cheese kept the creditors from our door when times were hard. With the price of corn so high, the sale of the cheese will provide for a rainy day. And she works as hard as Clem in the inn. She be a good lass. Unlike others of mine.' Her gaze dropped to the fire and her mouth became more pinched as she sucked in her cheeks.

'Do you count Mama amongst them?' Rowena blurted, the echo of Elspeth's words still carrying their sting. 'Am I like her?'

'Only by your looks. You have the bravery and goodness of your father.'

'Many say Papa was no better than Mama.' She could not control a heartfelt sigh.

'Ah well, they be blind.' Sal shook her head. 'The Lord be praised, I see Edward Loveday in you. You have a good heart.' She pointed to the honey and balm. 'Meriel would never have given such thought to her old ma for her likes and needs. As for Rose, the only thing she brought to us was shame.'

Rowena frowned. Sal rarely mentioned Rose, her elder daughter, who had run off with a soldier long before Meriel had married St John.

'That is the second time you have mentioned Rose. Have you heard from her?' her curiosity prompted her to ask.

'I were dreaming of my little ones when they were so sweet and innocent. Rose likely be dead, and good riddance too.' Sal folded her arms across her chest. 'At least our Clem has turned out right and much of that be due to Kezzie. And Zach be a blessing in my old age. He'll make something of himself, you see if he doesn't. Only boy in Penruan to go to that grand school in Truro.' Her head began to nod, but she jerked it up with an effort. 'And you will do me proud, my dear. You've the sense to learn from your ma's mistakes.' Her eyes closed and a soft snore escaped her.

Rowena placed the shawl back over Sal's knees and returned to the Dolphin Inn, where she had stabled her horse. Rose's story intrigued her. Had her aunt turned out bad and suffered a life of poverty, or had she used her wits and beauty to cock a snoop at convention and find love and fortune? Why would any woman who had broken away from the hardships of tavern life and found success wish to be reminded that her family were violent smugglers?

Chapter Eight

After a night tied up and captive, Bryn had no reason to trust his gaoler. But while he was bound, he had no chance of escape. When he heard the door open, he had the further disadvantage of lying on the floor. He rolled towards the wall and struggled to sit up. At each movement the rough rope scraped a layer of skin from his wrists until the flesh was raw. Once upright, he demanded imperiously, 'Who is your master? I would speak with the man who treats any unwitting traveller no better than a vagabond. It is outrageous that I was attacked and abducted whilst innocently visiting a church.'

'Don't mean to say you bain't no thief or miscreant.' A second voice further chilled his blood. He glanced up at the door and saw a stocky, bull-necked figure pointing a blunderbuss at him. 'There be odd sorts taken to the road, soldiers and sailors crippled in the war with no way of finding work.'

'Do I look like a miscreant or beggar?' Bryn scoffed. 'I demand to see your master. There are laws to protect the innocent as well as property owners.'

'Master don't live here no more.' The man with the gun had clearly taken charge. 'But he be most particular about apprehending any trespassers. They bain't never up to no good.'

'Who is your master?'

'You told my associate that you were looking at the church.' The man ignored his question and continued, 'It be locked up. Bain't been no services there for some years.'

'I never got as far as finding that out.'

Bryn studied his two gaolers. The first man would have posed no threat to a strong healthy opponent had Bryn not been bound. He was thin and hunched over and from his pallor looked to be suffering some debilitating malady. The newcomer was another matter. He was bald, with a pumpkin-shaped head and weasel eyes. Visible through a torn sleeve of his shirt were muscles that would rival those of any strongman Bryn had seen in a travelling show. Although Bryn did not recognise either of the servants, that did not mean that they would not recognise him from a description. Had they been given instructions to kill any stranger who had more than a passing resemblance to the young boy who had run away from this estate?

He tried to pull his thoughts together. A pounding headache, which had abated little since his attack yesterday, did not make coherent thinking easy.

'I saw no signs about trespass.' He decided there was no point in trying to get more information from his gaoler. 'I am travelling through England studying architecture. War in Europe has made it impossible to make a Grand Tour.'

When his plea appeared to have fallen upon deaf ears, he assumed his most authoritative tone. 'I have never been accosted in so dastardly a manner. Usually, under the laws of hospitality, I am welcomed in the homes of the gentry.'

'Happen I were a might too hasty.' The smaller servant eyed his companion nervously 'We don't need no more trouble, Savage.'

'Then untie me and allow me to continue on my way.' Bryn addressed the man with the gun. 'I shall put it down to an unfortunate misunderstanding. Clearly your master has issues about trespass and privacy. Though I thought I saw a desecrated village and the ruins of a manor house. What is there of value to steal if I were a thief, which of course I am not?'

'We have our orders.' Savage grunted and kept the blunderbuss pointed at Bryn's chest.

'I inadvertently trespassed,' Bryn conceded. 'For which I would crave your master's pardon. I suggest you put up clear signs in the future. Now if you would be so kind as to release me, I shall continue on my way.'

Neither of the men stirred and a dangerous tension was building. One false word or move and the blunderbuss would be fired and his body buried. It was no comfort to Bryn that it would be on his own land. It meant that once again Carforth had won.

'This has all become rather out of hand,' he blustered. 'You may have been over-zealous in your duty, but no man of property would condemn you for that. I have so far sustained no more than a crack to the head and some inconvenience. I suggest that in the future you question any traveller who has the bearing and dress of a gentleman before you attack them. Release me,' he demanded. 'No more need be said on the matter.'

He could almost hear the cogs in the servants' heads grinding to find a way of escaping any recrimination or persecution. He played on their uncertainty. 'You cannot go about attacking any traveller who stumbles on to your master's land. My family would be up in arms if any of our gamekeepers acted in such a manner.' He whipped his anger to give weight to his bravado. 'Dammit, man! I am on my way to visit Lord Ridgemount. This could have serious consequences for you, if I am not immediately released. I thought we had cleared up any misunderstanding.'

Bryn held his breath. The man who had attacked him was sweating profusely, his voice shaken. 'I were just doing my duty. I don't want no trouble.' He glanced anxiously at his accomplice. 'Master bain't here. What if Ridgemount sends out a search party? The man we were told to look out for were said to be fair. This one is dark-haired.'

Bryn breathed more easily. He had been blond as a boy, but his hair had darkened over the years to brown. He persisted in his reasoning, 'I should have taken more care. I had not realised the church was on private land.' He held out his arms. 'Cut these and I give my word I will not inform the authorities of your over-diligence.' He attempted a mocking laugh. 'Least said mayhap the better. It is somewhat humiliating for me to have been laid out cold. My guardian was against me doing this tour for another year. I was most insistent that I could look after myself. Made a poor job of it with you on duty here.'

'Untie his feet but leave his hands bound,' Savage ordered, his stare narrowed and calculating upon Bryn. 'One false move and I fire, understand?'

Bryn nodded. The rope about his legs was untied and he rose unsteadily to his feet, the blood rushing through his veins like molten lead. His limbs buckled under the agony and it took all his strength to remain standing.

Savage stepped back but kept the blunderbuss trained on him as

Bryn climbed the steps. 'This time I will let you off, young sir. But the laws of trespass are strict. There be some as would have shot you on sight.'

'Then I am indeed grateful to you.' Bryn remained civil. He squinted as he walked into the morning sunlight. Through the overgrown shrubs he glimpsed the ornamental dome of the old carriage house at Willow Vale. From its direction he realised he had been locked up in the cellar of the twelfth-century fortified manor house that had originally been built on this land. He had thought that his grandfather had blocked off the old ruins, but he must have been mistaken and they had been used as storerooms.

'I left my horse by the church.' He looked around as though he was a stranger unaware of the layout of the estate. The church would be behind him.

'Then head through yonder wood.' Savage indicated with the gun. As they approached the long grass, he snapped, 'Mind where you put your feet, there be mantraps hidden all over these grounds.'

Of all the shocks Bryn had experienced on his return to his home, this was the most horrifying, with its sinister implications. What dastardly deeds had Carforth committed, bringing dishonour to the estate and Bryn's Bryant ancestors?

Following yet another lecture from Felicity, this time about her lack of consideration towards other members of the family, Rowena was halted in a heated protest by the echo of Elspeth's words in the graveyard. Although she hated the constraints placed upon her at Reskelly Cottage, the old woman's words did make sense. The only way to protect her parents' good names was to act impeccably. She loved her father too much to bring further disgrace to his memory.

'You are right to show me the error of my ways, dear Stepmama.' She startled Felicity by her compliance. 'It is time I overcame my grief at the loss of Papa. He would be ashamed that I have neglected my brother and sister. You have dealt with your own loss with dignity and forbearance. I ask your pardon that I have added to your burdens when I should have been your helpmeet.'

Felicity seemed unable to answer, but her face lost much of its tension. Rowena dipped a curtsey. 'Let me start today. I will take Charlotte and Thea to visit Aunt Hannah at the farm. May I use the pony and trap?'

'Yes.' Felicity became flustered. 'That would be lovely for your sisters.' A tear appeared on her lashes and she dabbed it gracefully away. 'I hope this is how you will continue in your responsibilities.'

Rowena lowered her eyes demurely. 'It is what Papa would wish. I want only to be a daughter of whom he would be proud, and yourself, of course, dear Stepmama.'

Felicity nodded and embraced Rowena, gently touching her cheek as she pulled away. 'Your papa would wish for us to manage well together, would he not?'

Was it really that easy to get her own way? Rowena smiled as she ordered Mo Merrin to harness the pony to the trap. Since she had been sent away to the seminary she had outgrown her riding pony and Rhianne at Boscabel now used it. She had demanded a horse of her own from Adam to replace it, but he had been influenced by Felicity's complaints that she did not trust Rowena not to gallop about the countryside in the most unladylike manner and endanger her reputation, and had decided she must wait until her eighteenth birthday to have a mare of her own, when another servant would be engaged to accompany her on her rides. He had however allowed Jasper Fraddon to teach her how to drive the pony and trap, which had given her some freedom. Felicity, who was nervous of horses and poor at handling the reins, preferred Rowena to drive when they called upon family and neighbours. This also allowed Mo Merrin to continue with his duties at the cottage.

Today, although she did not relish having Charlotte for company, Rowena realised that it would be convenient for her stepsister to join them, as she could then supervise Thea, leaving Rowena free to enjoy her time at the farm with Abigail and Florence.

It was a fine Cornish day. The sky was clear of clouds and a light breeze kept the temperature moderate. Thea was excited about the visit, and having decided to make the best of the companionship of her sisters, Rowena led them in singing folk songs and telling stories until they were laughing and in high spirits.

She stopped singing when she saw a rider approaching as they reached the crossroads between Trewenna, Penruan and Polruggan.

'Is that not Wilbur Trevanion?' Charlotte giggled. 'What will Mama say when she learns that you have met your beau?'

'He is not my beau,' Rowena stated, yet she adjusted her straw bonnet and tucked a stray tendril of hair from her brow out of sight.

'You planned to meet him today.' Charlotte pouted. 'That is why you were so nice to us. I knew you were up to something, Rowena.'

'I did not plan to meet him.' Rowena was annoyed that her good deed had been twisted against her.

'Then do not dare leave us and go off and talk to him alone,' Charlotte warned. 'If you do, I shall tell Mama.'

'Miss Loveday and Miss Barrett.' Wilbur raised his hat to them as he drew level. 'This is an unexpected surprise.'

'Is it?' Charlotte muttered under her breath. Then, louder, 'We are visiting our cousins at the farm. We have to be home again by midday.' A jab in the ribs from Rowena made her yelp in pain.

Wilbur was on a chestnut gelding that he was having trouble keeping in check. An irritated flick of the whip from its master caused the animal to rear, almost unseating its rider.

'That is a spirited beast, but quite magnificent. A firm grip of the knee and hand will serve you more readily than the brutality of the lash.' Rowena did not like to see a fine horse ill-treated.

'He is more stubborn than usual this morning.' Wilbur's face was set with annoyance as the gelding pranced in agitation.

'Perhaps you should give him his head and allow him to gallop.' Rowena clicked her tongue and flicked the reins to urge the pony to a walk. With Charlotte spying on her she did not want the meeting elaborated to Felicity.

Wilbur circled his horse and rode along beside her, his voice coming in short pants as he struggled to control his mount. 'I was on my way to Trewenna to deliver an invitation to your family to dine with us next Saturday. My cousin Selwyn is visiting for a month and we thought it would be pleasant to meet our neighbours. Reverend Mr Loveday, his wife and your cousins Japhet and Adam and their wives are also invited.'

Rowena's initial glow of pleasure at their meeting was transient and her voice was touched with frost. 'My stepmother and myself could not accept so pleasant an invitation if you have also included the new master of Trevowan.'

'My brother is aware of your sensibilities,' he hastily assured. 'It is to be a small affair. There will be opportunity enough for Selwyn to meet other neighbours on subsequent occasions. He was very keen to make Japhet's acquaintance. Selwyn has an interest in horse racing and your cousin is gaining a reputation for his breeding from his stallion Emir Hassan.'

'I have no doubt that he will win the Derby with one of his foals in the future.' Rowena basked in the pride of Japhet's esteem amongst the top breeders and owners of the racing fraternity, many of whom were amongst the highest ranks of the nobility.

They were approaching the lane and the entrance to the farm. 'If the abominable Tristan is not to attend, I am sure my stepmama will be delighted to join you and your family on Saturday. It is a shame I will not be at Reskelly when you deliver our invitation.' She glanced up at him under her lashes. 'Good day, Mr Trevanion. My family are expecting us.'

She urged the pony to a trot and set off along the narrow lane at a rapid pace.

'You are too cruel, Rowena,' Charlotte giggled. 'Did you see his disappointment? He was quite discomfited that you did not linger and talk. How could you so treat your beau?'

'He is not my beau. And you will have no tales to tell your mama. I behaved with perfect decorum.' Rowena smiled in satisfaction. The handsome Wilbur was too complacent if he expected her to swoon at his slightest attention. He had not called at Reskelly Cottage since she had seen him at the May Day revels, though his brother Bruce had called on them twice while Wilbur was visiting an old school friend in Redruth.

Rowena did not like his neglect, and she hoped her coolness would teach him a lesson. She had been infatuated with him when they had first met two years ago. The five-year difference in their ages had made him seem dashing and sophisticated, and he had dominated her dreams at the ladies' seminary. Abigail also was enamoured of him and they would talk for hours about how handsome and charming he had been when they met. Each had fed the other's rivalry over which of them he had shown most attention. Rowena was certain that it had been to her, and this had increased her fervour, so that she had convinced herself that she was half in love with him.

Yet this year she had not been so besotted. She had seen that although he was quick to compliment her and seek her company at any social occasion, he was also equally attentive to other women. Abigail would not have a word said against him, her praise rekindling Rowena's interest. It disconcerted her that each encounter left her less enchanted. But an unexpected meeting like this morning could still set her heart fluttering. There was no mistaking the deep admiration that shone in his eyes. Could he be falling in love with her? A thrill of anticipation sent a delightful shiver through her body. Although she was not interested in the man, after enduring so much censure from her family, his adoration was exhilarating.

Chapter Nine

The experience at Willow Vale had shaken Bryn, and had brought up more unanswered questions than solutions to the mystery of his flight. They continued to disturb him on his journey to Boscabel.

He had been tempted to remain longer in Exmoor and learn more of events during his lost years. Innkeepers were notorious for knowing all the local gossip. But caution prevailed. Although he had talked his way out of his capture, the thicker-set of the two assailants had remained wary. If he stayed in the area and they found out that he was asking questions, it could alert Carforth that someone had an interest in the estate. That could be a short pace to his stepfather believing that he was alive and almost of an age to inherit the property. There were too many secrets bound up in Carforth's time at Willow Vale for his stepfather to allow Bryn to investigate. Carforth would have had no legal jurisdiction over the estate, but if he had deliberately allowed it to fall into ruin, then he would be accountable to the courts.

In the meantime Bryn did not want an assassin on his trail, which could also endanger the Loveday family. His only chance of bringing Carforth to justice for the death of his mother and brother was for him to work incognito in the background.

He reckoned he would have three or perhaps four days of grace before Captain Loveday would send out men to search for him, or undertake the task himself. It would not be right to drag his guardian away from the busy shipyard at this time. The last letter from Senara to Nathan had said that apart from a new brigantine they were building, three vessels damaged by French warships would provide six months' work for the shipwrights.

If his stepfather's watchmen were in any way suspicious, it would be better to lie low and avoid further investigations. He did not come into his inheritance for another three years. Captain Loveday would know how to find out how the house and hamlet had been destroyed.

Bryn arrived at Boscabel late in the afternoon to find the house in the throes of activity, preparing for Captain Loveday to leave the next day.

Cries of relief and pleasure greeted his appearance. Joel, who tore through the dwelling, yelling at the top of his voice, had seen his approach from an upper window.

'Mama! Papa! He's back. Bryn's not murdered or run off to join the circus or be a pirate. He's here. Bryn's here.' In his excitement his flights of fancy were limitless.

Throughout the house footsteps echoed on the wooden floors. Joel was the first to the entrance hall and flung himself into the young man's arms, almost toppling Bryn in his eagerness. Senara stood inside the entrance, a tear glistening on one cheek as she waited for him to put Joel aside and greet her. With pride she noted that he was now a head taller than herself.

'I said all along he would be safe,' Nathan declared, joining them, finally able to cast off his guilt that he should have read the letter Bryn had written to his father and informed the headmaster of the school of its contents. He had been terrified that his friend had been harmed.

The family settled in the great Tudor hall, which was cool in the heat of the summer afternoon sun.

'You had us all worried, Bryn,' Adam said sternly, as he joined them. 'Fortunately you are safe. Did you find out about your family and home? Has your memory returned?'

Ashamed of the concern he had caused them, Bryn could not hold his guardian's stare. 'I visited the estate in Exmoor but did not make my identity known,' he evaded. 'The house was closed up. My stepfather had not lived there in recent years and I recognised none of the servants. Seeing it made me recall everything about my childhood and family.' He glazed over the details of destruction, not wishing to worry Senara or the children, and simply told them the facts of his name and background.'

'So do you now wish us to call you Alexander or Alex Bryant?' Senara asked.

'I will always call him Bryn,' Joel remonstrated. 'I chose his name.'

Bryn smiled at the eleven-year-old, whose eyes flashed with defiance. 'For the present I would prefer to be known as Bryn Loveday. It will be easier to discover the whereabouts of my stepfather and any misconduct that way.'

'Was your house beautiful and as you remembered it?' asked Joel's twin sister, Rhianne. She was as fair and sweet-natured as Joel was dark and tempestuous.

Adam noted the slump to his ward's shoulders and the brief shadow of pain in his eyes. Yet Bryn did not allow his smile to waver. 'It was not exactly as I remembered it. But then I had only seen it through the eyes of a boy.'

He answered all their questions with carefully rehearsed half-truths that did not escape Adam's attention. Eventually Adam put up a hand. 'Bryn is tired from his long journey. Allow him to take some refreshment in peace and rest.'

Bryn gratefully escaped to his room to change his travel-stained clothes and stretch out on the bed. He rubbed his hands across his face. He had hated deceiving the family, but with each mile that had distanced him from Willow Vale, he had become more certain that if he was to bring Carforth to account for his crimes, he must do so in secret.

An hour passed and there was a light tap on the chamber door.

'May I come in, Bryn?' Captain Loveday enquired.

'Of course, sir.' He rose from the bed and stood stiffly to attention, expecting a lecture, which he fully deserved.

Adam closed the door. 'Sit down, Bryn. I suspect that for the sake of my wife you spared her any upsetting details.' He pulled an X-shaped chair away from the wall and sat next to the bed.

Bryn sat and faced Captain Loveday's patient stare while all the horrors he had experienced sent shudders through his body. Ashamed that he was not showing the fortitude his guardian would expect, he drew a sharp breath, but the words locked in his throat.

'Take your time, lad,' Adam prompted gently. 'It was foolish to go off on your own, but I probably would have done the same. We have always suspected that anything you discovered about your past would not be pleasant and could present many dangers.'

'I knew that what I had to face would not be easy.' Bryn swallowed against the desolation and anger scalding him. 'It was worse than my most horrendous nightmare.' He could not hold his guardian's stare and kept his own fastened to a knot of wood in the floorboard. 'I remembered that my stepfather had tried to kill my mother – and that in the end he succeeded in poisoning her. He also killed my older brother. He was evil and crazed. He had some bizarre notion that there was treasure hidden on the estate. He was prepared for us all to die to claim it.' His throat seized up, the tremors increasing.

Adam counselled, 'Take deep breaths. Tell me everything. This is indeed more horrific than I had feared. We are here for you, Bryn. You do not have to face this alone.'

Reassured, Bryn found it easier to breathe and control the panic that had threatened to unman him. He revealed all that he had remembered about his childhood, the beatings and his flight. His voice grew heavier at his graphic description of the desecrated cottages, the ruined house and neglected grounds. He was scathing of his own naivety at being captured. Then with characteristic modesty he played down how he had outwitted the guards and made his escape.

Adam had remained silent throughout the narrative, but as the events unfolded, his face tightened and Bryn could sense the outrage burning through his guardian.

'I did not mean to cause Mrs Loveday worry and I ask your pardon for causing you both distress,' Bryn finally concluded.

'You could have been killed,' Adam responded, 'but I would have done the same in your position. I am appalled at the incidents you have related. Carforth must be brought to account. But you must promise me that you will not go near Willow Vale again on your own. You are still under my protection and I regard you as a son. Japhet will support me in this. When we confront Carforth, it will be as a family.'

'Thank you, sir. But I am already indebted to you for my life and your care these past years. I would not have others place themselves in danger. Carforth is vengeful and evil. He destroyed the lives and reputation of my family. I must be the one to seek retribution. I will be eighteen in August. I am not as young as you believed.'

'You are still three years from your majority.' Adam lifted a dark brow to lighten his words. 'Time enough to find out a great deal about Carforth. His history before he married your mother, and what is known of him in recent years. With his connections with the government, my good friend Long Tom will be invaluable in tracing him. Can you remember the name of the lawyers who served your father's estate?'

Bryn shook his head. 'A Mr Hensby called upon my mother from time to time when she was a widow. I do not remember any visits after she married Carforth.'

'That at least is something to go on.' Adam sat forward in his chair. 'Promise me there will be no more charging across the country on your own. We are a family on this. Willow Vale will be restored to you and Carforth will pay for his crimes. I give you my word.'

Something was definitely not right. Each day since Hannah's return to the farm the feeling had intensified. Yet she could not nail down why she was unable to shake that impression. She had gone through the farm accounts. The livestock entries tallied. The production of the milk herd remained steady, and more inns and local kiddleys were purchasing milk and the cheese and butter made on the farm. The weekly takings for the dairy produce at market had also improved. The animals were free of disease. The outbuildings, dry-stone walls and ditches were well maintained. The dairymaids and servants seemed content enough in their work. Ample hay had been cut for the winter and the fields of corn would give a good harvest. Why then did her unease remain?

Her first inspection of the milking sheds and buttery had confirmed that the high standards of cleanliness that she insisted upon had been maintained. The storerooms were free of vermin droppings, the laundry was also immaculate and no mud had been trodden in from the farmyard.

The timber-framed farmhouse was a low-ceilinged, rambling structure that had been added to over the generations by those who had lived here. There had been Rabsons here before there were Lovedays at Trevowan, and Hannah was proud that Davey would continue in his father's line.

This morning she had re-checked every room in the house. No valuables were missing from the chambers or the locked silver and china chests. She had felt a twinge of guilt at her vigilance, but she never ignored her instincts, and they were telling her that all was not as it should be. Although she missed her husband, she had intended that her stay would last several weeks. Time enough to discover anything amiss.

The sound of whistling carried to her, and she grinned. Davey always whistled as he worked with the animals. His father Oswald had done the same. It had seemed to calm the beasts, and any cows grazing in the fields would walk in the direction of the sound when they heard it. The smell of pastry cooking filled the lower rooms, and Hannah hurried to the kitchen to check that a maid was on hand to ensure that it did not burn. As she passed the open yard door, the whistling stopped and she heard Davey talking to the gruff-voiced Cy Watkins. She had wanted a word with the manager herself, but was careful that she did not appear to act over Davey. It was important to establish with the servants that although a young man, Davey was now the one in charge of the farm.

It sounded as though Davey was giving Watkins orders for the far wood to be checked for poachers' traps. Watkins's answer was low-pitched, but Hannah sensed that he was arguing with her son. She walked in front of the window where her shadow would be visible from outside and raised her voice.

'Annie, the pastries are about to burn. Where are you?'

The kitchen maid, who was also the cook, came into the room from the larder. 'I was counting the eggs for market tomorrow, Mrs Deighton.' Her round ruddy face was flushed. She grabbed a wooden paddle and opened the bread oven set in the corner of the fireplace and lifted out the golden pies. 'They be saved just in time, Mrs Deighton.'

'Good work, Annie.' Hannah glanced outside and saw that Watkins was now listening to Davey's instructions without interruption. She kept a covert eye on the manager as she examined the vegetables that had been picked from the garden for their supper. All were plump and at their best. Watkins had his back to the kitchen and his manner was now deferential. He tugged respectfully at the brim of his felt hat when Davey dismissed him.

A milkmaid had come into the yard and dipped a curtsey to Hannah's son, her voice anxious. 'Could you look at a cow, sir? She be favouring her right leg. She slipped in the mud coming to the milking shed. Maybe she strained it.'

Davey disappeared into the shed and Hannah watched Watkins

hang back reluctantly from following. She went into the yard where the horse and cart had returned from the milk delivery to the local villages. While the driver led the horse into the field to graze, two milkmaids were unloading the empty churns and taking them to the pump to be washed. Watkins saw Hannah and tipped his hat to her.

'Mrs Deighton, it be a pleasure to see how able Master Rabson be in taking charge.'

'Thank you, Watkins. He learned well on the Eastley estate during his time there. It was a beneficial experience.'

'He will make a good farmer.'

'In that he takes after his father.' She was suspicious of his too ingratiating manner, and he did not hold her stare. If a man had something to hide, he would find that difficult.

'I trust you found no fault with my management this past year, Mrs Deighton?' Watkins challenged whilst his gaze travelled over the outbuildings and fields, anywhere but at her face.

'None at all.' She kept her voice light, unwilling to rouse any suspicion that she did not trust him. 'My late husband set high standards for this farm. The Rabson milk herd has long been one of the best in the county.'

She regarded Watkins's tidy appearance. He had a pleasant round face and was clean-shaven. His brown hair was touched with grey at the temples and cut short. His breeches and shirt were of a good quality and remarkably clean for work clothes. She had noted before that he changed his shirt every three days, earlier if it had become exceptionally soiled. Farming was dirty work and few workers took such care with their appearance. He was stocky of build and slightly below average height. He allowed nothing to slip his observation and was constantly ordering the servants to work faster and chatter less. Sometimes Hannah felt that his badgering was too extreme, but he certainly achieved results.

She judged him to be in his late thirties. He was not married and did not mix with the other servants, taking his meals alone in his cottage. He had been working at the farm less than a year. The previous overseer, Mark Sawle, and his wife had left to work at Tor Farm for Japhet. Mark had always wanted to work with horses again. As a youth he had been employed at Lord Fetherington's stables. He was conscientious and hardworking, and it had been a blow to lose him.

Watkins had come with good references from a friend of Bruce Trevanion. He might earn an occasional dour look from a servant when he criticised their work, and they certainly made themselves look busy whenever he was nearby, but Hannah had heard no word of complaint from them. During the years she had run the farm alone, she had often faced resentment and antagonism from male workers. She had always informed them plainly that if they did not like taking orders from a woman, they should find work elsewhere. A few had tried to disregard her orders. All of those had been given short shift. She had refused to be bullied or browbeaten, but it had made her wary, and she was ready for any confrontation. This was the first time she had been able to study the manager's work over a period of time. Any failing would soon be apparent.

'I have great faith in my son, Watkins. He may be young, but he is not without experience.'

She would have said more, but the noisy honking of geese made her turn in their direction. They were better heralds of visitors to the farm than any guard dog. She smiled with pleasure at recognising her brother Japhet riding through the entrance in the lane. He cut a distinguished figure on his black Arab stallion Emir Hassan. The horse was spirited and temperamental, but Japhet rode him as though he and the stallion were one. She could see from the dust on the muscles of his mount that they had enjoyed a long ride, and under her brother's skilful hands his prize stud was obedient to every command.

Japhet leapt nimbly from the saddle, his tall, slim figure lithe as an athlete. He tethered Emir Hassan to the hitching ring at the side of the house and loosed the girth. Hannah restrained the impulse to throw herself into his arms. Every time she saw him, she was proud of all he had achieved in the short time since he had returned to England. There had been a period when she had feared that they would never be graced with his company again. For eight years he had either been incarcerated in Newgate or facing the dangers of transportation to Sydney Cove after being falsely accused of highway robbery. Even now, the thought of that time made her shudder at the horrors he must have endured. But they were all behind him. A pardon had been obtained, and his brave and devoted wife Gwendolyn had sailed to Australia with it to gain his freedom. To their credit, the couple had stayed in the fledgling colony for a further five years, and Japhet had used all his cunning and skills to make a fortune. Hannah suspected that not all of his ventures would have been strictly legal. He had always been a lovable rogue.

'Good day to you, sister.' Japhet grinned. 'Gwen asked me if you and the children would dine with us tomorrow.'

'We would be delighted. Although I doubt Davey will drag himself away from the farm. He is taking his work here seriously, and I am not sure that he is not finding it easy to handle Watkins. The man too often questions his decisions.'

'Then Watkins must learn his place. Do you wish me to have a word with him?' Japhet's expression hardened, and for an instant Hannah glimpsed the dark side of her brother's nature. No man could have risen so high in a penal colony after suffering degradation and untold horrors without being irrevocably changed in some way. Once, the devil-may-care aspect of his personality had been light-hearted and irrepressible. Now the narrowing of his hazel eyes could also blaze with hellfire. Having tasted the fires of the damned, Japhet was more ruthless, more determined to avenge an injustice. She had to choose her words carefully until she had proof about her suspicions of Watkins.

'Not for the moment. It is one of the trials Davey must overcome to win the respect of the workers. He has to prove himself.' She frowned. 'The man is difficult to fathom.'

'Where is Watkins?' Japhet said, looking round. 'Were you not talking to him when I arrived?'

Hannah sighed. 'As so often happens, he appeared to vanish into thin air. He should be walking across that field. I heard Davey tell him to check for poachers' traps in the wood.'

'I called at the farm regularly when you were away to check that everything was in order. I could tell Watkins did not like my interference, but he seemed to be doing an excellent job. Although often he was not here when I visited; supposedly he was working in one of the fields on the far side of the farm. As everything appeared in order with the deliveries and animals, I did not follow up his absence.'

'I am probably worrying overmuch.' Hannah did not dwell on the matter. 'This is an important time for Davey, and I want everything to go smoothly.'

'Adam and I are on hand if Davey needs advice. I shall keep watch on Watkins when you leave. Will that make your mind rest easier?' The lines that had gouged deeper around Japhet's eyes and mouth were a sinister warning. The rugged features were still as handsome as those of a demigod, whose easy charm could draw anyone under his spell, but like all deities his vengeance could be terrible to behold.

She laughed. 'I know that look of yours, Japhet. You think I am fussing too much and mollycoddling Davey.'

Their manner remained light and teasing, but both were aware of the underlying seriousness behind the words. Japhet replied, 'I never ignore a woman's intuition. Neither do I trust a man who is too eager to please. It is often a smokescreen to cover their tracks.'

Chapter Ten

It was the first time Rowena had been inside Polruggan Manor, and she was not impressed. It was a gloomy square granite structure with mullioned windows. The entrance opened directly into a flagstoned hall with a dog-legged Jacobean staircase. Life-size portraits of men in ruffs or falling lace collars and half-armour in the style of Holbein or Van Dyck crowded the walls. The guests were led through an anteroom, which was dominated by a large red and green tapestry that was gloomy and dour.

The main salon was equally uninviting. The padded chairs were in bright gold brocade to match the window hangings, which were lavishly embellished with fringes. Huge brass firedogs adorned the inglenook fireplace, which was set with a large log that would burn slowly all day. Although the fire was unlit, the room smelt of wood smoke. An old-fashioned wooden cartwheel-shaped chandelier dominated the ceiling, and the dark floorboards were polished so highly that they reflected the light from the windows. More ancestors glared smugly from the walls. They were all so solemn and filled with self-importance. Did none of them smile?

Apart from the elaborate hangings, the room lacked the finesse of a woman's touch, and the only ornament was a large grandfather clock that chugged like a mine's pump engine as it paced out the seconds.

Felicity's praise was nevertheless effusive. 'How charming to see that so much of its original character has been retained.'

'I am delighted that it meets with your approval, Mrs Loveday.' Bruce Trevanion greeted them as he marched into the room, followed by Wilbur and another young gentleman. His voice echoed theatrically, and dressed in moleskin trousers, navy jacket and red and gold embroidered waistcoat, he filled the room with his presence. He was at least fifteen years older than Wilbur, and although their features were unmistakably those of brothers, his figure had vastly thickened and his hair, already grey, had receded to the crown of his head. His voice had an over-hearty boom that Rowena found irritating.

She curtseyed to the men, watching the response of the young ones through her lashes.

Felicity was talking far too quickly as she simpered, 'The manor is beautiful. I love these older houses. There is so much history attached to them. I daresay if these walls could speak they would have a merry tale to tell.'

Rowena cringed with embarrassment. Felicity was blushing and fawning over Mr Trevanion worse than an adolescent schoolgirl. Fortunately their host was either oblivious to her feelings, or too gentlemanly to act with similar lack of decorum.

Mr Trevanion had been addressing Rowena, and with a start she realised that she had not been paying attention.

'Your pardon, sir, I was distracted by the portraits of your ancestors. Could you repeat what you said?'

'Wool-gathering again, my dear,' Felicity reprimanded. 'Mr Trevanion was introducing you to his cousin.'

Rowena turned a bright smile upon the young man who had stepped forward to bow to her. Her heart skittered in an alarming fashion. She had never encountered a gentleman of such angelic beauty. A head taller than his uncle and cousin, he was broad-shouldered and athletically built. He was also impeccably attired in the latest fashion and was breath-stealingly handsome.

'Miss Loveday, may I present Sir Selwyn Trevanion?' Mr Trevanion repeated.

The Adonis smiled, causing Rowena's stomach to turn somersaults, and her mouth was suddenly too dry to reply.

'Charmed to make your acquaintance, Miss Loveday. Wilbur speaks often of you. I can understand why, now that I discover that he has been singularly blessed with so delightful and beautiful a neighbour.'

She moistened her lips with the tip of her tongue. 'Welcome to this part of Cornwall, Sir Selwyn. I understand that you are interested in my uncle's stables. He is unfortunately out of the county for the next week or so.'

'Then that will give me longer to further our acquaintance, Miss Loveday.' His smile was so beguiling, it tripped her heartbeat to a breathless pace.

'You are very forward, sir,' Felicity announced primly.

'Indeed, Selwyn, Miss Loveday is but recently out of the schoolroom.' Mr Trevanion was annoyingly pompous. He made her sound as naive a nincompoop as Charlotte, who was too young to have attended.

'It was a finishing school, Sir Selwyn. I am not such a child,' she answered.

'And you have spirit.' Sir Selwyn grinned. 'I would have taken you as nothing less than an accomplished young lady.'

Wilbur snorted derisively. 'Pay no heed to this silver-tongued rogue, Miss Loveday. My cousin is an abominable flirt. He cannot resist flattering every women he meets.'

Rowena smiled sweetly, but her voice carried the sting of censure. 'Sir Selwyn, I shall take your flattery with a pinch of salt, though it is ungallant of Mr Trevanion to suggest that I am unworthy of a sincere compliment.'

Wilbur gulped. 'My dear Miss Loveday, a thousand pardons. It was never my intention . . .'

Sir Selwyn laughed. 'Wilbur, you really do take life too seriously. Miss Loveday was but jesting.' He bowed to Rowena and his gaze caressed her ardently. Although she was delighted at his boldness, she would not allow herself to be so easily played.

'That is the art of flirtation, is it not, Sir Selwyn, to tease and coerce?' She raised her fan to cover the lower part of her face, her eyes alight with mischief. 'It can be a dangerous game, so I have been told.' She had summed up Sir Selwyn as worldlier than Wilbur and was resolved to be on her guard. She sketched a curtsey, aware of Sir Selwyn's interest, Wilbur's blush of discomfort and Felicity's glare of disapproval. Mr Trevanion's sharpened scrutiny was of no interest to her.

Further voices drifted to them from the entrance hall. Uncle Joshua and Aunt Cecily were announced and further introductions made. With Japhet at a race meeting, his wife Gwendolyn accompanied her sister Lady Traherne and her husband Sir Henry, from Traherne Hall. Adam and his family had sent their regrets that they had a prior engagement to dine with Squire Penwithick.

They dined in an oak-panelled room. On either side of Mr Trevanion sat Felicity and Aunt Cecily. Rowena was placed between Uncle Joshua and Wilbur and was directly opposite Gwendolyn, who had Sir Henry and Sir Selwyn on either side.

The conversation at the table was lively, but Rowena was irked that Sir Selwyn was talking animatedly to Gwendolyn about the stallion Emir Hassan and the foals he had sired.

'I fear I must disappoint you,' Gwendolyn replied laughingly. 'I am no authority on horses, but you are welcome to visit the stud whenever you wish.'

Wilbur was making up for his cousin's lack of attention and chatting incessantly to Rowena, although there was a strong element of boasting and bravado in his topics. To her surprise, on several occasions Mr Trevanion addressed a direct comment to her, asking for her observation upon a subject. Never short of an opinion on any matter, Rowena was twice cut short by Felicity, who reclaimed their host's attention with some trivial inanity. Sir Henry flirted outrageously throughout the meal with Gwendolyn and Felicity and included Rowena in many of his compliments. A childhood friend of her uncles', he was always free with his appreciation of a pretty woman, and if gossip could be believed, had kept several mistresses in style in Fowey.

Even to Rowena's inexperienced ear there appeared to be a friendly rivalry between Sir Henry and Mr Trevanion as they vied to flirt with the ladies present. Lady Traherne ignored her husband, her stony-faced comments directed at Aunt Cecily or Gwendolyn. She had none of her younger sister's vivacity and was too quick to criticise others for their shortcomings. Twice when Rowena laughed, she made a cutting remark about the impropriety of young women today.

Rowena bit back a tart retort. It was only the third occasion she had been permitted to join adult company when they were entertaining. Roslyn Traherne never had a good word to say about anyone and for years had ridiculed Gwendolyn for marrying a rogue, and she certainly would not have spared Rowena's mother in her condemnation of the Loveday family. Rowena stole a sideways glance at her. Lady Traherne's protruding teeth did nothing to improve the sour lines of a horsey face. She was talking loudly to Felicity, who looked uncomfortable.

'Why you have anything to do with Elspeth after the way she turned her back on you to feather her own nest and remain at Trevowan, I will never understand, Felicity. The woman believes herself to be a law unto herself. Where is her loyalty to your late husband, who gave her a home for all those years? She has always been somewhat eccentric, but this behaviour is—'

Felicity cut the older woman short, bristling, 'If you disapprove so strongly of my aunt's behaviour, I am sure she is more than able to defend her actions to you. Rather than you talk about her behind her back.'

Rowena was startled at her stepmother's flash of spirit. She had always been in awe of Lady Traherne. Now Felicity pointedly turned away from her ladyship to listen to Gwendolyn, who had all those around her at the table laughing at an anecdote.

Lady Traherne snapped her mouth closed, and the harsh lines about her eyes and mouth deepened. For the briefest moment the shadow in her eyes made Rowena sense her ladyship's unhappiness. Was that why she was always so critical of others? She recalled the words Elspeth had spoken to her in the graveyard about charm and sweetness achieving more success than recrimination; or something like that. Lady Traherne was certainly proof that no one warmed to a shrew who never had a good word to say about anyone.

As though sensing her glance upon her, Lady Traherne turned to Rowena. Her lips curled with disdain. 'Your hoyden ways seem to have been improved by your time at the ladies' seminary.'

The flash of anger was quickly suppressed. Rowena smiled demurely as she experimented with Elspeth's advice. 'To have won your approval means a great deal to me, Lady Traherne. It was unladylike of me to express my grief for the loss of my father in so volatile a manner. In honour of his memory I want only for my father to have been proud of me.'

'Very commendable. Let us hope that your wilful nature does not blight your good intentions.'

Again Rowena swallowed a retort, her smile as sincere as she could make it. 'And how are your children this summer? The boys are visiting Lord Traherne's cousins in Kent, I believe. You must miss them. And your three daughters, are they well? I saw them last at Lord Fetherington's June garden gala. Such pretty girls, and so polite. They are a credit to you.'

The stiffness left her ladyship's features. 'Anne is an exquisite dancer and sings like an angel. Dear Dorothea delights all our guests upon the pianoforte, and Mary . . .' Her face glowed with pleasure. Rowena had never seen her so animated, and was surprised when Roslyn Traherne leaned forward, lowering her voice in confidence. 'Mary has attracted the attention of Lord Fetherington's youngest brother, the Honourable Anthony Fetherington. There have been discussions concerning a match. There should be an announcement next month. Is that not wonderful? Although the wedding will not take place until she is eighteen. And I have great hopes for Dorothea that a match will be made with one of the Bracewaite cousins. There has been an understanding between our families. A pity both Wilbur and Selwyn have shown no interest in marriage. It would be perfect to have Anne settled as well.'

'She is but thirteen, is she not?' Rowena could not contain her astonishment.

'A mother cannot start casting an eye upon erstwhile suitors too early,' Lady Traherne sighed.

'I wish Mary every happiness. And Dorothea,' Rowena said sweetly, through a stab of jealousy. Both girls were younger than her and far less attractive, yet had won eminent and wealthy suitors.

The malicious glitter was back in her ladyship's eyes. 'I trust Felicity is equally diligent in introducing a suitable husband for you. Though the poor woman has her hands full with your siblings. It cannot be easy, especially as I assume your dowry has been severely diminished.'

'I would not want a husband who did not desire me for myself rather than for my dowry.' Rowena was indignant.

Lady Traherne sniffed. 'True life is no fairy tale. Pretty faces are two a penny. When a man comes to marriage, the dowry is what is important. That and good breeding, of course.'

Felicity laughed at a comment from Mr Trevanion. 'You have the drollest wit, sir. Has he not, Gwendolyn?'

Lady Traherne gave a sniff of disapproval. 'It would appear that your stepmother is too eager to snare a husband for herself to ensure your happiness. And your father hardly cold in his grave.'

'In your wisdom, Lady Traherne, you stated that it cannot be easy for Stepmama to manage on her own. She has been a widow more than two years. Her security and happiness would be my greatest wish for her.' It would certainly make life less onerous, Rowena reflected, if Felicity married Mr Trevanion and took up residence at the manor. She did not feel her thoughts were disloyal to her father. He would wish for Thea and George to be well provided for in their education and future. Neither would it do Rowena herself any harm to have the influence of the Trevanions to improve her own marriage prospects.

The dessert was finished, and as the highest-ranking woman present, Lady Traherne rose. 'Ladies, we shall leave the men to enjoy their port and cigars.'

'And perhaps one of you accomplished ladies would honour us humble men by playing for us,' Mr Trevanion insisted. 'The pianoforte has recently been tuned and I am eager to hear how well it sounds.'

'Then that had better be Felicity,' Gwendolyn insisted. 'My sister and I play no more than adequately. Though Rowena has a pretty voice. I am sure we can persuade her to sing for us.'

The men stood as the women filed from the room. Mr Trevanion watched them with interest. 'I suggest we do not dally upon our port and cigars. It would be ungracious not to attend upon so favourable an entertainment.'

Felicity played a sonata and a short piece by Mozart before inviting Rowena to join her.

'Pray continue to play, Mama. You are more skilled than I. Gwendolyn was too kind. I have never been noted for my singing.'

'Then it is time you performed. This is a small gathering amongst family and friends.' Felicity was proud of her musical skill and was also not averse to her stepdaughter being shown to be less favourable in her accomplishments. She had thought Wilbur Trevanion a little too enamoured of Rowena, and as a younger son he had only his name and no fortune to support a wife. Yet more disturbing was the impropriety of Wilbur paying court to Rowena when Felicity was certain that Bruce was about to announce his feelings for her. A sufficient time since St John's death had passed for it to be acceptable for her to receive an offer of marriage.

As Felicity played the introduction, Rowena composed her nerves by breathing slowly and deeply. Apart from her singing lessons at the seminary, this was the first time she had sung for an audience that was not her family.

Lady Traherne was talking loudly to her sister as she had throughout Felicity's recital. Rowena felt her heartbeat increase. Her mind raced. Please let me not be humiliated by forgetting the words or singing out of tune. The first notes of the song trembled uncertainly, then pride sustained her and she lifted her voice with growing confidence. There was a slight hesitancy on Felicity's part as she recovered her own composure as the gossiping was hushed. Rowena stared at a fixed point on the wall and imagined that St John was present, listening intently.

When the final note faded, loud applause came from the doorway and Mr Trevanion led the men into the music room.

'Bravo, Miss Loveday. Bravo indeed.' Their host smiled with pleasure. 'The sweetest and most delightful voice I have been honoured to hear. Another song if you please.'

Rowena's own smile faltered as she turned and encountered Felicity's set expression. Mr Trevanion eased the moment of tension. 'Are we not doubly blessed, gentlemen, to not only have this nightingale in our midst, but also Mrs Loveday, a most accomplished pianist? You delighted us all with your playing.'

He went on to insist that Rowena sing three more songs, but when he suggested a fourth, Felicity rose from the stool. 'Your pardon, gentlemen, but the hour is growing late. I would be home in time before my youngest children are asleep. Come, Rowena.'

Sir Henry, Joshua and Wilbur and Selwyn Trevanion had gathered around Rowena, praising her performance. Joshua was most effusive. 'You have kept that remarkable talent hidden from us all these years, my dear.'

Sir Henry announced loudly, 'Now that you are mixing with society, no soirée will be complete without the charm of your presence and sweet voice.'

'My music mistress encouraged me to sing, as my playing was so abominable.' Rowena brushed away the praise.

'You are too modest, Miss Loveday. I was entranced,' gushed Wilbur, his expression adoring.

By comparison Sir Selwyn was more aloof, although Rowena was certain she had glimpsed an appreciative glint in his eye. Then, in front of them all, he raised her hand to his lips. The pressure of his fingers circled in a shockingly intimate caress and the warmth of his lips tingled along her arm. 'Quite charming, Miss Loveday.'

Felicity called her name sharply and she reluctantly withdrew her hand. Sir Selwyn stepped back, his manner again cool. Had she imagined that charge of energy like a lightning bolt between them? Flustered, she hurried to her stepmother's side.

'Must you always be so brazen?' Felicity hissed beneath her breath. 'What will Mr Trevanion think of our family when your manners are so disgraceful?'

Rowena did not give a fig about Mr Trevanion's opinion; she was too excited about her reaction to Sir Selwyn and the certainty that she had not been alone in her response to their touch.

Lady Traherne also gestured to her husband and sister that it was time for them to depart.

There was a great fuss and bustling as pelisses were fetched for the ladies and Wilbur jostled with Selwyn to place Rowena's upon her shoulders.

They had gathered on the drive waiting for the carriages to be brought round. Joshua and Cecily were to return to Trewenna in the Traherne open carriage. While Felicity bade her farewell to Mr Trevanion, who escorted her to the trap, Rowena took Selwyn's hand to help her into her seat. Again the meeting of their flesh made her skin tingle and her breath catch in her throat.

'It has been a most delightful afternoon, Miss Loveday. One I shall remember for a long time.'

'It has been a pleasure to make your acquaintance, sir.' Rowena smiled sweetly. 'I trust you will enjoy many pleasurable days at the manor.' It took all her willpower not to make her attraction obvious. Felicity's judgemental eyes were boring into them.

Rowena settled her skirts and reached to take up the reins, but discovered that Felicity was holding them firmly in her grasp.

'Do you not wish me to take the reins, Mama?'

'I think you have made enough of a spectacle of yourself this day,' Felicity gritted between clenched teeth. She flicked the reins with an abruptness that startled the pony, and it set off so quickly that they nearly collided with the Traherne coach that was turning out of the drive.

Rowena gripped the side of the trap with one hand and put out the other to prevent Felicity from being unseated. Her stepmother's expression hardened. She was clearly furious about something, but Rowena had been on her very best behaviour and had spoken and acted in the most seemly manner. Clearly nothing she could do was right.

It was obvious that Felicity was struggling to control the mare. The sky had darkened since they had left Polruggan Manor. The stiffening breeze and a sudden cloudburst made the pony more nervous. At the inexperienced handling, she kept throwing back her head. They were taking a sharp corner when a loud crash of thunder caused the animal to start forward, taking the bend too fast. The wheels jolted over the grass bank on the side of the road and they were almost overset in a ditch. Rowena lost her patience. She grabbed the reins to halt the horse and allow the animal to calm down. There was saliva around its mouth where Felicity had been hauling too heavily on the bit.

'Are you intent on ruining the horse and injuring us?' Rowena demanded. 'You hate taking the reins; why are you insisting on doing so now?'

'Because you were making an exhibition of yourself as usual,' Felicity snapped. 'Now drive on. I do not want to miss the children's bedtime. And we will be drenched by the time we reach the cottage. As if I had not had enough to endure this day.' She fumed silently for the rest of the journey.

Rowena was bewildered. Why did her stepmother hate her so much? There could be no other explanation. She did not want to live at Reskelly Cottage. She must convince Adam that her place was at Boscabel. That would be no easy task. Her uncle considered that she should be with her siblings. She would fight for her independence.

Sweetness, compromise and adapt. Elspeth's words repeated in her mind in time to the horse's pace. Perhaps there was more wisdom in those words than she had at first considered.

Chapter Eleven

Adam had written to his old friend Long Tom, the government agent, about Bryn's discoveries. It could take months to obtain the information needed on Carforth. A man capable of murder and stripping an estate of its assets would be too wily to leave a trail. He had advised Bryn to enjoy this summer and consider his future studies regarding the law. From the destruction of Willow Vale, Adam did not hold out much hope that the finances put in trust by Bryn's father or any family fortune would not have been stolen by Carforth.

In the meantime Adam had his own family's concerns to deal with, not least the continued prosperity of the shipyard. A mail packet from Falmouth had recently been repaired in the yard. It had been severely damaged by a French warship and only saved from capture by a timely sea mist that had enabled it to escape. Fortunately it had not been holed below the waterline and had managed to return to port with its one remaining mast and sail. It was the second mail packet that the yard had repaired, and eager to retain the goodwill of the authorities, Adam had been on board when it was delivered to Falmouth. He had remained on the packet during the inspector's sea trials, when they had sailed under heavy seas to the Scilly Isles. He had been given a satisfactory report on the repairs and a promise that the yard would remain on the company's books for any refurbishment work in the future.

Adam had intended to hire a lugger to take him back to Fowey. The voyage by sea was faster than overland, providing the wind was with them. His experienced eye scanned the horizon. What he saw did not please him. The clouds that had been building all day were now dark and ominous, and any sails in the harbour were being hastily furled as the strong breeze that had carried him so speedily from the Scillies blasted across the sky in violent gusts. The waves had turned from green to pewter; the rising swell of the incoming tide was topped with angry white crests. A storm would hit before the hour. He was stuck in Falmouth for the night. No ship would put to sea in such weather.

He resigned himself to a long, lonely evening. As he walked along the quay, the first drops of rain started. At the same time he noted the slim figure of a well-dressed woman hurrying down the gangplank of a naval frigate. It was an occurrence uncommon enough to hold his attention. The woman's face was hidden by the hood pulled low over her eyes, yet there was something familiar about her gait that made him regard her more closely. When a gust of wind lifted the corner of her hood, he saw enough of her face to recognise the Lady Alys. What was she doing un-escorted on the quayside? It was a dangerous place for a gentlewoman, where women of the streets loitered amongst the crates and barrels piled ready for loading, hoping to entice sailors back to their rooms.

A quick scan of the noisy dock showed him Lady Alys continuing to walk alone. Out of concern for her safety, he followed. Although he did not associate with her husband, Adam had great respect for Lady Alys, who had worked as a spy for the government in France. He had heard that upon her marriage, Tristan had insisted that she give up such perilous work. So what was she doing here?

He closed the distance between them as she weaved through the horses, carts, and men rolling casks along the rough surface of the quay. A scruffy man in worn breeches stained with brine detached himself from an equally shabby companion, and they took up positions behind and either side of Lady Alys. Adam suspected they intended robbery and quickened his pace. He was too late to stop the larger of the men jostling her ladyship. In the space of a few seconds she first elbowed the man in the gut, and then there was a brief glint of steel as her dagger flashed towards the throat of his associate. He ran off at this unexpected retaliation, but the larger man was not so easily discouraged.

The rain had increased and figures on the dock were hurrying for shelter, adding to the confusion around Adam. Lady Alys continued her struggle. Although her assailant grunted in pain from her jab in his gut, he grabbed at her reticule. Lady Alys was jerked forward as she clung tightly to it and slashed at his arm, drawing blood.

Adam found his passage blocked by two sailors carrying a heavy crate between them. He shoved them ruthlessly aside. The crate fell to the ground; wooden splinters from its broken corner erupted like bullets, causing further shouts and scufflings amongst the confusion of bodies.

The delay forced Adam to jump aside, and he watched in alarm as Lady Alys's attacker slammed his fist into her cheek. She was knocked sideways before Adam had time to leap at him, and his own punch to the robber's jaw felled him to the ground.

Upon recovering her balance, Lady Alys spun on the ball of her foot and flashed the dagger towards Adam, not knowing whether he was a third attacker. The wind had blown back her hood, and she squinted against the rain running down her face. There was a momentary flicker of recognition in her eyes before she lowered her guard and ran towards a waiting coach, the blinds drawn at its windows. A crowd had begun to form around the thief lying prone on the ground.

Adam continued his pursuit. Lady Alys pulled open the coach door and, gathering her skirts above her ankles, leapt nimbly inside. As she turned to pull the door closed, her gaze met with Adam's.

'Get in!' she shouted, and banged on the roof for the coachman to whip up the horses.

Adam slumped back against the leather upholstery as the coach lurched forward and the door slammed behind him.

'That rain was a welcome blessing, as it cleared some of the crowd,' Lady Alys said as she struggled under her cloak at the lacings at the back of her gown. She twisted impatiently towards her companion.

'Help me,' she demanded.

He hesitated, shocked that she intended to remove her gown in front of him.

'I've a shirt and breeches on beneath as a disguise,' she informed him tersely. 'If the coach is stopped and searched, they will find two men instead of the man and woman they could be looking for.'

'Who is after you?'

'Anyone who does not want some information reaching the

government.' She had flung off her cloak and he saw beneath the gaping laces of her grey woollen gown the waistband of moleskin breeches and the folds of a cambric shirt.

He ripped the lacing from its eyelets and she stood up and wriggled the gown over her hips. Then she scooped up the cloak and dress and lifted the top of the carriage seat. A brown velvet jacket and beaver hat were hoisted out and the female garments hidden inside. She was already wearing top boots and her hair was closely pinned in a coil around her head.

The carriage lurched, and if his hands had not shot out to save her, Lady Alys would have fallen across Adam's lap. She panted as she slammed the hat over her hair and pulled on the jacket. Then she fell back on to the seat opposite, a low throaty laugh accompanying her actions.

'That was a near thing.' She grinned. 'I had not expected a welcoming committee when I landed. I was fortunate you were there to help me.' She drew a parchment scroll from the reticule. 'We would not want this falling into the wrong hands.'

'Are you still working for the government?' he said, incredulous. 'I thought you gave up such work when you married.'

'I keep my hand in now and again. Though Tristan would be furious if he discovered I had become a courier.' Her eyes shadowed. 'Will you promise me you will not tell him?'

'I make a point of telling Tristan nothing. But I do not like to see you again placing your life in danger.'

'This is only the second time I have done so since my marriage. Tristan is often away on business and I have never cared for the usual entertainments about town.'

'Why do you not accompany him?' Realising that he had been too forward, he held up his hands. 'Your pardon. The question was impertinent.'

'I am not privy to all my husband's business ventures.' The guardedness of her tone warned Adam to probe no deeper.

The carriage slowed and there was shouting ahead. Lady Alys pushed the scroll into an inside pocket of her jacket, her dagger again to hand. When the vehicle halted, she grinned at Adam. 'Make use of the coach if you wish. He will be returning for me later. Your help was appreciated.' Her hand was on the door handle, and as it opened she jumped down into a virtually empty street. The rain was torrential, detritus from the gutter floating in rivulets along the cobblestones.

Adam followed. They had left the quayside and Lady Alys was hurrying along a narrow street off the central thoroughfare through the town. He knew she was a competent courier and could handle both a dagger and a pistol. This might be a more prosperous quarter of the town, but the dangers of theft or molestation still could manifest for a woman on her own, especially as someone appeared to know she was carrying valuable information that an enemy of the government would pay a high price to obtain.

He hid his smile as he watched her strut through the streets with a confident manly gait with just enough swagger to pass as a young blood. For a woman who was so feminine, she carried her disguise well. He greatly admired her courage, and although he suspected that she did not need his further protection, he reckoned that now she was kin and Tristan had fulfilled his duty in protecting Aunt Elspeth, he would be failing the family if he did not keep her under observation.

To his relief she had doubled back on herself and entered the prestigious Pearce's Royal Hotel. It was the port's main posting inn and frequented by the captains and passengers of the packet ships. Lady Alys had taken a seat in a dark corner of the taproom; close enough to feel the warmth of the fire. Her training for the government showed: she sat with her back against the wall, so that no one could come upon her unawares and she had a full view of the room and entrance. On the table in front of her was a hot toddy of brandy, a quart jug of ale and a glass. As Adam approached, she knocked back the brandy and poured the dark foaming ale into the glass. He noted that her jacket and boots were sodden from the rain.

He paused by her table but she did not look up at him, her attention apparently rapt as she stared into the contents of the glass.

'Sit if you wish,' she said without raising her head.

'You should take a room and get your clothes dry.'

'I am not here on pleasure.'

'Then I will not jeopardise your meeting.' He intended to sit in the corner of the taproom and remain on hand if events became dangerous for her.

'I do not need a bodyguard,' she said testily. 'The ship docked earlier than expected. My contact will not be here for some time.'

'Landlord!' Adam shouted. 'Your best beer and a platter of hot stew and bread.' He seated himself on a stool beside Lady Alys, ensuring that his own back was against the wall.

She waited until he had been served before asking, 'Do you have business in town?'

'It has been completed. I planned to hire a boat to take me to Fowey, but no one will sail in this weather.' As though to confirm his prediction, a loud boom of thunder echoed overhead, swiftly followed by another.

'My work should be done here by mid-afternoon. Providing the rain eases, I shall take to the road. You are welcome to accompany me. Company always makes the journey more pleasant.'

Adam hesitated, and her tone became impatient. 'Just because you and my husband are at loggerheads, it does not mean that I do not regret the rift between our families. I owe you my life, Captain Loveday.'

He ate several spoonfuls before replying. 'This is good. You should have some to warm you.' He toyed with a piece of bread and went on. 'You enjoy such intrigue. It gets into the blood, does it not?'

A coach had just arrived and the room filled with shouted orders and demands for their rooms. Lady Alys kept her figure hunched over her ale glass, her voice low. 'Perhaps that is why I challenge your feud against my husband. I doubt you fear Tristan's displeasure.'

'I doubt your husband would approve that you offer me friendship,' he hedged, refusing to be drawn.

'And when did you ever trouble yourself for his approval?' She had lifted a brow and was being deliberately provocative.

'I would not be the cause of dissension between a man and his wife.'

'You are ever the gallant, Captain Loveday. When I married I did not relinquish my identity and total independence. My husband is entitled to his friends and enemies and I to mine. I prefer the role of peacemaker than adversary.' There was a flash of warning in her eyes, although she kept her voice light. 'My first loyalty is to my husband, but we are still kin, are we not, Captain Loveday? You proved in France that family loyalty is important to you. You also saved Tristan's life. Whatever your differences, I will never forget that you put your life at risk to save ours. In similar circumstances Tristan would act no differently. That is where the Lovedays get their strength.

Individually they may be adversaries, but in times of need their loyalty to uphold a united front cannot be questioned.'

Adam did not have so much faith that Tristan would risk his life to save him or his family, but he was prepared to give him the benefit of the doubt. Lady Alys ordered the stew and they chatted on safer subjects as they finished their meal.

A movement of Lady Alys's hand warned Adam that the man who had just entered the hotel was her contact. He left the table and crossed to the bar, where he began conversing with a shipping merchant of his acquaintance. Throughout he watched the expert exchange of a document under the table. If he had not known what to look for, he would have missed it. A few minutes later the newcomer had left the hotel and Adam returned to the table. To his relief the meeting had gone without incident.

'The worst of the storm has passed,' Lady Alys said. 'My coach will be here shortly. Will I have the pleasure of your company? My driver will take you on to Boscabel.'

Adam nodded. It would have been churlish to refuse, and he did regret that because of the ill feeling between Tristan and himself he had not got to know the intelligent and intriguing Lady Alys as he would have wished.

Chapter Twelve

'It will be dark soon,' Lady Alys commented as she lifted the leather blind at the coach window. 'The storm may have passed but it is still raining. Jarvis will change these horses at Truro for our own, which will be fresh. Do you prefer to press on through the night, or stop at the staging inn?'

'I leave the decision to you, my lady,' Adam replied gallantly.

'If when we reach Truro the rain has stopped, we will press on. I have been away for longer than I expected. I do not like to leave Elspeth alone on the estate for too long.'

'How do you enjoy the company of my aunt? Not everyone finds her forthright speech and manner easy to withstand.' The conversation had flowed naturally, and he did not want his concern for his aunt to sound like an inquisition or criticism.

Lady Alys laughed. 'She certainly calls a spade a spade, but if she called it a fork, woe betide any who would contradict her. She seems content in the Dower House and can take a great deal of persuading to join us in the main house. She remains passionate about her horses and they fill most of her days.'

'That has always been so,' Adam said with a smile. 'As long as she can ride and her mares are well cared for, she asks for little else.'

'She is fiercely independent,' Lady Alys said more soberly. 'Although she is free to come and go as she pleases, she keeps herself very much to herself. Sometimes I worry she might be lonely. For so many years she has been surrounded by a large family.'

'She made her choice,' he replied tersely. 'I am concerned when she is on the estate alone for what can be weeks at a time.'

'As to that, Tristan takes his responsibilities seriously. When the main house is not occupied, Mrs Nance attends upon her every day.

103

She would not hesitate to summon Dr Chegwidden or notify you if Elspeth was taken ill.'

'For that I am grateful, although I never thought Tristan would neglect her welfare.'

'He is very fond of her.'

Adam nodded, then, steering away from the problematical subject of Tristan and Trevowan, he asked, 'Do you spend much time on your own estate? I recall you saying something about property in France being lost to you, but do you not have a home in Wiltshire?'

'Yes, it is ten miles from Salisbury. Death duties have taken a toll on the estate for all that the manager is efficient. The house suffered as a consequence. Not all the rooms are inhabitable.'

'But it is still your ancestral home?'

'Yes.' She had caught the edge of bitterness in his voice. She wanted the enmity between her husband and his cousins to be reconciled, but Adam's tone revealed how deeply Trevowan remained a barrier between them. 'Its neglect saddens me, but most of all I miss my aviary. It will be moved to Trevowan, but I have so many birds, the task is not easy and the new aviary must be large to accommodate them. I have yet to find someone to design it. Some of the birds, such as the parrots, I have had since childhood.'

Intrigued, Adam sat forward. A lantern inside the carriage had shown the longing in Lady Alys's face.

'How many birds are there?'

'Over a hundred. Mostly finches, linnets, canaries. There are four parrots. I have also reared peacocks.' She shrugged. 'They are to me what Elspeth's horses are to her. I used to spend hours with them as a child. I miss having them with me.'

He wondered if her childhood had been lonely; there was certainly longing in her voice. 'They would require a great many small cages to be transported safely,' he advised. 'What of your old aviary? Can it be dismantled and reassembled?'

Lady Alys shook her head. 'It is an old barn. There is nowhere suitable at Trevowan and I would want part of it to be outside, with natural trees, so they can enjoy the sunshine. I had hoped that a special building could be built for them that would abut the orangery. They could then be allowed to fly freely in a sectioned aviary.'

Adam drew a pencil and small sketchbook from a deep pocket in his jacket. He flipped over the first pages showing drawings of war- and merchant ships, or intricate details of rigging.

'What beautiful drawings,' Lady Alys exclaimed. 'May I see?'

He handed her the book. 'They are sketches. I never travel anywhere without this, especially if I am visiting a port. In the past it has helped improve my ship designs.'

'I did not realise that you designed the ships you build. No wonder the yard is one of the best known in Cornwall.'

When she handed the book back to him, he flipped it on to a clean page and drew a rough outline of the back of the house at Trevowan with the orangery extension. He worked rapidly, adding several lines along the side and a solid structure.

'There is room for something like this to work. You would then be able to enjoy the birds' songs from the orangery. It would also be in keeping with the style of the extension.'

She stared at him in amazement. 'You would sanction these changes to Trevowan? They would be perfect.'

He shrugged. 'It is not my property to sanction or no. But they would be in keeping. These are only rough ideas.'

He tore them out of the book and handed them to her. She stared at them, her voice breathless with excitement. 'I cannot thank you enough.'

'No doubt your birds will give Aunt Elspeth a great deal of pleasure.' He shrugged off her praise. 'Get Nance to send me the dimensions of that strip of land and of the wall and orangery, and I will draw the plans up properly if you wish. I can also give you a list of materials your workmen will need.'

'That is very generous.'

'It is a different and interesting project. If the birds are to be transported in cages, you will also need some type of supportive structure that will fix inside a covered wagon. The dark will help calm them. Too much distress could kill them, as I am sure you know.'

'You have solved the problem for me. I do appreciate it, Captain Loveday.'

'Is it not time that it was simply Adam?' He sounded apologetic.

'And you must call me Alys.'

He leaned forward and tapped the paper in her hand, which she was continuing to study. 'There will be ructions at home if young

Sara learns of this. She will want her own aviary. She is passionate about all animals. We have quite a menagerie from the wounded creatures Senara has healed over the years. Nothing so grand as peacocks.' He grinned. 'A few owls. A one-legged raven and a few tame sparrows.'

'Then as a way of expressing my gratitude, I would like to present to your daughter a pair of young peacocks.'

'She will be delighted.'

Any remaining restraints between them dissipated as they continued to chat easily and found they shared the same humour and wit. They reminisced about their childhood experiences in France, which led inevitably to their missions for the government. Adam had always venerated Alys's courage; he now discovered that she was a truly amazing woman, and as the journey progressed in the close proximity of the coach, he was also extremely aware that she was beautiful and desirable.

During their brief stop at Truro she had changed back into a fashionable gown, and as they relaxed and laughed together, the air within the coach became charged with a very different type of tension. He was falling rapidly under her spell. Her eyes held the mysteries of Eve, her voice the song of the siren. He knew that under her gown she possessed an hourglass figure and long, slender legs, temptingly revealed whilst in her breeches, waistcoat and jacket. What had that devil Tristan done to deserve such an angel? From the amount of time he absented himself from Trevowan and she sought adventure in France, did it mean that their marriage was far from idyllic? They had been wed more than two years and there were no children. Had that put a strain upon the marriage? Tristan was obsessed with gaining respectability. Had he wed Lady Alys for the status her title would reflect upon him? If so he was a fool and did not deserve such a wife.

Adam's old anger surfaced. Tristan schemed to take what his pride demanded with no thought of the consequences or unhappiness to others. The chiming of a church clock cleared the sensual contemplation from his mind. They were approaching Penruan. The clock was a distinguished landmark. How quickly the hours had passed.

'We will soon be home,' Alys observed. 'I have enjoyed your company. If circumstances were other than the past had dictated . . .' She broke off, but her forthright stare held his gaze.

What had she implied? An attraction between them, or regret that the feud existed between their families? From the way the breath had dried in his throat, it would be dangerous to analyse her intention. He loved Senara and would never be unfaithful to her.

Then the coach lurched as it hit a rut on the highway. Alys was thrown forward and it was instinctive for him to catch her in his arms to prevent her being harmed.

For a long moment she clung to him, the perfume of her hair and skin a seductive musk flaying his senses. In that time their gazes fused, dark and translucent. He could feel the echo of his own trembling in her slender form, and then abruptly she lowered her stare and sat back on her seat.

She cleared her throat and lifted the blind on her side of the coach. The fading daylight revealed the tall chimneys and gables of Trevowan Manor silhouetted against a leaden sky.

'Jarvis will convey you to Boscabel.' She spoke with cool formality. 'Thank you again for your drawings of the aviary, Adam. I hope that one day you visit us when it is built.'

It was a reminder of the barriers between them. When the coach halted, she stepped nimbly on to the drive and walked into the house without looking back. As the coach continued its journey, Adam rubbed his hands over his face. He was shaken by the feelings that had almost been unleashed.

Candles were being lit within the Tudor house at Boscabel. A man wrapped in a dark cloak crouched behind the cedar tree studying the occupants of the property. He had been spying on the family all day. Now as darkness approached he hoped to gain greater insight into their home. Several windows of the house were illuminated, the internal shutters left open. The two women were in the drawing room, laughing as they bent their heads over their sewing. The female servants were in the kitchen, finishing their tasks for the day. The old coachman had bedded the horses down for the night and was dozing in his chair in his room above the stables. The large servant he had heard referred to as Rudge and the one-armed man Brown had finished their rounds, checking the animals were shut in for the night. Brown had rejoined his family in their cottage and Rudge was supping ale in his room behind the kitchen. The shadow of the nurserymaid passed across the upper window where the younger children were sleeping. Or at least had fallen silent after a noisy session of giggling that had resulted in the mother threatening them that they would not be visiting their cousins the following day if they did not go to sleep. The older boys were playing cards in their chamber.

This was the room that held his interest. For two days he had been lying in wait to seize Bryant and take him back to Willow Vale for questioning. Every day that his prey eluded him his work was more dangerous. This morning Rudge had nearly caught him as he climbed down from a tree and just managed to hide in the lower branches in time. Then this afternoon the family dogs had picked up his scent. They were almost upon him when a fox running across their path with a rabbit in its mouth diverted them and they had sped off in chase. His luck could not hold out much longer.

He'd seriously messed up, letting his captive go. How was he to know that it had been the man his master wanted dead? The description they had given him of a young man who would be no more than medium height with fair hair and a nervous disposition from years of being beaten was a far cry from the tall, brown-haired gentleman with self-assurance and indefatigable spirit whom he had knocked unconscious in the churchyard. This sharp-witted gentleman could see them all swinging on Tyburn gallows for their crimes.

Amos Savage scowled as he wrapped his cloak tighter around his aching body. The dozen whip marks, his punishment for allowing his prisoner to escape, were still raw and festering, and his coarse shirt stuck to them, reopening the wounds every time he moved. It did not help that it was raining again and he had eaten nothing since yesterday, when he had stolen a pie cooling by the kitchen window. The youngest lad had got the blame for the theft, although he had protested violently.

Savage shivered in his wet clothes. There had been little let-up from the downpour since he had picked up the prisoner's trail and followed him back to his home. He had been warned that this could be where young Bryant had taken sanctuary. He had read the notices posted in news-sheets about a boy found in a wrecked coach who had lost his memory. That had suited his master at the time. As the years passed, strangers to Exmoor were carefully watched. One day the prodigal would return. When he did, he must be imprisoned and kept alive until he could be interrogated. Savage had not been informed what information he would have that was so important. He could only speculate that the heir knew of the atrocities committed and had to be silenced. Why then was he not to be killed instead of being dragged back to Exmoor? That would be far less inconvenient than kidnapping him.

He had been given strict instructions that the heir was not to be harmed, or it would be Savage's life that was forfeit. His master was not a man to cross. The latest beating had proved that. Neither could he run away and refuse to serve him. Another servant in the past who had tried that had been hunted down, enduring hours of torture before his grisly end had released him from his suffering.

Savage dared not fail his master again. Bryant had tricked him. Savage did not like being made a fool of. His master might demand that Bryant return alive, but that did not mean that Savage could not beat him senseless during their journey. He would strike tomorrow, and this time he must succeed.

A distant rumbling brought a stream of curses to his lips. A coach drawn by four horses lumbered into the drive, and there was a shout from the driver calling out that Captain Loveday had returned.

Savage had lost his chance. He had better go back and check on his accomplice. Ratty Tribe, his cousin, was young and impetuous. He did not like taking orders, but Savage had needed someone to guard the horse and wagon and watch the prisoner on the return journey. Ratty would not hesitate to kill a man when necessary, but he lacked restraint. A job like this called for patience if they were not to be caught. Savage hoped that Ratty had stayed sober. Drunkenness was another of his failings

As he crept back through the undergrowth, he cursed that again fate had outwitted him. How long would they now have to wait until Bryant played into his hands?

Chapter Thirteen

The sun was high in the sky the following morning as Wilbur Trevanion nervously paced his brother's study, waiting for Bruce to finish examining the household accounts for the end of the month. He paused, picked up a small bronze of a greyhound on the mantelshelf, then replaced it and fiddled with a large conch shell.

'Sit down, Wilbur,' his brother snapped. 'I cannot concentrate with you fidgeting like that. I will not be a minute or two.'

Wilbur continued to pace. With an impatient snort Bruce placed his quill in its holder and sat back. 'Out with it then. Something is clearly on your mind.'

Wilbur turned to face him. As a younger son he was beholden to Bruce for his allowance, and all year his brother had been hinting that he should consider a career in the army and make his own way in the world.

'Is there any way you can increase my allowance?'

Bruce frowned. 'Has Selwyn led you into debt? Your allowance should be adequate for your needs.'

'It is not that. I have my future to think of. What if I were to consider marriage?'

'Then I strongly advise that you find either a wealthy widow or an heiress.' In the past Bruce had heard many excuses from his brother to get more money from him. Marriage was a new ploy. As usual, Wilbur expected him to provide for this latest whim. The boy was far too indolent to put himself to any great trouble, especially if it involved work and a curb on his leisure activities. Bruce continued caustically, 'Although it is unlikely that her parents will look favourably upon your own lack of income. Unless, that is, you intend to give your good name to a daughter of some jumped–up tradesman who is seeking respectability.'

'And if the woman in question did not fall into those categories? Would it not be possible for us to have rooms in the east section of the house?'

'And you would expect me to support yourself and a future family?' Bruce glowered at this unexpected turn of events. Did Wilbur believe himself in love?

'I am your heir.'

Bruce resented his easy assumption, and his expression darkened. 'Until I remarry and have sons of my own. And then only for the tin mines. This estate is not entailed. Tegen will inherit and will be mistress here. I have offered you the opportunity on several occasions to take over the supervision of two of the mines, but you refused. That leaves the navy, the army or the clergy. I am prepared to pay for a commission or a living.'

'I would not be suited to any of those. I could oversee an estate and its tenant farms.'

'There is no money in our coffers to purchase such an extravagance. Find your heiress, Wilbur, or look to some besotted father in trade willing to buy his daughter a manor and estate.'

'The woman I hope to wed is Miss Loveday,' Wilbur confided forlornly.

'I doubt the shipyard will provide income enough for Captain Loveday to afford such a generous dowry for his daughters. Are they not too young to even be considered?'

'Miss Rowena Loveday,' he blurted out. 'I adore her.'

Bruce rose abruptly and bore down upon his brother. 'Such a match would be totally inappropriate and out of the question.'

Wilbur had not expected to meet with such anger. 'But you have said how delightful she is, how dutiful and sophisticated she has become since her return from finishing school.'

'She is a wench who will need a firm hand to guide her, or she could be capable of leading her husband a merry dance. She is not for you.'

Wilbur stood his ground. 'I mean to marry her if she will have me.'

'Then find the means to support her.' Bruce was scathing. 'Make a career for yourself. Men of good standing can rise high in the

111

army. I am sure she will be impressed with the uniform. In times of war, promotion can come swiftly. I will buy you a commission. When you are given your first command, then would be the time to make your offer. If she cares for you she will wait a year or so.'

'I could lose her in that time.' Wilbur was distraught. 'My life would have no meaning without her. I love and adore her.'

'Passion blazes fiercely in young bloods' veins,' Bruce mocked. 'You must prove your worth. That is one young lady who will marry no pauper for love.'

He seated himself at his desk and from a drawer withdrew a piece of vellum. He placed the blank sheet in front of him and dipped his quill in the inkwell, the nib poised above the paper. 'I will write to General Kirkbridge. He is uncle to cousin Richard's wife. He is on the King's staff in London. The commission is as good as yours.'

Placing his life in danger on the battlefield was the last thing Wilbur wanted. But he loved Rowena. If this was the only way he could win her, then he would sacrifice himself. He saw himself in scarlet and gold. An officer's life could be a good one. He would win glory. Rowena would adore him.

'I will take the next stage to London,' he announced triumphantly. 'I will make Rowena the proudest wife alive.'

Nothing of his surprise at this passionate declaration showed in the older man's face as he rapidly penned the letter, then sanded, folded and sealed the document. He stood and handed it to Wilbur and shook him firmly by the hand. 'I am proud of you. Once you report back to me as an officer, I shall double your allowance. That and your pay would enable you and your wife to live in the east wing until you can establish a home elsewhere.'

Wilbur marched to the door. 'I will declare myself to Miss Loveday this very day.'

'That would be jumping the gun, would it not?' Bruce lost his geniality. 'My condition was that you receive your commission first. I doubt Captain Loveday would give his consent to a match whilst you have no visible means of supporting his niece. The girl is young. Time enough for you to return a hero and acquire an income that would make you acceptable in Captain Loveday's eyes.'

'Then I must at least tell Rowena of my feelings before I leave.'

Bruce snorted in derision. 'I have seen no sign from the young woman that she is enamoured of you. At her age they usually wear their heart on their sleeve. A handsome fellow in a uniform does much to sway a young maid's emotions. You would be better served to win her affection if you wait until you receive your new rank and status.'

Wilbur hesitated, his voice sullen. 'I suppose you are right.'

Bruce nodded. 'We will call at Reskelly Cottage this afternoon before you leave for Launceston to await the morning coach for London.'

Selwyn accompanied them to the cottage. Bruce sensed a greater camaraderie between the two cousins. Wilbur was buoyant, his mood expectant; Selwyn also had an air of anticipation. Bruce guessed that Wilbur would have confided in his cousin, and at least Selwyn did not appear to have discouraged him. Also, without Wilbur for companionship Selwyn would now make other plans to provide himself with entertainment. Bruce doubted that he would return to the restrictions imposed in his maternal grandfather's house. As his godfather Bruce would give him advice on his future. It was his duty now that the young man's parents were both dead. Selwyn had inherited his father's title but all that was left of a once great fortune was a town house in London and a small allowance provided by an investment in government bonds. His young cousin needed a military career if he intended to marry.

Felicity and Rowena were visible at the front parlour window as the men approached. While Felicity was diligently employed with her embroidery, Rowena stared despondently out into the garden. A smile lit her face with a radiant beauty at recognising their guests and she waved enthusiastically.

Following their greetings, Bruce suggested, 'After the last few days of rain I thought that upon so delightful an afternoon it would be pleasant to stroll down to the river. Make the most of my brother's company, Miss Loveday. Tomorrow he leaves for London with a view to securing himself a commission in His Majesty's army.'

'This is very sudden, is it not?' Rowena gasped.

'In times of war a man must do his duty to his country.' Wilbur did not sound very enthusiastic.

'How wonderful and brave,' Felicity gushed. 'He is a credit to your family, is he not, Mr Trevanion?'

'I will accompany Wilbur. We hope to serve in the same regiment,' Sir Selwyn declared.

Mr Trevanion did not hide his shock.

'I had no idea you had such an intention. Have you your grandfather's consent?'

'It will come as no surprise to him. Indeed, he has been impatient at my reluctance to purchase a commission.'

'Oh, how gloriously courageous of you both.' Rowena clapped her hands. She was not sure if she was pleased or not. These were the two most exciting men she had so far met. 'But I declare I shall be quite bereft to lose such gallant company.'

'May we dare to presume that you will think fondly of us when we are officers, Miss Loveday?' Sir Selwyn placed his hand on his heart and bowed to Rowena. The intensity of his gaze filled her with confusion. How could a look make her feel both hot and shivery at the same time in the most delicious manner?

'You will both be in my prayers daily, sirs.' She struggled to contain her disappointment for her heart was clenched in a painful vice at the thought of the danger they faced.

'I must also extend my good wishes to you both,' Felicity enthused once they had commenced their walk. 'Mr Trevanion, you must be exceedingly proud of these two brave men. This dreadful war with France will come to a speedy resolution in our favour now that our army will have men of such calibre.'

'They but do their duty when their country has need of them. I am sure they will serve with honour.'

'Great honour, Mr Trevanion,' Felicity enthused.

Wilbur had increased their pace and leaned towards Rowena to whisper, 'You know I adore you, Miss Loveday. I would like to think that you would look favourably upon me if I were to correspond with you whilst I am away.'

'I am not sure that my stepmama would regard that as within the proprieties, Mr Trevanion. She is very strict about such matters. But I would be happy to receive word of your progress through your brother. Be assured I shall listen with interest to any news he passes on to us.' She hoped that would appease him without giving offence.

'But you must know that I had hoped . . . that if it had been appropriate I would speak—'

'Pray, speak no further, Mr Trevanion. We are friends. I greatly value that.' She hoped that her smile was dazzling, assuring him of her interest and affection, but she could not resist a glance towards Sir Selwyn, who was absorbed in answering a question from Felicity. Was she reading too much into the way Wilbur's cousin had looked at her? Was he a natural charmer to whom no woman could fail to respond? The news of their departure had been too startling a shock. It had thrown her emotions into turmoil, she reasoned.

Felicity noted the intimacy between Wilbur and Rowena and her suspicions were aroused. Rowena was shameless in encouraging the young man's attentions. It was just as well that he was to leave for London on the morrow. The minx was a born flirt; did she have no care for her reputation?

She feigned a shiver and sighed dramatically. 'The breeze has freshened, Mr Trevanion. We should return to the cottage. I sense a dampness in the air.'

Mr Trevanion glanced at the sky and frowned. 'There are few clouds, but if you are cold, then we must return at once, Mrs Loveday. I would not have you contract a chill.'

'I hope you will take tea with us,' she offered.

'I fear not. My brother and cousin must leave in two hours for Launceston to reach the staging inn before nightfall.'

She was disturbed at hearing a harsh note to his voice.

He called to the younger men. 'Time that we left the pleasurable company of these ladies.'

'You will think of me, will you not, Miss Loveday?' Wilbur blurted to Rowena in distress.

'I shall look forward to your first leave, hopefully before you are sent abroad. You will look most dashing in your uniform.'

A blush crept up his neck and cheeks, but Rowena was more interested in the speculative gaze Sir Selwyn had directed upon her.

'Wilbur, be so good as to run ahead and fetch a shawl for Mrs Loveday,' Mr Trevanion ordered. 'She is cold.'

'No. I would not put you to any trouble,' Felicity protested as the young man hurried to her side.

'Wilbur will only be too delighted,' his brother insisted.

Rowena hung back as Wilbur cast a forlorn glance in her direction. 'Would Miss Loveday also require a shawl?'

She shook her head, annoyed that Felicity had ruined the last moments she would have with Wilbur for many months.

Making a mockery of her own claim to be cold, Felicity had now paused and was pointing out to Mr Trevanion a fish that had jumped out of the river to catch an insect, leaving a widening circle of water when it disappeared. 'My father was a keen angler. Is it a sport you enjoy, sir?'

Rowena was not interested in his reply and stooped to pick two wild flowers. They were red and yellow and a species she did not recognise. Sir Selwyn had come to her side as she lifted them to her face, but the blooms had no scent. 'I shall press these as a keepsake of two brave men about to don the scarlet and gold.'

'Wilbur is quite enamoured of you, you do realise, do you not?' Sir Selwyn surprised her by announcing. 'Do you feel the same towards him?'

'I . . . I could not say.' She hesitated. 'Indeed it would not be proper or appropriate. We are neighbours and I like to believe friends.'

Impatience darkened his eyes. 'I have little time and this is important. Wilbur is a great fellow and my cousin. I have immense admiration for you, Miss Loveday − more than that: from the moment I saw you, I knew that you would be the only woman for me. The one I would marry. But I will not press my suit in a contest against Wilbur. If you have the same regard for him as he has for you, then I will trouble you no further.'

Rowena was flabbergasted. 'Sir Selwyn, I do not know what to say, or how to take your declaration. I hardly know you.'

'Cupid's arrow can strike swift and sure. Dare I hope that you are not averse to my attentions? And that Wilbur is no more than a friend?'

She put a hand to her cheek. 'Sir Selwyn, how old are you?'

'Three-and-twenty.'

'I am but seventeen and I am quite overwhelmed.' Her gaze sought his, seeking reassurance that he was not mocking her innocence. 'I have a great fondness for Wilbur. But above all matters I have a very great regard for my reputation. It would be indelicate of me—'

Ahead of them Mr Trevanion and Felicity were hidden from view by a willow tree overhanging the river. Selwyn cut short her protest. Drawing her into his arms, he kissed her with passion.

Momentarily the world spun around Rowena and she felt herself floating, sensations of need and excitement coursing through her veins. The emotions were shocking in their intensity and warning lights flashed like lightning bolts through her mind. With a gasp, she wrenched herself free of his hold, her breathing ragged.

'How dare you, sir? I am no common doxy.' She stepped back, fearing that he had heard tales of the wantonness of her mother and believed that she was equally free with her favours.

'Truly, I meant no insult.'

He held out a hand to her and she stared at it as though it was a serpent about to strike.

'Your cousin and my stepmother will wonder what has befallen us.' She picked up her skirts to hasten her pace, her cheeks aflame with humiliation and something so much more dangerous – desire.

'Your kiss told me all I needed to know, my sweet Rowena,' he taunted as his long stride matched her hurried pace. 'I beg of you, we cannot join the others with you looking so distressed.' The gentle touch of his hand on her arm made her halt. 'Let me assure you I have only your reputation and honour as my highest regard. There is no time now, but at the first opportunity I will speak with Mrs Loveday, or Captain Loveday if it is more appropriate. It may be some weeks before I am in a position to do so. Just give me hope that I do not give my heart to you in vain. That you have no intention of marrying Wilbur.'

She was so stunned that she could only laugh at the absurdity of his words. 'Whatever gives you that impression?' Then she remembered Wilbur's earlier ardour, and her thoughts and emotions were again in turmoil. She also recalled that within their family, her step-uncle, Richard Allbright, had used his glib tongue to seduce a young gentlewoman, and then sought to abandon her when she was with child. Scandal had only narrowly been avoided when Adam had forced Richard into marrying her. Rowena had no intention of being so duped by an experienced rake. 'This is madness. I will make no promises to anyone. How can I accept any suitor without Captain Loveday's agreement?'

Despite her resolve, the wildness in her blood was luring her into temptation. Selwyn was so handsome, so charming, and far too worldly for her peace of mind. She fought the attraction and took a steadying breath. 'This is all too sudden, Sir Selwyn. It goes against all proprieties and convention. You cannot ask this of me.'

His expression froze into a steel mask and he bowed stiffly. 'Your pardon. I spoke in the heat of the moment. I was mistaken that there was a hope of something very special between us.'

'There could be, but . . .' She bit back her words. 'This is wrong. It is too soon.'

'I thought we were kindred spirits. Your pardon, Miss Loveday.' He strode away leaving her staring after him in astonishment and in complete confusion and dejection. Had she just made the biggest mistake of her life?

Chapter Fourteen

'Have you no sense of decorum?' Felicity raged as Rowena stood angry and defiant before her in the morning room of the cottage. 'First you throw yourself at Wilbur Trevanion, and then as soon as his back is turned you are flirting outrageously with Sir Selwyn. I do not know what Mr Trevanion must make of the morals of our family.'

The Trevanion men had departed and Rowena wanted to escape to her room to digest the unexpected proposals she had received. What had she done that had overset Felicity in this extreme manner? Clouds now obliterated the sun and at this time of the day the room had a doleful air.

'I have not thrown myself at Wilbur and I was not flirting with Sir Selwyn,' she defended. 'They are neighbours and Wilbur is a friend. Those two brave men are about to take up commissions and put their lives at risk to fight for our country. Was I supposed to ignore them?'

'A young gentlewoman does not have male friends. You may mix with your cousins but anyone else will only cause gossip. And what do we know of Sir Selwyn, or why he suddenly appeared here?'

'Is not Mr Trevanion his godfather? He lives with his grandfather and I should think is much in need of the companionship of a man of similar age.'

'That is enough of your impertinence, young miss. Go to your room.' Felicity refused to be reasonable. 'I will not have you leave this house until you learn to mend your manners. Your uncle Adam will have something to say about the lack of respect you accord to me. You have no shame in your scheming for a wealthy husband.'

'I should think Uncle Adam would have a lot to say about you keeping me a prisoner.' Rowena was too indignant to control her outburst. 'And if you condemn me for flirting, then in my defence I would say that I follow your example upon how a well-bred lady conducts herself with a gentleman not of her family. You were fawning over Mr Trevanion and lavish in your flattery. It was embarrassing to watch. If anyone is scheming for a husband, it is you. And scant respect you show my father's memory.'

The room echoed to the sound of the slap that stung Rowena's cheek. She veered away from her stepmother, her eyes crystallised with loathing, and ran from the room. Felicity threw herself down on to a chair and burst into noisy weeping.

Rowena fled the house. There was no point in going to Cecily for advice; Felicity had no doubt poisoned the older woman's mind against her wayward charge. In matters of decorum Uncle Adam always took Felicity's side. Everyone was against her. They saw only her mother's scheming and wantonness. Why were they blinded to her pride in her Loveday blood? She was not like her mother, nor would she ever wish to be.

Entering the stable, Rowena did not trouble to hitch the pony to the trap. She removed its halter and replaced it with a bridle, then jumped up and swung her skirts over the mare's bare back and dug her heels into its sides. The pony was a smaller mount than she would have favoured, but it was easier to ride without stirrups. She was desperate to confide her unhappiness and confusion, and needed the advice of someone she could trust. Hannah was at the farm until the harvest was completed. Her aunt would know what she must do.

The farmhouse was surrounded by golden fields of wheat and lush rolling meadows full of rich grass for the dairy herd that provided the county with its thick creamy milk and cheeses produced in the buttery.

When Rowena reached the farm, her hair was wild and tangled and her muslin dress covered in dust from the track. She saw Davey examining the leg of a cow in a distant meadow and hurried into the house calling for her aunt. Abigail appeared from the stairwell.

'Hush, Rowena. Melody has only just fallen asleep and she has been feverish today. Mama is not here. She has gone with Florence to visit Aunt Gwendolyn.' She paused, looking aghast at her dishevelled cousin. 'Whatever is amiss? Have you been attacked on the road? Did you not ride with a servant to protect you?'

'I need to talk to Aunt Hannah, urgently,' Rowena ground out in frustration. 'I cannot bear to live at the cottage. Felicity is impossible. She hates me.'

'You dramatise too much, Rowena,' Abigail sighed, clearly not taking her cousin seriously. 'Felicity does not hate you. What have you done now?'

'Nothing. Well, nothing so very dreadful. I tried to do what was right, to obey the proprieties, but there can be no rules for such an unusual situation.' She was babbling in her distress. 'Wilbur and Sir Selwyn have left to join the army. They both asked me to wait for them. Two proposals in one day; I am quite overcome. I had no idea that Selwyn had such interest in me.' She ploughed on, unaware of the misery shadowing her cousin's eyes. 'I was honoured and greatly flattered, but the shock threw me into panic.'

Abigail had turned away, picking up a discarded rag doll of Melody's and straightening the dress it was wearing. Rowena was distraught as she related the events of the walk and her quarrel with Felicity. She took Abigail's silence for stunned admiration, and clutched her hands together in front of her breast, her face glowing as she continued. 'Of course I refused both of them. I treasure Wilbur's friendship but have never seen him in that way – as a husband, I mean. As for Selwyn.' She sighed wistfully. 'Is he not so handsome? Oh, so very handsome, and so charming.'

She twirled ecstatically and giggled wickedly. 'He makes me feel that I am on fire when he looks at me. But that is absurd. He said that as soon as he saw me he knew I was the woman he would marry. Yet I hardly know him. I did not encourage him. Neither of them. I swear it.'

She stopped her spinning, her laughter fading at her cousin's lack of reaction.

Abigail had lost all her colour and her eyes were wide with alarm. 'Wilbur has left for the army?'

'They are staying overnight in Launceston and taking the morning coach to London.' Rowena frowned. 'Is that all you have to say? I thought you would be amused at my news.'

'Did Wilbur truly ask you to marry him? You are not making this up for attention?' Abigail glared at her.

'Why should I make it up? He has been hanging around me like a lapdog since May Day.' Rowena was affronted at the accusation.

Abigail flared in equal outrage. 'It was wicked to play with his affections in the way you led him on. It is just so you can pander to your vanity. I hate you.'

Rowena was appalled at the hostility in the younger woman's voice. 'I did not realise that you liked Wilbur so much. I thought you regarded him as a friend. Why did you not tell me?'

'Because it would have made no difference. You only think of yourself. I shall never forgive you for this. Go home, Rowena. I do not want to see you.' Abigail walked back to the stairs.

'But Abi, you are my dearest friend,' Rowena protested. Her cousin's outburst was unjustified. How could Abigail think her so mean?

'If this is how you treat your friends, God help your enemies.' Abigail burst into tears and ran upstairs to her bedchamber.

The outside door to the boot room closed and Rowena whirled to find Davey standing in his stockinged feet after removing his muddy boots. From his frown he had heard his sister's words.

'I never meant to upset her,' she said hollowly.

'Then I suggest you think less of yourself and more of others,' Davey replied. 'Everyone walks round you on eggshells. You fly off the handle at the slightest provocation and sulk if you are not the centre of attention.' He was the most serious of her cousins, taking after his father in his awareness of duty and responsibilities towards the farm. It hurt her more than she expected that he would so condemn her.

'I do not. Davey, how can you be so mean? I would never willingly hurt Abi.'

'The truth is not always kind, Rowena.' He showed no compassion. 'You never think how your words or actions affect others. The last two years have been difficult for you, we all understand that. You have always been spoilt and wilful. Lately you seem not to care about anyone with your demands for attention. You should apologise to Abi. Even I had noticed that she was smitten with Wilbur Trevanion.'

Belatedly Rowena remembered the way Abigail's face softened every time she looked at Wilbur. She had thought it was infatuation. It had become a game to draw Wilbur's attention away from her cousin to herself. 'I shall go to her.'

Ashamed at her callousness, she hurried to her cousin's chamber.

Abigail had thrown herself across the tester bed she shared with Florence, her face against the wall.

'Abi, I have been thoughtless.' Rowena sat on the edge of the mattress. 'I never meant to hurt you. I wish you had told me how you felt about Wilbur.'

'Go away. You would only have pursued him more if I had told you of my feelings.' She did not raise her head and her voice was sharp with hostility. 'You have to prove that men find you more attractive. That you are more popular than other women of our age.'

The words plunged sharp as knives in Rowena's heart. 'But you are much cleverer than I. You are the stepdaughter of Lord Eastley's guardian. That makes you far more important. You are witty and funny. Everyone adores you and sings your praises. And when you do not ruin your looks, like now by blubbering, you are pretty, sweet and kind.'

'You cannot even give a gracious compliment.' Abigail sniffed.

'Then you will have to teach me.' Rowena was genuinely contrite. 'You are my dearest friend. I would never hurt you. I was a fool to allow the flattery of Wilbur's attention to turn my head. You have a natural grace and dignity. Am I not always being accused of being a wilful hoyden?'

'Which is why men flock around you.' Abigail sat up and shrugged in a hopeless gesture. 'You are a challenge to them. You blaze across our lives like a comet, leaving everyone in awe of your beauty.'

'Do I?' Despite her remorse, Rowena was delighted by the compliment. Then she remembered her good intentions. 'Oh, that is not so. You and Florence are the adorable ones if you listen to Felicity, Amelia and Elspeth. Though I suppose you should be thankful that I am such a lost cause. The family applaud you as the fair saints destined for good marriages and contentment.'

With a groan Abigail gave her a playful shove. 'You are the most infuriating and self-centred of creatures. Even when you are in the wrong, you turn everything around so that it is about yourself.'

Rowena shrugged. 'Abi, I really could not bear it if you hated me. I will never flirt with any man if you are taken with him, I promise.'

'You will not be able to stop yourself.' Abigail swung her legs to the floor to regard her cousin. 'You are exasperating. But as a family we are all stuck with you. As a friend I suppose I shall have to put up with your histrionics, and tolerate that you draw all men to your bright flame. They are too blind to see that you are a siren luring them on to the rocks of their own self-destruction.'

Rowena frowned. 'Does that mean you have forgiven me?'

'I suppose it does.'

Rowena embraced her cousin enthusiastically. 'Oh, Abi, you are wonderful. I will never do anything to cause you pain again. I will be the perfect friend and cousin. I will always think of you first. I promise, I truly promise.'

Abigail kissed her cheek and taunted, 'You should not make promises your nature makes it impossible to keep.'

'Ever since your return from Exmoor you have been troubled, Bryn.' Nathan Loveday was concerned for his friend. 'Was what you found there not as you expected?'

They were sitting on the grass of the orchard where an archery butt had been set up. The quivers and bows were at their feet.

Bryn sat with his legs drawn up, his elbows resting on his knees. He stared at his feet, his voice raw with pain. 'My family honour is in tatters. My people were delivered into the hands of a monster. How can I return to my birthright when my name must be reviled and hated throughout the county?'

'But you have done nothing wrong. Your stepfather was evil,' Nathan replied. He was shocked at Bryn's despair.

When he lifted his head to regard Nathan, his friend's eyes were harrowed with self-loathing. 'I ran away to save my own hide. I should have stayed. I should have protected them.'

'You were hardly more than a child. You were ten. What could you do against Carforth's wickedness?'

'It would have been better that I had died trying to help them rather than run away like a coward and abandon them. God knows how they suffered. Their houses were razed to the ground. Someone tried to destroy the mansion by fire, for I doubt it was an accident. The fields are full of weeds. Everything my father worked for has been brought to ruin, and the people who trusted our family have been betrayed in the most foul manner.'

'That's stuff and nonsense,' Joel piped up before Nathan could reply. He crawled out from behind the tree where he had been spying on them. They had banished the eleven-year-old from archery practice after he had been fooling around and nearly shot one of the dogs with an arrow. 'You had to save yourself so that you could avenge the murder of your brother and mother. Now you can also avenge the ills that befell the people who trusted you. What good could you do them dead?'

'Clear off, Joel!' Bryn snapped. 'You're just a child. What would you know?'

'He's right, though, Bryn,' Nathan defended. 'You survived and can bring Carforth to justice. His treachery will be revealed and your family honour restored. And you will not face him alone. Our family is behind you. We have conquered our enemies before. United, nothing can stop the Lovedays bringing that villain to justice.'

'It will be a vendetta,' Joel crowed. 'You will return a hero.'

'It is not a game, Joel,' Bryn returned, but the light of battle was in his eyes.

'No, it is a real-life vendetta,' Joel repeated, and jumped up and down in excitement. 'What an escapade! You have a quest to bring Carforth down, like the knights of old. It will be the most exciting adventure ever to happen in our family.'

'Or the most dangerous,' Bryn warned. 'Carforth has no scruples or morals. He may be the most evil adversary this family has ever faced.'

Chapter Fifteen

Hannah was missing Sam and decided that an early-morning ride would chase away her longing for her husband. After Oswald Rabson died, she had never expected to feel such intensity of emotion for another man. She had been a widow in her early thirties and had decided to dedicate the rest of her days to raising her four children and continuing Oswald's dream of expanding the milk herd and the dairy foods produced on the farm. Sam Deighton had come into her life looking for work for the winter to provide for his young son Charlie. She had learned little about him that first winter other than the fact that since Charlie had been born he had not stayed in any place longer than a season. He was an experienced farmhand and she had offered him the job of overseer. At first he had appeared reluctant to accept. Matters had changed between them when her life had been in danger after she had refused to allow local smugglers to hide contraband on her land. She had been prepared to confront the dangerous gang rather than jeopardise the good name of the farm and all Oswald had worked for.

To her relief, Sam had stayed and supported her. In the following months he had become a mainstay of the farm, and it was some time before she learned that he could have sacrificed Charlie's safety by remaining. Charlie was not in fact Sam's son but his nephew; and he had become the heir to the tyrannical Lord Eastley, who wanted to manipulate the little boy for his own ends and ensure that Sam's father would never inherit the Eastley estate.

When Sam had to leave the farm and concentrate on protecting Charlie's inheritance from his own father, Hannah realised how deeply she had come to love him. Their lives were very different now, with Sam and Charlie forced by the covenants of the late Lord

Eastley's will to remain in Devon, while Hannah could not abandon the farm and risk Davey's future and security being jeopardised. Their love was too powerful to deny, however, and it had conquered both Sam's and Hannah's reservations that by being apart they were in some way failing each other. They had decided that to be together would also involve huge sacrifices, and that to honour their commitments to their families they would have to spend months every year away from each other.

It was true what they said about absence making the heart grow fonder. It certainly made their reunions passionate beyond ecstasy. Hannah felt the pulse of desire beat low in her groin and breathed deeply to suppress it. Harvest time was the busiest of the year; it would be weeks before Sam would hold her in his arms again.

She also missed her younger son Luke. He was the same age as Charlie and from their first meeting they had become inseparable friends. They were thirteen now, and Luke had stayed with his friend. Under the terms of the late Lord Eastley's will, Charlie would forfeit his inheritance if he did not spend his school holidays learning to manage the large estate.

Hannah urged her mare to a gallop to the farthest fields of the farm. With her thoughts preoccupied, it was some moments before she fully took in what she was observing. Or more to the point, what she was not seeing. Yesterday there had been a score of cows grazing on that land. Now there were only a dozen. Where were the others?

Her immediate fear was that rustlers had stolen them. When she rode to inform Cy Watkins, he was nowhere to be found. More troubling was that no one had seen him all morning. Unwilling to worry Davey unnecessarily, she decided that first she would count all the cattle on the farm. An hour later she was puzzled to find that all the cows were accounted for. Watkins must have moved half the number from the first field to another, yet that made no sense.

It was late afternoon before she could confront him. 'Where have you been working today? No one seemed to know where you were.'

'I were over the back field. One of the cows looked sick and I were checking no poisonous weeds had got a hold in the meadow.' His manner was surly at being questioned.

'I was riding that way earlier and did not see you.'

He shrugged. 'It be easy enough to miss a man. This farm be spread across hills. Is there a problem?'

She did not like his tone, which held the ring of challenge. 'In case of accidents you know full well that no one is allowed to work alone and not keep others informed of their whereabouts. We lost a man once who had tripped when climbing over a stile and fell on the spade he was carrying. He bled to death before anyone found him.'

'Some men be born careless,' Watkins sneered. 'A farm be a dangerous place. You have to be vigilant.'

'Which is why such rules are made to protect the workers.' Her suspicion was growing about this man. It was not just the disrespect in his tone but the slyness of his manner that aroused her distrust.

'I told the Jago lad where I could be found. He may be the farm simpleton but he can usually remember that much.'

Hannah knew he was lying, and she did not like the way he had used the Jago boy as an excuse. 'Why did you move only some of the cows from the far field and leave the others grazing the pasture?'

'You must be mistaken, Mrs Deighton. I gave no orders for cattle to be moved.' He held her stare through narrowed eyes.

'Yesterday there were twice that number in the field,' she stated, having trouble keeping her temper under control.

Insolently he shook his head. 'That be the heifers who'll soon be ready to be put to the bull. A dozen we raised and kept. Is that not right? Are any of those missing?'

'No.'

'Then what can I say, Mrs Deighton? How could there have been more in the field yesterday? Happen you confused it with the pasture on the other side of the wood. That be where I moved the cows from after one took sick.'

Hannah did not make such mistakes; or had her mind been wandering to Sam and Luke when she had ridden that way yesterday? Since no cattle were missing, this time she gave Watkins the benefit of the doubt.

For the three days after Felicity's scene with Rowena, neither of the women had spoken to each other. For once Felicity did not complain at her stepdaughter's habit of escaping her domestic duties. Rowena spent her time with her cousins at the farm and had twice stayed overnight. Without her disruptive influence, the atmosphere at the cottage was more peaceful, although Charlotte constantly complained that Rowena had abandoned her. Today her own daughter's whining had set Felicity's nerves on edge and she had sent Charlotte to help at the rectory for the morning. Cecily was making preserves from a selection of fruits and vegetables sent over from the farm.

Felicity was in the parlour writing a long letter to Amelia about her woes and requesting that Rowena stay with her and her son Richard's wife Emma in Bodmin until her nerves had settled. *Rowena needs a wiser head than mine to guide her*, she had written in desperation. *I have no one to turn to for advice. Adam is frequently away on business, and besides, if Rowena were to reside at Boscabel, it was likely that she would be encouraged in her wildness, for Senara places few restraints upon her own children—*

Her quill stopped in mid-sentence when she heard a horse approach and halt outside her garden. She gasped in delight, recognising Mr Trevanion. At least there would be no unseemly upsets today from her stepdaughter, as Rowena was at Tor Farm visiting Gwendolyn.

Felicity shook out her skirts, patted her hair to ascertain that no tresses had fallen out of place, and bit her lips and pinched her cheeks to add colour to her complexion. When Edna Merrin announced Mr Trevanion, the letter had been shut away in her lacquered writing box. Her good mood was restored and her smile was bright and welcoming.

'Will you take tea with me, Mr Trevanion? And do please sit.' Felicity frowned at the way he seemed to fill the small room by his pacing. Clearly something was on his mind. Then she noted that he had taken particular care with the fineness of his clothes, as would be warranted for a more special occasion. Dare she hope that today he intended to declare his feelings?

'Thank you, but no, I will not take tea. This is a short visit.' He crossed the room twice as she waited expectantly. Finally he said, 'The matter I would speak of is rather delicate.'

Felicity's heart leapt with growing excitement as he continued to pace. Surely that could only mean one thing? Modestly she lowered her gaze to cover her blushes. She realised that she had been staring adoringly at him.

He cleared his throat and said, 'Miss Loveday is not within the cottage, is she?'

'She is visiting her aunt Gwendolyn.' Felicity was puzzled by the seriousness of his expression. 'I must apologise for her conduct on your last visit. She can be young and headstrong at times. I was appalled at how familiarly she treated your brother and cousin.'

He waved aside her protest. 'There is no need to apologise, Mrs Loveday. Miss Loveday is, as you say, young, and she is without the stricter discipline of a man in residence to guide her impetuous nature. It can however be quite charming at times.'

'But not always appropriate. I fear her father rather indulged her.' She was eager to assure him that she did not approve of such lack of decorum. That she would not fail his daughter Tegen when it came to correct manners and deportment.

'As any man would with such a daughter,' he proceeded with no hint of censure. 'Miss Loveday is fortunate to have such a commendable example in yourself, Mrs Loveday.'

Felicity inclined her head in acknowledgement, her heart again fluttering at his compliment. Mr Trevanion was regarding her with a thoughtful stare that made her throat dry in anticipation. He had been a weekly visitor since he had returned to Cornwall during the May Day revels. Without the two older girls the cottage was quiet, except for Edna quietly singing a nursery song to Thea, and thankfully George was asleep for his morning nap and would not disturb them. This was the first time they had been alone without the bustle of family life surrounding them. It would be the perfect opportunity for him to declare his feelings and propose. She schooled herself to breathe calmly.

'My high regard for you . . .' He faltered and took a sharp breath to begin again. 'My admiration for you in the fortitude you have shown in your recent adversity . . .'

The pause set her body tingling as her expectancy built. She was finding it difficult to control her breathing as the words she had dreamed of hearing all year were about to be spoken. It took all her willpower to remain composed as he paced the room once more before continuing. 'I am uncertain if I should approach you first or Captain Loveday, who is now the head of your family.'

The rapid thudding of her heart had sent the blood rushing to her ears, all but drowning his words as he continued. 'But I have no wish to offend your sensibilities or appear forward in this matter.'

'You will not, I assure you, Mr Trevanion.' Her cheeks were heating as the tension in the room mounted.

His smile was dazzling. 'How understanding. I would have expected no less from you. I have the honour of asking your permission . . .' He again seemed overcome with emotion, and it took all her control not to blurt out, 'Yes. Yes. A thousand times yes, of course I will marry you.'

'. . . asking your permission to pay court to Miss Loveday, with a view to us marrying after her eighteenth birthday.'

The words crashed like storm waves over her head. She could not breathe, and a pain flared in her chest, suffocating her in its intensity. She could not have heard him correctly. This highly respected man who she had come to love was proposing not to her, but to Rowena. A child half his age! A rush of bile rose to her throat and she put a hand to her mouth to swallow.

'Rowena is too young for marriage,' she forced through clenched teeth. 'And is not your brother enamoured of her?'

'Wilbur has a career to carve for himself. It will be some years before he is in a position to marry. And he would not be at all suitable for Miss Loveday. As you have said, she needs a strong man. A mature man to mould her spirit.'

Felicity could not bear to look at him. It was the ultimate humiliation. Her hands flexed as she gripped the edge of the chair. She should have known that the selfish minx would ruin everything. It was not to be endured.

'Mrs Loveday, is that all you have to say at the honour I would bestow upon your stepdaughter?'

A dozen comments trembled upon her lips, none of which would be ladylike for her to speak. All the time Mr Trevanion had been flattering her and pretending an interest in her welfare and advice, he had been appraising Rowena as a future bride.

'Mrs Loveday?' he again prompted.

'This is a matter you should discuss with Captain Loveday.' Her speech felt as though she was chewing on crushed glass. 'You clearly have no regard for my opinion, and have overstepped any bounds of friendship. Your own daughter needs a woman of experience to teach her the proprieties, not a girl a few years older than herself.'

He stood rigidly to attention, clearly affronted by her reply. 'I regret that your opinion is so narrow-minded, Mrs Loveday. I would have thought you would want the best for your charge.'

'Please leave, Mr Trevanion. And I sincerely hope that you will reconsider before approaching Captain Loveday.'

'I bid you good day, Mrs Loveday.' He marched out of the cottage and Felicity slumped back in the chair, her dreams shattered. Mr Trevanion had deceived and betrayed her. How could she bear the shame if he approached Adam asking for Rowena's hand? The family had been speculating all winter that Mr Trevanion would wed Felicity. Pleading a headache, she shut herself away in her bedchamber and refused to leave the room.

A note was left for Rowena.

Ungrateful minx. Pack your things and Merrin will take you to Boscabel. I will not have you under my roof a moment longer. This final humiliation is too much. It is time Captain Loveday took charge of his responsibilities.

Chapter Sixteen

Amos Savage was desperate to accomplish his master's orders. The days were slipping past, but no opportunities had presented themselves for him to encounter Bryant when he was alone. Now that Captain Loveday had returned, he was desperate to get the job over and done with, but at all costs he must avoid discovery. He was hiding in the shrubbery, which gave him the best overall view of the house and grounds. Captain Loveday had left for the shipyard. The older boys were helping Rudge overhaul the haycart and sharpening the long-handled scythes. In a few days the harvesting would start. That would mean more workers in the fields and greater chance of discovery.

The younger of the Loveday boys had dragged out the archery butt and was practising with his bow and arrow. He kept calling to the others to join him. When an hour had passed, the boy was getting bored and his arrows were hitting the target more randomly.

'Nate, Bryn! Haven't you finished yet? You promised you would practise with me,' he shouted.

'Soon, Joel,' Bryant called from the yard outbuildings.

When a pony and trap arrived in the drive at a rapid pace, Savage recognised the boys' cousin. A pretty wench, and from the looks of her today, she was in a fine temper. Even before the trap had halted she leapt to the ground and flounced into the house, calling for her aunt. The driver alighted slowly and shook his head as he unloaded several coffers and carried them inside. In the house the young woman's voice could be heard, high, upset and demanding. Clearly something unexpected had happened here. That should keep the women distracted for a time, Savage reflected. Now he just needed to get Bryant alone.

It seemed that fate was with him. Nathan and Bryant came out of the outhouse and separated, the Loveday boy going off to one of the fields, while Bryant was immediately accosted by the younger brother, demanding he help him with his practice. This might be the only chance Savage got today to make his move. Even if he had to attack both Bryant and the lad to achieve his goal.

He watched Bryant walk into the orchard to join the youth. 'I can only help you for a short while, Joel,' he said. 'You have your own chores you should be doing.'

They walked to the butt, and after Joel fired off an arrow that hit the outer circle, Bryant stood behind him and helped the young lad reposition the bow and arrow for his next shot. A dozen arrows later the shots were still erratic and the boy was losing his temper.

'Take the bow and quiver indoors,' Bryant ordered. 'You are growing tired. We will set up the butt again tomorrow. I should be helping Nathan in the top field.'

'Just a few more shots, Bryn, please,' Joel wheedled.

'Tomorrow,' he answered, walking away.

Joel picked up the quiver full of arrows and fired one angrily at the target. With a loud thud it hit the bull's eye, and he let out a yell of triumph.

'Well done!' Bryant responded, but he did not falter in his progress. He had to pass close to Savage to climb a stile that would lead to a short cut to where Nathan Loveday was working.

A horse was already hitched to a covered wagon and hidden in a copse outside the estate. Ratty had better be awake and alert to what was happening. This might be the only opportunity Savage got today to overwhelm and kidnap Bryant. He drew the short heavy cudgel from his waistband and, bending double, crept towards his prey. Bryant had his head down, his expression drawn and troubled, obviously deep in thought. He did not hear Savage's final steps as he sprang out of the undergrowth and brought the club down on the back of his head.

Savage chuckled. The youth had learned nothing from the ease with which he had been captured at Willow Vale. Now all he had to do was drag him across the next field, where he could yell for Ratty to help get him into the wagon.

★

Within the house another drama was playing out. Rowena had been too impatient to await her aunt being summoned by a servant and had found Senara and Bridie in the morning room sorting through a pile of clothes outgrown by the children that would be given to those in need amongst the families working on the harvest.

'That woman has ordered me out of the cottage,' Rowena flared, her hands folded across her chest and her foot tapping in anger 'She has locked herself in her bedchamber and will not tell me what I have done wrong. She hates me. I have done nothing.'

'Then you will stay here for now,' Senara reasoned. 'I shall visit Felicity. But something must have happened.'

'I was with Aunt Gwendolyn at the farm.' Rowena shrugged in puzzlement. 'When I returned, Felicity was in her room and there was this note left for me.' She thrust it at Senara.

Senara read the note and frowned. 'Why does she call you ungrateful, and what is the humiliation she speaks of?'

Both women had stopped their work and were looking at Rowena in that annoying way adults had when they thought they knew where the fault must lie. She might have known they would believe the worst of her.

'I have no idea.' She stood her ground. 'Felicity was cross with me when the Trevanion cousins called upon us before they left to join the army. She said I had been flirting with them, but I was only being polite. Nothing has happened since, except that this morning, while I was at the farm, Mr Trevanion called on her. It was after his visit that she took to her room.'

The sisters exchanged troubled glances and Bridie observed, 'Oh dear, Felicity had been expecting . . .' She hesitated, unwilling to upset Rowena unnecessarily, as her relationship with her stepmother was so strained.

'Mr Trevanion has been a frequent caller. It is more than time that he made his intentions plain,' Senara said heavily. 'Is she upset because he did not ask for her hand, do you think?'

'What has that to do with me?' Rowena demanded.

'It has been obvious to me that Wilbur is very fond of you, Rowena.' Senara raised a questioning brow. 'If he expressed his interest to his brother, could it be that Mr Trevanion deemed that his own intentions would be inappropriate at this time?'

'Oh, both Wilbur and Selwyn asked me to wait for them. Selwyn asked for my hand. Of course I refused. I hardly know him. Though he is exceedingly handsome and charming.' She stared from one to the other of her uncles' wives. 'I did right to refuse, did I not?'

'Yes.' Senara continued to frown. 'I should visit Felicity. If what you say is the case, she will be very upset.'

'I do not know what she sees in Mr Trevanion. He is so stuffy and proper. Not at all like Papa,' Rowena replied. 'Can I remain here? I hate it at the cottage. Felicity is so difficult . . .' She decided it was diplomatic to say no more.

'A break from your stepmama for a week or so may be no bad thing,' Senara agreed. 'Though Adam felt that your father would wish you to grow up with your half-brother and sister.'

The window was open, and from outside came a shout that sounded like Joel, then a scream of pain.

'Now what has that child been up to?' Senara said as she hurried from the room.

'Mister, you leave Bryn alone, or I'll shoot you. I'll shoot you dead,' a serious voice ordered.

Savage froze in heaving the unconscious Bryant over his shoulder and then almost dropped him in astonishment to find that the steady hands of the young lad were aiming the bow and arrow at him. This was a kid and no threat to him. He could kill him with a slash of his knife. But if he harmed one of this family, a hue and cry would be up all over the south and west of England to find the killer.

'Ma! Rudge! Help!' The youthful voice was surprisingly shrill. 'Help! A man's got Bryn!'

Savage had to stop the cries before he was caught. He swung round and lurched at the lad, grabbing for the dagger in his belt as he did so. Before it was even free of its sheath, agony shot through his thigh and he screamed. An arrow had embedded itself in his flesh. The dagger drawn, he brought it up to press it against Bryant's throat. All he could think of was that he needed a hostage so that he could get away. But Bryant had become a struggling mass beside him and the young man's hand grabbed his wrist and wrenched the dagger from his grip before Bryant rolled away. Bryant shook his head to clear his wits as he rose to a crouch.

'Stop! Or you get another one of these!' The youth was advancing

136

slowly, his eyes gleaming with determination as he levelled the next arrow at Savage's heart.

Then the orchard was filled with shouts.

'Joel, put that bow away at once,' Senara demanded. 'Rudge, do not let that ruffian escape. Bryn, are you badly hurt?'

'I've got him covered, Mama,' Joel crowed.

'Don't kill me,' Savage whined.

'I am just a bit groggy, Mrs Loveday,' Bryn assured.

Before Savage could scramble to his feet, the burly Eli Rudge knelt on his chest and pinned him to the ground.

'Kill him, Rudge,' Joel demanded. 'He knocked down Bryn and tried to take him away.'

Savage was struggling wildly to throw off Rudge.

Senara stared at the macabre tableau with horror. She felt physically sick that Joel had shot a man. There was blood pouring from the wound.

'Joel, run to the barn and get some rope for Rudge to bind the man's hands.'

'But Mama, I've got him covered with my bow and arrow so he cannot escape. I stopped him taking Bryn.'

'You did well, Joel, but now I need you to get the rope. No arguments, and be as fast as you can,' she insisted.

She stared at the struggling man. 'You have lost a great deal of blood. Stop fighting or you could end up a cripple.'

Her command was ignored, and breathing heavily, Rudge planted a blow to the man's jaw that stunned him. Joel returned with some rope, and whilst Rudge continued kneeling across him, Bryn tied his attacker's hands and feet.

'Who are you, and why did you attack this young man?' Senara demanded.

The man's mouth clamped shut and his eyes were slitted with defiance.

'He is the man who held me captive in Exmoor,' Bryn said as he rubbed the back of his head, where a lump was forming.

Eli Rudge straightened and with a swift movement snapped off the shaft of the arrow an inch above the wound. The captive yelled in agony.

'Take him into the barn.' Senara took charge. 'There's a trestle table in there where I can treat him. Captain Loveday will want to question him when he returns from the yard. Send one of Billy Brown's lads to summon the master from the shipyard.'

She turned to Rowena, who had followed her. 'Fetch Gilly and tell her to bring my herb box to the barn.' As her niece ran off, Rudge heaved up the intruder, holding him under the arms, and dragged him across the grass. Any attempt by Bryn to lift the man's legs resulted in the captive screaming curses and kicking out.

'Stay still,' Senara commanded once he was lying on the trestle table. 'Or I will do you more harm than good. If the arrow is not taken out, the wound will fester and you could lose your leg.'

His eyes rolling with terror, the man nodded and stopped fighting.

Gilly had arrived with the herb box, and Senara poured an elixir into a cup and put it to the man's lips. 'This will take the edge off the pain.'

He shook his head, and when she tried to force it between his lips, he spat it out. 'Just cut it out,' he gasped.

She thrust a smoothed stick into his mouth for him to bite down on and gripped the shaft in metal pincers. Then, gritting her teeth, she extracted the arrow. A guttural screech was the only sound her patient made, although his grimy face was streaked with sweat. The blood pumped faster from the wound and she applied a tourniquet to stem its flow. Fortunately the arrow had missed the main artery. She packed the wound with a pad of linen and bound it tightly.

When she had finished, she instructed Rudge to keep the man's hands tied and lock him in the barn to await her husband's return.

Chapter Seventeen

Unaware of the dramas occurring at Boscabel and the danger that had faced his ward, Adam sat in his office at the shipyard and rubbed his brow against a building headache. The air was oppressive and a tang to the sea breeze proclaimed that a storm would be upon them by nightfall. For the moment the sun still shone and the clouds were far out to sea. The wet spell had delayed the progress of work on the two ships being constructed and the men were eager to make up time. School had been dismissed for the day, and the children had been given outside chores in the gardens of the shipwrights' cottages.

From the shrill shouts of the mothers and the yells of their sons, some of the boys had started a football game. Their cries rose above the sound of saws and adzes shaping wood, the hammering of nails and the squeaking of ropes from pulleys lifting heavy beams over the sides of the vessels. The door to the office was open and the aroma of burning tar and smoke from the forge drifted inside with the smells of the river. On days such as this the noise in the yard could be deafening. Orders were shouted, banter became a constant drone and somewhere a group of men were singing a sea shanty as they worked in unison upon some heavy task. The persistent cry of gulls added to the cacophony.

Adam worked in his shirtsleeves and breeches, his leather waistcoat unbuttoned and his long dark hair held back from his face by a black ribbon. He was completing the monthly orders to be sent to the timber yards, ropemakers and chandlers.

He rolled the order scrolls and heated a stub of wax to seal them. Older apprentices would deliver them tomorrow. There was a rapid knock on the door, and to his surprise Lady Alys entered. The noise outside had hidden the sound of her horse arriving.

Dressed in a blue riding habit, she pulled off her gloves as she exclaimed in a peal of excitement, 'You wonderful, wonderful man.' She laughed, clutching to her breast the plans that had been delivered to Trevowan earlier in the day. 'These drawings are perfect. I shall see more of my birds than ever before and it will be easy for other people to enjoy them. I cannot thank you enough.'

Adam grinned as he buttoned his waistcoat and picked up his jacket.

'Oh do not go putting that on purely on my account.' She impatiently dismissed his gesture. 'The day is too warm to be so formal. We are family when all is said and done.'

He replaced his jacket over the back of his chair. It was the naturalness of Lady Alys and her practical disregard for convention that he liked and admired. He replied with a smile, 'I enjoyed the work.'

She spread out the plans on his desk. 'These drawings are so detailed, and the way you have integrated the perches and suggested small trees to be grown within the cages is masterly. Especially here for the parrots. They have so much space. And you even included a shallow pool for them to drink and bathe in. Although I wondered if that would be better placed over here?' She bent over the drawing, pointing with her finger. 'And some more nesting boxes could go on this back wall. What do you think?'

Adam stood beside her, and as she moved her hand across the page, their fingers touched. The heat of her skin set his flesh tingling, and he tactfully placed a greater distance between them.

Lady Alys was peering closer at the plans. 'What are these marks here?'

'They show the places for nesting boxes.' Their heads were now very close together and the smell of her perfume and her hair teased his senses.

'So we do not need them on the wall.' She laughed, turning her head so that they were no more than a finger's breadth apart. 'I should have realised that you would think of everything.'

Her gaze lowered, focused upon his parted lips, and a small gasp sighed from deep within her. Like twin magnets their lips drew closer, and her eyes fluttered closed. A hair's breadth from their touch, Adam pulled back, raking his hands through his hair.

'We teeter on the brink of madness, my lady,' he said hoarsely.

140

She nodded, but her eyes remained dark with desire. 'Madness indeed. I should not have come. But the plans were so perfect.' She swallowed and turned her head aside, her voice shaky as she asked, 'What are your charges for these?'

Adam shook his head, the huskiness of his voice showing the turmoil of his emotions. 'It is payment enough to see your obvious pleasure.'

Lady Alys had not moved, her own voice breathless. 'But the time you have spent on them. I cannot accept them. I insist you charge your normal fee.'

The normality of their words belied the charged atmosphere sparking between them. He placed the width of the desk between them. 'Now you would insult me. Please accept them, with my goodwill.'

She continued to hold his stare for a long moment, her breathing rapid. Then she nodded, adding softly, 'Senara is a fortunate woman.'

Behind them was a loud clearing of a throat and Ben Mumford announced Mr Bruce Trevanion. The expression on the face of the owner of Polruggan Manor was sly and too speculative for Adam's liking. He had no great esteem for the man and was disconcerted at how much he might have witnessed.

'Have I interrupted a secret tryst, Captain Loveday? I can call back later if you are entertaining a guest.'

Adam resented the innuendo, and his outrage increased at Trevanion's lascivious grin as he bowed to Lady Alys.

'Lady Alys is here on business,' he curtly informed the intruder.

To her credit Lady Alys showed no discomposure and remained perfectly poised. 'Captain Loveday has designed this splendid aviary to be added to the orangery at Trevowan.'

At the man's look of disbelief, Adam could have slammed a fist into his pompous face.

'I have a collection of some hundred birds awaiting a bird flight for them at Trevowan,' Lady Alys continued with her usual charm. She appeared unruffled, but in her role as a government spy she had shown her skill as a consummate actress. 'Is this not marvellous?'

'I thought you designed ships, not pet cages, Loveday.' Trevanion's laugh was false.

'I have married into a family of many talents, Mr Trevanion.' Lady Alys rolled up the plans. 'I will leave you to your business, cousin.

141

Good day to you, Mr Trevanion.' She departed, leaving the scent of her perfume lingering behind.

'A fine filly that one. Lucky devil, your cousin Tristan.' Trevanion moistened his lips as he watched Lady Alys swing nimbly into the saddle without the assistance of a groom or mounting block. 'I did not expect you to have dealings with that family. Not with so much bad blood between you. Yet now you have designed an aviary for your old family home.'

'Trevowan remains within the Loveday family.' Adam struggled to conceal his rising anger. He could not see what Felicity saw in this man. Though he could understand her need for greater security. He might not relish welcoming Trevanion into the extended circle of his family, but Felicity's remarriage would certainly take some of the responsibility of her welfare from his shoulders. He would, however, never shirk his duties towards his twin's children. He diplomatically changed the subject. 'What is your reason for calling, Mr Trevanion?'

'Ah, a delicate matter.' Trevanion immediately became more ingratiating and amenable. 'Delighted to see that you are on such good terms with your cousin now. But I would speak to you on a very different issue. A subject dear to my heart and one that I trust will be to our mutual benefit.'

'Please take a seat, Trevanion.' Adam sat opposite him behind his desk. 'I did not take you as a man with interests of the sea.'

'Oh, I am not here to commission a ship,' he guffawed, his attempt at bonhomie as grating as chalk dragged across slate. 'Indeed not. That is not my line of business at all. Damned risky in these times of war, if I may say so.'

Adam folded his hands together and waited for the man to get to the point of his visit. Was it as he suspected that he wanted the hand of Felicity, and craved Adam's blessing on the match? It was not altogether unexpected, after the number of calls he had made upon her since her widowhood.

Bruce Trevanion assumed an air of self-importance. 'I wish to discuss with you, as head of your family, the great honour of asking Miss Rowena Loveday to be my wife.'

Adam could barely contain his shock. 'Good God, man, I thought you were paying court to my brother's widow.'

'How did you arrive at that misunderstanding?' Trevanion blustered. 'Mrs Loveday is a most accomplished woman. We have much in common, having both been recently bereaved. I was most impressed by how she has taken on the responsibility of Miss Loveday and raised so charming and delightful a creature.'

Adam swallowed his disgust that a man of Trevanion's age should seek a bride so young and innocent. 'Rowena is too young for me to consider any proposal of marriage for at least another year or so.'

'Surely not! Many women are wed and even with child at her age. It is not as though I cannot give her everything that she would wish for in comfort and social position.' His mouth had thinned with affront, accentuating the weakness of his chin and the fleshy jowls hanging over his tight high collar.

While Adam struggled to master his contempt, Trevanion blundered blithely on. 'Mrs St John Loveday knows of my intention. I thought it right to inform her. She was insistent that I approach you as head of the family. I take it that you have no objection? It is a good match. Better than Miss Loveday might receive in the future. I am prepared to overlook the scandal that surrounded her mother. And there was the regrettable circumstance of her father's death.'

'My niece is not a charitable case.' Adam stood and leaned his knuckles on his desk, his head thrust forward, his eyes flashing with outrage.

Trevanion blanched, visibly withering in his chair. 'Indeed not. She is beautiful, intelligent, witty.'

'Clearly you have reservations about her parents,' Adam challenged with a dangerous edge to his voice. 'Others of higher station than you have not been so bigoted or intolerant. Do you question our honour?'

'Your pardon, Captain Loveday. I would never presume . . .' Trevanion blustered, desperate to assure the younger man. 'I have the highest regard for Miss Loveday and your family. I merely meant to assure you that although others may judge her by the scandals, completely founded upon scurrilous gossip, I am sure . . .' His face was turning puce in his need to make amends, but he was too arrogant to realise that he was only digging a deeper trench between them. 'Her father died in debt. I am prepared to waive the usual dowry to prove that I revere her above all women. Do you not consider that an older, wiser man of the world would be a more suitable husband?'

'Not if you intend to crush her spirit.' Adam straightened in his outrage, ready to grab Trevanion by his lapels and throw the blackguard out of the office.

Sweat stippled Trevanion's upper lip and brow. 'I would be her devoted servant. I hold your family in the highest esteem.'

Adam was not convinced. However, it would serve no purpose to call this pompous ass to account. He mastered his emotions. 'As I said earlier, Mr Trevanion, I do not yet consider my niece to be of marriageable age. When the time is right, I will also respect her wishes in the choice of a husband.'

'A woman of gentle breeding should be aware of her duty,' Trevanion snorted. 'She is still young enough for fanciful daydreams of a knight on a white charger sweeping her off her feet. As men of the world, we know that no such possibility exists. I am prepared to wait until she has reached her eighteenth birthday. That is early next year, is it not? However, in the meantime a formal betrothal would be in order. I trust you will advise her wisely. A dutiful niece will marry as her family dictates.'

The man was insufferable and refused to accept that he was being tactfully rebuffed. Adam spoke plainly. 'I am no dictator. My niece will wed when she is ready. Neither will she go to her husband a pauper, as you seem to imply. My only concern is for her happiness and welfare.'

'You would refuse my suit, Loveday!' Trevanion's tone was belligerent as he rose and glared down his nose at Adam. 'After what I witnessed here on my arrival, I would say that you would be delighted to spare yourself further scandal. I am a broad-minded man. I may discount the gossip that has haunted your family in recent years; however, you may find other suitors less generous. Like mother, like daughter is no idle adage. I offer her an honourable marriage, not seek to treat her like a common doxy, which is how her mother ended her days.'

Adam rounded his desk and slammed his fist into Trevanion's jaw, stopping the words. 'Get out, before I am tempted to call you out for insulting my sister-in-law, my niece and my cousin's wife.'

Trevanion was staggering backwards, holding a hand to his bleeding mouth where Adam had dislodged a tooth. 'You'll regret that, Loveday.'

'I doubt it.' He was beyond controlling his fury. A second blow to Trevanion's chin floored the conceited lecher. 'On second thoughts, take that to convey the full extent of my contempt for a man who would wed a woman more than half his age and believe he was not governed by lust.'

'I'll have you for assault.' Trevanion struggled to his feet.

'If you had any backbone you'd call me out. Think yourself fortunate that I do not demand that we meet at dawn tomorrow for the insults to my kin.'

As Trevanion backed away, Adam warned, 'If I hear of any lies being spread about the Lady Alys, who has more courage and morals in her little finger than you possess in your entire body, or about my niece, or indeed any member of my family, I will know that they have come from you, and you will face me at swordpoint.'

Chapter Eighteen

Still fuming from his encounter with Trevanion, Adam stood outside the open door of the empty barn and rounded on his servants, his eyes dark with rage. He was horrified at the attack upon his ward. 'Where is the prisoner?'

Eli Rudge was holding the side of his head; half his bearded face was cut and swollen, the broken spade flung on the ground testament to the weapon that had knocked him out.

'I be sorry, Cap'n,' he groaned. 'I never saw what hit me. He must have had an accomplice.'

'That much is obvious.' Adam glared at Rudge and Billy Brown, who both had their heads bowed in shame. 'Did you not think to search for a partner? How did you think he was going to get Bryn away once he had kidnapped him?'

When they looked at their boots and did not answer, Adam flared, 'He would need a horse at the very least, and probably a cart.'

'There weren't no sign of strange horses or a cart,' Brown defended.

'They would have been hidden,' Adam snapped. He could not believe their stupidity. 'I know we are getting ready for the harvest and migrant workers are seeking employment, but the grounds should still be searched. We could have rustlers ready to run off our cows, or thieves lurking to break into the house and steal the silver. A member of my family has been attacked, and not only were you unaware that strangers had been stalking the grounds, but you then allowed his assailant to escape.'

The display of anger was uncharacteristic of their master, showing how seriously they had failed his family. 'I want the prisoner found,'

Adam instructed. 'My family continues to be at risk while that villain goes free.'

'He can't have got far. The man could barely walk. He were sorely wounded,' Rudge explained.

'He is on the run for his life.' Adam spared them nothing in his fury. 'I want every stranger travelling by cart or horseback stopped and questioned. I want every man working on the estate looking for them.'

The two men scattered to summon the others. Senara tried to reassure her husband. 'They could not have been gone more than half an hour. His partner would have had to drag him to their horses. There is also another matter for your attention.'

'I'll deal with it later. What can be more important than to discover why they were after Bryn?' His eyes continued to flash with angry lights as he turned to his wife. 'I cannot believe that you actually tended that villain. He could have killed Joel.'

'I could not let an injured man suffer.' Senara was unrepentant. 'He has lost a lot of blood, and by moving he would have reopened the wound. There should be tracks to follow. The other matter can wait. However, you should know that Rowena will be staying with us for a while.'

'There is a great deal to discuss about that young madam.' Adam scowled. His horse had been tethered to a hitching post in the barnyard and he swung into the saddle, impatient to begin his search. Any problems concerning his niece would be slight compared to what his ward might face. 'Will Bryn be all right?'

'He was not badly hurt,' Senara replied. 'He was more shaken than anything.'

Bryn had followed the others more slowly to the barn and had hung back whilst Adam issued his orders. He was pale and was slightly stooped to ease his pain. 'I am well, Captain Loveday. I want to join the search.'

Adam shook his head. 'It will place you in further danger.'

'Not now I am on my guard. I will not hide here behind women's skirts.' He was furious with himself for again being taken unawares. 'My stepfather must be behind this assault, I need to know what else he has planned. The attacker was Savage – the one who assaulted me at Willow Vale. I am no longer a child to be coddled and protected.'

'That was not my intention.' Adam regarded him for a long moment, and there was understanding and concern in his stare. 'If you are sure that you are strong enough, then I would expect no less from you. Your pardon, Bryn, I did not mean to question your courage.'

Bryn relaxed. He wanted to prove his worth to his guardian. 'I have delayed too long in searching for the truth. My stepfather has much to answer for. Let me at least ride to Tor Farm to call out your cousin and on the way will also rouse the men of Trewenna to join the search. I shall go armed.'

'Japhet has not returned from his race meeting,' Adam informed him as he wheeled his horse about to ride out. 'But go to Trewenna and then on to Traherne Hall. As a Justice of the Peace, Sir Henry can call out the militia. We will get this man. But Bryn . . .' He paused significantly, his expression carved with worry. 'Take a groom with you. On no account try and apprehend these men if you come across them. Follow them discreetly, and as soon as a time presents itself, inform the authorities.'

The attack had frightened Bryn. It meant that his stepfather still wanted him dead. Even more than the fear he felt for his own safety, he had placed in danger the family who had treated him as one of their own with unstinting kindness and generosity. He could not allow that to happen again. He was mortified that reckless, passionate Joel, who had a greater love of adventure than sense at his young age, could so easily have been killed. Or any of the women and children. How could he have allowed them to face such evil? He would never let his vigilance slacken again. Whilst Eugene Carforth lived, his stepfather could not afford for the wicked perpetrations of his past to become known. From the little that Bryn had learned in Exmoor of the years since his mother's death, it seemed that despite the devastation to Willow Vale, Carforth had escaped recrimination.

He galloped to Traherne Hall. The more people there were searching for the attacker and his accomplice, the more likely they were to ensure their capture. His head ached from the attack and his thoughts were so clouded by remorse that he almost ignored the dark form in a flooded ditch, discounting it as a dead badger. The whinny from his horse as he drew level focused his mind with a jolt. He reined the mare in so sharply that she reared and it took several moments to bring her to a halt. That was not badger hair partly concealed in the reeds; it was human.

He leapt to the ground and threw the reins over a hawthorn bush. The reeds were thick, and as he splashed into the ditch a large water rat swam away from the carcass. The head and shoulders of a man were visible, the rest of the body hidden by an uprooted tree stump that had fallen into the ditch. Bryn grabbed the sodden shoulders and flipped the body over. The face was covered in slime, but there was no mistaking that it was the man who had held him captive. His throat had been cut. So much for honour amongst thieves. He had been murdered so that he could not reveal the name of his partner in crime or his master and his motives.

Bryn scanned the track ahead. There were wheel marks on the muddy bank of the ditch, revealing that the accomplices had travelled by cart or wagon. They were travelling towards Traherne Hall, but a half-mile further on there was a crossroads that led to Fowey. It was a port large enough that a man could lose himself amongst the brothels and taverns. If you had enough money, you could hire a lugger to take you along the coast, or you could join a cargo ship as crew if you were desperate enough to escape capture.

Should he continue to Traherne Hall, or pursue the killer to Fowey, and hope to capture him on the way? Bryn did not pause to think of the danger of confronting a man who had not hesitated to murder to save his own hide. He would go to Fowey, unwilling to waste too much time. He ordered the groom to continue to Traherne Hall. He set off at a gallop, praying that he would overtake the slower-paced horse and cart before he reached the port.

A short distance from the crossroads there was a field with two haystacks in it. The muddy entrance near the gate was rutted with wheel tracks. Most were filled with rain, but one set of tracks held no water. Having almost missed Savage's body in his eagerness to pursue the men, Bryn turned in to the field. Behind the stacks was an abandoned cart with blood on its boards. Just visible tucked into the straw was the glint of a harness. The man he was after was headed to Fowey on horseback. God willing he would still be able to trail him and inform the authorities, though he had no idea what the murderer would look like. He did not think it was the weaker, more ineffectual man from his imprisonment at Willow Vale.

At first it was easy to follow the most recent horse tracks on the road to Fowey. Then he encountered two carters heavily laden with goods coming out of the port, and precious minutes were lost when he had to pull over and allow them to pass in the narrow lane. Both men confirmed that a single rider was on the road ahead of him.

'What did he look like?' he asked one of them.

'Unkempt. Bearded. Had a slouch hat pulled over his eyes and did not look comfortable on the horse.' The carter snorted. 'Bain't a horse thief, be he? Is that why you be after him?'

Bryn shook his head. 'How was he dressed?'

'Nothing out of the ordinary. Dark clothing, that be all I can say.' The beady eyes regarded him suspiciously. 'Why you so interested?'

'There's a dead body near the crossroads. Throat slit. Blood is still wet. I am on my way to inform the authorities, so any description will be of help.'

The driver became less antagonistic. 'Bad business. Sorry I can't be of more help. Wouldn't have noticed him if he hadn't been such a poor rider. Rode that mare like he were a sack of corn.' He tipped the brim of his hat to Bryn, eager to continue his journey. A man with access to a cart could easily be involved with local smugglers, and would certainly not want to draw attention to himself.

'Thank you for your help, sir.' Bryn bade him good day and clicked his tongue for his mount to continue its pace.

Less than a mile further along the track he found the horse abandoned and whinnying in pain. It must have taken a fall. Both its knees were bleeding and its head was down between its legs. He did not like to leave an animal in discomfort, but his first duty was to discover the whereabouts of the accomplice. He could not be far ahead of him now. If the horse was still loose when he returned from Fowey, he would take it back to Boscabel for Senara to tend.

He scanned the way ahead and the surrounding countryside. Either side of the track was wooded and the bracken was waist high. If the man left the road it would be impossible to follow him through that terrain. His misgivings grew when the next rider from the port had seen no one else on the road. That was worrying. The murderer could be anywhere in the woods.

He could not shake the guilt that he was responsible for the danger that had lurked at Boscabel. He needed to bring this man to justice and question him about Carforth and what had occurred at Willow Vale in his absence. Those deeds must be dark indeed if

Savage had been killed to prevent him divulging any information. This was the moment Bryn must prove himself worthy of his heritage and avenge the wrongs done to his family and the people who had relied on them for protection.

On his approach to the port, he realised that he would have travelled faster than a man on foot. It was now his time for subterfuge. He dismounted and tethered his mount out of sight, then climbed a tree to spy on any travellers entering the town. The port itself was busy. Two large sailing ships were docked and the quayside was teeming with sailors unloading the cargo.

After an hour, his muscles became cramped and ached, and he began to doubt the wisdom of lying in wait. His prey was wily and could have found another way into the port to avoid detection. The longer he delayed in reporting him, the greater the chance that the killer would escape. He abandoned his observation post and, now worried that he had wasted time, hurried to give a description to the authorities. He was sent to report to a captain of the militia lodged in a tavern.

The captain was in the taproom with other militia sprawled on the seats drinking ale. The tavern smelled of fish stew and its interior was gloomy.

'Captain Burlace.' Bryn addressed the middle-aged officer with a hooked nose and bushy side-whiskers. The officer had his feet on the table and his hands folded across a thick stomach. His eyes were closed and he was snoring. 'Captain Burlace,' he said, more loudly. 'I am here to report a murder.'

The man opened bloodshot eyes and started awake. 'What's that you say?'

'I am reporting a murder on the road. There's a man with his throat cut lying in a ditch.'

'If it was a vagrant it is of no concern to me.'

Bryn was outraged at the officer's attitude. 'His body was still warm when I found it. The tracks showed that the killer was making for the port. From another traveller I got the description of a bearded, unkempt man riding a horse. He should be arrested and questioned.'

'A bearded, unkempt man, you say, young sir?' Captain Burlace sneered and did not lift his feet from the table. He studied Bryn's flushed face, the good quality of his clothes. 'That description would fit any number of farm labourers or sailors. Do you wish me to arrest them all?'

'Does it not trouble you that a murder has been committed?' Bryn could not contain his outrage.

That got the officer to his feet, his face suffused with blood. 'I could throw you in the lock-up for insolence towards an officer of the King's militia.'

Bryn did not even flinch under the captain's threat. The man was an arrogant buffoon, his self-importance swelled by his rank. 'If you deem my words insolent, then that would be your right,' he said in a reasonable tone, for there was no point in antagonising the man further. 'Though that may lead to awkward questions from our family friend Sir Henry Traherne, Justice of the Peace. I would have to inform him that you allowed a murderer the freedom of the port to secure a passage and escape justice. If there were to be another murder in Fowey because of your neglect of duty . . .' He allowed the implication to hang in the air between them. 'Your pardon, Captain Burlace, if you took my concern for the welfare of the good citizens of this port to be insolence. I have reported the murder, where the body can be found, and a description of a likely suspect. I deem my duty to be done. I should have taken my findings direct to Sir Henry; he would not wish a murderer to remain at large.'

The officer reddened at the implication that he had failed in his duty. 'Get to it, men. Search the town for any man of such description seeking to take passage out of here,' he commanded tersely. 'The parish will not thank me for dragging back here a corpse to be buried at their expense.'

Angrily Bryn flipped a silver coin on to the table. 'That should cover the cost of a pauper's funeral, courtesy of the Loveday family. Good day, Captain Burlace.'

The satisfaction he had gained from putting the conceited officer in his place lasted no longer than walking out into the street. The murderer was still at large. Bryn still knew nothing of the events at Willow Vale. He had failed Captain Loveday and his family by losing track of the killer. The description was too vague to be of use to either the militia or the search party Captain Loveday would send out for him. He started for home with a heavy heart.

The injured horse had vanished from the side of the road, and even after a thorough search Bryn could find no sign of it. He doubted it would have wandered far on its own. A horse was a valuable animal, and although it had been an unremarkable beast, if tended it would serve a new master well. The body had also disappeared, although there were signs that it had been dragged from the ditch. Sir Henry must have sent someone to deal with the matter.

He expected to have the riot act read to him when he faced his guardian across the desk in his study and explained his failure and ineptitude. He stood to attention, his knuckles white as he gripped his hands behind his back.

'I let the murderer get away,' he raged. 'He was our only chance to discover what happened at Willow Vale, or what Carforth's plans are for the future.'

'Although you could have been in danger, you did what you thought was right.' There was none of the expected accusation in Adam's manner. 'I too would have followed the accomplice. You found the cart. That means they had intended to kidnap you and take you away. At least we are on our guard now.'

'But it is not right that my presence here puts your family at risk. I was already in your debt, Captain Loveday. I feel I should make my own way in life now—'

'There will be no more talk like that,' Adam cut in sternly. 'You are part of this family, Bryn. If it were not for his cursed war with France, my friend Long Tom would have been able to put men on to finding Carforth. Obviously his first duty is to our country and all his men are working in France. Carforth has covered his tracks well. And since no one seems to know first hand what happened on your estate in Exmoor, we can only assume that any perpetrators of that evil were put to death, or else the locals are terrified that the same could happen to them if they speak out.'

'But such injustice cannot be allowed to continue. I feel so responsible and ashamed.'

'You blame yourself too harshly, Bryn.' The arctic blue of Adam Loveday's eyes bored into those of his ward. 'Sit down, Bryn. This attack has brought matters to a head.' He unlocked a drawer in his desk and drew out a folded piece of parchment. He waited until Bryn sat down as he had commanded before he spoke again. 'I understand and sympathise with your feelings. They are worthy of you, and no less than I would expect. But we cannot just rush in. We do not know what we are facing.'

Bryn sat forward on his chair, his body coiled and tense.

Adam continued, 'After your return from Somerset, I visited our lawyer in Bodmin. I asked him to contact any associates that he was familiar with in Somerset requesting whether they dealt with the estate at Willow Vale under the name of either Bryant or Carforth. As yet I have received no information. When I do, I shall inform you. Until then we must be patient.'

Chapter Nineteen

Rowena sat on the swing that had been tied to a branch of a beech tree next to the orchard. Idly she moved backwards and forwards, still unsettled from her quarrel with Felicity. She did not miss the fraught atmosphere of Reskelly Cottage, but she had not found the peace at Boscabel that she had expected. The attack upon Bryn that had happened on the day she arrived had the family fussing over Adam's ward. She had hardly been noticed, but that had been a strange blessing. It had given her time to consider her future.

She had been horrified to learn that Felicity had turned against her because the detestable Bruce Trevanion had asked for her hand instead of her stepmother's. Even now the thought made her shudder. Thank the Lord that Uncle Adam had flatly refused him. Trevanion was old and grotesque. Besides, it was Wilbur who had asked for her hand first, or at least hinted that was his intention. Surely he would have requested permission of his brother, unless he had only been toying with her affections. Men were so difficult to understand. She had been warned that often a man was more interested in seduction than marriage, so how did she know who to trust if they paid court to her? It was too confusing.

And how was she supposed to trust Sir Selwyn? He was the most exciting one of the Trevanion family, but she had only recently met him and she was not sure that she should put too much faith in his declaration. She knew only too well from her own family that cousins thrived on rivalry and competition. She had even heard rumours that Adam and her father had both courted her mother until St John had won her hand when Adam was away in the navy.

Frustration rippled through her and she leaned back on the

swing, forcing it go higher. The motion was calming but brought no solution to her chaotic emotions. She had found Sir Selwyn thrilling and he had caused her heart to beat more rapidly than with any other who had flirted with her. But had his intentions been honourable? Even if they had been, Bruce Trevanion had ruined everything by his lechery. Had he lost his mind that he could even consider she would want him as a husband? It was so unjust. Why could he not have stayed true to Felicity, which would have made life easier for her stepmama? Now that he had been rejected, his pride would never agree to his godson marrying her. And Felicity would never forgive her for the fact that Bruce Trevanion had discarded her affection in favour of her stepdaughter. It all rebounded upon her, and it was not as though she had ever encouraged the old fool. It was too galling. Perhaps if some good could eventually come out of the debacle, it would be that Wilbur came to see Abigail for the loving, caring woman who would bring him happiness as his wife.

A movement by the house caught her eye and she saw Bryn walking slowly across the lawn. Rowena brought the swing to an abrupt halt to observe him more acutely. He was unaware of her presence, and believing himself unobserved, the slump of his shoulders showed his misery. From his frown he was deep in thought. Earlier she had heard raised voices from her uncle's study. Had the golden boy fallen from grace? She had often resented Bryn's popularity and how easily he had fitted in with the family. But yesterday's events must have unsettled him. The family had kept quiet about what had happened after the attempt to kidnap him. The men had been out until dusk, and her curiosity had made her spy on them. Listening at a closed door, she had learned that Bryn had discovered the body of the man who had tried to abduct him, dead in a ditch. There had been no sign of his accomplice.

Her own problems paled into insignificance beside what Bryn recently faced. His manner was usually so carefree that she was startled to see that he walked as though his body was weighted with copper ore. She was also surprised that she was looking at the figure of a man and not a youth. Bryn was taller than either Wilbur or Sir Selwyn. He must have grown six inches whilst she had been away at the ladies' academy. She had thought of him as younger than herself when the family had first taken him in. Now that his memory had returned, it was discovered that he was also seventeen, and three months older than her.

He walked with a languid gait, like the lions she had seen in a travelling circus. His hair was not as dark as that of her uncles and cousins, and in the sunlight it was crowned with a reddish-gold glow. The boyish softness of his features had been pared to a striking countenance that had both the hardness and beauty of a cut diamond.

'Bryn, you look all at sea,' she called. 'Come, be a charming gallant and push me on the swing.'

'I have better things to do with my time than pander to your whims.' His voice sounded odd, gruffer and rippled with anger. It was a far cry from the amenable youth who had irritated her intensely by ingratiating himself to be a favourite of the family.

They had never been close. She had regarded him as a rival for her uncle Adam's affection, and her cousins had all adored him. She had never liked competition, and had been particularly irked that it had been her father who had rescued him from the wrecked carriage. Everyone had cosseted the boy who was without a memory. Rowena had regarded him as a cuckoo in the nest, drawing the attention that should have been hers by right. He had sensed her antagonism and made no effort to charm her as he had the younger children. Looking back on his attitude, she would even go so far as to say that he had done his best to ignore her. It had never bothered her before, but now she was vexed.

Since St John's death, Rowena had faced so much criticism that she often felt excluded. It now irked her that Bryn had been so aloof towards her. Was he not the closest to her in age, and were they not both orphans? She had also been deeply shocked at the way he had been attacked yesterday.

'I thought it would lighten your mood and be diverting.' She tilted her head and favoured him with her most winning smile.

'For whom? Are you completely unaware of what has been happening here, that you only think of your own pleasure?'

His scathing tone froze the smile on her lips and put her immediately on the defensive. 'My thought was to divert you. I never regarded you as a curmudgeon. A gentleman does not display his ill humour to a woman. Has Aunt Senara not taught you manners? But then you have never liked me, have you, Bryn?'

157

'Why do you see everything as revolving around you?' He walked away more briskly.

His words stung like attacking hornets. She slid from the swing and ran after him. 'I'm not a vainglorious simpleton. I realise that you were in grave danger yesterday and that there is something very sinister lurking in your past. We Lovedays have more than a few skeletons in our own family closets that we would rather the outside world did not discover. I wished to take your mind from your worries.'

He halted, but his gaze was wary when he turned to regard her. 'You have never so troubled yourself ere this.'

'I had never felt an outsider within this family before,' she said, surprising herself that she had revealed so much. She shrugged. 'I wanted to make amends to you. I could have been more accepting of your anguish. Though my cousins had no such reservations. They more than made up for my failings. I ask your pardon, Bryn.'

He studied her for a long moment, his eyes veiled. The tension left his figure and he nodded. 'I considered you to be an overindulged minx who scarcely noted my presence.'

Flames flared along her neck and her face was hot as a torched beacon. She put her hands on her cheeks. 'Was I really that dreadful?' She attempted a light-hearted laugh and was mortified when it sounded hollow.

'You were secure and surrounded by those who loved you. You could be wilful and enticing and captivating when you chose.'

'Hardly redeeming virtues.' She gasped, and then caught a telltale glitter in his eyes. 'You are an abominable tease. Although I suspect that I deserved some of those comments.'

'Just some of them?' he queried.

'You are no gentleman, Bryn Loveday.' She assumed an air of righteous indignation, but in truth did not know whether to be annoyed or amused. No male close to her in age had ever treated her like that. The local boys were always deferential, and that had included Wilbur and Sir Selwyn. Her younger cousins tended to avoid provoking her temper and she usually got her own way with them. Her grandmother Amelia's son, Richard Allbright, was older and had shown a bullying side when crossed, and she had despised him. Fortunately, now that he was married and away with the navy fighting the French, she did not have to tolerate his presence. For once she did not know how to respond. She was used to compliments and admiring glances from young men. Bryn did not seem to either like or dislike her. She felt that she was merely being tolerated. And that was more aggravating than being ignored.

Yet that enigmatic glimmer remained in his eyes when he solemnly bowed to her. 'Miss Loveday, permit me to introduce Sir Alexander Rufus Bryant. Perhaps you would hold him in greater esteem.'

'Sir Alexander Bryant! You are titled?'

'A lowly knight baronet, a title that was conferred on my family in my great-grandfather's time.'

She dipped a respectful curtsey. 'Sir Alexander Rufus Bryant, I am delighted to make your acquaintance. Yet I was just becoming intrigued by Master Bryn Loveday. Such a pity he is no more.'

'I am honoured to remain Master Loveday. He has kept me alive and shown me the values of a devoted, caring family.' He crooked his arm to Rowena. 'Would Master Loveday's beautiful and delightful cousin deign to promenade in the garden with an unworthy interloper?'

She laughed at his formality. Although the assault upon him must have left him profoundly troubled, his manner was more confident and mature than she would have expected. His boyhood had slipped from him, and before her was a young man determined to embrace his destiny. Her admiration for him increased. She was also aware that in his fashionable clothes he cut a dashing figure. The line of the broad shoulders beneath his tailored cutaway coat was disturbingly masculine.

'You are no unwelcome participant in our family, Bryn.' Rowena was strangely at odds with herself in his presence. He was both familiar and a stranger. That was intriguing, and her interest was captivated. She wanted to know more of this new, more self-assured side of his nature. They were both orphans and living on another's bounty. They shared much in common.

She wished to reach beyond the shield that she sensed protected his emotions. Her voice lightened and became soft and coercing. 'I am ashamed that I have not been as kind to you as I would have desired. I was selfish and thought only of my own problems, and yours were much greater. I ask your pardon and would like us to be friends.'

'Only a complete bounder would refuse so delightful an apology.' He grinned. 'I take it that was an apology.'

'Surely a lady should never have to apologise, or explain?' A glint of battle was back in her eyes.

'Then it must have been I who was entirely in the wrong,' he mocked.

'Just so that we understand each other,' she replied with a peal of laughter. 'That would form the making of a firm friendship.'

Chapter Twenty

Three weeks after Adam Loveday had refused Bruce Trevanion's offer to marry his niece, the master of Polruggan Manor learned that Tristan Loveday had returned to Trevowan. He had been impatient for this moment.

He arrived at Trevowan and met Tristan inspecting the extension to the orangery. An attractive gabled structure had been constructed out of willow, with narrow panels, across which had been stretched a fine wire mesh. The design complemented the roof line of the back of the house.

'A structure worthy of a pleasure garden,' Trevanion observed.

Although Tristan nodded appreciatively, there was an edge to his neighbour's voice that put him instantly on his guard. 'My wife has long wished for a proper aviary. She has a collection of birds in Wiltshire that will be brought here.'

'Who is the architect? He should be recommended.'

Again Tristan detected a sneer behind the words. 'Lady Alys did not say. We discussed the idea before I had to leave on business. I did not expect to be away for so many weeks. My wife has wasted no time in putting the work into progress.'

'And where is Lady Alys, that I may congratulate her on her expertise and enterprise?' Trevanion grinned. 'Such an aviary could become very much à la mode.'

'My wife is in Wiltshire organising the removal of the birds.' Tristan was becoming uneasy at his neighbour's interest. Although he had encouraged a friendship with Trevanion to establish his own importance amongst his neighbours, he had never cared much for the man. He was a fop and a braggart. 'Transporting the birds is a delicate matter, as my wife is anxious that none will die during the journey. Some of the exotic popinjays have been her pets since childhood.'

'It is a fine construction and built with great knowledge and expertise. It would explain the intimate moment when I came upon Lady Alys closeted with your cousin at Trewenna Hard. I had not realised Captain Loveday was a designer of bird flights. Now I come to think about it, there were plans spread across a table.'

The narrowing of Tristan's eyes and the taut line of his jaw prompted Trevanion to push the matter further. 'It was refreshing to see them so attentive, laughing and conspiring like old friends. Your rift with your cousin is clearly over and forgiven.'

'You forget that before my marriage, Captain Loveday saved the life of Lady Alys when they were in France.' A barely concealed violence threaded through Tristan's tone.

Bruce Trevanion inclined his head. 'Indeed that is so. Lady Alys must find the days here when you are attending to business long and lonely. Old Elspeth mayhap connives to bring your families closer. Yet a word of advice from a man of the world, of which you also must be aware: it does no good to leave a beautiful woman alone and prey to the interest of circling predators.'

The speed with which Tristan's hand shot out, grabbed him by his stock and slammed him up against the trunk of a nearby tree caught Trevanion unawares. His head throbbed with pain and the air was cut off from his throat as Loveday's fingers dug into his windpipe.

'Careful how you speak of my wife, sir.' This time there was no mistaking the lethal intent.

Trevanion held up his hands. 'Your pardon, I meant no insult, just a word of friendly advice. An incautious word of gossip can irreparably harm a woman's reputation.'

'Not when she is with her own family, or are you insinuating that you caught my wife and cousin in flagrante?' The pressure on his throat increased and Trevanion's face turned puce, his eyes bulging.

'Indeed not,' he managed to croak.

Still Tristan did not release him. 'Then keep your filthy mouth closed on the subject, or I shall shut it permanently.'

Trevanion nodded and Tristan loosened his grip. 'News travels fast. Felicity Loveday has taken her family to visit a cousin of mine in Dorset, Tamasine Deverell. A loose tongue intimates that she had been expecting an offer from your good self. You have been a frequent visitor to the cottage. This loose tongue maliciously declared that you had instead offered for her stepdaughter, and that Captain Loveday turfed you from his office proclaiming you a lecher and worse.'

'Mrs St John Loveday was kind enough to give me much advice upon the health and raising of my daughter. Hearsay will always make idle speculation where a widow and widower are concerned.' Trevanion's voice was a high-pitched squeak.

'Only a fool crosses our family, Trevanion,' Tristan warned, his lips drawn back into a snarl and his hand again tightening on the stock. 'Watch your speech in future.' He released him abruptly.

Trevanion straightened his stock with shaking fingers. 'They are right what they say about you. You are no better than a guttersnipe. I would not taint my ancient lineage by association with your kind.'

His exit was made with undignified haste.

Elspeth walked purposefully towards Tristan from the Dower House. Her limp was more pronounced and her face flushed with anger. 'Was that wise, nephew? Trevanion is regarded as a pillar of society. We do not need him as an enemy. What made you threaten him in that way? Surely not over the way he treated Felicity.'

'It was not about Felicity.' His eyes were hooded and she could tell he did not intend to discuss the matter. That had never stopped her in the past.

'If you wish to be accepted by our neighbours, such conduct will go against you. Many remain suspicious as to how you became master of Trevowan.'

'Was Adam poking his nose round here while I was away?' The words were spoken too quietly and reasonably and did not fool Elspeth.

She glanced at the carpenters at work on the roof of the bird flight. 'It will be many a day before Adam sets foot on Trevowan land. He did design the aviary, though. He met Lady Alys in Falmouth when he delivered a repaired ship. There was a storm and she offered for him to accompany her home in the coach. That was when he made some sketches for the aviary. One of the apprentices from the yard delivered them. I believe Alys was so delighted with them that she went to the yard to thank him.'

'Why would he go to so much trouble on my wife's account?

Especially as it involves changes to his precious Trevowan.' Arrows of angry fire darted from Tristan's eyes, the tension in his body ready to explode.

Elspeth was determined to pacify him. Trevanion had been bent upon mischief and had deliberately intended to set the cousins at each other's throats. 'Alys has won the respect of everyone since your marriage. Do not regard it as anything more than Adam rising to a challenge to create something that will be fitting for its surroundings. Alys had been planning the bird house for months and had not found the right design.'

Her nephew's emotions were now carefully veiled from Elsepth. It was a trait she found disconcerting, and usually did not bode well for his reactions. He was hot-headed enough to confront Adam, and both men's volatile tempers could erupt in the most disastrous fashion.

'Do not make too much of this, Tristan. See it as an olive branch,' she counselled.

The hot balmy days of harvest time settled over Boscabel. A fine haze hovered over the fields as the labourers worked in a line with the long scythes. Although the toil was strenuous and back-crippling, they eased their labour by singing in rhythm to the momentum of their movements. Gilly Brown's father had come to live with the couple. He was too old to join in the work but he sat under a hawthorn, his gnarled hands beating time with a hand drum. Toddlers chased each other around the stooks and cried out in alarm if they spotted a weasel, rabbit or field mouse running for cover towards the hedgerows. Overhead hovered a kestrel, which dived from the sky like a lightning bolt on to a fleeing prey.

The labourers would end their working day in an hour. The field would be finished tomorrow and they would move on to another farm at the end of the week. The Lovedays had been fortunate with the weather. This was the last of their fields to be harvested and the rain had held off, giving them one of the best yields in years. Profit would be high, for the price of corn and wheat had risen because of the war.

As the workers continued their toil, the children distributed the last of the water from the stone jars. When the labourers trudged back to the barn where they would sleep, ale and food would be provided. The house servants collected up the last of the stone water jars and placed them on the cart to be refilled in the morning. Adam assessed the work with approval. It would be a lucrative year for both the estate and the shipyard. He should feel deeply satisfied that he was no longer haunted by debt, but there remained a nagging unease within him, something left unsatiated that gnawed like a caterpillar through leaves before its process of metamorphosis.

Why did he continue to feel unsettled? He had a wife and family he adored; he was proud of the expansion of the shipyard and also the rise of Boscabel from the ruin it had been when he purchased it after his marriage. With so much talk of the war with France and the threat of a Napoleonic invasion, however, the old craving for adventure kept surfacing. It was inappropriate with the responsibilities that lay on his shoulders. He wondered if his father had felt this way. Edward Loveday had always seemed content. He had enjoyed his role as shipbuilder and been in control of the successful management of Trevowan. He had become one of the most respected figures in society. Now Adam began to wonder if that respectability had not been a yoke to be endured. Edward had been driven by family loyalty and would always put his duty before all else. Had he also thirsted for adventure? He must have done, yet he had hidden it well. Adam was not so sure he could deny the call of his wild blood so easily.

With the restless mood continuing to plague him, instead of returning to the house he ordered Achilles, his young hunter, to be saddled, and set off for the coast. The smell of the sea was tantalisingly close and he missed the sound of the waves breaking over the rocks at Trevowan Cove. He headed east away from his old home to a long stretch of beach. The tide was ebbing as Achilles galloped along the shore. The waves were no deeper than his fetlocks and the water splashing over Adam's body was cooling and refreshing after a day in the fields.

He pulled Achilles to a halt and stared out to sea. Dotted on the horizon, several brigantines and merchantmen in full sail headed towards Plymouth or ports further along the south coast. From Penruan a cluster of fishing luggers were fanning out to sea for the night catch. The air was crystalline and in the far distance headlands stretched seawards, their colours fading to purple and grey.

For so many years he had taken this sight for granted. The

tumbling of waves against rocks and beach; a distant ship's bell were the sounds that had filled his childhood. Woven through these the smell of brine, kelp, a catch of fish recalled the years he had spent at sea. He closed his eyes momentarily, feeling the rise and fall of a deck beneath his feet. The whoosh and slap of the waves and the shriek of gulls turned to the song of a siren as his old mistress the sea lured him into her embrace.

He shook his head to clear the memories of exotic lands across the oceans; the challenge of the elements as he stood at the helm through gales and storms. It had been a hard life, but it was a fever that had never left his blood.

The clock in the church tower of Penruan struck the half-hour, its notes carrying to him on the breeze. It was time to return to the mundane routine and blessings of his present lifestyle. He left the beach and kept to the cliff path until he reached the woodland track. His mind was on the end of harvest tasks tomorrow, and as he entered a clearing, he was startled to find his passage blocked by Tristan standing in his way. His cousin's horse was tethered to a tree. The shadows were lengthening in the glade as the sunset streaked the sky crimson.

'Cousin.' Adam drew rein, regarding Tristan with wary deliberation. The older man stared back, his antagonism charging the air around him.

'Get down,' Tristan snarled.

Adam had no intention of being ordered like a servant by a man he could not abide.

'I said get down, or I'll drag you from that damned horse.'

'You can try. If you have something to say, spit it out,' Adam jeered. Tristan was bristling for a fight, and Adam felt his own blood stir. A confrontation was long overdue.

Chapter Twenty-one

Tension was running high for other members of the Loveday family. Hannah could not shake the feeling that all was not as it should be at the farm. The hens and geese had been laying poorly in the last week. None of the poultry appeared ill or off their food, yet there were a third fewer eggs than normal to be taken to market. Watkins had reported fox droppings around the coops. The cubs at this time of year were rummaging for their own food, and if they were pestering the geese by sniffing around the coops of a night, it was possible that they had disturbed their laying. Yet it was strange that the farm dogs had not barked at their presence.

She decided that this week she would take the cart to market herself, and relieved Watkins of his duty. He had looked disgruntled. No doubt he used the day to spend an hour in a tavern supping ale. Her wares sold quickly, her attendance drawing a crowd from the housewives she had not seen for many months, all eager for gossip about her life in Devon. Many were women she had known for eighteen years, since the first time she had come to market as Oswald's wife.

Once her produce had sold, she had an hour to wander around the market to make some purchases of her own. She was near the cattle section when an argument between two men turned into a fight. Usually Hannah avoided brawls, which could quickly turn nasty. She hated violence, but there was something about the angry outburst that held her attention.

'I tell you, that be my cow,' shouted the shorter, thicker-set of the two men as he lashed out at a younger, unkempt figure.

'And I tell you, I just bought her.' His opponent lurched towards the shorter man, grabbing him about the ribs in a wrestling hold.

'That cow were stole from me,' the first accused, swinging his fist wildly to land a punch.

'Someone call the constables!' another farmer demanded.

'I bought her, I didna steal her,' the unkempt man protested.

The accusations continued as the men rolled on the ground, kicking and punching. Other farmers had formed a circle, cheering on the opponents.

'There's been cows stolen regular since last winter,' one spectator shouted. 'Four of mine were took.'

'Same with me.' A deeper voice joined in.

The two men were dragged apart but continued to hurl abuse at each other. Hannah stared at the heifer in question. She was covered in a great deal of mud, which disguised most of her colouring. Suddenly Hannah's blood ran cold. The animal had a twisted horn that grew at an odd angle. She had seen that heifer in her own field last week, she was certain of it. It had been in the meadow from where she had believed cows had been moved. The horn deformity was not one she could remember from her visit to the farm in the spring, but then the heifer would have been too young for it to have been so noticeable.

'Break it up.' The constable had arrived and grabbed the arms of the thickset man. Another farmer held on to the second fighter.

'You are both in breach of the peace. A night in the lock-up will cool your tempers,' the constable threatened.

'That cow were stolen from my farm not two weeks back,' the thickset man accused.

'I paid good money for it,' the purchaser whined.

'Who did you buy it from?' the constable demanded.

'A man here had six or seven to sell.' The accused struggled to free himself from the hold on his arms. 'He wanted too much for them at first. This were the last one left. He sold it at the price I offered. He were eager to get away by then.'

'That be my cow. I want what it be worth, or it should be returned to me.' The thickset man was red-faced with his anger.

'Who was the seller?' the constable persisted, his temper rising as a wild punch from the thickset man struck his chin.

'I didna recognise him as a regular here.' The purchaser kicked out as he continued to struggle. 'Said he came from St Tudy way and was selling the cows for his brother who were sick. I bought that cow fair and square. This man here will vouch for that. He saw me.'

'That be right,' the man answered. 'I saw him hand over the money.'

'What did the man look like who sold him?' The constable was struggling for breath as his captive elbowed him in the ribs. 'Dammit, man. Stop struggling or I'll throw you in the lock-up now.'

The buyer finally stopped wriggling and now looked alarmed. 'Same as any other farmer. He were short, bearded, ruddy face.'

The constable glared at the gathering. 'Did anyone recognise the man who sold the cow?'

Several heads were shaken in denial.

'I want my property back,' the thickset man shouted.

'It be mine. I paid for her.'

The argument threatened to break out again as Hannah walked away. It was obvious that the cow had been stolen, and she was appalled to think that it could have been mixed in with her herd. But that was preposterous. Rustlers hid their plunder and would sell it far from their own locality to avoid being recognised. Yet the cow's horn was so distinctive, she was certain it was the one she had seen in her field. The implications of that were too dreadful to contemplate. Someone had exploited her absence to use her land. Either that or Watkins was in some way responsible.

She had not hesitated to denounce the smugglers who thought they could manipulate her. Whoever was responsible for this would find they had made a serious mistake in underestimating her. But she could not act until she had proof.

She would start tomorrow by checking every detail of Watkins's work. She would also make the milk deliveries herself, and by talking to the customers she might learn something of what had been happening at the farm in her absence.

Chapter Twenty-two

'Devil take you! You know what this is about.' Tristan strutted forward, his fist punching the air as he approached Adam.

A slow grin spread across Adam's face. 'I have many issues with you, Tristan. I would be happy to fight you over any of them.' He languidly threw his leg over the saddle pommel and slid to the ground. 'No formal duel. No seconds. No witnesses. It is better this way. Also I have no sword. There is a pistol in my saddle holster. A fit enough weapon to shoot a stray dog.' He stooped and with agile speed withdrew a dagger from the inside of his boot. 'Or we could fight like footpads or vagabonds – a form you would be more familiar with than I.'

With terse, angry movements Tristan stripped off his fashionable cutaway coat and embroidered waistcoat, tossing them impatiently over a fallen branch. 'You cannot bear that I am master of your beloved Trevowan. Accept that your wastrel twin gambled it away.'

He paced around the clearing as Adam discarded his leather work-jerkin and jacket whilst regarding his cousin through narrowed, calculating eyes.

Tristan continued his taunting. 'What is more, you must squirm with envy that I have the money to bring the house back to its original glory. How you must resent that I have married a noblewoman who will grace its halls; a woman whose family is as old and revered as that of Anne Penhaligan, Trevowan's heiress when Great-grandfather Arthur Loveday wed her to gain the estate. Lady Alys is a fitting mistress, whereas you and St John thought an innkeeper's daughter or a gypsy wench good enough to rule where once Anne Penhaligan was matriarch.'

Adam controlled his rising temper. Tristan was deliberately

goading him and thus seeking to gain the upper hand. A cool head would outmanoeuvre a hot, impetuous one in a fight. They continued to circle, and Tristan drew his own dagger, the first threads of a crimsoning sky turning the blade to the colour of blood.

At Adam's silence, Tristan showed signs of losing his composure. A muscle was pulsating along his jaw and the lines about his mouth had tightened.

'You think you are the better man, Adam,' he scoffed. 'Now we shall prove who is the more worthy master of Trevowan. We will make this a real test of skill and courage.'

Adam crouched. 'When you stop blathering we can start the fight. Or do you intend to talk all evening?'

'Ah, but the preparations are not complete.' Tristan grinned. He had circled until he reached his horse, and now with a quick movement he drew out a leather strap that had been resting across the saddle. 'Just to make it more interesting, we will wind each end of this around our wrists so that there can never be more than two paces between us. Or is that too dangerous a risk for you, cousin?'

He flicked out the end of the strap to Adam, who caught it and wound it several times around his left wrist. Tristan was left-handed, so he wrapped his end about his right wrist. Two feet of leather separated them. Adam had watched the gypsies fight this way when Senara's brother's band had camped on his land. He had never fought in this manner himself. He guessed Tristan would be accomplished. It was a brutal test of courage, strength and skill.

A vicious jerk on the strap caught Adam unawares, and only his quick reflexes enabled him to recover his balance.

'This is no time to be wool-gathering, cousin,' Tristan mocked. He swiped his dagger across Adam's chest. Adam avoided contact by leaping aside and then wrenched hard on the leather to pull Tristan off his feet. Lithe as a cat, his cousin stayed upright, his eyes glittering with ridicule.

Adam responded with a chuckle. 'Keep your own wits about you, Tristan. This is no child's game, but deadly serious.'

The blood was pumping through his veins, every one of his senses heightened. The scent of dew forming on the grass smelt sweeter, the evening song of a blackbird sounded sharper. His skin prickled from the buzz of excitement and danger, and he could taste the anticipation of victory, though not before old scores were settled.

'You still think that you are the better man.' Tristan shook his head in amusement. 'You have no idea what you are up against when you pit yourself against me.'

They exchanged short jabbing attacks, ducking and twisting as the lethal blades skimmed close to flesh and sliced through silk and cambric. No blood was drawn and both men were breathing heavily. They were of similar build, although his years of working in the shipyard had honed Adam's body to hard muscle. Tristan was naturally wiry and had the combat instincts of an alley cat fighting over its prey.

'How does it feel knowing you will never have Trevowan?' Tristan goaded.

'You grow as tiresome as a tolling bell. It was never my birthright,' Adam returned, jumping aside as his cousin's blade almost shaved the evening stubble from his cheek. His own dagger juddered as it encountered his assailant's steel. 'My pride is now Boscabel, resurrected from ruins by my own hands.'

The hilts clashed together, and the men's wrists locked in a trial of strength as the crossed blades pressed closer to their opponents' throats. Their teeth were bared, and sweat glistened on their brows. The interlocked daggers reflected the sunlight into both their eyes, and just as Tristan began to bring his knee up to strike Adam in the groin, Adam shoved his cousin away and twisted enough for the blow to glance off his hip.

'And gypsy brats will found your dynasty. Is that why you would cuckold me with Lady Alys?' snarled Tristan, the length of leather again separating them.

The statement was absurd even by Tristan's standards. Adam was so astonished that his reflexes did not counter a follow-through attack and he felt the edge of steel glance along his jaw. The wound smarted as blood trickled on to his shirt. He lunged wildly, but a kick behind his knee dropped him to the ground. Tristan threw himself on top of him and again their dagger hilts fused. Only strength would save a mortal blow.

'You have the mind of the sewer rats you grew up amongst,' Adam grunted as he managed to push his cousin aside and roll on top of him. He spat his disgust. 'Have you no respect for your wife? A lady of virtue and integrity. I always knew she was too good for you.'

There was a demonic twist to Tristan's features as he strained to press the edge of his dagger into his cousin's throat.

'Curse you,' he spat. 'Trevanion saw you. You want Alys because you cannot have Trevowan.'

Adam could feel the tremor starting in the older man's wrist as his blade nicked the flesh above his adversary's stock. Tristan's blood mixed with Adam's own on his shirt. The men rolled across the dew-sodden grass and Adam claimed the advantage of kneeling across Tristan's panting body. 'Would that be at the time I refused the lecher from marrying Rowena? He would not be bearing a grudge, would he?'

'Lies. You wanted Alys for yourself to make a fool of me.'

The strength of both men was sapping fast, their arms trembling from their exhaustion. 'Your wife is more worthy than that, and so is the honour in which I hold Senara.'

Tristan bared his teeth, the tendons in his neck standing out as he pushed Adam's hand back. Using his weight, he shoved Adam from him and sprang to his feet. 'Would you have me think you designed the bird house out of the kindness of your heart! I think not.'

There was enough give in the leather strap for Adam to uncoil from the earth like a striking snake. Upright, he yanked their binding, striving to bring Tristan to the ground once more. He failed, and although both remained standing, they were breathing heavily.

'I designed the aviary because it was a project that interested me,' Adam raged. 'Also the structure was in keeping with the house.'

'Lies,' Tristan spat again. 'It was to win her favour. You put yourself out to save her life in France. Did you have your eye on her then?'

Jumping back to avoid a dagger thrust to his chest, Adam twisted round so that Tristan faced the setting sun. It shone directly into his eyes.

Adam ground out, 'Like myself, she was one of Long Tom's agents. Japhet and I were after the man who tried to kill her. I also saved your worthless hide out of a misplaced sense of loyalty.'

'You have to be so damned superior.' Tristan slashed wildly, the blade nicking Adam's side as it glanced off his rib. A half-inch either side and it would have pierced his gut.

Through his rage, Adam wanted to dominate the fight and bring it to an end. He had not originally intended to kill Tristan. The consequences of that would be too serious to avoid. Too many knew of their enmity, and he would be the first suspect. Now, however, the cut had roused his blood lust, and he rushed Tristan. His dagger found the flesh of Tristan's arm, but the attack had thrown him off balance, and his cousin's weight crushed him as they both fell to the ground.

Adam landed awkwardly, the breath knocked from his lungs. Tristan's wounded arm had smashed against a small boulder and the dagger flew from his grasp, disappearing into some nearby bracken. Unarmed, he was now at Adam's mercy. But the feral light glittering in his eyes remained murderous. A lesser man would have been in too much pain to do more than beg for his life. Not Tristan. He gritted his teeth and used all his strength to slam his fist into Adam's nose with an impact that broke the bone, blood gushing forth.

A red haze formed before Adam's eyes and he shook his head against the explosion of pain. He threw aside his own dagger and grabbed his cousin's neck, his hands pressing into the windpipe. Tristan pushed his thumb into Adam's eye.

Locked in their battle, each refused to give ground, until a bullet thudded into the soil an inch from their heads. Momentarily they both froze.

'What does it take to get you two to come to your senses?' Lady Alys demanded, the smoking pistol in one hand, Adam's discarded dagger in the other.

'You could have killed us both,' Tristan snorted in derision.

'Give me credit for being a better shot. If I had wanted either of you dead, you would be.' Her glare was incensed, and as she studied her husband, she showed no pity at his bloody wounds. 'Is this the way to thank Adam for his generous design for the aviary, husband? I despair of you. Aunt Elspeth said you had galloped out of Trevowan with the devil riding your tail after Trevanion called on you. I can guess what evil that vicious weasel planted in your ear. But I did not think to find you brawling like wayward children.'

'We were settling a gentlemen's disagreement.' Tristan scowled as he rose stiffly to his feet and cradled his injured arm with his hand. Blood oozed from a cut on his neck, which was also reddened and showing bruising. Grass and bloodstains covered his ripped shirt and dead bracken and leaves clung to his hair.

Adam looked scarcely better. His shirt was splashed with blood, there was a tear to the knee of his black breeches and a stream of blood smeared his nose and cheek.

Lady Alys folded her arms across her chest and regarded them severely. 'A gentlemen's disagreement indeed! Perhaps this charade has finally cleared the air between you and we can resume a civilised approach to being neighbours.'

The men both drew in lungfuls of air. Tristan bent over and put his hands on his knees to help recover his breath. Adam unwound the leather strap from his wrist and retreated to lean against a tree. The clearing was revolving slowly before his eyes, his body heaving with exhaustion. He spread his hands in supplication.

'It is Tristan's call,' he said. 'He is the one with bats in his belfry. He accused us of being lovers.'

'As if you would ever betray Senara,' Lady Alys derided, but there was a telltale flush to her cheeks, which fortunately her husband did not see as he was too busy scowling at the ground.

She quickly recovered her composure. 'This foolish rivalry has to stop. You do not have to act as best friends, but you could at least be civil with each other and stop thinking the worst over any matters concerning you both. I am grateful to Adam, who took the time and trouble to design the bird flight. No one else would have been so sensitive that it would not look out of place beside the orangery.'

Tristan resignedly held up his hands. The leather dangled from his wrist and he pulled it off and flung it into the bracken. Then he went to search for his dagger.

Lady Alys was far from finished. 'And you can swallow your pride, husband. I expect an apology for believing Trevanion's lies. Your cousin also deserves no less.'

'You have my unreserved apology, my lady.' Tristan bowed to her. He remained stiff and unbending as he regarded his cousin and continued to rummage through the undergrowth.

Lady Alys tapped her foot impatiently. 'Leave that! Now apologise to your cousin.'

Tristan baulked. Adam had enjoyed witnessing his discomfort. However, he could not silence his own conscience that an attraction had been sparking between him and Lady Alys. An attraction that would dishonour them both and all he loved most dearly. In the circumstances he was prepared to be magnanimous. He stepped forward and held out his hand.

'I am as much to blame,' he said. 'This fight is long overdue.'

His hand was gripped in a bone-crushing hold and he tightened his own grasp. It was an unspoken warning that all was not forgotten or forgiven between them. He caught a glimpse of sunlight reflected amongst the undergrowth and picked up Tristan's dagger and returned it to him.

As he turned to walk away, Lady Alys called after him. 'You should ensure you do not greet your wife until you have washed the blood from your face, cousin. Or her tongue will serve you no more lightly than mine did my husband.'

Adam laughed, and Tristan joined in. For the moment the tension was eased between them.

Lady Alys put her foot into her husband's cupped hand as he assisted her into the saddle. She nodded briefly to Adam as he rode away.

'I am not a fool, wife,' Tristan said, having mounted his own horse and reining it alongside her. His stare was piercing. 'Happen I have neglected you overmuch of late. It has been difficult for me to come to terms that much as I love you, you may never give me an heir.'

Alys hung her head, ashamed of her failing. Twice since her marriage she had thought she had conceived a child, only to have her hopes dashed at the third month. 'That is even more reason why I would never betray you with another man, my love. Yet I admit that your cousins are interesting and entertaining. I also feel that continuing the feud between our families is wrong.'

'Your wifely duty is to accept my wishes in this. Adam Loveday has given me no reason to trust him.'

'Yet in France he killed a man and saved your life. Why must you be so unreasonable?' From the first moment of meeting Tristan's cousins and their wives and families, she had wanted to be a part of the closeness they shared. As an only child, and with no cousins of her own, she had always dreamed of the companionship a large family would give her. Perhaps there was no such reality, and feuds and rivalry governed all family life, but Senara, Bridie, Gwen and Hannah certainly provided a united front. They had accepted Aunt Elspeth's decision to remain at Trevowan. They even showed little censure when the old woman could be difficult to tolerate in her outspokenness, though there was no doubting her fearlessness and courage. Felicity too continued to be supported by them, yet from

176

what Alys had seen and heard of St John's widow, she was the least amenable and most intransigent of the family.

She loved Tristan, but there was a side to him that he never opened up to her and she was certain that not all his business deals were strictly legal. And she still had to tell him that she was again working for Long Tom and if called upon would return to France.

Chapter Twenty-three

The sound of a man's and a woman's laughter carried through the open window. Senara peered out of the casement in the long gallery. She had been mixing a bowl of dried rose petals and rosewater to freshen the mustiness of the infrequently used long gallery. At witnessing another peal of merriment, she smiled contentedly and turned to her sister, who was sitting in the afternoon sunlight making lace.

'Bryn and Rowena are often laughing together. Do you think romance is blossoming, Bridie?'

The younger woman halted the rapid clicking of the bodkins as they flew across the cushion covered in pins. A wide half-circle that would form a delicate collar was spread in front of her. She acknowledged the smile with a grin. 'Who knows? They certainly spend a great deal of time in each other's company. I am sure that Adam would approve of a match. Though Bryn could be a pauper and will need to make his way in the world before he can support a wife. Nothing more has been learned about his estate.'

'They could live here,' Senara said wistfully. The more family she had around her, the happier she was. Bryn was a good influence on Rowena; her niece had changed and been more considerate of late.

'I cannot see Bryn allowing his inheritance to be even further neglected,' Bridie counselled. 'He will wish to restore Willow Vale and make good the devastation wreaked by his stepfather. Adam has taught him much about family pride and responsibility. For that to happen he may have to marry a heiress, and not for love.'

'It would be a nice dream, though, would it not?' Senara sighed.

Bridie laughed and shook her head. 'Bryn may be good for

Rowena, but is Rowena good for Bryn? You cannot keep filling Boscabel with waif and stray members of our family.'

There was a catch in Bridie's voice, which made Senara regard her more sharply. 'Do you feel like a waif or stray, Bridie? I love having you here and I forget that it cannot be easy for you. You must miss Peter dreadfully.'

'He is doing what he must. It would be selfish of me to keep my husband from God's work now that he has found his vocation again. But yes, I do miss him. The wilds of Canada are so far away. He has our brother with him, and when he is not preaching he is trapping. They spent last winter in the mountains, which is why I received no word of him for months. He has regained his faith. It was always so important to him, and now he wishes to spread the word as a missionary in the wilderness.'

Bridie was so accepting and brave, Senara's heart went out to her. She felt that Peter was being selfish, but since his wife did not so judge him, what right did she have to criticise? Peter and her gypsy brother Caleph were unlikely companions, yet they had much to offer each other. After Peter lost his son, and with Michael's death his faith, he had craved adventure, and was the only Loveday male not to have sought it before marriage. Caleph also had lost his family, through persecution of his race. Their loss had formed a bond between the two men. When Caleph had decided to start a new life in Canada, Peter had been moved to join him. While Caleph taught the preacher's son how to survive in the wild, Peter taught the gypsy the ways of a gentleman and, during the weeks of the voyage, also how to read and write.

'I have my teaching,' Bridie continued, cutting across her sister's thoughts. 'That is my vocation. If I can help some of the children from the villages and Trevowan Hard move on from the poverty their parents have suffered, then I am content.' She frowned at Senara. 'I truly do not begrudge Peter this chance to follow his vocation. I have been blessed with his love and I was fortunate to have his and Adam's support to overcome being lame and receive an education. I am content. Our lives could have been very different if such honourable men had not loved us.'

Through the window Senara continued to watch Rowena and Bryn. They were walking through the Tudor knot garden, the low hedges thinned and cut back to reveal the intricate original designs.

They had their heads together as they sauntered arm in arm and made an idyllic couple. Her eyes glazed and a mist formed around the young companions. Pictures like the pages of a book being opened darted into her mind. The heaviness of sorrow, danger and great tribulations pierced her senses. The couple seemed to merge and part and merge and part as though coming together in an elaborate dance. There was longing and hope, tears and fleeting ecstasy, ebbing and flowing like waves . . .

'Senara, you have gone quite pale. What do you see?' Bridie's anxious voice penetrated the vision and the mist dispelled, again revealing a sunny afternoon. The couple were now engaged in a disagreement. Rowena looked flushed, and from her dramatic hand movements was overset by some matter. Then Bryn leant forward, and whatever he said made her laugh.

'Nothing. Just two people enjoying each other's company.'

Bridie put aside her work and joined her sister by the window. 'You *saw* something and it troubled you. Do not hide your sight from me. I have seen it happen too often. Are they star-crossed, or will they face some tragedy?'

'Few couples escape some tragedy in their lives,' Senara began, but at encountering the seriousness of her sister's expression, she shrugged. 'I did not see their future as such. It was more feelings. Their lives are interwoven; there will be no escaping that. But whether through love, hatred or danger . . .' She broke off, her voice husky as though the words were drawn unwillingly from her. 'There will be danger. Death . . .' She felt suddenly as though she had been doused in icy water and her body trembled uncontrollably. Her heart was thudding so fast she thought she would suffocate, and she drew great gasps of air.

Bridie held her in her arms. 'Senara, what is it?'

Senara shook her head and leaned against her sister's shoulder as her breathing returned to normal. 'I could not see but only feel that danger will overshadow them. I love them both so dearly. I pray that God will spare them. I can warn them, but I fear it will make no difference. Both are driven by their own need. Their passion.'

In the knot garden the young couple were oblivious to any sense of danger. Rowena was more light-hearted than she had felt in years. She enjoyed the way Bryn would tease her, yet never ridiculed or criticised the wildness of her nature. She had never felt this close to any of her cousins, and would have spent all her spare time in his company given the opportunity.

Bryn found he could relax and be himself when he was with Rowena. He admitted to her that because of his gratitude at his guardian's generosity, he tried too hard to please and impress him. Whereas before he had regarded her as a nuisance, always demanding attention, she was now exciting, vivacious, and there would be a huge void in his life if he could not spend the day in her company.

They discovered that they had the same sense of humour. He was enthralled at her courage and willingness to engage in any wildcap adventure. Every morning he was devoted to his chores, but the late afternoons were free, and they had taken to riding across the moor or along the shoreline. Every ride ended in a race, and he found he was hard put to beat her. Rowena encouraged him to think of his plans for the future and what he would do to restore his home and estate. She surprised him with her insight into the needs of his people, for this was a side of her nature he had never expected. She never disappointed him and never failed to surprise him with some new enticing venture. Yet he never felt that he quite knew her. It was as though she was always holding something of herself back. He could understand that. There was that same element within him. Part of it was a shield. Having once been hurt by those you trusted, your heart was never fully opened; it kept an intrinsic part of you wary and suspicious so that you would never allow that trust to be exploited by another.

'Have you decided what you will do now that you will not be returning to school with my cousins?' Rowena broke through his reflections with her abrupt question.

'Captain Loveday has urged me to take up my place at Cambridge, but I am reluctant.'

'I hated the restrictions of the seminary.'

'It is not that.' He paused as Rowena regarded him quizzically. 'It would mean that I would be accepting more of your family's bounty. I would rather repay Captain Loveday for all his generosity.'

'I am sure my uncle feels that your education is repayment enough. Unless you do not intend to take up a profession. What are your other options?' She felt a stab of alarm. 'Please tell me you would not consider the army or navy.'

'I may not have a choice. I do not intend to live on your family's charity.'

'You could be killed whilst we are fighting this war.'

'I am gratified that you are concerned for my future.' He continued to tease, then his expression sobered. 'I have neglected finding out the truth about my past.'

'But how does that help you financially at this time? You do not come of age for some years. You said your estate was deserted and neglected. Even if there was an income, it would be under the control of your stepfather.'

'Who is unfit to even set foot on that once honoured soil.' His anger erupted, revealing the depth of his frustration and pain.

Rowena took his arm, drawing him to a halt. Her other hand was laid against his chest. 'I understand your pain, Bryn. There are so many mysteries and uncertainties to be resolved. Uncle Adam desires only what is best for you. Unless you remain and help run the estate to gain that experience, or work in the shipyard, whatever you decide will take you away from here.'

'You will be telling me next that you will miss me.' He attempted to jest; he did not want to give in to the bleakness that the future might hold for him.

'But I *would* miss you. You have become like the brother I never had. A friend I can talk to who does not judge me.' Her eyes glistened with tears and she struck him none too gently on his chest.

He was taken aback at her fervour and grabbed her wrists. 'I did not know you cared.' He still made light of the matter.

'I do not. I hate you. You are selfish. Where is your gratitude to this family?' High colour flooded her cheeks and her lower lip trembled. She stamped her foot. 'I have just got to know you and you would desert me . . . as everyone does in the end.' Wrenching her wrist from his hold, she ran through an arch into the walled garden and flung herself down on a crescent-shaped stone seat.

The crunch of gravel told her that Bryn had followed her, and mortified at her outbreak of emotion, she turned her head away.

'Leave me. You are hateful and unfeeling.'

'I did not mean to overset you. I am so used to your spitfire retorts, I could not resist teasing.' He sat beside her, unsure of what to say or do. When he saw a tear roll down her cheek and form a droplet a shade darker on her pale blue muslin dress, he burst out, 'I do care, Rowena. These last weeks have meant a great deal to me. I can talk to you as to no other.'

Still she did not respond above a stifled sniff. He passed her his handkerchief. 'Dry your eyes. I cannot bear to see you cry when I have been so thoughtless.'

She dabbed at her eyes. 'You just feel guilty now that my eyes are swollen and my face all ugly and blotched.'

'You could never be ugly, Rowena,' he soothed. 'You are the most beautiful woman I know.'

'Am I?' She turned towards him but kept her head lowered. 'You were mean to mock me. I will miss you. But I am nothing to you.'

He cupped her chin with his forefinger and made her look up at him. Her eyes sparkled like diamonds and the scent of her filled his senses.

'You are so much more than I could ever hope you could be.'

'Do not play games with me this way,' she moaned. 'Too many people say one thing and mean another.'

'Then mayhap I have said too much. Forget my words.' A shutter came down over his eyes, and she could read nothing in his expression, though perhaps there was regret.

'Bryn, we have shared so much these past weeks. Do not talk in riddles.'

'Bryn, where are you?' Joel's high-pitched demand was impatient. 'Sir Henry said we could pick a puppy from the litter of his spaniel bitch.'

The boy tore into the walled garden, gabbling excitedly, his face flushed with exertion. 'There you are, Bryn. What are you doing with Rowena? She is no fun and never joins in our games. Mama said Nathan and I cannot go to Traherne Hall unless you accompany us. If we do not go now we will have to wait until the end of the week as Sir Henry and his family are leaving for Truro tomorrow.' He grabbed Bryn's hand to pull him away.

'Go away, Joel,' Rowena snapped. 'Bryn and I are talking. He will come to you shortly.'

'Mama says we are to go now,' insisted Joel, and behind Bryn's back he poked his tongue out at his cousin.

'Just give me a few minutes, Joel.' Bryn concealed his irritation at the intrusion.

Joel stood his ground, the stubborn jut of his chin declaring that he would not go away until Bryn went with him.

Bryn stood up. 'I shall need my riding crop. Would you fetch it for me? You are so much quicker than I. It is on my bed.'

'Very well, but don't be long. You spend all your time with Rowena now. You used to be fun to have around.' Joel ran back to the house.

'That child!' Rowena groaned. 'Does he never stop his demands? Do you have to go now, Bryn?' She smiled, hoping to entice him from his duty.

He chuckled and, taking her hand, raised her to her feet. 'You are too much the temptress. You would turn any man's head from his obligations.'

Her eyes clouded with annoyance. 'Go then, if Joel is more important to you than me. You do not care about my misery. I thought you understood . . .' Her voice cracked and she walked rapidly away.

He caught up with her in the doorway of the walled garden. 'You mean a great deal, but you must see that some things can never be.'

'There you go, speaking in riddles.' She was becoming too angry to be placated.

'Because the truth can never be spoken,' he continued cryptically. 'I would give my life to protect you from pain, Rowena.'

This time it was Bryn who broke away, and hurried towards the stables. Rowena stared after him in confusion. There had been no mistaking the tenderness in his avowal.

Chapter Twenty-four

Davey rose before dawn. Holding his boots, he crept through the farmhouse in his stockinged feet, careful to avoid any creaking stair or floorboard. Although each room was as dark as pitch, he did not risk lighting a candle. He knew the position of every piece of furniture and could walk through the house blindfolded without colliding with a chair, footstool or table. The need to be away from the land and buildings before anyone stirred sharpened his senses. In the kitchen there was a dull red glow from the dying embers of the fire that threw the objects in the room into relief. This part of the house was filled with the aroma of woodsmoke and of the hams hanging on hooks from the beams above his head. It also smelt of strong soap, where the surfaces and flagstones had been scrubbed before the kitchen maid retired for the night.

He paused to sit on the bench by the table and pulled on his boots. A snuffling outside the door as one of the dogs sniffed the threshold made him freeze momentarily, his heart thudding in alarm, then there was a soft whine as the dog recognised his smell. Davey opened the door, and as he stooped and ruffled the animal's ears, he quietly ordered it to be silent.

Swiftly he ran across the yard to the stables. In a nearby field a cow lowed, its sound mournful in the pre-dawn light. The white underbelly of a barn owl flashed overhead as it returned after a night's hunting to its roost high in the rafters. The ghostly spectre startled him, for there had been no sound of its approach. He held his breath as he opened the stable door. Fortunately, the hinge did not betray him with a squeak, as he had rubbed whale oil on to it before locking up last night.

A few minutes later he had saddled his gelding and was riding out of the farm gate. He glanced back at the house and cottages. The sprawling Tudor farmhouse was clearly defined by the spreading rays of the sun, and the first blackbird was trilling its opening to the dawn chorus. The more strident crow of a cockerel followed. Then a shiver of trepidation smote him.

A figure was running across the yard into the servants' quarters. It was a woman, and she had come from the direction of Watkins's cottage. Had she seen him? He did not want the man's suspicions aroused. It could ruin his investigations. He was not sure that he approved of Watkins seducing the female servants. Some of them were not much older than his own sisters, and men in positions of authority too often used their power to gain sexual favours, or threaten a reluctant companion with dismissal.

A candle flickered in the room above the barn, where the milkmaids were waking. He hoped the woman had been too interested in avoiding detection to have observed his departure.

He felt like a thief stealing away in the night, but he had his reasons. On a neighbouring farm he could discern the winking eye of a rushlight flaring behind shuttered windows. The light from a lantern bobbed across a field as a farmhand went to herd the cows for milking. It made Davey hasten his pace. He disliked deceit, but he was aware of his inexperience in many matters concerning the farm. It was important to prove that he could overcome them and not lose the respect of those who relied on his judgement.

By the time he reached his destination, the sun had risen above the distant hills, the trees casting long shadows across the track and meadows. Rabbits and badgers darted for their burrows and setts, while a stealthy fox padded along the hedgerow.

The three-storey granite-built farmhouse was bathed in the dawn light that softened the harsh stonework to the colour of dark amber. The slate tiles, moistened by the earlier mist, glistened against the backdrop of wooded hills. Smoke was streaming from the kitchen chimney. The stable lads were emerging from their quarters, some rubbing the sleep from their eyes. The head groom was shouting, and the bang of stable doors opening and the ring of iron shoes on the hard earth carried to him.

A tall figure in moleskin breeches, shirt and leather jerkin emerged from the house, his long stride marching to the stables. He was the first to notice Davey's arrival.

186

'Nephew, this is an ungodly hour for you to be abroad. There is nought amiss at the farm, I trust,' Japhet demanded.

Davey dismounted. 'There is a matter I would discuss with you, Uncle. Is it convenient to talk now?'

Japhet grinned. 'Only something of extreme importance would take you from the farm at milking time. Am I right in thinking your mother does not know of this visit?' His voice had attracted the attention of several of the horses in the limewashed stables and their heads appeared over the top of the half-open doors. Some neighed a greeting, whilst others shook their heads and drew back their muzzles, hoping for an apple titbit from their master as he passed.

Japhet guided Davey to a side door that led directly to a small office at the end of the stable block. It contained a wooden chair and an oak table piled with racing pages from news-sheets and ledgers with performance details of the stables' colts and fillies in their racing training. There was a schedule of exercise times on the wall and another of the dates of race meetings.

'We will not be interrupted here.' His uncle gestured for Davey to take the chair, and he himself propped one hip on the edge of the desk. 'If my sons learn that you are visiting, they will be all over you demanding attention. So what is troubling you?'

Davey shifted in the chair. 'I have so much still to learn about the running of the farm. Not the everyday management, for Mr Deighton taught me well both here and on the Eastley estate.' He paused, and then blurted out in a nervous rush, 'It is the other problems. Dishonesty or misconduct by the workers. I realise that they will be watching and testing me for my reactions to unforeseen events or misadventures, but it is difficult to know how to deal with such matters wisely.'

'That comes with experience. I am always willing to give you advice or help you sort out any matter. So what is bothering you now?' Japhet leaned forward, encouraging him to be honest and open.

'I do not believe that the farm books reflect all that has been happening in Mama's absence. But as yet I have no proof.'

His uncle's expression darkened. 'You cannot act without evidence, or you will lose the trust and respect of your servants. Clearly you have suspicions.'

Davey nodded and sighed. 'Watkins often disappears for hours at a time. If questioned, he has a plausible excuse involving work on the farm. I know I am young and he probably resents taking orders from me.'

'You are his master, Davey. You are in control,' Japhet reminded him firmly, and there was an amber flash of anger in his hazel stare. 'I take it you listen if he offers you advice on a matter when he may have felt your orders were not in the best interest of the livestock or management of the farm?'

'He can be arrogant and sullen. But yes, I am prepared to listen if what he says makes sense. Though there is something in his manner that I do not trust.'

'It is a good intuition to follow. Do you believe he is dishonest in his dealings, perhaps keeping money from sales back for himself? That cannot be allowed to happen.' His uncle's earlier carefree manner was replaced with an edge of steel. Japhet would never tolerate any injustice or wrongdoing.

Davey became more confident that his kin was not ridiculing what he sensed rather than could prove might be wrong. 'A few days ago I discovered the imprints of the hooves of several cows that appeared to have been led through the wood at the far end of the farm to where it joins a track that would take them to the Bodmin road. No cows, just the tracks, you understand. The ground of the wood was still moist from the last rain. Little light penetrates that area. The trees are chopped down when we need to replace fencing, otherwise no one goes there. That was not all . . .'

Davey stood up and paced the small room. 'The meadow that backs on to the wood has a dry-stone wall all around, except where the gate leads to the fields near the farm buildings. The meadow is used for grazing for the heifers, which will be added to the milk herd next year after they have calved. The wall at the back looks like it has been tampered with. There is a corner section where the old stones have been replaced by larger ones, as though to repair it. It would take a man just a few minutes to remove enough of these stones to allow some cows to be herded through, and then replace them. That corner is out of sight of the main pastures or ploughed fields.'

'That was a good observation to have made. How many heifers were taken?' Japhet demanded.

'That is what is a mystery. None.' Davey rubbed his hand over his cropped hair in a way Japhet had often seen Oswald do when he was troubled. 'I have checked all the cows. None are missing.'

'Have you an idea of what you think may have happened?' Japhet encouraged.

'It sounds absurd, but all I can think is that rustlers have used the field to hide their cattle amongst our heifers.'

'That sounds like good reasoning, Davey.' The lines about his uncle's face had tightened. This early in the morning Japhet had not yet shaved, and the dark stubble on his jaw hardened his handsome features with a menacing air. 'Yet it would be a risk. They could be discovered if someone from the farm was not a party to them using that field.'

'I agree.' Davey stopped pacing and held his uncle's steady gaze. 'Therefore I suspect that Watkins is involved. When I questioned him about the wall and the cow tracks through the wood, he said that some of the heifers had escaped from the field when that part of the wall collapsed some weeks ago. He said that was why it had been repaired, but those hoof imprints were fresh.'

'Have you spoken to Hannah about this?' Japhet asked.

Davey stood tall with his shoulders squared. 'I do not wish to cause her concern. Mama is to return to Devon in three weeks. If she believes Watkins is in league with rustlers, she will want him dismissed, and she will stay at the farm until a new man has proved his experience. She worries that the work will be too much for me without a man who has knowledge of dairy farming. I have to show by my handling of this that she need have no fears of my capabilities.'

Japhet stood up and gripped Davey's shoulder, conveying his solidarity and concern. 'For that you will have to find answers. You are right to suspect Watkins. But he is a man who will have covered his dishonesty well. If discovered, the consequences could cost him his life. That could make him a dangerous adversary.'

'I am not afraid to face my responsibilities.' Davey was pale but resolute.

'He cannot be allowed to get away with abusing his position at the farm, for it reflects upon the reputation of your family.'

'That is another reason why I need to resolve this myself. What do you advise, Uncle Japhet?'

In his mind, Japhet still regarded the eighteen-year-old standing before him as no more than a self-conscious youth. Those veils were lifted now. It had taken maturity and insight to make those deductions. The curl of his nephew's mid-brown hair flopping over his brow might soften his features boyishly, but his brown eyes were keenly intelligent. He might not need to shave the faint outline of a moustache and beard more than twice a week, but his self-consciousness had been replaced by self-assurance and awareness. The stubborn tilt of his chin was a recognisable Loveday trait from his mother, and the proud squaring of his shoulders showed the family pride of both his parents. Japhet would never think of him as a youth again. The young man was less than a head shorter than Japhet's height, and he was some inches over two yards. Those young shoulders now carrying the weight of responsibility had also been broadened by the muscles of his labours. His actions today had shown him to be a man who commanded respect.

'You can but keep a discreet watch on Watkins,' Japhet advised. 'Give him duties that should not take him out of sight of the farm buildings, and make regular rounds of all the fields to ensure that nothing is amiss. I doubt now that you are in residence that Watkins will risk allowing the rustlers to use your land again. If he is stealing from you in other ways, you must check all the quantities of produce and the money from deliveries. Do not hesitate to query any discrepancies.'

'You will not tell Mama that I have been here, will you?' Davey insisted. 'She will see it as a reason to stay. I must prove that I am a worthy master of the farm.'

Japhet nodded, his eyes warm with pride for his nephew. 'Promise me that you will do nothing against Watkins without again consulting me. He could be dangerous. It is no weakness to gather your resources around you when about to enter combat. We Lovedays are united in adversity and will never fail one of our own. I am proud of you, Mr David Rabson, gentleman farmer.'

Davey blushed. 'I thank you for your advice, sir.'

'If you do not object, I will call at the farm on a more regular basis. It will be a visual warning to Watkins that you have the support of your family at all times.'

'I would appreciate that, Uncle Japhet. You have many responsibilities of your own here at the stud.'

'It will be my pleasure.' Japhet grinned. 'I admire your sentiments in not wishing to concern Hannah that not all is as it should be at the farm.' Diplomatically he did not mention that his sister had already spoken to him about her own worries involving Watkins. He could at least reassure her that Watkins was unlikely to try anything unlawful if he realised that Japhet was a regular visitor to the farm.

Chapter Twenty-five

Japhet was not the only one to express his support for a younger member of the family that day. When Adam returned from the shipyard in the afternoon, he summoned Bryn to his study. They sat either side of the unlit fireplace in two padded high-backed baroque chairs with carved wooden arms. A robin sang outside the diamond-paned windows, and the branches of a rowan tree heavy with red berries, scratched against the glass. The room smelled of leather from the bound books lining the walls. There were several carved models of ships, a recorded history of the vessels built in the shipyard. The estate ledgers were locked in a glass-fronted cabinet behind the heavy desk, which also held a silver tankard filled with quill pens, and an inkstand.

'I received this today.' Adam passed a letter to Bryn. 'It is a reply from a Mr Parfitt of lawyers Messrs Parfitt and Hensley of Taunton. They handled the legal matters of the Willow Vale estate in your father's time. He is not prepared to put any details in a communication and suggests that a representative of the estate attends at their offices with proof of their credentials.'

'That does not sound as though they are willing to help us.' Bryn groaned in disappointment.

'It is the formal language lawyers use to conduct their business,' Adam reassured. 'It is a start. When would you like to leave? I will need a couple of days to organise the work at the yard. It is fortunate that the harvest is finished. Rudge will deal with any matters concerning the estate.'

'If you are busy, Captain Loveday, I could go to Taunton alone.'

Adam tapped his long fingers on the polished arm of his chair. 'That would be unwise, considering recent events. And since I am your guardian until you come of age, Mr Parfitt would need me to confirm your story and the facts about your flight from your home. They may even need details of the woman who was killed in the coach accident.'

'Now that my memory has returned, I am certain that she was Arabella, my stepfather's younger sister. Carforth was forcing her to marry a man she despised.' Bryn sat forward in his chair. 'If Parfitt has news of my mother's maid Josephina, she could tell me why the estate was so neglected. If she is still alive, she would be in her late forties.'

Adam rose from his chair and picked up some papers that he had been working on. 'That is among many questions you may wish to put before Mr Parfitt. I suggest you spend tomorrow writing down everything you can remember about your home and estate: descriptions of the rooms, or any details about the family that only you would know. We have to prove to him that you are not an impostor and that you are who you say you are. There may also be questions you wish to ask him about how the estate matters were handled after your father's death. We will leave for Taunton on Thursday. I have informed my wife that we could be away for a week or two. Any information we are given will have to be followed up.'

Bryn was grinning. 'I will start a list immediately. I would also find out what Mr Parfitt knows about Carforth's whereabouts now. My stepfather has a great deal to answer for.'

Two days later Adam and Bryn left by carriage for Taunton.

Dearest Papa,

If only you were here to tell me what to do — tell me whom I can trust.

I have heard nothing from Wilbur or Sir Selwyn, though it would be wrong for me to believe that they would write. The rumours I have heard about Sir Selwyn have been disquieting and there is no one I can confide in. Felicity has said that for all his title he has no estate or establishment of his own. His inheritance is described as barely substantial to keep himself, let alone a wife. He had no choice but to enlist in the army to make his fortune.

Rowena frowned as she wrote, the tip of her tongue protruding above her lower lip as she concentrated on her writing. It had been some weeks since she had felt the need to express her uncertainties to her father in this manner, and she could feel the tension in her body relaxing. The script became more scrawling as her troubled thoughts gathered momentum.

Selwyn is handsome and exciting, and I would wait for him if I thought he truly loved me. But that old lecher Bruce Trevanion has ruined everything. How can Selwyn marry me when our happiness would be a slight and insult upon his uncle? That also applies to Wilbur, and there was a time when I thought it would be romantic to be mistress of Polruggan Manor. Of course it is not so fine as Trevowan, Papa, but I would have had a grand mansion close to my old home and family. I hate Bruce Trevanion: he has destroyed two chances of my making an agreeable marriage. It is so unfair.
Then there is Bryn.

The pen hovered above the paper, and she was overcome with the sense of loss mixed with yearning. Impatiently she clutched a hand to her breast, where her heart felt that it was squeezed in a cider press. The pen again flew over the paper.

As to Bryn . . . there are times when I could throttle him. He drives me to lunacy by never quite saying what he means. He can be charming and my best friend one moment and then provoking beyond measure the next. I thought he could be my confidant and friend. I have never felt such pleasure in another's company, except for yours, my dearest Papa. Then like the wind he changes. He knew I was upset. The thought of that lecher Trevanion wanting to make me his bride made my flesh cringe as though slugs and snails were crawling across it. Just when I need him, Bryn has gone away with Uncle Adam, and no one will discuss why. I suspect it is to do with his past. It was so dreadful that someone had been sent to abduct him. He has his own problems and no one troubles to explain them to me. I am no longer a child, and yet everyone treats me as one.
I thought it would be easier living at Boscabel, Uncle Adam used to be kind to me when I was a child. But I am now another responsibility to him — an orphan like Bryn and dependent upon Uncle Adam's bounty. It is obvious he prefers Bryn to me. He has been locked away

with his protégé for hours since my arrival, and with all the distress I have endured because of Trevanion, he has barely given me a second glance, let alone been supportive and understanding. Oh, Papa, why can no one see my pain . . .

The agony of her grief gripped her in its relentless vice. A wayward tear that she angrily brushed away smudged the words on the paper. She despised any show of weakness. With a snarl of frustration, she crushed the page into a ball, then reached for the bowl and drew her father's silver tinderbox from a drawer. Clasping it in her hand, she could feel his presence and love as her fingers caressed the warm metal.

She opened the tinderbox and struck the flint until it sparked, setting the tinder within smouldering. Her palms cupped around the box and she blew softly on the tiny red glow, watching as it flickered into a flame. An eternal flame that linked her father to her for ever.

'I love you, Papa.' She breathed a kiss and the flame became brighter, touching against the crumpled missive. Once the paper had blackened, she ground it to ashes with the pestle until her outpourings turned to a fine dust. When she opened the window and allowed the breeze to carry the particles away, the ritual was completed.

She had never felt so alone – never missed St John more profoundly. Never felt that there was no one she could trust and rely on.

When Rowena awoke the next morning she felt the lightning bolt of grief strike again. She had been dreaming of St John; he had lavished her with fine gowns and jewels and proudly escorted her to her first ball. Those dreams would never come true, but she remembered also that in the dream her papa had been searching through the revellers and calling for Thea and George. Her half-brother and sister were too young to attend the ball, but Rowena remembered St John's anxiety.

She threw off the bedcovers, and after splashing her face and hands in cool water from a jug on the washstand, she dressed in her riding habit. It was as though St John had reminded her that if she felt deserted by her family, she must be more loving and caring towards her siblings. They too were without a loving father. She would ride to Reskelly Cottage as soon as she had broken her fast.

And then she would visit Grandma Sal and her cousin Zach. It had been wrong of her to neglect them in recent weeks.

Rowena also resolved to be more considerate of Felicity. Now that she did not have to live with her stepmother and tolerate her petty restrictions and rigid adherence to all things conventional, she could afford to be more magnanimous.

The sun was shining and it was a warm day. She would make the most of what was left of the summer, before the autumn storms and gales set in. Catching sight of her reflection in the windowpane, she smoothed the lines of her red velvet military-style riding habit. In this Uncle Adam had been generous, providing her with a new wardrobe of clothing. He had also given her a grey mare with a pure white mane and tail that she had called Misty. The mare was her most prized possession and allowed her more freedom.

Perhaps she was being too harsh on her kin. Throughout her childhood she had adored her dashing uncle. She had been awed by his tales of sea battles and his exploits in France rescuing émigrés from the terror of the Revolution. She supposed that she was grateful to him for dealing with the obnoxious Mr Trevanion in no uncertain terms. Yet even the daring sea captain Adam Loveday could do nothing to turn back the clock, so that it would not affect how Sir Selwyn and Wilbur would now regard her. She also still had to deal with Felicity's resentment. Her stepmother was unlikely to forgive her for some time for having stolen Trevanion's affection, even though none of that had been her doing.

A chill atmosphere settled over the interior of Reskelly Cottage when Rowena arrived. She chose to ignore it. She presented Felicity with a bowl of sugared violets made by Winnie Fraddon, who was now cook at Boscabel. They were her stepmother's favourite. Charlotte eyed her sulkily and picked up Thea as though protecting her from her elder sister.

Felicity had been seated at a table writing a long entry in her diary, and made no move to accept the sweetmeats. With a false smile Rowena placed the bowl on the table. Felicity continued to eye her coldly and did not invite her to be seated.

Charlotte pouted. 'I suppose you have upset them all at Boscabel and expect us to welcome you with open arms. You spoil everything here. You made Mama cry.'

Rowena curtseyed to her stepmother. 'No one was more mortified than I when Mr Trevanion called upon Uncle Adam. I expected him to wed you.'

'Charlotte, take Thea into the garden. I would speak with Rowena,' Felicity ordered stiffly.

She waited until they were alone, and to make sure that no one could eavesdrop outside, she closed the door. Her stare was hostile. 'Mr Trevanion proved himself to be a false friend. Though I shudder to contemplate how seriously wayward your conduct must have been to induce a man of such esteem to save your honour.'

The accusations were no less than Rowena had expected, and she bit her tongue to remain outwardly cool and composed. 'I did nothing to be ashamed of. I certainly did not encourage Mr Trevanion. He is older than my father. I thought he was wooing you.' She could not stop the shudder of disgust that Trevanion now aroused in her. Then, noticing the tight line of condemnation to her stepmother's mouth, she realised that her words had offended Felicity and attempted to make amends. 'Wilbur and Sir Selwyn were my friends. Mr Trevanion has ruined that. I despise him. He certainly did not treat you with the respect and honour you deserved.'

'Mr Trevanion has taken pains to ensure that neither his brother nor his cousin continue their misalliance with you.' Felicity was unmoved by the protest and turned away from her stepdaughter, the high colour of her cheeks revealing her disdain. Through the window she kept her gaze upon Mo Merrin, who was digging in the kitchen garden. 'Polruggan Manor has been closed up. Mr Trevanion, his daughter and her nurserymaid have taken lodgings near his brother's and cousin's barracks. He intends to remain there until they take up their commissions.'

It was a relief to learn that the objectionable man had left the district and Rowena would not risk a chance encounter with him. It would have been too embarrassing. Her spirit lightened and she resolved to let nothing stop the reason for her visit. 'Where is George?'

'You have finally remembered that you have a brother,' Felicity scoffed, and sucked in her cheeks. 'You paid no heed to Thea when you arrived.'

'She was whisked away before I could do more than greet her.'

Rowena felt her anger rising. She had come here intending to make amends to her stepmother. She should have known Felicity disliked her too much to be other than contrary. 'I trust you do not intend to prevent me seeing my father's son.'

'George is sleeping. He was awake in the night, fractious with a summer cold. I would not have his rest disturbed,' Felicity informed her tartly.

'May I at least look in upon him?' Now that she was being thwarted, Rowena was determined to fulfil her duty as a devoted sister.

'I would prefer that you did not. The slightest disturbance could awaken him. I need a rest from his crying.' The older woman's lips turned down as she eyed the new riding habit Rowena was wearing. Her words oozed venom. 'I suppose you had the choosing of so unsuitable a garment. The style and colour are too old for you. Also that mare of yours is far too showy for good taste. Adam is a fool to allow you to twist him around your finger. You father was also weak and could deny you nothing.'

'My father loved me. And Uncle Adam is not a fool,' Rowena hotly defended. 'He is kind and generous.'

'And you remain brash and wilful. I suppose it is too much to expect that Senara is able to teach you manners and decorum.'

'Senara is tolerant and compassionate.' Rowena clenched her fists so hard that her nails dug painfully into her palms. She refused to rise to Felicity's baiting. 'Since my company brings you no pleasure, I will disturb you no longer. Good day to you, Stepmama.' She turned on her heel and strode out of the cottage with her head high.

Chapter Twenty-six

The offices of Parfitt and Hensley were on the second floor of a timber-framed building in the same street as the St Mary Magdalene church in Taunton. It was mid-afternoon, and having taken rooms at an inn close to the Market House, with its assembly rooms, they attended the lawyer's establishment. Bryn was hoping that they might obtain information that would give them an insight into current events at Willow Vale, which could be acted upon. The sooner he could break his stepfather's hold on the estate, the sooner the good name of his family could be restored.

The stairs were narrow, and every step groaned as Adam and Bryn ascended. The old building smelled of damp and dust, and on the second landing the floor tilted towards the overhanging front of the property. A clerk sat at a high desk inside the entrance of the offices, his fingers smeared with ink from copying a legal document in neat copperplate writing.

The creaking staircase had announced their arrival and the clerk was wiping his hands on a rag, a nervous tic contorting one eye as they approached. He stood by the side of his stool, bald of head and stooped of shoulder.

'I am Frobisher, Mr Parfitt's clerk. How may I be of service, gentlemen?'

Adam briefly surveyed the cracked and deteriorating plaster on the walls, the original wattle struts visible where the daub had crumbled. 'Mr Parfitt is expecting us. I am Captain Loveday and this is my ward. Is Mr Parfitt available at this time?'

'Mr Parfitt made no mention of an appointment, Captain Loveday,' Frobisher replied officiously.

'Perhaps you would inform him that I have called. I arrived

earlier than anticipated.' In his work for the British government, Adam's life had depended often on an instant appraisal of a man's manner. There was a shiftiness to Frobisher that he did not trust. The fact that Mr Parfitt had not written in any detail about his connection with Bryn's family also made Adam wary. He lifted a querying brow, and his voice was clipped as he ordered, 'Be so kind as to inform Mr Parfitt that I am here. If he is otherwise engaged now, I can return in the morning at a more convenient time for us both.' He had spoken loud enough for his voice to carry.

Frobisher shuffled away on spindly legs, his figure resembling an arthritic beetle. He scratched on his employer's door, but before he could enter, the portal was flung wide and a man in an old-fashioned bagwig hailed his visitors. He had a round, affable face, but the tautly stretched skin and the yellowy tinge to his complexion showed the frailty of his health.

'Captain Loveday. I thought I heard your name mentioned. How good of you to call. Erasmus Parfitt at your service, gentlemen.' The lawyer greeted them as though they were old friends. He was holding a flat-topped hat and a walking cane. Despite the warmth of the day, he wore a red muffler tied about his neck.

'I was about to leave, but would welcome you and your companion joining me in more comfortable surroundings. I always take refreshment at the coffee house at this time of day. Lady Winterbourne informed me that you wished an introduction to her cousin. I shall of course be happy to oblige.' He gave a sweeping gesture towards the stairs. 'Shall we away to the coffee house, gentlemen?'

If Adam thought his actions and the falsehood of the reason for their meeting odd, he gave no sign. There were too many mysteries surrounding Bryn's past, which could have dangerous repercussions to his ward if revealed to the wrong person. It was, however, disconcerting that Parfitt was being so cautious. Neither did Adam like the way that Frobisher was twisting his claw-like fingers together in an agitated manner.

Erasmus Parfitt addressed his clerk. 'I will not be back to the office today. Make sure that copying is finished. Mr Kendal will be in tomorrow to sign the conveyance for the land he has purchased.'

To add to the subterfuge Mr Parfitt had projected, Adam assumed a more foppish air. It would do no harm to give Frobisher a false impression of his true character. 'A sojourn at a coffee house would be most pleasant, Mr Parfitt, I do so abhor the trappings of business around one. Lady Winterbourne was most effusive about your standing in the community.'

'This building is very old, is it not, Mr Parfitt?' Bryn remarked as they descended the stairs.

'Indeed, sir. It was built in the time of Henry VII, I believe, and sadly is riddled with dry rot, wet rot and death-watch beetle, and is in danger of sliding down the road into the gutter, as you can feel from the tilt of the floor.' Parfitt wheezed. 'Bit like myself. But the old place will last out my time here.'

Adam was aware that Frobisher was hovering by the banisters above them, and he kept the conversation to vague pleasantries until they entered the coffee house. Once inside and seated on a high-backed settle in a corner far from the window, Mr Parfitt visibly relaxed. He scrutinised Bryn closely.

'You have more of your mother's looks than your father's. Though you have his colouring, and there is no mistaking the Bryant nose.'

Bryn rubbed the appendage and smiled wryly. He was aware that his nose was larger than he would have liked, and rather hooked in appearance. Senara had said it was imperious and in no way detracted from his good looks. But Senara would never make anyone self-conscious about their appearance.

Mr Parfitt was about to speak, but paused when the serving maid arrived with their order. He waited until she had left and sipped at his drink. 'Your prompt arrival in reply to my letter is estimable, Captain Loveday. Also that you realised at once that Frobisher is a man who takes too much interest in his master's business. It heartens me that this unpleasant matter will be dealt with discreetly until you are in a position to act.'

'Why do you employ him?' Adam asked.

The lawyer gave a resigned shrug. 'Better the devil you know. He has been with me for many years. He knows the general legal work as well as I do myself. I attend few clients these days. But I suspect that a mutual acquaintance of Mr Bryant and myself is paying Frobisher for information concerning certain property and finances.'

'My stepfather?' Bryn tensed.

'No names. I would rather speak in generalities.' Mr Parfitt looked nervously around him at the other customers. 'As you know, a client's confidentiality cannot be breached in my profession, but suffice to say that I am no longer in the employ of our mutual acquaintance.'

He looked again at Bryn. 'There is little in you of the small boy I remember. You have your grandfather's height. However, I would have passed you in the street and not recognised you. That may work well in your favour.' He now regarded Adam. 'How did Mr Bryant come to be your ward? Carforth let it be known that his stepson was visiting relatives abroad.'

Adam briefly outlined the story. 'My brother discovered a coach that had met with an accident on the road not far from our home. The driver and a well-dressed female passenger were dead. The horses had broken their shafts and bolted. Bryn – sorry, I should say Alexander. We named him Bryn. When he was found unconscious, he had no memory of his name or background. That lasted for many months. My wife nursed him back to health. From his nightmares it was obvious that something traumatic had happened to him in his childhood. We did put notices in many news-sheets describing the accident, but there were no replies. It was obvious that Bryn . . . Alex was of good family and well educated. I was happy to give him a home. I have never regretted it.'

'There must have been some papers or identification within the coach.' Mr Parfitt eyed them fixedly.

'My brother was concerned to save the boy's life. He brought him straight to us. When servants were sent to collect the passengers' possessions from the vehicle, everything had gone. Smugglers or other itinerants must have passed that way and stolen every-thing. No trace was found of any of the property. It was most unfortunate.'

'Unfortunate indeed,' Parfitt snorted. 'Although your ward resembles the Bryant family, I cannot divulge the information I possess until I have asked him some pertinent questions about his childhood. Would you leave us to speak privately for some ten minutes, Captain Loveday?'

Adam nodded and left the table. He went outside to stretch his legs. They had been seated in the coach too long and his joints had stiffened. Wryly he reflected that he was not as young as once he had been. The weather had changed and had become overcast, and he decided that he would leave exploring the castle and river until later.

In the town, the tower of St Mary Magdalene church was the tallest he had seen. He decided to walk in that direction. He had not progressed far when the first splatter of rain made him retrace his steps. If Parfitt was still questioning Bryn, he could take a table in the front of the coffee house until the lawyer had finished.

He was drawing level with the coffee shop when he saw the beetle figure of Frobisher emerge from the offices ahead of him. Adam ducked into a doorway as the clerk scanned the street both ways before hurrying away in the opposite direction. He checked his watch. It was a quarter before four. Frobisher should be at his desk until dusk, and that was not for another three hours or more. Parfitt had certainly given him enough work to occupy his time. Instinct told Adam that the clerk was up to no good, and he decided to follow him.

Frobisher moved fast, and was on the opposite side of the road to Adam. The thoroughfare was busy with carts and coaches moving quickly. Waiting for a gap between the vehicles, Adam kept pace with Frobisher and saw him disappear down an alley between two shops. The flow of carts remained brisk and he was forced to curb his impatience before running across the street. The shafts of a wagon pulled by two horses brushed his shoulder.

'Clodhead!' the driver shouted. 'Watch your step. You could have been killed.'

The rain turned to a sudden downpour and Adam sped down the alley, which led to the next street. It was filled with pedestrians hurrying back to their homes before they were soaked. There was no sign of Frobisher. He ran several yards in either direction but the clerk was nowhere in sight. He waited in a doorway for several minutes but the clerk did not reappear, and Adam decided to return to the coffee house.

Back inside, Mr Parfitt saw him enter and beckoned him to rejoin them. 'You are drenched, Captain Loveday; I had not intended to send you away in the rain. However, I am satisfied with your ward's answers,' the lawyer said, looking more cheerful.

'I am a trifle damp, nothing more,' Adam replied. 'I saw your clerk leave your office. Did he have errands to run for you? I followed him but lost him amongst the crowd.'

Erasmus Parfitt frowned. 'He was not fooled by our ruse. We may then have little time if he is sending word to Carforth. As soon as the rain eases, you must come to my house. I have information there of benefit to you.'

Fortunately the shower passed quickly. The lawyer's house was two streets away and almost as old as the office. The windows were small and the panelling had aged to a dark murky brown. The interior smelt of pipe smoke, testifying to Mr Parfitt's main weakness, and also a mouth-watering aroma of roasted chicken.

'You will do me the honour of staying to dine,' Mr Parfitt insisted.

A large woman in a plain grey gown, white apron and mobcap, her grey hair pulled back in a tight bun, waddled from the rear of the house. 'Ah, Mrs Appleby, we have two guests to dine. My housekeeper is a estimable cook, most estimable indeed.'

Mr Parfitt led them into another dark-panelled room, brightened only by the flames of a fire and the pale faces of four portraits; two with stern features who wore large white Puritan collars. Mrs Appleby appeared carrying two candelabra, the six candles changing the atmosphere of the room to a more homely feel. Even the two Puritans looked less austere. A bright red and blue Turkish carpet and gold brocade-upholstered chairs also made the room less formal. Mr Parfitt poured three glasses of claret and waved his visitors to be seated upon two padded chairs. He then lifted a rack of pipes from a table.

'Can I offer you a pipe and tobacco, gentlemen?'

Adam and Bryn both declined, and Parfitt spent a few moments filling and lighting his pipe, finally blowing a canopy of smoke into the air.

'As to your enquiries I had been unhappy about certain legalities being contravened after your mother's remarriage, Mr Bryant. That displeased your stepfather. My partner and I were curtly told to do what we were paid to do and otherwise keep our opinions to ourselves.' He shook his head and drew on his pipe. 'We had the reputation of our practice to consider and felt it our duty to protest at the unethical procedures he wished introduced. As a consequence we were summarily dismissed as Mr Carforth's lawyers.'

Adam respected the straightforwardness of Parfitt's manner. 'You said in your letter that Mr Hensley died shortly after my ward fled his home, and that it was he who had mostly dealt with the Bryant estate.'

'That is sadly true.' Anger and sadness flashed briefly across the old man's eyes. He finished his claret in one gulp and again drew deeply on his pipe. When he next held Adam's gaze, he had regained his composure. 'His death was untimely and suspicious. I could not prove it, but I believe he was murdered. Poisoned. He had refused to hand over the deeds of the estate. We were trustees to Master Alexander and his brother Howard. The estate was entailed to them.'

'You believe Carforth was behind your partner's death?' Bryn demanded, clearly shocked at the information. 'Mama believed that Howard's demise was not an accident. She wanted me to run away, fearing that my death could be next. Mama was also poisoned; she had a slow and lingering death.' His head was lowered into his hands as he struggled to overcome the grief that assailed him.

'Shortly after your disappearance there was a fire at our offices,' Mr Parfitt confessed. 'It was in the cellar where we stored our papers. Many of them were destroyed. Including those relating to Willow Vale. Or that is what Mr Carforth was led to believe.'

Bryn raised his head, and drew several harsh breaths to regain his composure. 'So Carforth gained possession of the estate by his marriage to my mother?'

'No court of law would allow him to break the entail,' Parfitt corrected. 'Only by the death of your brother and yourself could he lay any claim to the estate. Your loss of memory probably saved your life.'

'Yet I posted notices in all the news-sheets at the time. Did you not see them?' Adam accused.

'Not at first, for then I believed that young Mr Bryant was abroad, but something about the continued appearance of the notice nagged at my mind and I did write to you.' He puffed on his pipe, and when he continued his voice was gruff with emotion. 'You will appreciate that at that time I knew nothing of Carforth's implication in your brother's and mother's deaths, Mr Bryant. I was puzzled when I heard nothing from you, Captain Loveday, and lest the original communication had gone astray I wrote again some weeks later. That letter also received no reply.'

'I never got those letters.' Adam sat more upright in his chair, becoming mistrustful.

Parfitt dragged deeply on his pipe and released the smoke with a great sigh. 'I did not learn for some years that one of the clerks at the time was in the pay of Mr Carforth. I believe the letters were never sent. The clerk, Mr Tucker, was killed outside his house by a bolting horse a month later.'

Bryn leapt to his feet and paced the room, his expression dark with rage. 'Is there no end to Carforth's treachery?'

'Please be seated, Mr Bryant.' The lawyer refilled their glasses and waited for Bryn to return to his chair. 'All is not lost. My partner did not like or trust your stepfather. When we were ordered to hand over all papers concerning the estate to a lawyer in Bridgwater, we refused. We also made copies, and these were the deeds and papers lost in the fire. I have the originals here.'

Adam closed his eyes in relief, and Bryn let out a cry of delight. Mr Parfitt smiled benevolently.

'Well done, sir.' Bryn crossed the room to shake the lawyer's hand. 'In that at least Carforth has been outwitted. But I deeply regret that your stoicism may have been the cause of your partner's death.'

The old man sobered. 'I want your stepfather brought to justice. Not just to avenge the deaths of your dear mother and brother, Mr Bryant, but also that of Wallace Hensby. I am too old to cross such an adversary, but I have to confess that I did not write to you recently, Captain Loveday, without making enquiries into your own reputation. Any man who brought the smuggler Harry Sawle to trial will not hesitate to act against Carforth's infamy. I shall give the Bryant documents into your safe keeping. You will know best how to proceed against Carforth.'

When they got back to their room at the inn, a piece of paper had been slipped under the door. Bryn picked it up, and as he read it his blood ran cold. Seeing his pallor, Adam took it from him, and his own gut clenched in foreboding. The paper had been torn from a larger piece and the writing was poorly formed. Its message, though, was clear.

Bain't nothing for you at Willow Vale. Only death.

Chapter Twenty-seven

Rowena could not settle. She paced the walled garden at Boscabel, which was scented with pink and yellow roses climbing along two of its high walls. As she walked, she flicked the skirt of her riding habit with her whip with growing impatience. Misty was saddled and ready for her to ride, but she had darted into the enclosed garden hoping to give the slip to the groom who had been ordered by Senara to accompany her. She intended to ride to Penruan, and did not wish to be spied on and her visit reported. It had been some weeks since she last visited Sal and Zach.

She glared towards the horses, where the groom continued to loiter. Rowena willed him to be distracted or called away; then she could make her dash to her mare.

The delay increased her discontent. Bryn and Adam had been away for five days. What was keeping them so long? She was cross with herself that she missed Bryn's company. Once again she felt a stranger among her family. Senara and Bridie were always together, and she could not help but feel excluded in the company of the sisters.

Close by in the orchard she could hear Nathan and Joel at archery practice. As usual Joel was fiercely competitive and demanding that, as he was younger and shorter than his brother, he should be allowed to stand closer to the target. Rowena could tell by the growing excitement in the younger boy's voice that within minutes his temper would erupt and he would throw down his bow and stamp away. She wanted to get away from Boscabel before that happened. If Joel were bored, he would insist that he accompany her as he had often joined her when she and a groom rode over the moor.

A glance towards the waiting horses showed her that the groom had been called away to help another in a task. Rowena picked up her skirts and ran to her mount. She could hear the grooms talking in the stables as she untethered Misty from the hitching ring and climbed on to the mounting block. They were galloping towards the end of the drive before a yell behind her told her that the groom would soon be following. She had already informed him that she intended to ride to Trewenna. To maintain her deception that this remained her destination, she headed in that direction whilst still in sight of the estate. There was a narrow track that cut through a wood that would take her on to the Penruan road, and when she disappeared down this she was relieved to hear no sound of pursuit behind her. With luck the groom would reach Trewenna before he realised that she had changed course.

She laughed at how easy it was to dupe the servants. She hated being constrained. Her ride took her past Trevowan and Squire Penwithick's land, where everyone knew her, so she would be perfectly safe. It was liberating to feel the wind on her cheeks as Misty sped onwards. All too soon the first houses of Penruan could be seen marching in single lines each side of the combe leading down to the harbour. Rowena slowed her pace; the jowters and their pack ponies were spread across her path as they carried the gutted and smoked fish from the harbour on their way to Bodmin. The large wicker panniers on the ponies' backs creaked from the weight of the catch.

She wrinkled her nose at the sharp smell of the fish. Even after the harbour and sheds were swilled down, there was never any escaping the smell of a fishing village. It clung to the very walls of the cottages and the tree branches.

She pulled over to the side of the road and allowed the jowters to pass. Most of the men were bearded, their faces darker than chestnuts from their long treks from the sea to the towns. Rowena did not look at them and held her head high as they passed. From the corner of her eye she noted that a few tugged their forelock in deference to her class. Two or three muttered bawdy comments, which caused laughter amongst their companions. In response Rowena's expression was glacial. When the youngest, a scrawny man in his twenties, had the audacity to blow her a kiss, her fingers twitched around her whip, tempted to strike the knave. She curbed the impulse, refusing to react like a fishwife; instead her chin tilted higher and she trotted regally into the village.

Another surprise awaited her. An open carriage was blocking the road outside Blackthorn Cottage, and the driver was having trouble keeping the village children from clambering on the wheels or jumping inside. Two bay mares pulled the carriage, and for a moment Rowena's heart plummeted, fearing that Bruce Trevanion was back in Cornwall. She quickly dismissed the notion. What would he be doing in Penruan, outside the cottage where Sal lived with her Clem and Keziah? The couple would be busy at the Dolphin Inn at this time of day, especially since the jowters had just left and the fishing fleet was in the harbour. The fishermen and their wives would be enjoying a quart or more of ale with the money they had received from the catch.

That did not solve the mystery of the carriage or its occupant. There was a high gloss to the yellow paintwork of the barouche, and she could still smell the newness of the pale leather upholstery. It belonged to someone of wealth and status, which made it even more intriguing that they should visit Sal Sawle and her family.

Rowena tied the reins of the mare to the gatepost of the cottage. Usually she left Misty at the Dolphin, but she was too impatient to meet the visitor to further delay her entrance. As she shook out the folds of her riding habit and patted the blond curls that had escaped her caul and formed tendrils around her face, she considered that a slight dishevelment made her more interesting than appearing immaculate, without a hair out of place. The cottage was never locked, and she stepped brazenly into the front entrance, calling out to Sal. The welcoming smell of baking bread was overpowered by a heavy rose-scented perfume.

There was an abrupt hush to the voices in the kitchen. What was Sal doing entertaining so important a guest in so humble a room? Although it was her grandmother's favourite place, and she preferred the comfort of her rocking chair by the hearth to the padded settle in the parlour. What was also suprising was that Sal's voice had been sharp and accusing. Again, not how she would have expected her to address such a visitor.

Rowena paused at the door to the kitchen to survey the scene before her. Sal was in her rocking chair facing her; and the guest, a woman in an amber velvet pelisse and bright yellow gown, had her back to the door. The bright curls were of a brassy hue and the brim of her elaborately feathered hat was as broad as her shoulders. When the visitor turned, following Sal's stare, Rowena was shocked at the bright patches of rouge on her cheeks. The woman might once have been beautiful, but the skin was now stretched too tightly across her cheekbones and there were deeply scored lines about her eyes, nose and mouth.

The woman's movement bludgeoned Rowena with the rose scent that had been so heavily applied it made the younger woman's eyes water.

'Lawks a mercy, Meriel, you bain't changed at all.' There was a thick Cornish burr to her vowels, though she had attempted to hide it with a theatrical cultured tone.

'That bain't Meriel,' Sal remarked. 'It be your niece Rowena. Though I had hoped you would be gone afore she learned you be here. This be your aunt Rose, child. Your ma's elder sister.' Turning to her granddaughter Sal loosed her scorn. 'Rose ran off with a lover when she were no more than your age, and brought disgrace to us all.'

If Sal had intended to shame her daughter, it had no effect on the visitor. The younger woman sneered. 'The disgrace would have been to stay here suffering the abuse of a bully. How is my evil father? Dead and in his grave, I hopes.'

Rowena knew that Reuben Sawle had been a brutal man who had ruled the local smugglers by fear and violence. He had been a drunkard who regularly beat his wife and children until Clem was strong enough to defend his mother.

Rose scrutinised her niece with a gleam in her eye as she appraised the expensive velvet of her habit and the pearls in her ears.

'Looks like Meriel did well for herself. She always said she'd wed the richest man she could snare. You mentioned the Lovedays, Ma. Which one of those did she trap? Peter were the young and innocent one. Were it him? Though as I recall, my sister was always sweet on Master Adam.'

'My father was St John Loveday and he loved my mother very much,' Rowena defended, anger heightening the colour in her cheeks. 'How dare you malign my mother, madam!'

Rose laughed, a spiteful sound that reminded Rowena of her corrupt uncle Harry Sawle. 'She have spirit, I give her that. Now that she be mistress at the manor, do you see much of Meriel, Ma? Or does Edward Loveday still rule the roost at the great house? A good-looking man like he must have remarried by now.'

'Edward, St John and Meriel are dead. All in tragic circumstances,' Sal informed her daughter with sadness.

'Meriel dead.' Rose shook her head. 'God rest her soul.' She recovered herself with remarkable speed – a sign of the many hardships she had weathered.

'So Adam be lord of the manor, be he?'

'Many things have changed since you ran away.' Sal heaved her thickened body out of the chair and waddled to the oven. She inspected the two loaves within before lifting them out with a wooden paddle and setting them on the table. 'I doubt that handsome soldier wed you. Have you brought further shame to our house by how you came by such finery as you be wearing?'

Rose shrugged, surprising Rowena by taking no offence at her mother's accusation. 'My handsome lover had his way with me and in the manner of such scoundrels moved on.' She lifted a brow at Rowena. 'You heed my words, niece. A beautiful young woman is the prey of such rakes. They may profess love and devotion, but they all want one thing, and I be sure you be old enough to know what that be.' She laughed coarsely. 'But there be no need for you to fret on my account, Ma. That handsome scoundrel I ran off with did me a favour.' She proudly smoothed her hands over her velvet gown and then touched the diamond earrings and pendant at her throat. 'I've done all right for myself. Look outside and you'll see the fine carriage at my disposal. I be Mrs Colonel Sebastian Harwood-Smythe, with a grand house in Tunbridge Wells and a country estate near Winchester. The colonel can deny me nothing. He agreed to accompany me here before we took the waters in Bath for a change from those in Tunbridge Wells. The dear lover do have a terrible leg wound from a skirmish in India that will not heal. We spent several years in Asia. It was where we met.'

'So you became a camp follower when your handsome scoundrel, as you calls him, discarded you.' Sal sniffed her disapproval.

'I survived, Ma.' There was a heartfelt catch in her voice. 'Don't that mean nothing to you? The colonel be a good man. Bain't got no hoity-toity airs and graces. Served the army for forty years. He wants to meet you. He be down at the Dolphin now. Heard tell on the road here that Clem be in charge now and it do the best meals for an inn outside of Truro.'

At the praise, Sal's expression softened. 'Clem didna hold with his pa's ways. His wife would have nothing to do with him if he continued with smuggling. They worked hard to bring credit to our name. Not like afore.'

'I wager that did not sit well with Harry.' Rose laughed. 'By the time I left he were a right little rascal. Used to bully the village lads and was always in fights.'

'Harry got his just deserts,' Sal snorted. 'God rest his soul. Reckon by his standards you've lived a saintly life, my girl.' She sank back down in her chair and there were tears on her cheeks. 'He were hanged at Bodmin and folk cheered at his death. He were worse than your pa.' She threw her apron over her head and burst into sobs. 'The shame were too much to bear.'

'Gran, you must not overset yourself so.' Rowena knelt at Sal's side, taking her into her arms. 'No one blamed you for Harry's evil. You are justly proud of Clem, and his boy Zach will make something of himself. And Uncle Mark has never given you cause for grief. He has a good job with horses now. You are proud of him, are you not?'

'Mark was always a good lad.' Sal wiped her eyes and lowered the apron, her stare upon Rose. 'He be groom for Japhet Loveday at his racing stables.'

'He weren't no more than a yard high when I left.' Rose wiped a tear from her own eye. 'Pa were always beating him for being too soft. But a groom be something. Do you reckon he remembers me?'

Sal rarely showed a loving gesture; for too many years Reuben would have ridiculed or cuffed her for being soft and useless. Now she reached out and squeezed her daughter's hand. 'I feared you were dead, Rose. You did right. There were nothing for you here, my lover. But I be glad you haven't forgotten your old ma.'

Rose flung her arms around Sal's neck. 'I could never forget you, Ma. When I came back, I wanted you to be proud of me.'

Embarrassed by the outpouring of affection, Rowena stood and moved to the door. 'Perhaps I should come back another day, Gran. It has been interesting meeting you, Aunt Rose.'

'Lawks, child!' Rose straightened and drew away from Sal. 'No need to run off. What will you think of me?'

Rowena dipped a hasty curtsey. 'You and Gran have much to catch up on. I would not intrude.'

Rose chuckled. 'You've more manners than your ma, that be for sure. Meriel would want to know everything. She loved gossip.' She held out her hand, which was covered in a black lace fingerless glove. 'Come closer into the light, my lover. I would see you more clearly.' Her glance took in every detail of Rowena's features, figure and clothing. 'You be taller than Meriel, and I suspect even prettier. You have her colouring and something of her looks, but there is more – a natural dignity and bearing. That must come from your father.' Briefly a frown lined her brow, and her gaze was thoughtful. Then she smiled. 'Aye, there is much of the Lovedays about you.'

'Are you staying in Penruan, Aunt Rose?' Rowena could no longer contain her curiosity about this woman's adventures; perhaps in some ways she was very much like her mother. It was exciting to learn that Rose had led something of a scandalous life, and yet if she was now married to a colonel, no one could dispute that she had turned adversity into success. That was fascinating.

'That be up to Clem and Ma,' Rose said softly. 'I have no great fancy to take a room at the Dolphin. It has too many unhappy memories for me. The colonel and I can take rooms in Fowcy. If the Lovedays have no objection, mayhap you could visit us there. I'd like to get to know my niece while I am here.'

'You and your husband are more than welcome to stay here. There is a large bedroom spare,' Sal offered. 'Or mayhap this bain't be the luxury you be used to and you'd prefer Fowey.'

'When the army is on the move, even a colonel's wife lives in a tent for most of the time,' Rose declared. 'This will suit us very well.'

'May I come and visit you tomorrow, Aunt Rose?' Rowena was breathless in her anticipation. She sensed a kindred spirit, one who would understand the torment of her thoughts; that was, if she had the chance to confide in her new-found aunt.

'If your uncle Adam does not object,' Rose responded.

'It be Captain Loveday now,' Sal snapped. 'I am not sure that another meeting is a good idea. Miss Elspeth would not approve.'

'Be that old dragon still alive?' Rose grinned. 'Now that was a woman who knew how to run with the hare and hunt with the hounds.'

'Rose!' Sal glared at her daughter. 'Less of your disrespect, if you please.'

Rowena lowered her eyes so that she did not reveal her satisfaction that her aunt knew something about Aunt Elspeth that the family had concealed. Rose would definitely be an interesting person to know better.

'I suspect gossip will reach Trevowan of my arrival,' Rose sighed. 'Captain Loveday will not approve of my furthering an acquaintance with his niece.'

'My uncle is away from home. I shall look forward to our meeting tomorrow.'

Rowena had stayed longer than she intended, and she did not want the groom searching for her in Penruan when he discovered she was not at Trewenna. Her aunt's arrival would be the talk of the village; the groom would not keep such gossip to himself, and that would be the end of another meeting. Now she hoped that she would waylay him on his return to Boscabel. She would tell him that she had been riding along the beach.

Her blood tingled with excitement. A little harmless deception had gone a long way to alleviate her boredom, and she suspected that tomorrow would be even more revealing.

Chapter Twenty-eight

'Who do you think sent that note, Captain Loveday?' Bryn hunkered on the floor beside Adam, who was seated on the bed going through the documents given to them by Mr Parfitt. 'Do you think it was that clerk, Frobisher? There was something sly about him that I did not trust.'

'I think you are right not to trust him,' Adam replied. 'I saw him leave the lawyer's office when you and Mr Parfitt were in the coffee house. But this writing is not neat copperplate; that is how he makes his living.'

'He could have disguised it to make it look like someone else wrote it,' Bryn suggested. He was chewing his thumbnail and doing his best to keep a brave face, although his eyes were troubled. 'That note does not scare me. It makes me more determined to bring Carforth to justice. If he has spread it abroad that I am dead, he would have laid claim to the estate as my mother's husband. There is no other family.'

'Anything that Carforth has stolen from your inheritance will be repaid, and with interest. That knave has a great deal to answer for.' Adam's eyes were stormy, the colour of a tempest-lashed sea. 'There is no shame in feeling fear when dealing with a man such as your stepfather. He is cunning, manipulative and completely without scruples. A dangerous adversary in many ways. But now you have become a man, he is more likely to pay others to harm you than face you himself. You will need to keep one eye on your back in future.'

Adam continued to study the deeds. Dusk was approaching and he drew the single candle that had been provided closer to the papers and nodded in satisfaction. 'You are the undoubted heir to Willow Vale. But it would not have benefited Carforth to declare you dead. From what I can decipher from this complicated legal language; the estate is entailed, and once your line is extinct, it reverts to another branch of the family living in Scotland.'

'I have never heard of such relatives.' Bryn shook his head.

'It is strange that Mr Parfitt did not mention them.' Adam frowned. 'We will call on him again.'

'And what of Frobisher?' Bryn uncoiled from the floor and paced the room, the uneven floorboards creaking with each step.

'He could give us some very interesting answers.' Adam smiled grimly. There was a hardness to his handsome features that Bryn had never witnessed before. It made him glad to have his guardian on his side. That expression was of a man who would get to the truth and would not shrink from using any persuasion necessary. It made him remember that Captain Loveday had fought several sea battles whilst captaining his own ship as well as during his time in the navy. Although his guardian was no braggart, Bryn had overheard several of their neighbours commenting on his exploits rescuing refugees from France when the country was in the grip of bloody revolution.

Adam carefully refolded the documents and put them into a flat leather bag. Then he rose from the bed and stretched his arms above his head, his knuckles grazing the black beams of the ceiling. 'I need to step out for a while and get some fresh air.'

'I'll come with you,' Bryn offered.

'I need to think about things. I do that better alone.' Adam strode purposefully to the door, and paused before he opened it. 'I will not be long. That note disturbs me. We do not know who is watching us. I would ask you to stay in this room until I return. Do not answer the door unless you have your dagger to hand. There is also a spare pistol in my saddlebag on the bed. I hope you will not have to use the skills I made you practise so ardently in recent years.'

Bryn quelled the stab of panic that twisted in his gut. Captain Loveday would not so warn him if he did not believe that there was a chance that their lives could be in danger.

It took Adam some time of questioning passersby before he discovered the home of Mr Parfitt's clerk, Frobisher. It was in a dark, shabby street consisting of a dozen terraced cottages. The moonlight revealed that many of the windows were broken and stuffed with rags and most of the paint had flaked off the doors. The street stank of stale urine where the children must run wild and squat in the central gutter. As a precaution Adam's hand closed over the hilt of his dagger. There was no way of discerning which house was Frobisher's.

An old woman shuffled along carrying a wooden pail of water drawn from the pump. She glared warily at Adam when he stepped in front of her and enquired, 'In which house does Frobisher live?'

She hawked and spat on the uneven cobbles. 'That bastard be in end house. May our landlord rot in hell.'

The smell of mildew and decay rose from her tattered clothing. There were several holes in the musty, faded shawl tied around her frail shoulders. He noted that she wore only one shoe. The other foot was bare and bleeding. Compassion made him press a few pieces of silver into her hand. She snatched them and cowered away as though expecting him to steal them back.

'My gratitude, madam. May the coins bring some ease to your advanced years. Did you say that Frobisher is your landlord?'

'Aye, devil take him. But then Satan looks after his own,' she said without looking back, and hobbled through an open door where a couple could be heard shouting obscenities at each other.

The end house was larger than the others in the narrow street. A gaunt, nervous-looking woman finally opened the door after Adam's third knock. She was holding a screaming baby, and two half-naked toddlers peered out from behind her frayed and grubby skirts. They wore only shirts that reached to their hips, and their legs were covered in sores.

'Is Mr Frobisher at home?' Adam demanded.

'He bain't here.' The woman looked terrified.

'When will he be back?' The unappetising smell of boiling turnips drifted from the interior.

She shook her head. 'He never says. Left town this afternoon.' The baby in her arms screamed louder. One of the toddlers tugged her apron. 'Ma. I gotta pee.'

Before she could react, a trickle of water ran down the girl's legs and pooled around her feet. The woman clipped her ear. 'That bain't no way to behave. Get a cloth and wipe it up.' The girl ran off sobbing and her mother began closing the door in Adam's face.

He put a booted foot against it to stay her movement. 'And you have no idea where Frobisher has gone?'

'No,' she wailed in distress. 'Please go, sir. You'll only make trouble for me.'

She had stepped forward as she again tried to close the door and he saw fading bruises on her face. There was also a bald patch at the front of her straggling scalp where a hank of hair had been pulled out.

He removed his foot and the door was slammed. Adam would wager a year's income that Frobisher was in the pay of Carforth and the minion had gone running to his master. In a distant street a bell clanged and the town watchman called.

'Nine of the clock and all's well. May the good Lord bring peace to our land and defeat to our enemies.'

All was far from well. Adam fumed silently as he marched back to the inn. Halfway there, he made a detour to visit Parfitt. He was concerned that the elderly lawyer might have retired for the night, but he had a nagging feeling that another meeting was too important to delay. He and Bryn could then leave at first light; whether it was to Willow Vale or to the lawyer to whom Carforth had ordered Parfitt to send all the Bryant papers depended on Parfitt's answers to his questions.

The lawyer's house was in darkness, except for a pale light showing through the shutters of an upper window. Adam pulled an outside chain that rang an internal bell, and while he waited, he ran through in his mind the questions that had arisen as he read the deeds. After a long wait, he rang the bell again. Then, more impatiently, a third and fourth time. Perhaps Parfitt and his housekeeper were sound sleepers or hard of hearing. His frustration getting the better of him, he banged once on the door with his fist. The wood moved under the impact of the blow, and as the door swung open, an uneasy feeling clenched his stomach.

Adam stepped inside the house, calling out, 'Good evening, Mr Parfitt. Mrs Appleby. Good evening.'

There was no answering greeting or even a sound. He moved further inside to stand at the foot of the stairs. On the landing above him a door was open, and the light from a candle flickered palely on the walls.

'Mr Parfitt. Mrs Appleby. The door was open,' he called again to attract attention.

The only response was the scampering of tiny claws as a mouse skittered into its hole in the wainscoting. A growing dread now gripped Adam, and he drew his dagger as he ascended the stairs. He paused as he spied a white shape inside the open door of a darkened room.

'It's Captain Loveday, Mr Parfitt,' he warned as he stepped closer.

The blood froze in his veins. The white shape had been the outline of Mrs Appleby's Puritan collar. She was lying unmoving on the floor, her legs twisted under her. Adam knelt and gently turned her over. The front of her collar was dark with drying blood. Her throat had been cut.

'Dear Lord!' He sprang to his feet and hurried to the second room, where a candle had burnt low.

One side of the hangings around the bed had been drawn back. Mr Parfitt was lying on his back beneath the covers. His mouth gaped; his eyes were open and bulged sightlessly at the canopy above his head. On the floor was a discarded pillow, the torn edging of lace testament that this had been the weapon used to smother the old man, and that he had tried in vain to save his own life.

Adam's initial shock was replaced by the necessity to select between two choices. He could raise the watch and report the crime, which would mean that he and Bryn could be delayed for a day, if not longer, as investigations were made. Or he could leave the house as he had found it, closing the outer door behind him, and he and Bryn would leave Taunton at first light.

It was no coincidence that Parfitt had been murdered within hours of the Willow Vale heir arriving to lay claim to his inheritance.

Chapter Twenty-nine

Lady Alys returned to the window of the winter parlour at Trevowan, which overlooked the entrance to the stables. Unfortunately, the rain lashing the panes obscured her vision. The downpour had been continuous for two hours. A large puddle had formed to one side of the stables and a stream of water cascaded from the overflowing guttering. She chewed her lip, unable to dismiss the unease, that had been with her since the rain had started. The weather had changed drastically since Aunt Elspeth had left for her morning ride. Then the day had been merely overcast, but within a half-hour gales had battered the house and the rain had been torrential. Lady Alys had ordered the grooms to inform her the moment Elspeth returned. Now she was on the point of sending out a search party for the old woman.

'You are worrying unnecessarily, my dear,' Tristan spoke, making her start at his silent approach. 'Elspeth will have taken refuge with one of her family. She is probably with Japhet. She rarely misses an opportunity to visit the horses and watch their training.'

Alys turned to her husband. His words would have been reassuring if his own expression was not tight with concern.

'Why does she refuse to ride with a groom? It is foolish. Riding accidents are common. A tree branch could have come down on her. She jumps the highest stone walls and ditches, and at a fast gallop a horse can put a hoof into a rabbit hole and throw its rider.'

'Elspeth would not appreciate your lack of faith in her riding ability,' Tristan taunted. 'She regards herself as too fine a horsewoman for any mishap. No horse would dare to unseat her.' He attempted a strained smile.

'She damaged her hip in a riding accident when a young woman. She could be lying unconscious somewhere.' Lady Alys refused to be pacified and rubbed at the window where the glass had misted inside, obscuring her vision.

'It does no good to imagine every ill that could befall her.' Tristan put his hands on his wife's shoulders and massaged the tension in the muscles. He kissed her neck before saying, 'I will send a groom to ride to each of the family homes and find out where she is staying. It will be dark in a couple of hours and the rain looks set in for the night. She will probably stay until the morning.'

It was not just to put his wife's fears at rest that Tristan rang the bell cord to summon a servant. His aunt's stubborn refusal to be accompanied by a groom vexed him. If anything happened to the old woman, too many in his family would hold him responsible, at a time when some of the tensions between them were beginning to lessen. The opinion of others did not usually concern him, but his wife disliked the feud with his kin, which undermined his position in the community.

'Oh thank the Lord, she is here!' Alys proclaimed with relief. 'Tristan, she is in a dreadful state and can barely stand.'

Tristan hurried to the stable yard. Before he reached his aunt, he too was drenched to the skin. The exasperating old woman was following her mare into the stable. The horse was hobbling and Elspeth was clinging to the arm of a groom, shouting instructions for the animal to be tended at once. Her clothing was saturated, the skirt of her riding habit clinging to her slender form and further impeding her walking. Her hair was moulded to her skull and grooves of pain were etched around her mouth and eyes.

'You'll be the death of yourself, old woman,' he snarled. 'Get yourself into the warm. I'm sending for Dr Chegwidden.'

'I need a horse doctor. Kara is lame,' Elspeth snapped. 'A bit of rain is not about to harm me.'

Tristan grabbed her arm. Her flesh was like ice, her lips were blue, and she could not control her shivering. 'While you live under my protection, you will do as I say. The horse will be cared for and Dr Chegwidden will attend upon you. You are frozen and will take a lung fever.'

The head groom had lifted the mare's foot and examined the hoof and swelling. 'There is no cut, Miss Loveday. A poultice and rest

221

should make the mare as good as new in a day or two. I shall attend to her personally.'

Elspeth tried to wrench her arm free, and when her nephew held it fast, she lost her temper. 'Unhand me! How dare you presume to lecture me! Kara is in distress. I will not leave her . . .'

With each word her voice became weaker, and then to Tristan's alarm his aunt pitched forward, her eyes rolling upwards as she fainted. He caught her and lifted her into his arms, and was shocked at how light she was as he carried her to the Dower House. At the sound of a servant riding fast to Penruan, he hoped that Chegwidden would not be delayed.

Alys must have been watching from the window. Her hair and gown were wet from the rain as she followed him up the stairs to Elspeth's bedchamber and ordered a maid to bank up the fire. After Tristan had laid his aunt on the bed, she shooed him out of the room and began to remove the old woman's saturated clothing. Once the fire was lit, she instructed the maid to bring buckets of hot water and towels and a warming pan to heat the sheets.

She was frightened that Elspeth was so cold, and her own fingers shook as she struggled with the wet buttonholes of the tight-fitting jacket. The senior maid, Bess Moffat, appeared and took over. She was older and more used to dealing with her mistress's ill humour and temper.

Lady Alys waved smelling salts under her aunt's nose, and was relieved when Elspeth pulled a face and slapped them away.

'Will you both stop fussing?' she snapped, unappreciative of the care that could prevent her taking a fever.

Bess grunted as she pulled off the sodden riding boots, muttering, 'Miss Elspeth, you take better care of your mares than you do of yourself.'

Elspeth was so slender she never wore a corset, and although now conscious, she was too weak to sit up unaided. Once she was naked, Alys rubbed vigorously at the old woman's chilled flesh with warmed towels, until Elspeth revived enough to voice her indignation.

'What the devil are you about, Alys? I will not bear this indignity.' She grabbed a towel and held it against her figure, her eyes blazing with fury.

'You are frozen half to death. We are bringing the warmth back to your limbs.' Alys was equally incensed at Elspeth's lack of cooperation. 'Stop fighting me, Aunt. Dr Chegwidden will arrive soon. Be still so that Bess can put on your nightgown.'

'Nightgown! It is the middle of the day. I am not an invalid.' Elspeth pushed Bess away, glaring at her. 'Fetch me a hot toddy that will warm me, and I will have a clean chemise and my green velvet dress.' She pulled a cover around her and swung her legs to the floor, biting her lip as pain shot through the old injury to her hip. 'I don't want that fool Chegwidden near me. Fetch Senara. Then she can look at Kara as well.'

'You should not expect Senara to come over in this weather.' Lady Alys paused, and the sound of the rain hammered on the window. At her nod, Bess hurried downstairs to prepare a hot toddy. If the maid made it strong enough, it might calm Elspeth and make her sleep.

Elspeth braced herself to stand, and only Alys's quick reflexes prevented her falling backwards. Irritably, Elspeth shook off her aid. 'Then I shall prepare a poultice for my mare. I do not trust that fool head groom who took over from Fraddon. He is far too heavy-handed with the horses, as I have told Tristan many times.'

Bess returned with the hot toddy, and whilst Elspeth sipped it, the maid removed the net caul and pins from her mistress's hair and set about drying the dripping locks. The grey hair was streaked with white, and although no longer thick, it curled around her narrow hips. Elspeth insisted on wearing her velvet dress, but had allowed Bess to seat her by the fire as the maid helped her on with her hose and shoes.

Downstairs, Tristan could be heard greeting Dr Simon Chegwidden. 'Good of you to come so promptly. My aunt is upstairs but is refusing to take to her bed. I am concerned she has taken a chill.'

'I will not see him.' Elspeth raised her voice and ended with a coughing fit.

Bess placed a shawl about her shoulders, which Lady Alys held in place as Elspeth tried to shrug it off.

Dr Chegwidden had served Penruan for nearly twenty years, taking over his father's practice when he left the navy after a short service. Tristan accompanied the physician, who hesitated by the bedchamber door. 'Miss Loveday, your servant, madam.'

'You have made a wasted journey.' Elspeth scowled at the two men. 'It is a horse doctor I need, for my mare.' Her terse speech again caused her to cough.

'As Dr Chegwidden is here, he will examine you,' Tristan insisted.

'Not without my say-so he will not.' Elspeth fixed her most withering glare upon her nephew. The warning flags of fever, or perhaps anger, had reddened her cheeks.

Tristan stood over his aunt. 'You are in my care, and Dr Chegwidden will attend upon you to reassure me that you have taken no ill effects from your drenching.'

When she opened her mouth to speak again, he added with a warning look, 'I would not have it said that I neglected my duty to you.'

Elspeth and her nephew locked horns in a battle of wills on a regular basis. Both were obstinate, and each believed the relevance of their own authority and opinion. Tristan might be master of Trevowan, but Elspeth had never spared her younger brother Edward a tongue-lashing when she considered that he was in the wrong, and Tristan was but a whippersnapper compared to Edward. Elspeth played on her age and the knowledge that her continued presence at Trevowan gave her nephew the degree of respectability he needed to make the unscrupulous manner of his acquiring the family home acceptable to the local gentry.

The inflexible jut of her chin did not waver. Elspeth never admitted that she was wrong, never apologised and never backed down from a confrontation. But she was beginning to shiver, and her head now ached and her hip throbbed with an abominable pain. She twitched the shawl more firmly about her body, and eyed with disdain the physician who was standing timidly behind Tristan. For a moment a coughing fit rendered her speechless. When it passed, she condescended, 'Since Chegwidden has ridden here in such foul weather and will be paid for his attendance whether he examines me or no, he may as well confirm that I am as hale and hearty as yourself, my dear nephew.'

She refused to meet the physician's eye, and his examination was cursory and clearly nervous.

'There is as yet no sign of fever or phlegm. Though it may be advisable to bleed Miss Loveday to release an excess of spleen.'

'My aunt very clearly suffers an excess of spleen,' Tristan replied caustically. 'Being bled will benefit her.'

Elspeth sat stiff and mutinous, her eyes narrowed as Chegwidden poised the knife over her vein. His hand shook, and with a tut of disgust she turned her head away and suffered the procedure in silence.

When the doctor handed the bloody bowl to Bess to dispense with, he added, 'Mr Loveday, I shall of course send my servant with a preparation to stave off the ague and alleviate the cough. I shall call again in the morning, but if there is any sign of a fever, do not hesitate to summon me. I am at your disposal. Good day to you, Miss Loveday. You would be wise to take the precaution of taking a day or two in your bed.'

Tristan escorted Chegwidden out of the room, but returned within minutes as Elspeth was ordering Bess to bring her cloak so that she could return to the stables.

'Your mare is being well cared for, Aunt.'

'When did you become an expert on horse medicine?' She scowled, and another bout of coughing racked her body.

'That cough must not be neglected.' Tristan glowered. 'I will send word to Adam and his wife to inform them that you are indisposed. Also that you are concerned about your mare. It is their decision whether they wish to call upon you to reassure themselves that your condition is not serious, and whether my cousin's wife chooses to tend your horse. Neither of them has stepped foot on Trevowan land since it has been in my possession.'

None of the men in Elspeth's family had ever dictated to her in so high-handed a manner. How dare Tristan presume to intimidate her in the home where she had been born? She rose, refusing to allow him to tower over her. The pain shooting through her hip from the long walk made her clench her jaw to restrain a gasp. 'And does not Adam have good cause?' she accused.

Even the fading afternoon light could not hide the malicious glitter she had never before witnessed in his eyes. His hand gripped her shoulder and the pressure forced her to sink back down on to the chair.

'I am displeased with you, Aunt. You forget your place and mine. Today you defied my orders yet again that you were never to ride without a groom. It was for your own safety and welfare.'

'I came to no harm.' Her cheeks heated with outrage.

He maintained the pressure on her shoulder, his body stooped and his face inches from her own. 'That remains to be seen. I forbid you to ride alone. At all times a groom will accompany you. If you disobey me, the groom will be whipped.'

'I will not be made a prisoner,' she countered.

'And I will not be disobeyed. It is for your own good, old woman. If you do not like my terms, you are welcome to live with Adam. I am master here, and it is time that you acknowledged that my word is law. To ensure your recovery, Bess will serve your meals in your room while you rest as instructed by Chegwidden.'

'The man is a fool,' Elspeth muttered. She had never backed down from a verbal fight or threat, but inwardly she could feel her body shivering. The ache in her hip was becoming intolerable. That long walk had taken too much of her strength, and Chegwidden bleeding her had not helped. Her forthright stare held that of her nephew. The only relief she would receive from the pain in her hip would be if she lay on her bed. 'You are master of Trevowan. It is difficult for me to change the habits of a lifetime, but I shall defer to your wishes. Mayhap I will rest for an hour. The walk was tiring.'

'See that you do.' Tristan marched from the room, and Elspeth found that she was more shaken by the contest of wills than she was prepared to admit.

It made her all the more determined to prove that he was making a fuss about nothing concerning her health. Time enough to rest later when she had assured herself that Kara was properly cared for. She waited until Tristan would have returned to the main house before she limped to the stables. Fortunately the rain had finally stopped, but every step sent daggers of pain through her hip and leg.

The mare was favouring her front leg, but the forelock was tightly bandaged, and from the smell of the herbs coming from the poultice, she had been treated correctly. Kara whinnied softly and nuzzled her hand, searching for the chippings from a block of sugar that Elspeth always carried with her. Satisfied that the mare had suffered no lasting damage, she hobbled back to the Dower House. A leaden weariness was making every step torture, and Bess cried out in alarm when she saw how pale and shaken her mistress had become.

'Get me to my bed, Bess. I will have another hot toddy and a light supper, and some of Chegwidden's potion when it arrives.'

Her constitution did not fail her. When she awoke the next morning, she was stiff and in pain, but there was no sign of a fever or even a cold. When Tristan visited her, she was aware that he was watching her closely.

'You appear to have sustained no ill effects from yesterday, Aunt Elspeth.'

'Apparently not.' She kept her silence on the resentment she felt at their confrontation. Better to let him think that he had won the battle for now. In a war of wills, she was confident of her own victory. She had forgotten that so often pride comes before a fall.

Chapter Thirty

A moral dilemma tested Adam's conscience. His honesty and sense of right urged him to report the deaths of the lawyer and his housekeeper, but a deeper instinct nagged him to get out of Taunton with Bryn as soon as possible. If he reported the murders to the authorities, they would not only be delayed to answer questions, but could also be under suspicion as they were the last people to see Parfitt and Mrs Appleby alive. He was also certain that Frobisher, or someone else acting on Carforth's instructions, had murdered the pair. He could not release that information without explaining Bryn's past. It was too complex a matter for local magistrates.

Above all, he could not shake off his sense of urgency that Parfitt had been killed because Carforth now knew that Bryn was alive. Bryn's life was in danger. Their best defence if they were apprehended over the lawyer's death was to have the evidence against Carforth in their possession.

By the time he returned to the inn he had formulated a plan, and prayed that they would have the time to carry it out. To leave the town at this time of night would make them look suspicious of the murder. They must hope that Parfitt and his housekeeper were not discovered until late tomorrow, when they would be far from Taunton. Tonight they had to act naturally, take their meal in the inn parlour and leave once they had broken their fast. He decided not to tell Bryn of the murders until they were out of the town. That way, if they were questioned, the boy's shock would likely convince the authorities of his innocence.

It was one of the longest nights of Adam's life. Bryn was wound up like a clock spring. He was impatient to act against Carforth.

'Now we have these documents from Parfitt, we should go to

Willow Vale,' he demanded on Adam's return to the inn. 'Do we need Parfitt to accompany us? He could prove to any who doubt it that I am the legal heir. As my lawyer he could take out proceedings against my stepfather.'

'Whoa!' Adam halted him. 'You go too fast. Our moves have to be carefully planned. Carforth has had since your flight to safeguard his interests in the estate.'

'All the more reason that we no longer delay bringing him to justice.' Bryn's tone was rising in his agitation.

'Keep your voice down. Anyone in this inn could be a spy for Carforth,' Adam warned.

'Therefore we must go to Willow Vale,' Bryn insisted. 'Someone from the villages must know what happened there.'

Adam shook his head. 'It is too risky with just the two of us. Whatever we discover, it will place you in danger. Carforth cannot afford to allow you to live and give evidence against him, or even have enquiries made into the deaths of your brother and mother. We have the papers. We need to plan strategically. I would be happier with my own men backing us when you return to your estate.'

The disappointment was stark in Bryn's face and he struck his fist hard against his thigh. 'I have waited so long, Captain Loveday. I want my mother's death avenged. Every day Carforth lives is an insult to her memory.'

Adam put a reassuring hand on the young man's arm. 'You are not legally of age to take up your inheritance. Carforth has proved his evil. To bring him down will take guile. If we show our hand too soon, he could slink into some foreign lair and escape our justice.'

Rowena was excited about meeting Rose again. It would be a wonderful chance to learn about her mother's life. Sal and her father had never been forthcoming, and the villagers of Penruan had been cagey if she had probed them about Meriel's childhood. She dressed and arranged her hair with care and asked Winnie Fraddon to prepare Sal's favourite confection, which she could take as a present. She also took one of Senara's specially prepared lavender soaps and hand balm as a luxury for her grandmother.

She was eager to leave Boscabel early and was nervous that somehow news would reach them before she left that Rose Sawle had returned to the fishing village. Thankfully Adam was still away, and Senara was unlikely to hear the news until she attended the sick at the shipyard later that morning. By then it would be too late to stop her.

However, to extend her stay in Penruan, she made no secret of the fact that she was visiting her cousin Zach and her grandmother, and would not be home until afternoon tea. She would have to tolerate the presence of a groom for such a long a visit, but he would spend his time drinking at the Dolphin.

Throughout her ride she was anxious that Rose and her colonel might already have left Penruan. Sal's attitude towards her elder daughter had not been exactly welcoming yesterday, and Clem Sawle could be a surly cur when it suited him. Would he tolerate the visit of a sister who had disgraced their family?

When she rode into the yard of the Dolphin to stable Misty, she was relieved to see the yellow barouche, protected from the weather by the old wagon barn.

'I will send for you when I am ready to leave Blackthorn Cottage, Gimlett,' she ordered the groom. He was young and had not been working at Boscabel long. During the ride he had been making sheep's eyes at her, and she felt he now needed to be reminded of his place. She had found it amusing to flirt with the grooms when she was younger, but an indiscreet boast from one of them could easily damage her reputation. With the arrival of Aunt Rose there were bound to be stories circulating about Meriel, and Rowena had no wish to have her mother's wayward morality linked with her own conduct. Her parting words to the groom were clipped with authority. 'Make sure that Misty is properly rubbed down and watered in my absence.'

As she passed the open side door of the inn, a boom of male laughter came from within. Rowena could not resist a glance inside to discover who had caused such merriment. The taproom was gloomy, as little light penetrated the small windows, but the limewashed walls reflected some sunshine into the interior. The inn had changed considerably since Clem had become landlord. The smell of chickens roasting on a spit, together with the aroma of baking bread and of a thick pottage full of vegetables bubbling in a cooking pot over the fire, wafted from the kitchen. It helped to mask the smell of stale ale and tobacco that was ever present in such establishments. The upturned half-barrels that had once served as tables and the rickety stools had been replaced by comfortable settles and polished tables. In the darkest corners candles burned in wall sconces, their flames flickering up the walls to reveal the carpentry holes in the old ship's timbers that formed the ceiling and frame of the building.

Another outburst of laughter drew her attention to a corpulent, well-dressed man standing by the bar. He had a shock of white hair and wide side-whiskers.

'Another round for the good folks of Penruan. Make them brandies,' he bellowed. 'I had forgotten how the cold and damp can eat into your bones in this part of the world. It was a very different story in India. I remember when . . .'

So that was Colonel Harwood-Smythe, Rowena mused. Rather too old, too fat and too full of hot air for her taste. But if he made Aunt Rose happy, that was what was important. The booming voice retelling a battle was pompous and bragging, and she did not stay to listen further.

Rowena skirted the quayside, where the stench of fish as the women gutted the catch that was being hauled ashore was overpowering. Unfortunately she did not escape discovery. Several heads followed her progress to the cottage, and there was an increase in gossip from the fishwives. Twice Rowena heard her mother's name mentioned. Her anger flared and she was on the point of retracing her steps and demanding that the women repeat to her face the tittle-tattle they found so absorbing. She could be as cutting as Aunt Elspeth when either of her parents needed defending. It took all her willpower not to retaliate. Even Felicity would have been proud of her restraint.

Taking several deep breaths, she regained her composure. She was determined to enjoy her visit with Aunt Rose, and no vicious tongues would spoil it.

She called out a greeting as she entered the cottage. The raised voices from the parlour instantly stilled. Were her grandmother and aunt sniping at each other again? Zach bounded down the stairs leading into the hall like an excited spaniel.

'Rowena, we have a visitor. Aunt Rose is here. Her husband is a colonel. He has fought in the American colonies and India.' He pulled her into the little-used parlour, where a fire burned to banish the musty smell from the room. Keziah was standing stiffly by the door, Aunt Rose and her mother seated either side of the hearth. The atmosphere could be cut with a knife.

'Aunt Rose, Keziah.' Rowena bobbed a respectful curtsey to the younger women, then went over to Sal, who was wearing her Sunday gown and an enamelled brooch Rowena had given her one Christmas. She put her straw basket by the old woman's side. 'I have brought you some of your favourite soap and that balm of Senara's that is so good for your hands.'

'Thank you, my lover,' Sal said in a voice more restrained than usual.

'You are very generous, Rowena,' Kezzie said tersely. 'We provide very well for all your grandma's needs and do not require your charity.'

'I often bring Gran a gift. I would never consider it charity.' She rounded on Keziah Sawle.

There was pride in the set of her aunt's features. Kezzie was as tall as a man, and whilst not over large, was impressively built, with a buxom figure. The auburn hair that had hung in corkscrew curls when she first married Clem was now tamed by dozens of pins and a lace cap. Her complexion had the rosy glow of health, but her lips were compressed with displeasure. She loved Clem, but had never approved of the seedier side of his lifestyle, when he had worked with the smugglers. This was her second marriage; her first husband had been a farmer. She had never shirked honest hard work, and the present success of the Dolphin Inn was due to her insisting it was refurbished and the finest meals served.

'There you are at last with my shawl, Zach,' she said. 'We must not miss the tide. Old Joe is waiting in his lugger to ferry us to Fowey.'

'Ma, do you really need me with you?' Zach protested. 'I have not seen Rowena for ages. And Aunt Rose will be gone by the time we return.' He could not hide his disappointment.

'You are leaving so soon, Aunt Rose?' Rowena was crushed by the news.

'I have overstayed my welcome as it is.' Rose did not appear unduly concerned. 'I have done my duty by Ma. I should have known she would not forgive me for shaming her. Anyone would think we were a family of innocents. There be not one of us who'll not need a silver tongue to convince St Peter we deserve to pass through the Pearly Gates.'

She turned her stare upon Kezzie. 'I can't say it's been a pleasure meeting you. A woman as prim as the likes of you would never approve of me. I will say you've been a good wife to Clem and you've raised a grand boy in Zach. Perhaps on your way to the quay you'd get him to run down to the inn and inform the colonel I be ready to leave and have the carriage sent up.' She stood up and shook out her skirts.

In the corner of the room was a stack of valises and travelling chests ready to go on the coach.

Keziah ignored Rose and gave a brief nod to Rowena. 'Come visit Zach another day soon, my dear. And if you are wise, you will take your leave now, before this woman taints you with her corruption.' She marched from the room, her stout shoes ringing on the flagstones.

Rowena was dismayed at the frosty reception her aunt had received. 'Do not go, Aunt Rose. I have so much I wish to ask you. About Mama when you knew her. I do not think you are corrupt. You have indeed led an interesting life.'

'Many would have another word for it,' Sal snorted.

Rowena seated herself on a padded settle and patted the cushion beside her, smiling when Rose eased herself on to the seat. Rowena's eyes sparkled and her cheeks were flushed with expectancy as she dropped her voice to a confiding whisper. 'Sometimes I feel as though I do not fit in amongst either of my parents' families.'

She glanced over at Sal and saw that the heat of fire was sending the old woman to sleep. Her eyes had closed and her chin rested on her chest. 'Sal, Clem and Kezzie are never at ease in my company, for they are too aware of the difference in our stations. Zach is natural with me, but then he does not have many friends in the village now that he attends school away from home. The children here know that he will rise above them. Kezzie makes no bones about expecting him to become a physician or a lawyer. I know Mama hated living at the inn. Your father was a cruel man; few of the villagers have a good word to say for him now he is dead. Was the soldier you ran away with handsome and dashing? Was he good to you?'

Rose also checked that her mother was sleeping before she answered, and she kept her voice low. 'Lawks, my lovely, so many questions.' She laughed. 'My soldier were like any other man who had a fancy for pretty women and the money to seduce them with false promises. I thought I loved him, but he were as false as could be. Once he had his way with me, he soon lost interest and threw me out on the street.' Pain shadowed the older woman's eyes.

'How awful. Were you frightened? Life must have been so difficult for you.' Rowena tried to imagine the agony that such a betrayal and desertion would bring. It was terrifying.

Rose shrugged. 'I were lucky that another in his regiment took a shine to me, or for sure I would have been destined for a life on the streets. He were older and kinder, almost grateful for the loving I gave him. If the women with the army have no particular protector then they fall prey to the common men for the price of a meal. I was spared that.' She leaned forward and patted Rowena's smooth cheek. 'You heed that warning about men and false promises. Your ma were lucky that your father did the right thing by her and wed her. Though Ma said her brothers did some persuading.'

'What do you mean?' Rowena was affronted.

'She were already carrying you when they wed.' There was a glint of satisfaction in Rose's eyes, as though to prove to her niece that she was no worse than her sister. 'Pa and my brothers were not about to let another daughter shame them. Though Sal said your pa loved Meriel, so happen a shotgun wedding were not such a tragedy.'

'Papa adored Mama,' Rowena hotly defended. She was not shocked at the comment, for others had made certain that such gossip reached her ears many years ago. 'It would have been my grandfather who would have refused to permit the wedding. They wed first, then told him.'

'Happen it was that way.' Rose smiled indulgently. 'Your ma were pretty as a princess and spirited enough to get her own way. It's true, your face and figure can be your fortune. Not that you'll have any trouble making a grand match. The Loveday name will take you far.'

Sal snorted in her sleep and woke herself up. She glared at Rose. 'What you be saying to that girl? Don't you be putting ideas in her head. She be too strong-willed by far. There be some things the Loveday name can't save her from, especially if she be careless with her reputation.'

Someone outside was singing a bawdy song and it was getting louder.

'Lawks, that be the colonel. He be in his cups again.' Rose ran to the window and stared out.

Curious, Rowena followed her. The colonel was singing at the top of his voice, his face ruddy and the elaborate folds of his stock askew. The words were slurred and his feet dragged. He would have been unable to walk if it were not for the two fishermen on either side of him, his arms over their shoulders. There was a shout as the carriage pulled out of the inn yard and halted behind them.

'Colonel, sir, get yourself on board,' the liveried driver suggested. 'You don't want the villagers seeing you in this condition.'

The colonel waved a hand drunkenly at his servant. 'You're a good man, Parsons.'

With much heaving and pushing from the fishermen, the colonel was settled into the carriage. Rose sighed. 'At least he seems to have enjoyed himself. As long as there is a drink and an interested audience, he can relive his former glory. It bain't right to deny a man that bit of pleasure.' She chuckled.

Sal had fallen asleep again and Rose rolled her eyes. 'At least I be spared Ma witnessing the colonel's grand exit from her life. He bain't such a bad old codger. I knows how to handle him, and providing I keep him happy, we fadge famously together.'

Rowena hid her own dismay. Her aunt might have made the best she could from the cards she had been dealt, but it was scarcely a life to envy.

The driver loaded the luggage and helped Rose into the carriage. Rowena stood by its side as her aunt settled blankets around the stout legs of her husband. The colonel leered at Rowena.

'Now if that lass is not the prettiest filly I've seen in a long year.'

'She be my niece and her family be lords of the manor,' Rose informed him.

He eyed Rowena with greater interest. 'You have your aunt's looks. Wonderful woman. Best bedmate and companion I ever encountered. Take after her and you will not go far wrong, my dear.' His words slurred and trailed off as the carriage turned in a circle to leave the village.

Rose leaned forward. 'You take care those pretty looks don't attract no bounders who would lead you astray.' She waved as the carriage pulled away.

Rowena regretted that she could not have spent longer talking to Rose. She admired her for the spirit that had carried her through unmentionable adversity to find happiness later in her life. When she had fussed over her husband, there was no mistaking the love in her eyes, and the adoration that he returned as he regarded her.

The progress of the carriage through the village had drawn a group of women, their eyes narrowed as they watched it pass. Walking almost level with it, Rowena was hidden from them by the vehicle as she made her way down to the Dolphin. When the carriage pulled ahead, the women had formed a huddle outside the general store and were conversing heatedly.

Rowena had her head high, her mind still upon Rose.

Nell Rundle, Rowena's old wet nurse, bow-backed and stooped over a stick, sucked on her toothless gums. Rearing seven children had aged her rapidly, and she looked a score or more years older than her mid-fifties.

'That one bain't no better than she should be,' Nell was quick to accuse. 'Sawle women be all the same. Sal carried another man's child when she wed that old misery Reuben. Though the woman paid a heavy price for her sins.'

Her daughter Biddy waggled her head. 'Those girls of hers weren't no better. Look at Miss High and Mighty riding in a carriage. A dung cart would be more fitting. And as for Meriel . . . I never did believe St John fathered the child. That hussy had eyes only for Master Adam all that summer and the previous one.'

'I suckled the child and my ma birthed her,' Nell wheezed. 'Ma reckoned that when Meriel were in labour she screamed Adam's name. I wager when he went back to the navy she were with child. By then she had the heir to the manor sniffing round her like she be a bitch in heat. She'd lost the man she loved and were sly enough to trap the one with a fortune awaiting him.'

Moira Warne, another fishwife crone, snorted with spite, 'If old Edward Loveday suspected, he would have taken some comfort that at least Loveday blood were in the child she carried.'

Rowena stopped in her tracks. With an outraged snarl she threw herself at the women. Shoving the two younger fishwives aside, she thrust an accusing finger in Nell Rundle's face. 'Vile, filthy liar. How dare you spread such gossip?'

Nell sidled behind her daughter and spat maliciously. 'There bain't no smoke without fire. Meriel were wild for Adam, and St John always had to have what his brother wanted. You ask my Sarah if you wanna hear the truth. She be wife to Isaac Nance, the bailiff at Trevowan, and many a time she said you had the look of Adam when the wildness were upon you.'

'Then Nance should be sacked for allowing his wife to spread such lies,' Rowena raged. 'St John was my father.'

Biddy put her arm protectively around her mother. 'Why should we cover for your whoring ma? She always thought she were better than us. Neither Captain Loveday nor St John be master of Trevowan. It be their cousin who be our landlord now and there bain't no love lost between him and the captain.'

'Hush, Biddy.' Moira Warne nervously wrung her hands. 'It don't do to stir up trouble with our betters. Don't heed them, Miss Loveday. That colonel been buying the men drinks all day, and Nell and Biddy had more than their share. They be drunk, Miss Loveday. They don't know what they be saying. Mr St John were your pa, course he were.'

Nell tittered. 'That be what they would have us believe. Why d'you think the twins were always at loggerheads?' The old woman eyed Rowena maliciously. 'We know all about the Lovedays' big secret. Your ma made a fool of that family.'

'A day in the stocks will put an end to your lies,' Rowena threatened. Nausea had gripped her stomach and she battled not to throw up. These rumours that Adam and not St John was her father, were ridiculous. She adored St John. Adam had never paid her great attention, and although he supported her as his niece, that was his duty. Even though she refused to give credence to such lies, she could not escape the feeling that her world was caving in around her. The blood was thundering through her head, making her skull feel as though it would explode. Her fists were clenched at her sides, and it took all her restraint not to throw herself at these creatures, pulling their hair until they admitted they had spoken false.

The drink had made the Rundle women belligerent, and jealousy towards Meriel ran high among the villagers. Amidst the fumes of stale cider thick on her breath, Biddy retaliated, at that moment feeling that a day in the stocks was worth putting this uppity miss in her place. 'Go and ask Sal. She knows.'

'You lie. You evil crones. The stocks are too good for you.' Rowena was hanging on to her temper by a thread, remembering that as St John's daughter she must not shame his memory. But her outrage was too fierce to allow her to back down without reminding them of their place. Her voice was icy with authority and scorn. 'I'll have you paraded through the streets in scolds' bridles for a week. That will stop your vicious tongues.'

When Biddy laughed, Rowena's body trembled from the force of controlling her fury. Words were now beyond her, and if she stayed a moment longer, she would disgrace herself by venting her wrath. Tipping up her chin, she spun on her heel and stormed back to the cottage. Her chest felt so tight she was struggling to breathe as she burst in on Sal. The old woman was still asleep by the fire.

'Is Adam my father, Gran?' she blurted out, unable to hold back the pain.

When her grandmother was slow to wake, she grabbed her shoulders and gently shook her. 'Wake up, Gran. Wake up!'

'What! What's amiss?' Sal was wide-eyed with alarm, her wits slow to return.

'Is Adam my father? The village women say he is.' Rowena stood with her arms folded across her chest in a protective gesture against an expected pain.

Sal struggled to collect her thoughts. 'Adam? What you be talking about, child?'

'Is Adam my father?' Rowena demanded again.

'What does it matter?' Sal waved a dismissive hand. She stared round the room as though uncertain where she was. 'No one can prove it. Why bain't I in my kitchen?' Her eyes cleared, and belatedly aware what she was saying, she shook her head and her face crumpled in despair. 'What madness has filled your mind, my lover? I knew Rose would stir up trouble. Of course Adam is not your pa. St John adored you. He were besotted with Meriel.'

'But did she love him? Or was it Adam she loved?' Rowena persisted. She realised that Sal was still bewildered by sleep and would be less inclined to hide the truth. 'Did St John marry her because Clem or Harry forced him at gunpoint?'

'What nonsense,' Sal gasped, but the deadly pallor of her cheeks and the fear in her eyes told Rowena all she needed to know. The man she had known as her beloved father – the only man she had truly believed she could trust – had been a victim of her mother's greed and treachery.

Sobs racked her body as she whirled and ran from the cottage. Avoiding the quayside, she sped through the back streets to the

Dolphin, heedless of the women who paused in their work scrubbing steps, cleaning their windows or sweeping dirt from the house flagstones into the street to stare at her.

'Miss Loveday, what be wrong?' Only one of them shouted in concern.

Rowena ignored her, and as she ran into the stable yard, she passed young Gimlett sitting propped up against the wall, sleeping off the unexpected bounty of Colonel Harwood-Smythe. Moments later she was riding out of the yard, the clatter of her mare's hooves not even disturbing the groom's drunken slumber. Blinded by tears, she urged Misty to a gallop. She gave the mare her head, and was unaware when her mount took the wrong road.

Chapter Thirty-one

In the Dolphin Inn, an angry Keziah shook Rob Gimlett awake. His head was pounding from a hangover and he winced at every word of her harsh demands.

'How long have you been asleep?' she shouted, striking his shoulder. 'Miss Loveday's mare has gone. Ma said she were upset when she left the cottage.'

'I've not seen her.' Rob raised his hands to protect his head as the innkeeper's wife continued to slap him.

'You be drunk and in neglect of your duty. Your mistress could have been missing for over an hour. That was when she was seen running in this direction. Clem thought he heard noise from the yard at about that time but he was down in the cellar bringing up a barrel of ale. Get back to Boscabel at all speed. It will be dark soon. You had better pray your mistress is safe, or they will have your hide, and you'll also face my husband's fury for failing his niece.'

The groom jumped to his feet and staggered into the stable.

The last of the light was fading when he skidded to a halt in the stable yard at Boscabel. His gelding was sweating and foaming at the mouth from the ride. Jasper Fraddon hobbled out of the stables. A single lantern burned by the door, illuminating his bow-legged figure and craggy features.

'Where the devil is Miss Loveday? You should have been back hours ago. Mrs Loveday is out of her mind with worry.'

The groom's face twisted with fear. 'She left the Dolphin without me. Gave me the slip.'

Fraddon limped forward and grabbed the gelding's bridle.

'Drunken sot, I can smell you've been drinking. This will be the last day you work for this family.'

He shouted for another groom to take the horse. 'Now you will tell Mrs Loveday of your incompetence.'

The large figure of Eli Rudge came out of nowhere. He grabbed Gimlett by his shirt collar and rammed him against the wall. 'If anything has happened to Miss Rowena, you'll wish you'd never been born.' Then he marched the groom to the house.

Fraddon shouted for Billy Brown and his son to ride to the farm, the stud and Reskelly Cottage. Then he saddled a horse to go to Trevowan, although he did not hold out much hope that Rowena would be there.

Rudge propelled the groom into the room with such violence that he almost landed at Senara's feet. She was pacing across the front of the fireplace and her sister was reading a passage from the Bible, trying to find some comfort. Both their faces were gaunt from worry.

'This tyke got drunk.' Rudge was seething with rage. 'Miss Loveday was overset about something after visiting Mrs Sawle and took off without rousing him.'

Rob Gimlett had pulled off his cap and wrung it in his hands. 'I didna mean no harm. It were the colonel; he were insistent we all took drinks with him. I bain't used to spirit. I passed out.'

'What colonel was this, Gimlett?' Senara demanded.

'He be family of sorts to Miss Loveday, I suppose.' The groom hung his head, unable to meet her stare. 'He be married to Sal Sawle's daughter Rose, who be visiting.'

'Rose?' Senara frowned. 'Sal has no daughter Rose, does she, Rudge?'

'Unfortunately she do.' Rudge scowled at the groom and looked ready to give him a thrashing. 'She'd not be the company you'd wish Miss Loveday to keep. Rose were the eldest. She took off with a lover long afore the first Mrs St John Loveday were wed.'

Senara drew a sharp breath, remembering that when she and her family returned to her mother's old home, there had been gossip about Rose Sawle and her disgrace. Many said that Meriel had been no better.

'Was Rose Sawle with Sal when Miss Loveday visited?' Senara rubbed her brow, wishing that her husband was here to deal with this.

'Happen so.' Gimlett groaned. 'It be Mrs Colonel Sebastian Harwood-Smythe now. The Colonel has not long returned from duty in India. He was flush with his money and would not take a refusal when he ordered drinks for everyone. I meant no harm. I only had two drinks. Miss Loveday said she'd not return until the afternoon. Let me join the search to find her.'

'That is the least you can do.' Senara dismissed the groom and turned to Rudge. 'Send men to everyone Miss Loveday is acquainted with. If she is in a taking, it is most likely that she would seek out Mrs Deighton and her cousins at the farm. But she could be anywhere. Let us pray she has not gone on to the moor. There is a mist forming.'

'She could have fallen from her mare and been hurt,' Bridie moaned. She put aside her Bible and came to her sister's side. 'She rides like a madwoman.'

'Rowena is a skilled horsewoman,' Senara corrected. 'I am certain she will be with her family. It might have been almost dark when she reached there and they would have insisted that she stay overnight.' She made her voice calm and positive, but all afternoon she had had an uneasy feeling that something dark was holding a loved one in its clutches. She had assumed that her fears were connected to Bryn. At least he had Adam to protect him. Rowena had no one, not even a dull-witted groom.

'I do not understand why she took off like that.' Bridie had gone to stare anxiously out of the window and wiped a tear from her eye.

'She is a Loveday,' Senara said with a sigh, as though that explained everything.

A commotion outside had both women hurrying to the side door that opened out on to the approach to the stables. A blur of white and scarlet pounded towards them along the drive, and Rowena jumped to the ground, her face rigid with fury. She flung the reins at Gimlett and at whirlwind pace ran into the house. At some time during her ride she had lost her hat, and her net caul had slipped back on her neck so that her hair was loose and dishevelled. For a terrible moment Senara feared that her niece had been assaulted.

The young woman did not meet her stare and pushed past her.

'Just a moment, young miss.' Senara grabbed her arm to halt her furious passage. 'We have been out of our wits with worry since Gimlett returned without you. What possessed you to flee Penruan? And look at the state of you. Have you been harmed in some way?'

Storm-coloured eyed glared back at her as Rowena wrenched her arm free. 'From your questions, my welfare was the least of your worries.'

'Obviously it is our main concern, but your conduct was hardly becoming of a gentlewoman,' Senara reasoned. Rowena was capable of twisting every word or action to suit her own ends. 'Where have you been?'

'Just riding. What is this – a witch hunt? Or do you think I have been seeking to trap some besotted wealthy heir into wedlock? As did my mother . . .' She headed down the narrow corridor to the stairs.

'What has made you say that, Rowena?' Senara hurried after her. 'You are clearly upset. Was someone spreading lies in Penruan?'

As Rowena continued up the stairs, words were hurled over her shoulder like stones from a slingshot. 'Mayhap I learned the truth. The most despicable secret locked tightly in the family closet.' She made it to her bedchamber, slammed the door and bolted it in her aunt's face.

Senara tapped softly on the wood. 'Rowena, what has upset you? Let me in so that we can talk.'

'I am sick of the lies. Go away. I do not want to talk to you or anyone.' There was a crash, which sounded as though Rowena had scooped all the toiletries on her dressing table to the floor. Then came the sound of violent weeping from within.

What had the unhappy young woman heard? The wild behaviour and outbursts of temper were clearly related to her grief for her father, which had not subsided after over a year and a half. She had idolised St John, and the manner of his death had made him the gossip of the county. There would always be some malicious person throwing his failings back in her face. Felicity had not helped, for she could be bitter in her recriminations at her husband's weaknesses.

The sobs continued unabated, and Senara attempted again to calm her niece. 'Nothing can be so bad you cannot talk of it. Let me help you, Rowena.'

'Go away. You do not care about me. No one does. No one ever did. I hate you. I hate you all.' The sobs turned to hiccoughs. Then the bedding muffled a low growl of rage as the coverlet was pulled over her head.

'We do love you very much, Rowena. Never forget that.' Senara stared anxiously at the wood in front of her, her heart agonising over the pain the girl must be suffering.

The reply to her entreaty was the thud of a pillow being hurled at the door. 'Go away.'

Senara gave up, hoping that the outburst of tears would be a form of healing in itself.

Exhausted from her anger and misery, Rowena at last fell into a doze. She slept briefly, but the weight of despair continued to press on her heart. A light, persistent scratching at the door eventually roused her from her torpor.

'Go away.'

'Miss Loveday.' Carrie Jensen spoke softly. 'You have missed your meals. Mrs Loveday would have you eat something. There is a tray outside your door.' The sound of footsteps retreated.

Rowena continued to glare mutinously at the door. The room was growing cold, the fire having burned low. She had always had a robust appetite, and her stomach was complaining that she had eaten nothing since breakfast.

She rolled on to her back and gazed at the unshuttered window, where a full moon was rising above the trees. Sleep had sustained her. The heat had faded from her anger, but the icy depths to which it had plunged were far more lethal and dangerous. Her thoughts remained in turmoil. To make sense of them she moved from the bed to her writing table, which stood in a beam of moonlight, and drew a sheet of paper from the drawer.

So this is what it has come to, Papa. I call you Papa, but that is the final mockery, is it not? You lied to cover the shame of your betrayal. You played your part well, for you even fooled me. Though once George was born, I saw what a true father's love should be like when you gazed at his tiny form. I thought it was because you finally had your heir – your true heart's desire. I was blinded by my love for you. I became but another encumbrance. Countless times I heard you cursing that you were condemned to a house full of women. Your gambling was a way to escape us. I thought it was Felicity's shrewish tongue that drove you from our hearth. Was I also the cause? How could you look at me and not see my mother and despise the dishonour she had brought upon you? And how could you say you loved me when I was a symbol of lies and deceit?

The flow of writing paused. The script had become scrawling and barely legible in places as her feelings of betrayal poured from her. She lifted her gaze to stare at the moon. The darker marks on the bright orb resembled a face. At first it was benign, watching her like a guardian. Then, as her vision lost focus, it changed, transforming to the image of her mother. The face was smiling, sweet and beguiling, until a sliver of cloud passed over its surface. Then the smile turned to one of mockery, and she could hear the cruel laughter that Meriel had frequently used to taunt St John.

Rowena clasped her hands over her ears to silence the sound. Briefly the moon was revealed free from the clouds, and the image upon it altered to the face of St John when he was at his most charming. Then, as more clouds drifted across the sky, the likeness turned his benevolence to a scowl – the face dark with disgust and hatred.

However much she wanted to believe to the contrary, the marriage of her mother and father had been no love match. She was the reason they had been shackled together in perpetual resentment and misery. Rowena's fingers clenched over the paper and she screwed it into a tight ball. 'I hate you. I hate you all,' she groaned. 'I adored you, Papa. I trusted you. Yet you betrayed me. There is no one I can trust. No one.'

She tossed the missive on to the fire, turning her back on the flames as they consumed it. Her lovely face was hardened as she regarded the partly hidden moon.

'Hide your treacherous face,' she accused. 'All is but an illusion.'

An inner voice continued to mock her. 'Whoever your father was, do not forget that Loveday blood ran hotly in their veins.'

The lethal ice of her anger drew her lips into a smile, her eyes glittering with resolution. She was a fool to fall prey to the weakness of tears. They solved nothing. Her head lifted higher and her shoulders squared as though ready for combat.

'Yes, I am a Loveday.' She uttered the words with the vehemence of a sacred oath. 'And I shall never forget it. I swear by that proud and zealous blood that even if I must stand alone amid a family who demand loyalty of each other, I shall show the world what it means to be a Loveday who has felt the bitter edge of a loyalty betrayed.'

Chapter Thirty-two

Davey had been keeping a watch on Cy Watkins. The more he observed him, the greater his suspicions were that the man could not be trusted. Yesterday the overseer had slipped away from his work when he should have been cleaning and sharpening the scythes for the last field of hay to be cut. Davey had almost missed his departure, and Watkins had been climbing over a stile that led to the Fowey road when he had seen him and hurried after him. Once out on the road, Watkins was walking at a brisk pace. He did not go far before he stopped and glanced over his shoulder. Davey barely had time to conceal himself by leaping behind a hawthorn tree, his hand snagging on brambles in the hedgerow.

When Watkins jumped over a dry-stone wall of the neighbouring farm, Davey held back. There were fewer trees to give him cover that side of the track, and he cursed his ill luck. Then to his surprise he saw the manager duck down out of sight behind the wall. Impatience gnawed at the young farmer as the minutes stretched out. Watkins had not crossed the field, as that would have again made him visible. Certain that the man was hiding behind the wall, Davey dared not show himself and move forward.

His frustration increased when a lone rider approached. The bearded man was a stranger, in a worn greatcoat and patched breeches. The battered brim of a felt hat hid most of his features. From the shaggy coat of his mount, it was a moorland pony, a typical packhorse used by smugglers or the poorer farmers who eked a living from the moor.

The rider halted where Watkins had jumped the wall. He drew a large kerchief from his pocket and made a great show of wiping his face. Davey could just hear the low rumble of his voice, but the words were indistinct. After returning his kerchief to his pocket, the rider kicked the pony into a walk, and Davey drew back, crouching down in the waist-high bracken.

The pedlar was out of sight before a scraping of boots on stone warned Davey that Watkins was back on the road. He remained hidden as the older man sauntered past to return to the farm. Davey was certain that the odd manner of the meeting meant that something illicit had been planned.

Tonight, with the moon bright, Davey had kept watch on the overseer's cottage from the darkened kitchen of the farmhouse. The younger children were asleep and his mother had not long retired to bed. The lights in the servants' room and the milkmaids' dormitory were extinguished, and Davey did not have to wait long before the candles in Watkins's cottage were doused. Another few moments passed before the moonlight revealed a dark shadow moving along the side of the dwelling.

Picking up his father's blunderbuss, which he had already loaded, Davey hurried across the yard. His heart was thudding loudly and there was a coating of sweat on his palms. His hand was tight on the gun and Japhet's warning words were pounding in his head. 'Do nothing on your own. Send word to me.' Yet Watkins was already in the first field, heading towards the meadow with the damaged wall.

At this time of night it was too late for Davey to send word to his uncle. He could rouse the farm labourers but he did not know if any of them were in league with Watkins. All he hoped to achieve tonight was to discover who Watkins was working with, and try and overhear their plans. He swallowed against the dryness of fear in his throat. If he was discovered they could kill him, but how else could he get the information he needed to deal with the situation?

Watkins crossed two more fields and Davey followed, keeping to the shadows as much as possible. As far as he could discern in the moonlight, Watkins was so sure of himself that he did not even trouble to look back to see if he was being followed. That roused the farmer's anger. Watkins thought him a boy not capable of a man's work or respect. Davey was young, but he had worked with the gamekeepers on Lord Eastley's estate and he knew how to track men. Since rustling was a more serious crime than poaching, he had to demonstrate that nothing illegal would be permitted on his property. That would also send out a warning to the smuggling gangs that he would not tolerate contraband being hidden there.

Even so, he jumped at every sound, and was now suspicious that the tramping he heard ahead was cattle being led through the wood on the far side of the meadow. There followed the scrape of stones being removed from the wall. He crouched in the shadows, shielded from the rustlers, and strained to catch the words of what sounded like four men.

'You sure this place be safe now the woman and boy are here?'

'They did not notice last time,' Watkins answered contemptuously. 'This be safe. I reckon we could risk bringing in more cattle next time. The boy bain't got a clue. Struts about the place like he be cock of the roost. That suits me fine. Long as he thinks he be in charge, I get my takings on the side.'

'Luck were on our side when you were hired here.' Another man sniggered. 'But it don't do to let down your guard. The lad may still be wet behind the ears, but he's got some serious help with his uncles close by.'

'They got their own problems with their upstart cousin causing trouble for them. They won't worry about what goes on here.' Watkins snorted. 'Now, how long these cattle gonna be here? You be right, there bain't no point in pushing our luck.'

'Two days, that be all,' replied another voice, clearly the leader. 'Then we can move them on to the moor with the others ready to be driven to market.'

There was a crashing through the undergrowth. Davey froze, his heart leaping to his throat.

Watkins snarled, 'Who goes there?' There was alarm in his voice.

'It be a deer.' The leader snorted. 'You losing your edge, Watkins, for all your bluster?'

'Damn you, Jowett! I be the one taking all the risks while the cows are here.'

The name sent a shiver through Davey. For generations the Jowetts of Bodmin Moor had been the scourge of the countryside. Most folks reckoned they were part of the wreckers' gang in the area. They were a family of some half-dozen bloodthirsty villains, who, if rumours were believed, were behind the disappearance of several unwary travellers on the moor who had likely been murdered for their money, the bodies rotting in a moorland grave.

Davey remained in the shadows until the sounds of the rustlers and Watkins returning to his cottage had died away. An inner shaking had gripped him that was not entirely due to the chill of the night. The Jowetts were not a family you took on lightly, but he knew that if he did not show his strength now, they would continue to use the farm. If rustled cattle were discovered in his fields, not only would his own life be in danger, but he could also lose the land that had been in his family for generations.

He was troubled and still shaken when he returned to the farmhouse. His mind was reeling as he wrestled with the problems ahead of him, and knowing that sleep was impossible, he flopped down on a chair at the kitchen table and held his head in his hands.

'Something serious is troubling you, my son. What took you into the fields in the middle of the night?'

His mother's softly spoken voice startled him. He had wanted to prove himself a man and deal with this alone. He did not want her worried. 'I could not sleep. I went for a walk to clear my thoughts.'

'With your father's blunderbuss?' she questioned, rising from where she was seated in the darkest corner of the room and coming to the table to touch the butt of the breeched gun.

'It is nothing for you to concern yourself with, Mama.' He wiped the worry from his voice. 'I have to deal with this myself.'

He could sense the inner wrestling that Hannah fought. She had run the farm successfully for many years and was fiercely protective of her family. 'If it is to do with Watkins, I believe he could be trouble. There is a strained atmosphere among the servants that was not present before he was put in charge. Yet the books show that he does his work efficiently and profits have not been affected.'

'I have it in hand, Mama,' Davey replied firmly.

Hannah squeezed his shoulder, surprised at the broadness and hardness of the muscle. There was mistiness in her gaze as she regarded him. She had first met his father when Oswald was Davey's age. At eighteen his own father had just died and Oswald had taken over the responsibilities of the farm. He had been so strong, capable and hard-working. Davey possessed the same traits. It was difficult as a mother to relinquish her need to nurture and protect. Her son was a man now, not a child. He was taller and broader than Oswald at the same age. The resolution and the fierce need to prove himself and win the respect of his neighbours and servants were set into the stubborn line of his shoulders and jaw.

Her throat tightened with love and pride. 'You are your own master now, Davey. Your father would be proud of you, as I am. Yet no one expects you to deal with potentially dangerous situations alone.'

Davey hesitated only briefly. 'I will discuss my findings with Sir Henry Traherne. As Justice of the Peace his advice can be trusted.'

'That is sound reasoning.' Hannah nodded approval and left Davey to his thoughts. It took all her willpower to keep quiet about her own discoveries and allow her son to deal with whatever problems he had encountered. If they were to do with the repaired wall of the far meadow, he had made a wise choice in consulting Sir Henry.

Adam and Bryn alighted from the London coach at Launceston and retrieved their horses from the inn where they had been stabled all week. If they rode hard they could be home by dark. Tomorrow Adam intended to visit Japhet, and they would raise men to return to Somerset and take control of the Willow Vale estate. Although Bryn had said the place looked deserted and that only the two men who had captured him protected the land, Adam wanted no further confrontations if they could be avoided. Too many people had died to prevent Bryn inheriting.

Before they departed from Taunton, they had discovered that Frobisher had left the town early that morning. It was reasonable to assume that he had murdered Parfitt and his housekeeper, and would be seeking Carforth to tell him that Bryn was searching for his stepfather and was intent upon claiming his inheritance.

The two deaths weighed heavily upon Adam and Bryn, and the younger man was appalled at the murders, guilty that they had been a result of their investigations and both looked forward to a joyful family reunion before bringing Carforth to justice. Such a simple longing was not meant to be. Adam had barely shrugged off this greatcoat in the hall when there was a screech from the top of the stairs. Expecting an unceremonious greeting from his younger children, he was startled to see a whirlwind of flowing blond hair speed down the stairs and launch itself at him, the hysterical words babbled and incoherent, her fists pounding his chest.

With a wry grin Adam put his hands on Rowena's shoulders. 'If this is how young ladies of honour conduct themselves, there is clearly no hope for future generations.'

'. . . liar . . . blackguard . . . hate you . . .' His smile faded as he discerned a few of the words.

Rowena continued to beat his chest, and he gripped her wrist in one hand. 'What is all this? What has so overset you?'

'You lied . . . How could you? Papa trusted you . . .' She continued to shout, her body shaking with fury.

'Calm yourself, Rowena.' Bryn tried to intervene.

Her furious glare turned upon him. 'What do you care? No one cares . . .'

'Rowena, that is enough,' Senara ordered, shocking Adam by her sharp tone. She rarely lost her temper. 'We will go into your uncle's study and discuss this rationally.'

'And what lies will you concoct to save our family name? Is it too much to expect honesty and the truth?' Rowena flung a defiant stare at Adam. The man she had known all her life was suddenly another enemy whom she was wary of trusting. She marched to the study, the proud tilt of her chin portraying vulnerability as well as a challenge.

'What am I supposed to have done?' Adam groaned to his wife.

'She has heard gossip that you and not St John are her father, and is hurt and confused,' Senara said softly. 'She deserves the truth. Talk to her alone. It changes nothing between us, my love. You and St John were rivals for Meriel's affection long before we became lovers.'

Adam had become very pale. There was remorse at the pain he had caused Senara as he stooped to kiss her cheek. He whispered, 'You never condemned me. I love you. Now I must ease my daughter's pain if she can forgive me.' He followed Rowena.

Bryn was standing rigidly still, shocked by Rowena's revelations. 'Is it true?'

'Some believe so. For Rowena's sake none can publicly admit it.' Senara linked her arm through his. 'You must be exhausted. Adam will deal with this, then we will talk of your journey to Taunton.'

'How can you take it so calmly?'

'It does not affect Adam's feelings for me or our children. What you cannot change it is best to accept with good grace.'

Joel was shouting as he ran down the stairs. 'Bryn, you're back!

Tell me your adventures. Did you slay your wicked stepfather? Are you master of a vast estate with a hundred vassals to obey your commands?'

'I am sorry, Bryn.' Senara sighed. 'I will send Joel back to his room until you have had a chance to rest and gather your wits.'

But Bryn was smiling fondly at the young boy. 'If I entertain him, it will stop him troubling his father at this time.'

Senara nodded, and he tickled Joel until he stopped asking questions. As he led the boy away, Senara stared anxiously after her husband as he closed the study door behind him.

The walk to his study felt more like a final walk to the gallows. Clearly Rowena was hurting, and Adam could only guess at the wild exaggeration of the gossip she had heard concerning the months leading up to St John and Meriel's wedding.

'Are you my father?' She attacked without even a warning shot across his bows, her heels clicking on the floor as she paced angrily between the bookcases lining the walls and the window.

Adam gestured to the two padded chairs either side of the hearth and stood by one. 'Sit down, Rowena. I will not discuss this matter whilst you prowl like a caged tigress.' He waited for her to take her seat.

'You will just tell me lies. Like everyone else,' she raged as she continued to pace.

'You deserve the truth.' He nodded to the chair and held the lapels of his jacket in a solemn stance.

'Just tell me!' Her voice rose and her stride lengthened.

Adam held her stare in silence until finally she seated herself, her fingers locked together in her lap. He sat opposite her before speaking. 'There is a possibility that I could be your father. I was courting Meriel during my shore leave before St John took up with her. I was recalled to my ship, and by my next leave your mother was already wed to St John. The only one who would know the truth of your parentage is your mother. Sadly she is unable to verify it.'

'Sal says I have your look.' Her glare was hostile. 'And there are the number of weeks from conception to birth.'

'St John and I were twins. Although not identical, we both had the Loveday colouring and build. As to the weeks Meriel had fallen on the stairs, you were an eight-month baby.'

'But it was you Mama was said to have loved.' Her gaze did not flinch as she accused him.

Adam crossed his legs and sat back in the chair. 'And at that time I believed myself in love with her. But it was St John she married.'

'Because you were at sea and she would have faced shame!' Rowena continued her challenge. 'Reuben Sawle would have beaten her senseless.'

'That is likely, but St John would not have wed her if he had not believed that you were his child.' Owning to this young woman that the wild oats of his youth had caused such havoc in her life was more difficult than Adam had envisioned.

'And of course he could make my mother mistress of Trevowan. A far grander life than being the wife of a naval officer.' Her scorn whiplashed across the space between them.

Whatever his feelings about Meriel marrying his twin, Adam was not about to reveal them to her daughter.

'You should never doubt that St John loved you, Rowena,' he reasoned.

'To save face. It was a sham.' The pain crackled in her voice. 'If Mama had been forced by her brothers to marry St John, she would have told you if I was your child.'

Adam steepled his fingers and chose his words carefully. He had promised to be truthful to her. 'She once told me that you were mine. And on the occasion of an argument with St John, she told him that you were not his. It was part of the games she played. It suited her if St John and I were at each other's throats, especially after I met Senara.'

'Were Meriel and St John ever happy together?' she surprised Adam by asking. 'I remember they quarrelled all the time, and Papa . . . St John would storm out of the house. I hated Mama for that. Then she ran off with a lover and I wanted so much for Papa to love me. There were times then that I think he hated me. No wonder he resented me, for I was the cause of their disastrous marriage.'

'Do not blame yourself.' Adam had not been aware that Rowena had taken in so much of the emotion that had threatened to destroy both her parents at that time. 'St John was proud to own you as his daughter.'

'But you were not!' Her eyes blazed with a challenging light he

253

had seen all too often from other members of his family. Rowena was smarting with rage, and who could blame her?

'It was not my place.' This was the hardest conversation he had ever been a party to, but he had to put his own discomfort aside in order to comfort the young woman who looked so wretched. 'My dear, I have always held you in the greatest affection. And if you were my daughter I would be proud to own you, but that would only cause scandal and harm to your reputation. St John is your father. There must never be any question to that.'

Her stare was bleak as it held his gaze. 'Where does that leave me? Are Thea and George my brother and sister, or Nathan, Rhianne, Joel and Sara?'

'They are all linked to you in a very special way.' He hoped that would console her.

'And where are my loyalties to lie with regard my kin?' she persisted. 'Our family put much store by such matters.'

Her expression had hardened and there was a dangerous edge to her voice, and Adam feared he was not reassuring her in the way she needed. He tried a different approach, though he felt that he was wading through water out of his depth.

'My father, who is undisputedly your grandfather, held that the family should be united in loyalty. It was Amelia's wish that St John's family should remain together. If you are unhappy at Reskelly Cottage, I am sure that Felicity will not object if you wish to remain here. That is your choice. It will not change my deep affection for you and the honour in which I hold you as my father's grandchild.' He stood up. 'I have been as honest as I can be with you. St John deserves the right to have your love and devotion as a daughter. As his twin, the blood we shared in the womb binds us in a unique closeness. His blood is my blood.'

'And is that your answer?' She rose, her figure stiff with affront.

'What more do you want from me? I will treat you no differently from Rhianne and Sara.'

'But you will never love me in the way you love them, as St John did not love me as he did George. My mother delighted in causing dissent with the power she wielded over you and St John with the secret of my parentage. She did not love me and she made sure no one else would as a child deserves from their parents.' Her voice was iced with pain and derision. 'For the sake of propriety I shall accept that St John was my sire. He deserves that for the misery my mother put him through. And I thank you for your hospitality and generosity, *Uncle* Adam.'

She swept regally from the study, but the air behind her was charged with her tension.

'We do love you, child,' Adam called after her.

She threw up her arms in a gesture of defiant disbelief. Adam rubbed the back of his neck and let out a harsh breath. 'I made a mess of that.'

'She will come round in time.' Senara entered the room. 'I listened at the door. Meriel has a lot to answer for. And you were as truthful as you could be in the circumstances.'

'I feel that I failed her.'

'She spoke out of hurt. Her faith in the family has been damaged and she is struggling to come to terms with the changes in her life. She will be happier here than at Trewenna. And she must never doubt the love of our family.'

His conscience smote him as he stared at his wife. Senara was beautiful, more compassionate than he deserved. How could he have been momentarily tempted by the attraction of Lady Alys. Senara was the woman he loved and he would always love her. He drew his wife into his arms and kissed her.

'As ever your words are wise, my love.' Adam still remained troubled. 'But just when I should be here for Rowena, I have to return to Somerset with Bryn. Matters there cannot be left unattended.'

Chapter Thirty-three

'Rowena, let me in so that we can talk.' Senara tapped on the locked door of the bedchamber.

Within, Rowena stopped the pacing that had overtaken her need for sleep. She glared at the door without answering. The moonlight provided all the light she needed when the candle had burned itself out and the creak of the floorboards became a comforting companion through the lonely hours of turmoil. She could not come to terms with the information that Adam had imparted to her. He and St John had always been rivals, and to them, proving which of them was the more worthy, whether to inherit Trevowan or win the affections of a spirited woman, was no more than another contest. And she had been the consequence of their tomfoolery and stubborn conceit. It was hardly a heritage of which to be proud. At least St John had not condemned her to the fate of bastard that would have made her despised by all classes.

Senara knocked again. 'Rowena, we want only what is best for you. And we do love you.'

The young woman hugged her arms about her waist and ignored the entreaty. The night was warm and she wore only a thin nightgown. Eventually she heard Senara return to her own chamber. Only then did she resume her pacing. Her mind was sharp and focused. She refused to be a victim, but her trust in her family had been destroyed. She was still too angry to sleep. She had adored St John, and now her faith in him was in tatters.

What had the moment of her procreation meant to the two brothers? She fumed. The arrogance of conquest? The vanity of seduction? Vanquishing the desires of a foe? Self-importance? Pride? Lust? Undoubtedly lust . . . As for the other reasons, they were no different than any other man used to prove that his manhood was more potent than another's.

It made her sick to her gut. Men cared only for their own gratification and nothing of the consequences to others. Armed with that knowledge, she vowed that no man would use her to his own ends.

Yet what use to rail against the twins, or even fate? The hours of pacing had brought a new resolve. There was only one person she now felt she had to answer to, and that was herself. She would show the arrogant Lovedays that she did not need their approval to make her way in the world.

The first sounds of stirrings in the house could be heard from the servants' quarters when tiredness finally claimed her. She lay on the bed and wrapped the counterpane around her, and when sleep came it was deep and dreamless.

The sun shining into her eyes eventually woke her. It was high in the sky and the echo of voices that had risen to a crescendo and slowly brought her back to consciousness were fading into the distance. Below her the grandfather clock chimed noon. The lateness of the hour shocked her, and she rose stiffly from the bed.

Joel was shouting. 'Why would Papa not let me go with them? It's not fair.'

'Papa would not even let me accompany them.' Nathan tried to pacify him. 'It will be too dangerous.'

Rowena ran to the window to see Senara wrestling with her younger son to stop him running after a group of riders trotting down the drive. Her heart clenched. Adam and Bryn led a group of half a dozen other men. With growing shock she realised that Japhet rode beside Adam. She could just make out the saddlebags on each mount.

With a sob of dismay, she tore through the house. Senara blocked her from running into the stable yard.

'Rowena, you are not dressed. You cannot go out there.' She grabbed her shoulders and held her back.

'Where have they gone?' Rowena demanded.

'To Somerset.'

'So soon?' Rowena was wild-eyed with growing anger. 'They cannot go. I have not spoken to Bryn.'

'If you had not shut yourself in your room last night—' Senara began, but was cut short by a distraught wail from her niece.

'But they have only just got back.'

'They feel that they must act at once if they are to bring Bryn's stepfather to justice,' Senara explained. 'Bryn's life could be in danger if they delay.'

'Could they have not said goodbye?' Rowena put a hand to her mouth to cover her anguish.

'You were sleeping. You had been upset and were pacing all night. And Bryn did not need to witness another scene from you.'

'You should have woken me. No one cares about my needs. Bryn is my friend. What if he does not return? What if he is killed . . . and I never had the chance to say goodbye?'

Senara looked stricken. 'I did not realise that you felt so strongly about him.'

'I do not. Clearly to go off like that shows that he cares nothing about me. No one does.' She wrenched herself free of Senara's hold and ran back to her bedchamber.

Half an hour later, without having eaten, she had dressed in her riding habit and was galloping out of the stable yard. The grooms had gone with the men and the only male servants at Boscabel where the one-armed Billy Brown, the heavily set Eli Rudge, who was a poor rider, and the ageing and arthritic Jasper Fraddon. All of them were too slow to follow her as Misty headed towards the moor. A hard ride would chase the anger and frustration from her body and mind. There was freedom within the vastness of the moor, and she had no one to answer to but herself.

The figure on the white horse the next morning was distinctive. Elspeth smiled as the rider gave her mare its head and galloped across the moor. The older woman was enjoying her early-morning ride. The mist, which lay as high as her mount's knees, was lifting and the sun was breaking through the last of the clouds, casting long shadows and an intensity of light and colour on the gorse and heather. The sound of skylarks was an uplifting accompaniment, and it was one of the rare mornings when the ache in her hip was negligible and the joy of riding and the sense of freedom it brought made it good to be alive.

Elspeth frowned when she realised that Rowena had no groom

in attendance. The remoteness of this part of the moor made it the haunt of vagabonds, who could pose a serious threat to a beautiful young woman riding alone. That Elspeth had escaped the vigilance of her own groom was a different matter to the older woman. Who would dare to harm her? She was certainly too old and unattractive to be considered fair sport to the more lecherous-minded.

Even so, she admired the spirit of her great-niece. At that age, Elspeth too had escaped whenever the opportunity arose to ride alone. It was the feeling of freedom that she had craved. The young woman was all Loveday, Elspeth chuckled. She had a spirit that the old woman could relate to and respect.

All at once her smile faded. Two other riders, men this time, had broken cover from the copse behind Rowena and taken off after her. Without hesitation, Elspeth touched her riding whip to Kara's side, galloping at a furious pace to follow the riders. She had a sickening dread that her niece was in serious danger and now cursed that independence that had left both of them without the protection of a groom. There was no time to return to Trevowan or Boscabel to summon help, and no other neighbours' estates were close enough to call upon for aid.

'Dear Lord, protect Rowena and let no harm come to her,' Elspeth prayed, careless of the danger that would also threaten her own safety.

As she closed the gap between them, the terrain became rougher and each stride of her mare jarred Elspeth's injured hip until it was throbbing with agony. She did not allow the pain to slow her pace. The two male riders were drawing level with Rowena and one was reaching for Misty's bridle.

'Get away from me!' Rowena screamed, and lashed out with her whip to strike her assailant across the cheek.

It served no purpose. Elspeth could only watch in horror as her great-niece's bridle was grabbed and Misty was pulled to a halt. The men were now on either side of her, and one had a pistol pointed at her head.

'Stop that at once!' Elspeth shouted. 'How dare you attack a gentlewoman?'

One of the attackers turned a face twisted with alarm towards Elspeth. Then, seeing who had shouted, he grinned evilly. 'How's one old woman going to stop us?'

Elspeth rode straight into the one who had jeered, lashing him furiously with her whip. 'We are Lovedays, one of the most important families in Cornwall. Release my niece unharmed and I will allow you to ride free. Otherwise a hue and cry will be raised searching for us and you will spend the rest of your days in prison.'

'We know this is Miss Loveday,' the one with the pistol sneered. 'Our master has an interest in her.'

The threat increased Elspeth's alarm. Never in all her years riding the moor alone had she been endangered in such a manner. Few men were foolhardy enough to attack one of her family. 'I do not have much on me, but take my gold brooch and this ring.' She stripped off her riding glove to show a sapphire and diamond band. 'Take these and let us go.'

The pistol was pointed at Elspeth. 'You are unimportant.'

'No!' Rowena screamed. 'You cannot kill her. The family will pay a ransom for our return. More than your master is giving you. My uncle owns the shipyard. Name your price.'

'You don't cross our master,' the man announced coldly.

'Please, let my aunt go.' As the man hesitated, Rowena lashed out with her whip.

Elspeth continued her own attack whilst braced for a shot to slam into her body. In the skirmish the horses jostled each other in panic and the weapon was knocked from the attacker's grasp. Then Misty crashed against Elspeth's side, and a fiery pain like the tongs of an inquisitor's red-hot pincers was the last thing she remembered before she blacked out.

Rowena screamed as her great-aunt swayed in the saddle and slid slowly to the ground, her foot remaining hooked into the stirrup. Kara was wild-eyed with fright and took off. In horror Rowena watched Elspeth being dragged several yards over the rough ground until her foot was wrenched from the stirrup.

In the tussle a rope had been hauled over Rowena's shoulders and pulled tight, whilst the other man, still holding Misty's bridle, dragged them away. As she was rushed past Elspeth's unmoving figure, Rowena saw the side of her aunt's face covered in blood. Kara had bolted and was heading back in the direction of Trevowan.

Davey left the farm while Watkins was busy delivering the milk to their customers in the cart. When he arrived at Traherne Hall, he was dismayed to learn that Sir Henry and his family had gone to Truro the previous day and would not return for another week. That ruled out acting against Watkins and the Jowetts with the aid of the militia or constables authorised by the magistrate.

It seemed that just as he needed to make a stand against the rustlers, ill fortune had played its hand against him. Hannah had been at Tor Farm yesterday, as Japhet was departing to join Adam and Bryn when they returned to Somerset. To make matters worse, both uncles had taken their best fighting men with them, and Davey did not know how many of his own workers he could trust. To prove that he would not be duped by the rustlers or by smugglers, he could not afford to allow the Jowetts to get the better of him this time. It would brand him as weak.

As soon as he walked into the farmhouse, his mother dismissed the two maids working in the kitchen, ordering them to separate the whey from the curds in the cheese room.

'Did you talk with Sir Henry about the cattle?' she said without preamble.

'He is in Truro and will not return for another week.' Davey tried to make light of his anxiety but knew that he had failed miserably when his mother frowned.

'With Japhet and Adam away, we must deal with this ourselves.' Hannah's grim expression showed her determination.

'Ma, I do not want you involved. It is too dangerous.'

Hannah shot him a look that was now scathing. 'I have dealt with worse than Watkins and the Jowetts.' She placed her hands on her hips and stared fixedly at her son for some moments before announcing, 'There are two ways we can deal with the cattle. We can take the easy route and release them from the meadow and drive them towards the moor to wander as they will; or we can confront Watkins.'

'He will deny any involvement, even though I will say I saw him with the Jowetts.' A muscle pumped along Davey's jaw in his frustration at feeling so powerless. 'They cannot get away with this.'

Hannah suggested, 'I could visit some of the villages and find out if any farmers have reported their cattle stolen in the last week.'

'That could take too long. What if the Jowetts return tonight?' Davey groaned.

'You could inform another Justice of the Peace, though I trust none of them as I would Sir Henry,' Hannah replied. 'They are ready enough to spend an occasional day in court but loath to exert themselves in arresting a culprit.' She chewed her nail as she tried to find a better solution. 'I will visit a few of the villages. Watkins will be returning soon, and you do not want to alert him that we are aware of his deceit. The farmers will help us if they have lost cattle. I shall go before he returns.'

Davey did not hold out much hope that his mother would succeed.

Hannah had ridden no further than a mile when she was hailed by a farm worker shouting and waving to attract her attention as he ran across open land. The urgency in his voice made her canter towards him. She did not recognise him as he held up a hand and bent over, taking great gulps of air to recover his breath.

Finally he managed to gasp, 'Mam . . . a woman's been hurt . . . a gentlewoman . . . and she looks bad. Blood on her head . . . not moving . . . not sure who she be . . . I be new to this part of Cornwall but I think her be a Loveday . . . old woman . . . often rides on the moor.'

'Aunt Elspeth,' Hannah croaked in fear. 'Where is this woman?'

'On the edge of the moor . . . that way.' He pointed. 'Open land near a copse.'

'You did well, sir. Do you work on a farm that is close?' He nodded, still having trouble getting his breath. 'Mr Verryn's place.'

'Tell him it could be Miss Elspeth and to bring a cart so we can get her home. Was her mare nearby?'

'No, mam.'

'I am Mrs Deighton. My father is the Reverend Loveday of Trewenna. Thank you, I am grateful to you. Return as fast as you can.' She kicked her mare in the direction he had gestured. In her concern for her aunt, all thoughts of her ride to the villages was abandoned.

The search seemed to take hours as she combed the moor, the rough terrain with its scattered rocks hindering her search. As her desperation was making her frantic with fear, the breeze lifting a pennant of white caught her attention. It was Elspeth's petticoat that had fluttered, marking where she had fallen. Hannah threw herself down beside the old woman. One side of her face was bloody, the other white as the linen that had been blowing in the wind. Her eyes were closed and she did not seem to be breathing.

Hannah ripped open the buttons at the front of her aunt's riding habit and put a shaking hand over the old woman's heart. The beat was weak but Elspeth was alive.

Hannah examined the head wound, which was still weeping blood. The gash was not deep, but a large swelling surrounded it. She was also alarmed at the odd angle of one of her aunt's legs, and hoped that it was not broken.

How long had Elspeth been lying there? A glance at the sun showed Hannah that it was long after noon. Her aunt often rode early in the morning. That her riding habit was saturated from the morning dew probably meant that she had been unconscious for a few hours. The wet clothing would not have helped her condition.

Hannah sat up on her haunches and scanned the moor for sight of the cart. There was no sign of it, but a lone rider was heading in her direction. She stood up and waved her arms, and prayed that he could at least help her get Elspeth's body across the saddle of her horse.

As the rider neared, she recognised Tristan and gave a sob of relief. Although she had the same distrust of her cousin as other members of her family, she knew he would not fail Elspeth. Behind him she could now see the cart approaching. It would be the easiest and least uncomfortable way to convey Elspeth to Trevowan.

When Tristan lifted his aunt and laid her carefully on to the floor of the cart, Elspeth groaned in pain but still did not regain consciousness.

'Would you ride with the cart while I go ahead and summon Dr Chegwidden?' Tristan asked Hannah.

'I know Chegwidden is close, but we usually engage Dr Yeo of Fowey. If Elspeth has broken a leg or damaged her hip, I would say he was the more competent,' she replied.

Tristan nodded, his face white with strain. 'I will ride to Fowey. I cannot say I have much faith in Chegwidden.'

'Shall I inform Senara too?' Hannah suggested. 'Elspeth is likely to need special care. It would be difficult to find a more proficient woman to tend her.'

'If Senara has no objection to tending Elspeth in the Dower

House, she is welcome to call upon her aunt.' There was stiffness in his manner as the cart slowly turned around.

'I will inform her.' Hannah rode beside the cart as it headed to Trevowan. The pace was slow to avoid jostling the patient too roughly as the vehicle lurched over the uneven ground. They had not covered many yards when Hannah cried out and snatched a ribbon of scarlet velvet that had caught on a gorse bush. She recognised the material. Had Rowena been with Elspeth today?

She kicked her horse to a gallop and shouted as she set off after Tristan. Her Arab mare bred by Japhet easily outpaced his heavier hunter, and she held up the material. 'This is from Rowena's habit. She could be in danger. I do not believe that Elspeth's fall was an accident, if the two women were together.'

Tristan frowned. 'Rowena must have gone for help. Surely that makes more sense. She will be at Boscabel.'

'Then why are there no servants from Adam's estate searching the moor? Boscabel is closer than Trevowan.'

'Your niece is often on the moor. She could have caught her skirt at any time.' His impatience to be on his way was obvious.

Hannah turned her mare to cut across in front of him. 'There was an attempt to kidnap Bryn recently. What if Rowena has been taken?'

'Then Adam will be dealing with it.' Tristan's eyes snapped with impatience. 'Elspeth needs a doctor. God knows how long she has been unconscious. She could be dying.'

Hannah continued to block his way, her voice cracking with fear. 'Adam is not at Boscabel. He and Japhet have gone to Somerset with Bryn and several armed men.'

Tristan cursed roundly, then apologised. 'I will do what I can. What hare-brained escapade are Adam and Japhet engaged in?'

'It is to do with Bryn's estate and bringing to justice the man who murdered his mother and older brother. And Sir Henry is in Truro. Davey was at Traherne Hall earlier on another matter.' There was no point in telling Tristan of their concerns for the farm. Others were in greater danger.

'Then pray that your niece is at Boscabel. My first duty is to summon a physician for my aunt. I will call on Senara on my return from Fowey. If the girl is not there, I will do what I can to find her.'

'Rowena is a young woman, not a girl. Her life and reputation are in danger. Adam and Japhet could not be away at a worse time.'

Tristan no longer hesitated. 'When you arrive at Trevowan with Elspeth order my men to search for your niece.'

They parted company each locked into new fears that now threatened the family. Whilst Hannah was concerned for her aunt and for her niece, she would have to trust Tristan to deal with a search for Rowena if she was indeed missing. As to the Jowetts and Watkins, she cursed the ill timing of another looming conflict. It would be up to her and Davey to bring those rogues to account.

Chapter Thirty-four

After his frantic ride to Fowey to summon Dr Yeo to attend Elspeth, Tristan left the physician at the crossroads. Dr Yeo galloped on to Trevowan and he took the road to Boscabel. It was not a meeting he was looking forward to, but at least he would not have to confront Adam, and he had every confidence that once Senara recovered from her fears for Rowena, she would not hesitate to tend Elspeth. Even so, with his family he took nothing for granted. By informing them of Elspeth's accident he would have done his duty.

It was the first time he had been near or in the house and it was very different from his expectations. He tried not to let his curiosity get the better of him, but human nature hoped to find that Boscabel compared unfavourably to Trevowan. In that he was disappointed. He had assumed that because all the Tudor houses he had seen in towns were timber-framed, this also would be a black and white structure, but it was built in local stone with a wide sweeping drive, complete with dolphin fountain and a sundial above the porch. The tall oriel window of the old hall and solar above dominated one side of the courtyard. Inside the panelled entrance a large marble fireplace would warm it in winter, and several doors led off to the downstairs rooms. The staircase was not as impressive as that at Trevowan, but its dogleg design was ornately carved and many of the portraits that he remembered had hung at Trevowan now graced these walls.

'Mrs Loveday will receive you in the main salon,' the maid said as she turned away for him to follow her.

Aware of the dust from the road covering his boots and clothing, he hesitated. 'This is not a formal visit and I would not normally pay a call besmeared with the dust from my ride. I also cannot delay returning to Trevowan. Be so kind as to ask Mrs Loveday to speak with me here,' he returned. 'It is a matter of extreme importance.'

'Leave us, Carrie.' Senara had heard the conversation and came into the hall. Her lovely face with her dark hair in an elegant chignon was taut with worry. 'Only something of great seriousness would bring you to Boscabel. Is it Elspeth?'

'She met with an accident on the moor and was found unconscious. Her mare returned alone to Trevowan and I immediately sent out a search. Fortunately Mrs Deighton was also on the moor at the time and had been notified of the incident. She had managed to commandeer a cart by the time I came across the scene. Mrs Deighton returned to the Dower House with her aunt and I rode to Fowey for Dr Yeo.'

'Adam is not here. But I will come at once.' Senara paused with uncertainty. 'You do not object?'

He shook his head. 'I had hoped for your expertise in attending her. Her injuries could be serious.'

'Then I will get my box of herbs and bandages.'

'There is another matter.' Tristan remained uncomfortable at giving further bad news. 'Has Rowena returned from her ride?'

Senara put a hand to her cheek in alarm. 'Has something has happened to her as well? She has been gone since morning. Often she joined Elspeth on the moor. If she was not with Hannah, she might still be at Trewenna.'

'Mrs Deighton found a strip of material she believed came from Rowena's riding habit. The ground around where Aunt Elspeth was found was trampled, as though by other horses. As a precaution, my men are looking on the moor for her.'

The woman before him swayed and threw out a hand to the wall to recover her balance. He caught her elbow. To his relief she quickly recovered her composure and showed no sign of swooning or hysterics, as many would have done in the circumstances. 'Your pardon, I should not have blurted that out as I did, especially on top of the news of your aunt.'

'I am recovered, Mr Loveday,' she was at pains to reassure him, although her smile was strained. 'And I am indebted to you for all you have done.'

'Are you?' he fired at her with obvious exasperation. 'Yet I am still Mr Loveday, excluded from the courtesy of the title of cousin.'

Senara coloured, and her gaze slid from his. 'I did not wish to offend. But circumstances . . . the rift between . . .' She faltered, her shrug one of impatience. 'In the present situation it is ludicrous not to abandon the formalities. Welcome to Boscabel, Cousin Tristan. And please, I am Senara.'

He smiled bleakly. With two serious situations threatening the welfare of the family, it was a hollow victory. He bowed. 'I will accompany you to Trevowan when you are ready.'

Rowena lay hunched on the prickly straw pallet, battling to overcome her terror. She was bound and blindfolded and had no idea where she had been taken. For what seemed like an eternity but was only in fact little more than a couple of hours, she had been alone. She could hear birdsong so knew that it was still daylight. The ride with her assailants across the moor had been frightening. After wrapping a rope around her to get her away from the site where she and Elspeth had been attacked, they had stopped in a coppice and she had been blindfolded and tied more securely. One of the men had taken her bridle to lead Misty. Fortunately Rowena was an accomplished rider, or the wild pace over the rough terrain would have tipped her from the saddle. But she had no idea what direction they had taken.

She suspected that it was an isolated farm somewhere in the depths of the moor. There was the distant lowing of cattle when they had first arrived, and a strong smell of pigs. That stench continued to pervade her nostrils. No one had come to her since she had been thrust into this room. The blindfold was a rough piece of cloth that also partially obscured her hearing, and the gag tasted foul as it cut into her tongue and jaw. No amount of wriggling her hands had enabled them to twist free of the bonds, and the flesh around her wrists was raw and inflamed from her efforts.

Yet above her fears for her own safety she was haunted by the bloodied figure of Aunt Elspeth. The old woman's unconscious body had been dragged over several yards of hidden rocks and tussocks as hard as bricks. She had lain still and twisted, her face white with its terrible splattering of blood. Her leg could be broken. How long had she been left on the moor before someone had found her? And what if she was still there now? She could be dying. Or God forbid, already dead.

And who was behind this kidnapping? Was it some sick retribution by Bruce Trevanion for rejecting his proposal? Surely no gentleman would act in so perfidious a manner. But who else could it be? Her family had enemies, but what had they hoped to gain by apprehending her?

Rowena's head was throbbing, but with her hands bound she could do nothing to ease its discomfort. A thirst was also building, increased by the pressure of the gag. She had been given a drink of sour small ale when she had first been locked in this place, but nothing since.

It was impossible to work out who her captors were. Those men were working for a master, but which one? She shuddered to dispel the labyrinth of thoughts her mind was negotiating. A spurt of anger made her tussle frantically at her wrists. The rope did not budge and the flesh was now bleeding and raw.

At least she had not been molested. A fate worse than death, as Felicity would consider it. Her pent-up frustration and outrage manifested in a growl of fury muffled by the gag. When it was spent, she assessed her injuries. Apart from her aching head and sore wrists, only her pride and dignity were hurt. Yet if knowledge of this got out, her reputation would be in tatters. Some would gloat that she had deserved it. Curse them. If Papa were here, he would save her, protect her . . .

That thought cut deepest of all. There was no Papa – not St John and not Adam. Whichever twin was her sire, fate had taken both of them from her when she needed them most. Her head jerked up. The meeting with Rose Sawle had struck a chord within her. There was a woman with fire in her blood and a heart full of courage. Rowena admired how she had survived and conquered the adversities life had thrown at her.

She squared her shoulders. That same fire and courage sped through her own veins. To stand any chance of escape, she had to keep a cool head. With Adam and Japhet away, who was there to save her? Her mind began another circle of reasoning. Senara would send out a search party when she did not return. But it would need the ruthless guidance of the Loveday men to really accomplish her rescue. At least Aunt Elspeth might yet have been saved. Tristan would not rest until his aunt and charge was found. Rowena did not have the same faith that he would do as much for her. Why should he? Her family had done nothing but pour scorn on him since he had stolen Trevowan, and she had not lost any opportunity to show her disgust and disapproval.

Rowena was determined not to wait for anyone to rescue her. She would follow Rose's example. Her mother's sister never gave up without a fight and had been ready to seize any opportunity to use to her advantage. She would escape, and those curs who had dared to abduct her would pay dearly for her humiliation.

At Trevowan, Tristan anxiously paced the landing outside his aunt's bedchamber in the Dower House. Dr Yeo was examining Elspeth with Senara in attendance. Alys sat on a chair by a table opposite the bedchamber, her hands locked together and her face drawn with fear.

'I should have gone riding with them more often, Tristan.' She blamed herself. 'They would not have attacked three women. Besides, I would have carried a pistol and a dagger.'

'My niece would never ride with you, and that is my fault,' Tristan grated. 'It was a time that Elspeth cherished and that kept her in touch with her family. It was also her way of keeping a closer watch upon Rowena. There have been too many rumours of her wildness this summer.'

'All likely founded on spite.' Alys twisted the rings on her fingers. 'Why did Elspeth refuse to ride with a groom?'

'Because she is stubborn.' Tristan groaned. 'If she dies, she is my responsibility. I have failed her.'

'She will not die,' Alys affirmed with a desperate edge to her voice. 'She is a tough old bird. She will fight this.'

'She is no longer young and it is time that she realised she is not invincible or immortal. This is the second time recently she has placed herself in danger. I would have thought that last drenching would have made her see sense.' Tristan halted in his stride as he heard movement behind the door. It opened and the stocky figure of Dr Yeo approached them. His heart felt crushed at the seriousness of the physician's expression.

'I have set her ankle in a splint and given her a sedative to help her sleep through the pain. The signs of a growing fever are what concern me most. Mrs Loveday has agreed to stay and tend her. If anyone can get her through such a malady, she will. We must pray that any infection does not settle in her lungs. It could be fatal in a woman of her age. I will call back in the morning, but Miss Loveday is in the best of care.'

Tristan showed the doctor to the door. 'What is her chance of a fatal infection?'

'It is a strong possibility, that is all I can say. She will also be in a great deal of pain from the old injury to her hip as well as the ankle.'

When the physician had left, Tristan returned to the bedchamber. Senara and Alys were seated on either side of the four-poster bed. Jenna Biddick, who had served as a maid at Trevowan for over twenty years, hovered in the shadows, her round face wet with tears.

Alys looked up at Tristan. 'Jenna will make up the bed in the next chamber. Both Senara and I will stay with your aunt through the night and take turns to rest.'

'I am indeed indebted to you, Senara.' Tristan stood awkwardly by the door. He was at a loss how to deal with any illness and was relieved that Elspeth was in good hands.

'I owe Elspeth a great deal,' replied his cousin-in-law, placing a cooling cloth upon the old woman's brow.

'Yet this is a difficult time for you, with Rowena missing. I promise you, if someone has abducted her, they will pay dearly for this infamy.' He walked to the door. 'Anything you need of me, you have but to ask. I am you servant, cousin.'

He went to check that all the workers were out on the moor hunting for his niece. The low angle of the sun was alarming, the daylight was fading fast and he feared that nothing would be achieved until the morrow. A great many fearful and frightful things could change the life of a young and innocent girl in that time.

Chapter Thirty-five

Davey followed Hannah into the stable when she returned to the farm. He dismissed the servant hovering to unsaddle the mare and led the horse into its stall. 'You have been gone for hours. I have been worried.'

'We are not the only ones with problems this day, my son,' she whispered. 'Aunt Elspeth was seriously injured in a fall from her horse on the moor, and Rowena is missing. She could have been kidnapped.'

'Or eloped with one of the Trevanion cousins.' Davey gave a wry laugh. 'Wilbur and Sir Selwyn pursued her ardently.'

Hannah glared at him. 'She is not that foolish. Besides, they are in the army now and in training. I encountered Tristan searching for Elspeth on the moor.' She explained the events of her meeting. 'He stopped the workers at Trevowan from their haymaking and has sent them out to look for her.'

Davey was immediately contrite. 'She really is missing then? Your pardon for being so flippant. Should we also be looking for her?'

'We will send as many as we can on the horses. It will be dark in a couple of hours and too late to search far on foot. Tristan is also rousing the villagers of Penruan and Trewenna. Senara is now at the Dower House tending to Aunt Elspeth. She has recovered consciousness, but her ankle is broken and the old injury in her hip inflamed. She was also starting a fever.'

'There is no danger to her life, is there?' Davey said, alarmed.

'That is in the Lord's hands. Elspeth is a fighter and she could not be receiving better care.'

'This is terrible.' Davey dragged a hand through his short hair.

'And I would never have expected Tristan to rush to Rowena's aid after what he did to her father.'

'He has also risen in my estimation,' Hannah confessed. 'His quarrel then was with St John. Perhaps we judged him too harshly. Family lives are at stake. We need to all pull together in this and put our differences aside. With Adam and Japhet away, he offered his services to us if we had need of him.'

'I would rather call on the devil than go to him.' Davey bristled. 'Does he seek to take the role of head of our family now he is master of Trevowan?'

'His offer was by way of an olive branch. Nothing more, but it is hard to put aside all distrust.' Hannah chewed her lower lip. 'But we cannot afford to allow stubbornness or false pride to hinder the search for Rowena.'

'And what about the cattle?' Despite his fears for his great-aunt and cousin, Davey could not shake his own troubles from his mind. 'Obviously any danger to Rowena is more important. Do we therefore allow the Jowetts to get away with their lawlessness this time?'

'It goes against everything I believe in,' Hannah assured him. 'Who knows what new drama tomorrow may bring concerning Rowena? There is little that we can do ourselves for her today.'

'Then we must deal with the problem with the cattle differently than we intended.' Davey watched his mother closely, gauging her reaction. 'We do not need to wait until the Jowetts can be caught red-handed. I shall tear down the wall and drive the livestock out of the field towards the moor now. They can wander at will.'

'And Watkins?' Hannah challenged.

Davey was adamant. 'I want him off the farm as soon as possible. He can go today. Once the Jowetts discover that the cattle are gone, they will go after Watkins and mete out their own justice. If Watkins has any sense, he will flee the district. And the Jowetts will get the message that this farm in not a haven for their stolen livestock or contraband.'

Hannah nodded approval, but her stare held a warning. 'We also could face the Jowetts' retribution.'

'Then we remain on our guard. Rowena has to be our main priority.'

'When do you plan to drive off the cattle?'

'Immediately, then I shall come back and deal with Watkins.'

'I shall work with you,' Hannah insisted. 'And we had both better be armed.'

They were both breathing heavily by the time the gap in the wall was large enough for the cattle to push through. Davey had his father's blunderbuss under his arm and Hannah carried a loaded pistol. Once the livestock were in the lane away from the farm, Davey struck several of them across their rumps, causing them to stampede. He ran alongside them for a mile until the common land of the moor opened before them, then with a final strike on their rumps sent them careering ahead. It would be some distance before they halted to graze, and Davey hoped that they would be far enough away to escape recapture by the Jowetts.

He ran back to the farm to where his mother had been standing guard by the wall to ensure that Watkins did not put in an appearance and try and warn his accomplices. They were both flushed from their work and there was a gleam of satisfaction in Hannah's eyes as she regarded her son.

'Let us hope that the Jowetts and their ilk learn that we will not tolerate such use of our land.'

'Now to deal with Watkins,' Davey said grimly. 'There is another hour before dark.'

'He will not get far on foot so late in the day, but he could run into the Jowetts if they intended to move the cattle tonight. They could cause mischief to the farm. We would not be the first to have the hayloft fired and lose the winter feed for the cattle.'

'Then he must be apprehended. We could tie him up and lock him in an outbuilding,' Davey suggested.

'That is one way.' Hannah nodded. 'You are running the farm, so the choice will be yours, but I remember Grandpapa George Loveday had a similar problem with a family equally as unsavoury as the Jowetts. His cattle were being rustled with the aid of a tenant farmer of Trevowan. He discovered where the livestock had been hidden, moved then to another place and kept watch on the tenant farmer. When his associates discovered that their plunder had been moved, they turned on the farmer, for it had been his duty to safeguard it from discovery. Their punishment was severe. The Jowetts will serve Watkins in no less a manner if we allow him another night or so of freedom.'

Davey digested her advice. 'I am not afeared to face the Jowetts, or Watkins.'

'No one doubts your courage,' she insisted. 'If Japhet and Adam were here, it would be a different matter. I would support you in taking on anyone who would bring disrepute to this farm.'

'Yet I have to prove myself to those who would serve us ill.' His voice was tortured with uncertainty.

'It is not always brawn that wins a battle for justice, but wisdom,' she offered. 'But it is for you to decide. This way Watkins appears the one at fault, and it does not set the Jowetts immediately seeking retribution upon us. There will be other times when strength and battle will be the only way to deal with such men. There is a chance that if Watkins discovers the cattle are missing, he will make a hasty departure from the district to avoid a confrontation with the Jowetts.'

'It would still be prudent for me to keep a discreet eye on Watkins for the next few nights.' Davey was resolute. 'But I shall heed your advice, Mama. George Loveday ruled his estate with an iron hand. I would bow to his wisdom.'

Chapter Thirty-six

The raucous cawing of numerous crows drowned out the sound of Bryn's return to Willow Vale. He was ashamed of the dilapidation and neglect that were the first impressions his guardian and Japhet Loveday would receive of his ancestral home.

'It has seen better days,' he observed as they trotted through the weeds that rose to their horses' knees on the once immaculate drive.

'There is no need for you to apologise,' Adam returned.

Rearing sinisterly through the trees, the first turret of the house was visible. It was stained black from the fire, the glazing blasted from its frames by the heat and the roof open to the sky.

'Someone has much to answer for,' Japhet muttered ominously.

To divert attention from the desecrated house, Bryn nodded towards a clearing where a church and cemetery were now visible. 'Over there is St Michael's church, where I was struck down. And there you can just make out some of the rubble from the razed hamlet.' His voice caught at this point and he led the riders to the steps of the house without further comment.

'The place looks deserted,' Japhet observed.

'It's a ruin.' One of the men snorted and was silenced by a glare from Adam.

'Now is the time to find out if it is habitable,' Adam suggested. 'Fortunately we have ample provisions for tonight. This part of the house looks to have been untouched by the fire and the structure should be safe.'

'There is a thin trail of smoke coming from the kitchen chimney,' Bryn warned them. 'Someone is here. They are likely armed and instructed to shoot trespassers.'

The solid oak double doors in front of them were closed. Bryn

276

leapt to the ground, ran up the steps and turned the heavy iron ring, and one of them swung open. 'Two men stay with the horses. The rest of you ensure that you are in two or threes if not with us.'

The door creaked ominously as it was pushed further open and the Lovedays and their men entered the old building.

Adam saw immediately that it was more ancient than Boscabel by two hundred years at least. He had also seen the signs of a filled-in moat around the perimeter of the building. The sound of their footsteps echoed hollowly on the worn flagstones.

The room smelt musty and unused and cobwebs draped like long grey beards from the chandeliers and ceiling. Yet the tables displaying empty Chinese vases were free of dust and the floor had been swept.

'Good day there,' Japhet shouted. 'Anyone at home?'

Silence.

Bryn strode towards the back of the house to the kitchen. The place was clean and tidy and a cauldron of simmering pottage hung on a hook over the embers of the fire. He opened the kitchen door and looked around the courtyard leading to the stables and wash-house. There was no sign or sound of any servants.

Japhet and Adam were continuing to call out as they explored the lower rooms. As Bryn reached the bottom of the staircase, a floor-board creaked on the landing.

'Who is there?' he demanded. 'Show yourself. I am Alexander Bryant, the son of this house.'

'Master Alex. Is it truly you?' Several floorboards creaked in quick succession and a short, buxom white-haired woman paused at the top of the stairs. Her complexion was swarthy and she wore plain servant's clothes, the skirt frayed and ragged at the hem but her large apron was spotlessly clean. She stepped cautiously down the stairs, her gaze searching the faces of the men gathered below her.

Bryn stepped forward, his voice tight. 'Josephina! Yes, it is me.'

'Master Alex!' She shrieked again and quickened her pace. 'The Lord be praised you are safe and well.' She burst into copious tears and was almost incoherent as she sobbed, 'How tall you have grown! And so handsome. I would never have known you.'

'It has been a long time, Josephina.'

'Where have you been?' Her hands fluttered as though she would have caressed his cheek, then drew back as she recalled her place. 'Master Alex, how proud your mama would have been to see you now. The Lord saved you and blessed you. You have grown to a fine gentleman.'

'This is my guardian, Captain Adam Loveday, and his cousin Mr Japhet Loveday.' He turned to the men. 'This is Josephina, my mother's lady's maid.'

'I am but a humble servant now.' Josephina's lips trembled. 'Such terrible things have happened. Such evil. I am alone in the house. The last of the male servants disappeared a few weeks ago.' She wiped her eyes on the corner of her apron. 'This is a miracle. I thought you were dead.'

'Soon after we left, our coach was in an accident,' Bryn explained. 'I lost my memory. Arabella was killed.'

'Miss Arabella, dead!' the woman wailed. 'The Lord have mercy on her soul. She was such a sweet creature, and so beautiful and so young. Oh, the evil that has struck this family. But you are alive, Master Alex. For that we must be thankful. This is indeed a joyous day. A joyous, joyous day.'

Josephina laughed, her eyes bright and inquisitive upon Adam and Japhet. 'Your pardon, good sirs. In my excitement at discovering that Master Alexander is alive and has clearly been well provided for by your good family, I forget my manners. I am but a simple maid, and the only servant at your disposal and service. Once you would have been honoured as princes in this proud home. I can only offer you simple fare. If your men would be so kind as to light a fire in the parlour, it will chase the chill from the house and be more welcoming. And if two chickens could be caught and plucked I will cook them for later. Your men may also find some vegetables in the kitchen garden. The bedchambers are damp, but if you do not mind bedding down in the parlour for tonight, I can air them. I am ashamed that I can offer so little on behalf of my young master. Oh, but I believe there is still some wine in the cellar.'

'Do not fear, Josephina,' Adam assured her. 'My cousin and I have both served our country and suffered far worse hardships than good food and a dry roof over our heads. The services you have offered are very much appreciated. We did not know what to expect . . .' He let the statement hang ominously in the air. 'Are you indeed the only person in attendance on the estate?'

'I fear so, Captain Loveday.'

'And what of Carforth?' Bryn demanded.

The woman's face puckered and her eyes rolled with terror. 'Do not mention that monster. He is the devil incarnate. Have you seen the destruction he has wreaked upon your home, Master Alex? Your poor mama and papa would turn in their graves.'

'I have seen little but the neglect and the damage to the house,' Bryn replied.

'I fear he has ruined you, Master Alex. The villagers were driven out of their homes and the cottages destroyed.'

Adam stepped forward. 'Our journey has been long. Some of the wine would be reviving. We dined at an inn not three hours past. I believe your master may wish to inspect the house and estate. After our evening meal we would hear your story of what transgressions have been perpetrated here.'

Josephine bobbed a nervous curtsey, and Bryn ushered them into the parlour. It was a large room but was strangely devoid of furniture. Adam saw his ward's expression tighten and counselled, 'This will not be easy to accept. Let us inspect the property while your servant prepares a meal. You will have many questions to ask her. I would not mention that you were here before, unless she has knowledge of your capture and mentions it. You cannot be too careful.'

'But I would trust Josephina.' Bryn voiced his shock. 'She helped me to escape. She was a friend to my mama.'

'She was in your mother's employ. You had been away at school for some months before your last visit to this place. Is it not strange that she is still here?'

'Where else would she go?' Bryn frowned.

Japhet, who had wandered into several of the downstairs rooms before returning to the parlour, said softly, 'You were a young boy and upset over the way Carforth beat you and the manner of your mama's death. Things may not have been as you believed. I would make no judgements until we discover why there has been so much destruction. Mayhap you should also be asking why the maid was allowed to stay when you and Arabella escaped. Would Carforth not have punished her, or at the least dismissed her? After your mama's death, her services were no longer required.'

Bryn paled but nodded agreement. 'Josephina always showed me great kindness, and she was devoted to Mama.'

Japhet smiled thinly. 'That could still be the case.'

A tuneless singing from the kitchen followed the remark. Japhet

279

shrugged. 'I am always suspicious. She sounds happy that you are here.'

For two hours Bryn and Adam rode over the estate checking the devastation. Japhet and five of the men travelled to the nearest villages to learn any gossip in the taverns. The rest of the Loveday servants and workers were told to assist Josephina and to make sure that she was unaware of the investigations being made by the other members of their party.

Adam was as sombre as his ward on their return to the house, where they examined the central section and the south wing that had been damaged by the fire. The wing was too unsafe to enter. It was here that the roof and floors had fallen through. The blackened chimney stacks were cracked and in danger of tumbling to the ground.

'You will have no choice but to tear the wing down and rebuild,' Adam advised.

The central section had lost its roof, exposing a burnt-out long gallery. The rooms beneath were also damaged, from the elements attacking the first floor and the ceiling of the lower floor.

'How could a house that has stood for centuries be reduced to such a state in a few years?' Bryn groaned.

Adam studied the brickwork and any cracks. 'Nature soon reclaims its own. You can save the first two floors and the upper storeys can be rebuilt. The north tower seems to have sustained little more than smoke damage.'

They walked through these rooms. Some contained blackened hangings and mattresses that could not be saved. Although the wooden four-posters and furniture remained intact, it would all need a thorough cleaning. However, Bryn was relieved to discover that his mother's bedchamber was undamaged, and the anteroom next door was occupied by Josephina's truckle bed and her few possessions. Bryn's old room was thick with dust and cobwebs, as was Arabella's room above. In some of the chambers the wainscoting had been smashed and floorboards wrenched up.

Bryn let out a harsh breath. 'It looks like some avenging fury has tried to obliterate our existence here.'

'Or they were searching for something,' Adam sombrely observed.

'Were they looking for the treasure Carforth believed was hidden here?' Bryn snorted in disgust. 'He was obsessed by it. But there was no treasure. It was just a myth surrounding an old house.'

'A pity.' Adam attempted to lighten the mood. 'A hoard of treasure is exactly what it will take to restore your estate. A visit to the lawyers appointed by Carforth is overdue. We need to know exactly how much of your fortune is left.'

A gong echoed through the house and Bryn said, 'That will be Josephina summoning us to dine. Not that I have much of an appetite.'

'This has been a bad business, but at least you escaped with your life and will bring your stepfather to justice.'

After the meal was finished, Adam, Japhet and Bryn dismissed their servants for the evening and summoned Josephina to join them in the parlour. The maid hovered awkwardly by the door until Bryn gestured for her to be seated opposite them as they relaxed in front of the hearth.

'Tell me what happened here after I left,' he demanded.

'It was a terrible time. I can only tell what I know, which is not much.' She bit back a sob and steadied her voice. 'The night your mama died, Carforth left here in a towering rage. That enabled you and Arabella to escape his clutches. I prayed all night for your dear mama's soul and that Carforth would not come back until you were far away and safe from his evil. In that the Lord smiled on us. He did not return until after your dear mama was buried. She was laid to rest in the family vault beside your papa. It was what she wanted.'

She paused and dabbed at her eyes with the corner of her apron. Bryn bowed his head and waited for her to continue. Her voice became more distraught. 'I knew that when your stepfather discovered I had allowed you to escape, he would kill me. I ran away and found work at a house the other side of the moor. I thought I was safe. I should have known that monster would not let me escape punishment. I was found and dragged back here.'

Adam crossed his legs, watching her through narrowed eyes. 'That was several years ago, and yet you are still here and there is no sign of Mr Carforth.'

'I am but a weak woman and not so young in years.' Her eyes again filled with tears and she let them flow. 'For months I was locked up, beaten and starved. He was convinced my mistress had told me with her dying breath where the treasure was hidden. He

281

also thought I knew where Master Alexander and Miss Arabella had fled. He wanted the young master a prisoner so that he could control the estate and his fortune as his guardian.'

'Yet I posted notices in all the leading news-sheets when your master was found,' Adam persisted. 'He had no memory of his home or his family. Why did Carforth not answer them?'

'I could never fathom how that man's evil mind worked.' Josephina sighed. 'He did mention once that if the boy had lost his memory then he could trouble him no further. I was grateful that if that young lad was Master Alexander, he was at least safe and being cared for.'

Japhet shifted in his chair. 'He could just as easily have been placed in the poorhouse or an orphanage if there was no response.'

'I prayed every day that he would be safe.' She wrung her hands. 'He was indeed blessed that such a generous family took him into their care.'

'You did not answer my cousin's question.' Japhet remained uncompromising. 'Why have you remained here if your master was so evil? Where is Carforth now?'

'Where would I go? He threatened that if I ran away, he would hunt me down. He is a vengeful man. My health began to fail. Who would employ me? At least I had food and a bed. Carforth was seldom here.' She held an imploring hand towards Bryn. 'And I thought that if Master Alexander recovered his memory, he would return. How else would I see him again – warn him of the danger? Carforth had sworn to kill him. I thought his mama would wish me to stay. She had always shown me great kindness, and Master Alexander was such a dear, sweet boy.'

Japhet and Adam did not reply but exchanged tense glances. Josephina continued to wipe her eyes, which were now red and swollen. Bryn smiled at the old woman. 'You were very loyal to Mama. It saddens me that you suffered so much because of your devotion to my family.'

'Where is Carforth now? You did not say,' Adam cut in.

Josephina shook her head. 'He has not been here for many months. Even the henchmen who guarded the grounds have gone.'

'What happened to the hamlet?' Bryn could barely keep the anger from his voice, he was so incensed at the destruction. 'And what of the fire here?'

'That all happened while I was his prisoner. Carforth was hated. The house and grounds had been ransacked in his search for the treasure. Your stepfather was insane with rage. He even ransacked the church. The tenants and servants were treated no better than slaves. They stormed the house one night and set it on fire. Carforth's revenge was to destroy the village and drive them out. He had still found no sign of the treasure, but I think he had found a way to steal money from the estate. He had vowed that you would have nothing.'

'Thank you, Josephina.' Adam stood up to pace the room. 'That will be all for this evening.'

When she reached the door, Japhet too stood up and said loudly, 'How did Carforth maintain his hold on the estate as Bryn's guardian when the young master was not here?'

There was a pause before Josephina turned to face them, and the expression on her face was in shadow. 'To any who enquired, Master Alex was away finishing his schooling or visiting relatives.'

'But surely some were suspicious that he was never seen?' Japhet persisted.

'The estate is large and there would be little reason for the young master to mix with the locals,' Josephina added. 'The servants would know better than to talk. They were in terror of Carforth.'

When Bryn would have asked more questions, his guardian shook his head to silence him.

'What was that about?' Bryn asked when Josephina had left them. 'We were starting to get somewhere.'

'I would rather make our own enquiries to verify what we have been told.'

'Why should Josephina lie?' Bryn was shocked.

'I did not say that,' Adam corrected. 'There are still too many unanswered questions. I would also have Carforth's lawyer's opinion about recent events on the estate.'

'Is it wise to leave the place?' Japhet observed. 'If Carforth still has spies in the area, he will be notified that Bryn has begun investigations. Bryn and I could remain here while you visit the lawyers in Bridgwater.'

'And I keep feeling that I am missing something somewhere.' Bryn frowned and rubbed his brow. 'Yet for the present I cannot think what it is.'

Chapter Thirty-seven

So great was Cy Watkins's faith in his ability to deceive a woman and the young master of Rabson Farm, it had been arranged that it would be two nights before he was to move the cattle for the Jowetts. He had been annoyed when during the day he had been given orders to carry out work on the far side of the farm to where the cows were hidden. There was no way he could escape the vigilance of Davey Rabson, as he would be working alongside him throughout the daylight hours clearing a drainage ditch. If he could not check on their welfare, at least no one else would be sniffing round where they were not wanted. Hannah Deighton had also been taking too great an interest in his milk and dairy deliveries, and she was again making the round herself today. She might say she wanted to visit old friends and customers, but Cy was on edge that she had discovered how much profit he had been gleaning from those deliveries himself. It was time she went back to her new husband on his fancy estate and stopped interfering with the work here.

He was also no longer so certain that Davey Rabson would be an easy target to cheat in the future. It could be time to be moving on to more profitable work. He had a good business going with the Jowetts and he had put almost enough aside from his dealings here to purchase a small farm of his own on the moor. The smugglers would pay him well if he allowed them to hide their contraband on his land.

Unaware that he was being followed, there was a bounce in his step as he neared the hiding place of the cattle.

Davey held the blunderbuss firmly as he pursued his prey. His eyes were scratching from lack of sleep, but he had seen Watkins sneaking from his cottage and was determined to bring him to account tonight. He did not need to pursue him closely. A cry of outrage piercing the night told him that the loss of the cattle had been discovered. When Davey reached the field, Watkins was running through the trees in a panic and swearing profusely.

'They are long gone,' Davey announced loudly.

Watkins spun round. Despite the chill of the night, his face glistened with sweat and his eyes rounded with fear. 'What you be talking about? What be long gone?'

'The cattle, and this is the end of you using our farm in your dealings with the Jowetts.' Davey held the blunderbuss in front of him. 'You can pack your things and leave, and do not expect any references.'

'I never had no dealings with the Jowetts, and what is this about cattle?' Watkins blustered, edging closer and eyeing the gun in Davey's hands.

'Stay back and no fast moves,' Davey warned. 'And do not add insulting my intelligence to your deceit and treachery. You may have got away with using this field to hide stolen cattle when I first arrived here, but the one with the broken horn was spotted at the market. When I realised that none of my own livestock were missing, it did not take much investigation to see why this wall had been repaired in the manner it had, and why there were so many hoof marks and droppings in this field.'

Watkins took another step closer.

Davey raised the blunderbuss. 'I followed you the other day when you met that pedlar in the lane. I was watching when the Jowetts brought the cattle here and you sealed the wall. If my uncles or Sir Henry Traherne had been at home, then tonight would have been a very different story. They would be here with me, waiting to arrest you and the Jowetts for rustling. As it is, you have had a lucky escape. I am letting you go. You'd be wise to be as far away from the farm as possible before the Jowetts learn that your incompetence has cost them their profits.'

'They will hold you responsible for that,' Watkins sneered. 'No one crosses them and escapes their brutal justice. Once they find out that you sold their cattle—'

Davey cut in. 'But I did not. I merely released livestock that did not belong to me back on to the moor. And I have left a letter with

Sir Henry about my suspicions that you are involved in rustling. If you remain in the district, your arrest will be ordered on Sir Henry's return.'

'You won't get away with this,' Watkins snarled. 'The Jowetts will kill you.'

'Why should they risk their freedom by acting against a family of such high regard as mine? If they want a scapegoat, it will be you.'

'Bastard!' Watkins rushed towards Davey.

'Stay where you are,' Hannah ordered. 'I have a pistol.'

'Do you think I am afeared of a woman and a callow youth still wet behind the ears?' Watkins jeered.

Davey pulled the trigger and staggered back from the kick of the blunderbuss as its ignited shot flared in the air. He saw Watkins's mouth open in shock and then his face contorted with pain as the pellets tore into his shoulder and arm. The man keeled over on to the ground, screaming in agony and clutching his bloody sleeve. Davey stood over him, the gun now raised to be used as a cudgel if Watkins tried to attack him again. 'Think yourself fortunate that at such close range this wet-behind-the-ears youth chose not to kill you.'

'He is a crack shot.' Hannah came out of the dispersing smoke from the gun and handed her pistol to her son. He pointed it at Watkins, saying, 'Leave this farm immediately. You are making a great deal of noise over a flesh wound.'

'You are both dead meat over this,' Watkins fumed as he struggled to his feet and staggered away.

Davey and Hannah followed him, but Davey paused briefly to shout into the night, 'I know you are out there, Jowett. Your cattle are on the moor. Round them up again if you wish, but I identified their owners from their brand marks and sent word to them of what occurred here. You may find an ambush awaiting you. Stay away from our land in future.'

He held his breath at hearing the rustling on the far side of the wood. Then to his relief the sounds faded into the distance. He caught up with Watkins, scathing in his warning. 'Not very loyal, your friends, are they? Now leave. If I see any sign of you within five miles of the farm tomorrow, I shall drag you to the lock-up in Fowey myself and press charges. I would not leave it too long before you get someone to tend your wounds. The scattershot may not have been deadly, but you could lose the use of your arm through infection.'

'What about my things?' They had reached Watkins's cottage.

'I will give you to the count of a hundred to collect them,' Davey granted.

He followed the man inside and watched every movement until Watkins tossed a cloth that was wrapped around his few possessions over his shoulder. Hannah had stood guard at the door, a second pistol in her hand. He glared at them as he lumbered past. 'I'll get you for this.'

'The law will get you first,' Davey returned with confidence. 'I would make the most of the hours of darkness to get far from here. Word of your treachery will be all round the markets by the end of the week. No one will employ you. I have given you your life, which is more than you deserve. Now go.'

They watched as he staggered away, and Hannah let out a harsh breath. 'I would rather have seen him face trial, but to take on the Jowetts without help would have been foolish. They know you will not stand for their lawlessness. You have done well tonight, my son. Your father would have been proud of you. You have proved that you are a force to be reckoned with. You are more than able to run this farm on your own. I shall return to my husband at the end of the week, once Elspeth is out of danger and Rowena is safe.'

'I could not have succeeded without your help tonight, Mama.'

'I did nothing of merit.' She smiled and put her arm around his waist as they walked back to the farmhouse. 'You made the right decisions and were in control.'

'I did not want to kill him. Was that a show of weakness?'

Hannah shook her head vigorously. 'It is all too easy to kill. You have given Watkins a second chance. If he chooses not to mend his ways, then he will end his life soon enough at the end of a rope. The law is harsh for such transgressors. You have proved that you will not hesitate to use force to any who would strike against you.'

It had been a long and scaring day for Rowena, but she was now confident that she could outwit her captors. When late that morning one had brought her a flagon of water and some bread and cheese, her captor had also removed the gag.

'Scream all you want. No one will hear you.' He had chuckled sinisterly, but his voice had sounded thin and reedy. If he was puny, she might be able to overpower him. There was a slowness to his words that told her that outwitting him should be no problem. But first she had get free of her bonds

'You'll hang for this,' she had returned defiantly. 'My aunt lies injured. She is one of the most respected women in our community. A hue and cry will be raised by the whole of the county.'

'And you will not see another dawn if you keep talking like that.'

The room was filled with the stench of his unwashed body and her skin prickled as he moved closer to her. 'Who is behind this outrage?' she demanded, hoping that the frantic pounding of her heart did not betray her growing fear. 'Is it Trevanion?'

'So you have more than one enemy? How interesting,' her captor sniggered. 'Mayhap we will auction you to the highest bidder.' She could smell the foulness of his breath, and when his hands squeezed her breasts, she lashed out with her foot, catching him on the thigh with her riding boot.

A vicious slap to her face sent her sprawling back on the bed, and her blood had iced with the fear that he intended to rape her. She had lashed out again with her feet but encountered only air. The cruel laugh added to her shame and humiliation.

'A woman with spirit and a beauty. You could fetch enough to keep us in comfort the rest of our days.'

'And those days will be short-lived. Why have I been abducted?'

'You keep a poor choice of company. You are bait to draw him out.'

The door slammed behind his chilling chuckle. This was to do with Bryn. Her captors did not know that he and her uncles had gone to Somerset. If they discover that would they kill her, or run off and leave her to starve to death. With no one to rescue her, she had to rely on her own wits to escape.

Once alone, Rowena had swallowed against the sobs of fear that stifled her throat. She struggled to sit up and draw in great gulps of air. A tress of hair was irritating the tip of her nose and she tossed her head violently, sending the last of her pins hurtling from her curls as they tumbled about her shoulders. The anger now speeding through her body refocused her thoughts on escape. In her tussle with her captor, the blindfold had slipped to one side, and by rubbing her head along the straw pallet, she managed to push it down from her eyes.

She had gone straight to the window to peer out through the grimy pane. Her view was distorted by dirt, but she could make out the hazy outline of a tor in the distance that she recognised. With the sun now in the west, she calculated that she was about seven miles from Boscabel. She examined her prison. Apart from the straw pallet, there was a rickety table and nothing else. Her gaze returned to the window, now trying to judge how high she was from the ground. There was a one-floor drop to an outbuilding below her. That looked like the stables. So far she had heard no sound of dogs that would betray her escape.

But how to rid herself of the bonds? The walls were rough and much of the plasterwork had fallen off, revealing the wattle struts beneath. She attempted to rub her bound wrists against these, but only succeeded in scraping more flesh from her arms. Then her stare had fallen upon a broken nail at the corner of the window frame.

She had to crouch to get her wrists in position and her legs and arms were cramping in agony by the time the rope started to fray. Though her arms felt like they had been wrenched from her sockets, she continued to saw the binding over the nail. When it eventually gave, she toppled to the floor and lay panting with exhaustion. With no idea what her captors planned for her, her alarm increased as she heard them arguing below. The window was divided into two panes of glass. She could smash one of them, but the sound of the glass breaking was bound to alert her abductors. The latch was stuck fast, the wooden frame warped and refusing to budge.

Chapter Thirty-eight

Tristan could not rest while the men who had injured his aunt and abducted his niece were still at large. Elspeth was still slipping in and out of delirium and Dr Yeo was worried that the old woman's strength was failing. Every breath rasped in her throat and her thin body trembled in the throes of fever. He was helpless against stopping the onslaught of illness and channelled all his energy into rescuing Rowena. He vowed that if his aunt died or his niece had been harmed in any way, those men would wish they had never been born by the time he had finished with them.

He refused to call off the search party until every isolated farm, barn, byre, hut, cave and abandoned mine had been searched. As the second day dawned, there was murder in his heart that the villains had not been found.

He pushed his men hard and himself harder. They could not have vanished into the mists of the moor. No one close to Rowena's description had been seen on the main roads and tracks of the wild and open land. That must mean that they remained nearby. As each hour passed, Tristan became more desperate. His feelings for his niece surprised him. Rowena had never shown him anything but loathing; hating him for St John's death and the loss of her home. She had rebelled against her family and fate, and for that alone he admired her. If she had meekly accepted the changes that he had wrought in her life, he would have despised her for a weakling. Her fighting spirit had won his respect and stirred his family loyalty. That in itself had startled him, for he had mocked his cousins for burying the hatchet of their feuding and rivalry to band together in a crisis. Yet finding himself the only Loveday capable of rescuing his kin, it was a matter of pride that he succeeded.

By the second afternoon, Tristan realised that a blind search would never lead them to Rowena. He needed the expertise and knowledge of men who knew this moor better than any other. He rode alone to the Jowetts' run-down hovel.

This was only the second time that he had visited it, and the stench of rotting manure and urine from both man and beasts lying in the churned-up ground of the yard turned even his hardened stomach. The walls of the granite house were covered in ivy, and one wall, where the gutter had leaked for a decade, was coated in moss. The sparse thatch was ancient and mildewed. A milk cow and a few chickens and geese foraged for food. Even before he reached the vicinity of the house, the stench from the pigsties was overwhelming, making his eyes smart.

At his approach, four mangy, bony dogs snapped around his horse's hooves and barked hysterically. Tristan drew his pistol from the saddle holster and shot one of them dead, and the others ran off yelping. He took out his second pistol and laid it across his knees as the door opened and a bearded giant of a man lumbered out, a musket raised to his shoulder. The menace in his face turned to a scowl at recognising his visitor.

'Damn your eyes, Loveday. You shot my dog.'

'The cur was upsetting my horse. What are you going to do about it, Ezekiel?' The threat crackled in the air between them.

'That depends on what brings you here,' Ezekiel grunted. 'You bain't in much favour. That nephew of yours be interfering in our business. You said there'd be no trouble from the Rabsons.'

'Hannah Loveday took on the Sawles and stopped them using her land. It was for you to decide if her son was any less of an opponent. But I am not here to discuss cattle rustling. My business is with Malachai.'

Two more thickset bearded figures shambled outside, each clutching a musket. Tristan remained on his horse and nodded to Malachai and Gabriel.

'The Rabson boy loosing those cattle cost us plenty,' Gabriel snarled.

'Then your quarrel is with Watkins. You got greedy using the farm once my cousin returned.' Tristan was dismissive.

'Word is Watkins has run off. We were about to go after him, then pay a call on your nephew. Time he learnt we bain't to be messed with.' Gabriel stared Tristan down.

Tristan held the glare, unimpressed by the bluster. 'If you want to continue with our arrangements, then you stay away from my family,' he warned. 'There are higher profits at stake than your petty rustling. Deal with Watkins if you wish. He is no concern of mine. There are others on the moor setting up against us. They could be a problem in the future. My niece has been kidnapped. Have you heard anything about where they would have hidden her? There has been no demand for a ransom as yet, but Captain Loveday had intruders on his land after his ward recently. They could have taken the girl to bargain for the lad. I want them found and I want them dealt with.'

'What it be worth to us?' Malachai demanded.

'Any information you discover I will make worth your while. You would not want to lose my goodwill, would you?'

The Jowetts liked neither taking orders nor being given ultimatums. The three brothers glared murderously at Tristan as he faced them down. Tristan did not flinch under their scrutiny. Although they had had several dealings together and he had turned the brothers' petty thieving into a far more profitable business for them all, they remained distrustful of each other. The Jowetts were brutal and without conscience; though they were slow-witted, they were quick to take offence. Tristan could almost hear the cogs of their minds creaking over the benefits involved in retaining his favour.

Finally Ezekiel nodded. 'Happen we've done as much for you as you've done for us.'

'And I have always paid you well.' Tristan shrugged.

'Happen you have,' Ezekiel pondered.

Tristan waited patiently until he could feel the tension lessen in the three men. He then pressed his point. 'So would it not serve both our purposes if you were to find these kidnappers who have taken over our territory and use them as an example to others that the moor is our hunting ground?'

Rowena rested her head against the window and listened for signs of movement below. Earlier her captors had been arguing and it had helped cover the noise of her attempts to break open the window.

She had used the broken nail again, pulling it free and managing to dig out a pane of glass. It had taken hours, and her nails and fingers were sore and bleeding. It would be a tight squeeze to pull herself through the opening, but she prayed it would be possible. The voices below had fallen silent and she had seen no sign of the men in the yard outside her window. Should she wait until it was dark to better cover her escape, or did every minute she stayed in this room risk the kidnappers discovering that she was free of her bonds and could escape through the window?

She had to chance it now. She glanced out of the window, gauging the distance to the roof below. It looked a long drop, but there was no sheet or coverlet on the straw pallet that she could use as a rope, and even if she used her petticoats, there was nothing to securely tie them to. Despite the danger she dared not delay, and she prayed that she would not break any bones.

With her heart thudding in her chest, she pulled herself on to the narrow sill and pushed her legs out of the window, wriggling through the narrow gap. For a moment her shoulders stuck and she thought she would never get through; the pressure on her shoulder blades was intolerable as she used all her strength to work herself free. Then gravity aided her, the weight of her body dragging her forward. The pain was released and there was a brief time of weightlessness and falling, then fresh agony jarred through her leg at landing heavily, and she was unable to stop herself rolling and sliding down the roof. She bit her lip to halt a scream as her body gathered momentum and the ground hurtled towards her.

The breath was knocked from her body, and she almost fainted from the stench of the old soiled straw from the stables, which fortunately had cushioned her fall. She rolled over it until her feet touched solid ground. To her relief, no bones were broken and there was no sound within the house that her escape had been heard. She scrambled up and ran to the front of the stables. The horses were not there.

For a moment she panicked. Then the door to the house opened and she just had time to duck behind the wall of the outbuilding before one of the men appeared. The sound of trickling water as he urinated made her wrinkle her nose in disgust. When the door clicked shut behind him, she risked a peek and found the yard empty. She dared not chance searching for the horses, as it would mean crossing in front of the house.

Using the late-afternoon sun for guidance, she set off to the south-east, which would take her towards the tor she had seen from her window. Within a few steps she knew she had not escaped entirely unscathed. Her right ankle was aching and swelling tight within her boot. She must have sprained it during her fall.

She clenched her teeth to overcome the pain as she staggered through the wet mud of the yard and towards the covering gorse of the moor. She had been limping for almost a mile when the sound of galloping horses sent her diving for cover. The light was beginning to fade as she peered through the prickly branches of the gorse to see if she could recognise the riders and call for help. Her heart sank. The thickset figures of the Jowett brothers were all too easily recognisable. To call out to them would be to jump from the frying pan into the fire.

When they had passed, she staggered onward, cursing her ill luck that she had been unable to ride Misty to safety. Had she been too hasty in her need to get away? Now she faced a long walk home and a night on the moor. And what of her beautiful mare? She had been so proud of Misty and the freedom the horse had brought to her life. With Bryn away she had found the mare to be her only confidante, and she could not bear to think of her suffering.

When darkness descended, it did so swiftly. There was no moon, and all around her was like staring into a dark abyss. She stumbled forward for several yards until her boot squelched in water and moisture began to seep up her leg. With a gasp of horror she jerked her foot free and reeled back. The moor was notorious for its bogs, which could drag a person under their lethal slime to their death.

In this obsidian darkness she would lose all sense of direction. Panic built in her breast, her breathing becoming sharp and ragged. Her injured ankle was throbbing and felt as though it would burst through the leather of her riding boot, and her heart was racing so fast that she no longer felt attached to reality. Whichever way she turned or moved, her next step could pitch her into fresh danger.

She sank to the ground and her hand touched a granite boulder. Feeling carefully around her, she could ascertain that the stones spread towards her left and also rose higher. By scrambling over them, she found a hollow filled with rainwater, which enabled her to drink, and there also seemed to be a ledge that would afford her some protection from the elements if she lay beside it. Thankfully the late-September night was warm, and although she would face discomfort and fear, she would not freeze to death.

Rowena lay down and tried to shut out the night sounds and snufflings that were alarming by their unfamiliarity. There was no animal on the moor that could harm her. She must hold that thought and be brave. Although she was exhausted from her walk, sleep would not come, and as solitude and night rustlings set her heart bolting with terror, she felt the presence of St John watching over her. It brought a strange comfort, for she was still angry with him for what she now regarded as the betrayal of her birth. To keep her fears of isolation and danger at bay, she mentally raved at all the members of her family who had abandoned her and brought her to this sorry fate. Most of her anger was directed at Adam Loveday. How glibly he had renounced his parentage. Clearly he did not want her as a daughter. He had shown where his concern and loyalty lay, and that was with Bryn.

Convinced that she would be unable to sleep a wink, she nevertheless fell into a doze as the Jowetts retraced their tracks, and was thus unaware that they were leading Misty and two other riderless horses. Behind them in the direction of the isolated dwelling an orange glow lit the sky, until the flames burned themselves out.

Chapter Thirty-nine

Too many memories and images from his return to Willow Vale crowded Bryn's mind and made sleep impossible. The recollections of his last night here before he fled with Arabella were the most potent. He could not shake the death scene of his mother from his thoughts. It was almost as though her ghost was calling to him. The passage of years had made the vision of her lovely face difficult to recall. He needed to recapture it and was drawn to her bedchamber. He carried a single candle to light his way, and it threw distorted reflections of shadows along the panelled walls, conjuring emotions of that night of terror when, sore and beaten by Carforth, he had followed the sound of weeping.

He pushed wide the door of his mother's bedchamber and was transported back to that night. The room was exactly as he remembered it, except that no figure lay beneath the embroidered coverlet. Everything was spotless. The bed was made, the furniture glowed with the sheen of recent polishing and filled the room with the smell of beeswax. On the dressing table lay his mother's hairbrush and comb, a bottle of her favourite perfume, boxes of face powder and hair pomander, the tiny silver trinket casket where she kept the face patches that she had worn in the early days of her first marriage.

Draped across one chair was her favourite Indian silk shawl. A pair of crimson brocade shoes with a gold buckle was placed beside the chair as though waiting for her to step into them. The lid of the enamelled jewellery casket was closed, and when he raised the velvet lining he found it was bare of gems and pearls. Carforth's greedy hands had looted them, and Bryn angrily snapped the lid shut.

He was drawn to the great carved armoire that had held his

mother's dresses. When he opened it, his heart swelled with grief as the scent of her perfume wafted over him. He swallowed hard as his hands slid over the velvet, lace and silk and he raised a sprigged muslin sleeve to his face. It was the last gown that he remembered his mother wearing. He closed the armoire and raised the candle to where a portrait of his father still hung on the wall.

Bryn stepped closer. Sir Rufus Bryant was in knee breeches, hose and a shot silk azure dress coat and waistcoat edged with gold braid. The background of the portrait was dark, showing the hamlet and church on the estate through a window. His father's hand rested on a table, and beside it was a small carved Celtic cross and a spread of three silver coins. Bryn vaguely recalled that they were Roman denarii that had been found in a field in his grandfather's time when ground was cleared.

He remembered his father showing him the cross, which had always been in the reading room, while the coins had been in a drawer of a table. They were part of the heritage of the ancient people who had once populated this land. He had forgotten about the coins, and seeing their image now iced his blood. His father had considered them of more interest than great value, but had Carforth found them and become fixated that they were part of some larger treasure trove hidden on the estate? The idea was laughable if it did not carry so many horrific memories of his stepfather beating him to discover what he knew of the secret of the treasure.

A sound behind him made him whirl round, ready to use the candlestick as a weapon in case of an attack. He sighed dramatically.

'Josephina, you put the fear of my stepfather into me. When I heard you, I was remembering his cruelty and how often I was beaten.'

Despite the lateness of the hour, the maid was still in her work clothes. 'I sleep in my old bed in the anteroom where I could answer your mama's summons. I wondered who was in your dear mama's bedchamber in the middle of the night.'

'You have kept everything as it was,' he said as his breathing returned to normal after his fright.

'She was more than my mistress; she treated me as her companion. I knew that you would one day return. I wanted everything to be as you remembered.' She put her hands over her eyes and her shoulders shook with silent sobs.

Turning the room into a shrine for his mother was something Bryn found rather unsettling, but Josephina had always been devoted to the murdered woman. He suppressed an inner shiver. The candlelight was playing over the hollows of the woman's face, and when she lowered her hands, her dark eyes reflected the candle flame with a sinister light, which made him uneasy. He dismissed it as foolish, for the coldness of that light was merely the reflection of the servant's tears.

'I noted that Mama's jewellery is missing.' He changed the subject.

'It had all vanished by the time Carforth brought me back to the house. But there is one thing . . . She went to the bedside table and from a drawer took out a velvet pouch and handed it to him.

Bryn opened it, and again his heart threatened to stifle him with emotion. In his hand lay a miniature painting of his mother in a gold frame, which his father had carried everywhere with him.

'I found it wedged in a corner under a chair. Carforth must have missed it when he carried out his looting. I was pleased to be able to save it for you.'

'You have been the most loyal of servants, Josephina. To me this is priceless.'

She bobbed a respectful curtsey. 'Is there anything I can get for you, Master Alexander? A warm drink might help you to sleep.'

'I have all I need. Get some rest yourself. So many unexpected guests has given you a great deal of extra work.'

'To have you here at Willow Vale is the answer to my prayers, Master Alexander. I would willingly serve twice as many to see you take your rightful place.' She curtseyed again and returned to her sleeping quarters in the adjoining anteroom.

Bryn sat a long while on his mother's bed, staring at the miniature, until the candle burned out and he finally fell asleep. His dreams were troubled and disturbing. When he eventually awoke and ventured downstairs to rejoin his companions, he tried desperately to recall the message he felt had been conveyed in those dreams. It continued to elude him as he joined Japhet in the parlour.

'You look like you had a rough night,' his guardian's older cousin said, raising a quizzical brow.

Before he could answer, Josephina bustled in carrying a large plate of eggs, devilled kidneys, sliced ham, freshly baked bread and a tankard of ale, which she placed before Japhet. 'Can I get the same for you, Master Alexander? Oh hark at me, completely forgetting myself all day yesterday.' She bobbed a deep curtsey. 'It is Sir Alexander Bryant now, I suppose.'

'Not until I reach my majority,' Bryn corrected. 'My new family call me Bryn.'

'You will always be Master Alexander to me. I'm sure that your new family meant well in the circumstances.' Her tone was dismissive. 'It has all changed now, and as I recall, devilled kidneys were a favourite of yours, sir. Would you like extra?'

'That would be kind of you, Josephina.' Bryn was uneasy that she might have unwittingly offended Japhet. She seemed to have forgotten her place as a servant.

Japhet appeared not to have noticed her slip and was eating heartily. His expression only sobered as he studied Bryn. 'You do not look like you have had much sleep. It cannot be easy seeing the destruction that has taken place here.'

'It no longer feels like the home I loved.'

'If you feel up to it, we could stroll around the grounds and you could tell me something of its history,' suggested Japhet.

'Is there any point?' There was more anger than desolation in his voice. 'My home has been ransacked of valuables, the servants all but Josephina driven off, and the tenants deprived of their homes and livelihoods.'

Japhet continued to study him before replying. 'When I returned to England, I thought that I had lost everything except for the dream of starting the stud. Even when I discovered that Hannah and Elspeth had continued to raise my mares and first foals and ensured that Tor Farm prospered with a reliable tenant, I did not feel that the stud farm or horses were mine. My family had done so much, yet I felt alienated from the dream. It took me months of working with the horses, and I must have walked miles over the land in that time. Gradually I felt its power return and seep into my bones and my heart, and the changes I instigated put my seal upon the stud. There is no other place I would rather live and work to bring my dream alive now.'

'You had the loyalty of your family behind your years of exile, and their faith that you would return.' Unable to hold Japhet's stare as raw emotions churned through him, Bryn stared at a damp patch on the wall. His voice was stark with yearning. 'They loved you and wanted you to be accepted at Tor Farm as though you had always been its owner. Everything my parents and ancestors worked for was destroyed by the greed of my stepfather. He hated being thwarted of the riches he mistakenly believed were concealed here, and ensured that I would never have the means to rebuild and re-establish the estate.'

'But you had your own dream that Willow Vale would rise from the neglect and corruption Carforth caused.'

'I did not then know the extent of his vengeance.' Bryn picked a cobnut from a dish on the table and hurled it angrily at the wall.

'That dream can still happen,' Japhet urged. 'Carforth could not take the land from you. The land is the soul of this estate. It will provide you with the income you need to return it to its former glory.'

Japhet ate for a time in silence and Josephina brought Bryn's food. He picked at the kidneys, his appetite clearly deserting him.

Japhet said more sternly. 'Eat up. The food will revive you. Then we will walk the land and you will tell me your plans.'

Bryn forced himself to take a few mouthfuls and Japhet resumed talking, his light-hearted banter and the food soon restoring Bryn's spirits. When he had finished eating, the older man stood and grinned at him.

'Do we then walk the grounds and you can give me a history lesson on your ancestors and the estate?'

At first Bryn felt his feet dragging with reluctance, but as they walked through the grounds, Japhet's sharp mind continually prompted him to recall his early childhood. 'How old were you when your father died, Bryn?'

'Six.'

'Do you remember him?'

Bryn closed his eyes, a shadowy image filling his mind and a feeling of love and security that the Lovedays had never been able to replace in his life. 'I remember him well. My brother and I were often at his side when he visited tenants or inspected the work on the estate. In those days there was always laughter.'

'How did he die?' Japhet asked.

'A stupid tragic accident. He was brave, healthy and strong. The lake had frozen and he was teaching my brother and me how to skate. Mama joined us. It was a wonderful time. We spent every day for a week on the ice. There was a small frost fair for our friends and the servants and workers.' The memory of a day of such joy turning so rapidly to misery clutched at his heart and his voice cracked. He paused in their progress across a field and stared in the direction of the lake, which was hidden from sight by a steep bank. 'Mama and Papa were skating arm in arm. She never had very good balance and they were laughing hard as she clung to him and swayed precariously on her skates. Then her legs went from under her and she screamed with laugher, her arms wheeling wildly to regain her balance. Their legs tangled as Papa tried to catch her. He went over backwards, pulling Mama down on top of him. There was a crack like a pistol shot when they hit the ice and they were both giggling that they could not get their footing and had to be hauled to their feet by the servants. The mulled cider had been brought from the house and Papa urged everyone to drink it while it was still hot. Shortly afterwards he complained of a headache and he collapsed as he walked back to the house. Dr Wedlake was a close friend and present at the frost fair, but he could do nothing to save him. Papa was dead before nightfall from hitting his head on the ice.'

'A terrible tragedy,' Japhet commiserated.

Bryn walked on in silence, his thoughts centred upon his father, and he felt the hairs on the nape of his neck tingle. They had been such happy times. He did not want the persecution of Carforth's tyranny to be Willow Vale's epitaph. In honour to his father, the estate must flourish and happy times return.

Eventually he said, 'Mama told me many times that my father was always telling my brother and myself stories about our land. I do vaguely remember sitting on the floor at his feet or walking through the fields, when he would often stop and point out certain landmarks. I cannot remember much of what he told us, I was too young, but one thing I do recall him frequently saying was that the land would always provide for us, that we would never be hungry or poor.'

'He was right. What did the first owner of this estate possess other than the land when he settled here? Or was he immensely wealthy?' Japhet taunted.

'The Bryants never came here until 1560,' Bryn replied as they continued to walk 'The land belonged to a small convent that was destroyed several years earlier by the dissolution of Church lands. It was given to a courtier for his diligence in hounding the nuns out of England. I forget his name. The courtier lost the land in a wager to Sir Ancel Bryant, who gave it as a wedding present to his second son Rufus on his marriage. All that was on the property at that time was the old convent chapel, which was later incorporated into the church.'

'Your kin turned this land from desecration to prosperity,' Japhet pronounced. 'You survived when your stepfather wanted you and everything your family had achieved destroyed. You cannot allow Carforth to win. It may take your lifetime, but you have the courage and strength to restore Willow Vale to be even greater than its former glory.'

Japhet never made empty statements, and as Bryn heard the words, he felt his blood firing with the need to prove this man's faith in him.

'Is that the church through the trees?' Japhet said, striding towards it. 'Why do we not start there? A family vault or tomb is a good place to reconnect with ancestors.'

'The tomb has been smashed. I saw it when I came here and was taken prisoner,' Bryn raged as he matched Japhet's long stride. 'Carforth could not even leave the dead in peace.'

The main door remained barred, and his anger increased when he noticed that another two windows had been smashed. The chancel door was open to the elements, and when they stepped inside he was again assaulted by the stench of rotting vegetation and decay. The marble effigies on the desecrated tombs were ghostly silhouettes in the gloom of the interior.

Bryn was drawn to the mutilated figures, and behind him he heard Japhet curse at the destruction. He sank to his knees and laid his hands over the broken image of his father's fingers. The shock of Carforth's violation was no less a second time, and a sob tore from the depths of his body. He was vaguely aware that Japhet had walked softly away to give him privacy, but he had no concept of how long he knelt in prayer asking for guidance.

When he rose stiffly to his feet, his hand closed over the shape of a cross carved beneath his father's fingers. It was the same as the one in the portrait. It had clearly held great significance to his father and must have been an heirloom that perhaps dated from the time of the convent. The altar was bare of religious artefacts; obviously they had been looted at some time. As his first act of contrition and of pledging a vow to restore Willow Vale, he would find the cross and bring it here. He hoped that St Michael and his angels would then once again bless this land with their love and bounty.

He found Japhet examining the long, low, coffin-shaped gravestones in the far corner of the churchyard. 'These look old,' he said as Bryn joined him.

'They date back to the convent. Out of respect we kept the nuns' graves separate from the later ones.' He pointed to the church, where there was a clear delineation in the two styles of stonework. 'That is the original part of the church, which was the nuns' chapel.'

Bryn was flooded with a sense of pride and history. Japhet had been right earlier when he said that the land was the soul of the estate. The importance of heritage and all that had gone before on this land was important.

He climbed over the low wall at the rear of the churchyard and began searching through the long grass. He called to Japhet.

'Here are the stones from an old temple my father said was Roman.' The childhood memories made him laugh. 'Howard and I spent hours searching for bits of pottery. It was in a dew pond over there that three Roman coins were found. We never found anything.'

Japhet had walked in the direction Bryn had pointed. 'Where was this dew pond?'

He ran to show him. 'Here. There is nothing to see now.'

Japhet crouched down and touched his fingers to the earth. 'The ground is wet and it is late summer. I would not be surprised if this was an old holy well. We have them in Cornwall. They are pagan in origin but the Romans built temples over them and sacrifices were made. Those coins would have been an offering to the old gods.' He stood up and dusted down his knees. 'If Senara were here, she would probably tell you to give them back to the old ones to appease them. I'd say that they were released from their watery depths for a reason. If only to buy a jug of brandy or two to warm a cold heart through the winter.'

They laughed together and Bryn's mood was restored. Japhet could be outrageous, but he had been right to make him recall the happier times from his childhood. This was his land and he would not neglect his responsibilities.

When Bryn later searched the upper rooms, he found the wooden cross along with the Roman coins in the corner of a drawer. They were black with age. It would be dark soon and he wanted to visit the church and state his oath of ownership before the altar. He scooped the coins into his pocket and made a detour to throw them into the damp earth near the old stones.

'It is little enough to give back to you for the plunder that has taken place here.' He paused to say a prayer. 'But it is a token of my faith that I will restore the riches again to this land.'

He was about to enter the church when he heard Adam calling him. He was not aware that his guardian had returned and he was eager to hear his news. Still clutching the cross, he ran back to the house.

Chapter Forty

When the morning mist rising from the land penetrated her clothing, Rowena awoke shivering. The mist was low-lying and the dawn's light was throwing the landscape of the moor into clearer relief. She stood up, determined that when she reached Boscabel she would raise merry hell for all the trials and tribulations she had suffered. But first she had to ensure that her captors did not find her. Her stomach growled with hunger, but at least she was able to quench her thirst with the rainwater in the hollow.

As she climbed down from her ledge on the boulder, fiery agony shot through her injured leg. Lack of food made her light-headed. She had to get away from danger. Warning bells clanged in her mind. She must escape. Forget the pain in her ankle. Keep walking.

Her sore ankle twisted and she bit back a cry of frustration and pushed herself onwards. She checked the direction of the rising sun and the position of the tor to guide her home to Boscabel. It would take her hours to walk and at every step pain lanced through her leg. Every few paces she spun round to ensure that she was not being followed. Her abductors must have discovered by now that she had escaped. She knew where she had been imprisoned and could testify against them. They dared not let her live.

Her heart was pounding so loudly she thought she was hearing galloping horses. Was it her captors, or a search party? The early-morning shadows were playing tricks with her vision. A lone horseman was cantering towards her. It was her father. Confused, she rubbed her eyes. It could not be St John; it must Uncle Adam, but her uncle was not in Cornwall. The image wavered. Her pain and tiredness had created an illusion.

'Oh, Papa. You would have saved me.' She reached out at the

305

spectre, gaining strength from the image. Her father's ghost would guide her home.

But a ghost rode in silence. The pounding hoofbeats vibrated over the ground. Adam had returned in time to save her. Her heart leapt. He did care. It was a sign that as a parent he had sensed her danger and rushed to her rescue.

As rapidly as joy flooded her, it drained. This was no bond of parenthood. It was the ultimate humiliation. Tristan Loveday skittered to a halt, his dark features quizzing and sardonic.

Defiantly she lifted the hem of her riding skirt to speed her progress over the rough terrain and, controlling her grimace of pain and the need to limp, proceeded to walk past him.

To her further mortification, he laughed. 'Stubborn to the core, and I would be the last person from whom you would wish to accept help.'

Her chin tilted higher and ignoring him she struggled on. Every step was torture, her swollen foot feeling it would burst through the leather of her riding boot. From the corner of her eye she saw him wheel his mount and follow behind her.

'As I see it, you have three choices,' Tristan said with infuriating smugness. 'You can swallow that pride and accept a ride to your home now, or I can follow behind you for a mile or so until pain breaks through the dislike you bear me and you accept my assistance. Or I could treat you as the wayward child you are and hoist you protesting and undignified up before me.'

'Put a finger on me and I will lay charges against you for assault,' she seethed.

'I am your uncle, and while I admire your spirit, I am bound to ensure your safety.'

'You are nothing to me.' Her haughteur was scathing. 'You tricked and cheated my father out of our home and he is dead because of you.'

'That is your opinion and I certainly will not explain the truth to you if you are too blinded by hate to acknowledge it.' The reasonable tone increased her determination to discount the objectionable creature.

She tossed back her head and stamped onwards. Her ankle protested at its brutal treatment and twisted over. As she corrected her balance, she gave an involuntary cry of pain. At least she had not fallen to the ground. That would have been the final degradation before her enemy.

Tristan cursed at her foolhardiness. 'Confound you, young miss, I have one woman of your family seriously ill and I have no desire to sit back and see another suffer.'

The words halted her and she spun round. 'Aunt Elspeth! Is she alive?'

'Yes, but it is no thanks to her stubbornness of not riding with a groom. A trait you share. Elspeth is recovering at the Dower House and your aunt Senara is attending upon her. She will be confined to her bed for some weeks.'

The news broke Rowena's resolve to pay no mind to him. 'I feared that she was dead.' Tears ran unashamedly down her cheeks. 'Who found her?'

'Your aunt Hannah. I was searching the moor for Elspeth and came upon them and rode for Dr Yeo. Hannah had arranged for a cart to convey Elspeth to the Dower House. At that time she was still unconscious.'

'And you sent word to Senara?' Rowena continued her suspicion and antagonism.

'Of course,' he clipped out, his exasperation at her obstinacy and rudeness no longer concealed. 'Now do we persist in wasting time in getting you home? You have clearly shown great fortitude in escaping from the men who abducted you. Will you now use your intelligence to conceive that I intend no ill will upon you? Also it would greatly aid Elspeth's recovery for her to learn that you are no longer in danger.' He held out a hand for her to mount behind him.

The prejudices she felt for Tristan warred within her. Adam and Japhet had tempered their own animosity and allowed a truce with him when family matters took precedence. There was a time for maintaining a point of principle and a time when family loyalty overrode past differences. She needed to see Elspeth to assure herself that her great-aunt would survive. If both Hannah and Senara had also buried the hatchet for the sake of unity, she would show her maturity by doing the same, but only for this one occasion. Upon that she was equally determined.

She gripped his hand, and placing her good foot over his boot, sprang nimbly up behind him. He held a silver hip flask over his shoulder.

'It's brandy but the only refreshment I have. It will revive and warm you, but I advise only a few sips.'

She was about to refuse, but now that she was rescued, the events of her kidnapping seemed to swamp her and she could not control her trembling. 'I am grateful, sir. I did find some water in the night.'

He drew a pistol from the saddle holster and fired it in the air. 'That is to inform my men that you have been found and to return to Trevowan.'

She took a long gulp of the brandy. The fiery liquid burned her throat, making her cough and splutter. Her eyes were watering as she handed the flask back to him.

'I did warn you.'

The laughter in his voice rekindled her anger and she turned her head stiffly away to avoid his gaze. She suspected that he set off at a fast gallop just so that she would be forced to place her hands about his waist to ensure that she did not fall off.

'How did you escape?' he shouted back at her.

'My captors were simpletons. But I could not get to Misty. Uncle Adam will make those clodhoppers pay for their crimes.'

'They have already been dealt with.' His words disconcerted her. 'Unfortunately your mare was not at the farm where it was reported you had been held. The house had been burned to the ground and the men's bodies were found inside. You were lucky to have got out. Likely they were drunk when the fire started. You would have died with them.'

'How did you learn where they were?' Her suspicions instantly ignited. 'Were you a party to this outrage? Stop this horse. I wish to dismount.'

As she began to slide her leg over the mount's wide rump, Tristan urged the horse to increase its pace. They were crossing ground splattered with granite boulders.

'Stay where you are? Why the devil would I want to kidnap you? I organised the search party. It was a matter of family honour.' His scathing tone silenced the rest of her accusations, but she still did not trust him, and they rode the rest of the way to Trevowan in silence.

'There is no lawyer in Bridgwater dealing with this estate in either your father's or stepfather's name.' Adam paced the parlour, which was the only habitable community room in the house at Willow Vale. 'A bank admitted that they held the estate's account, but would not reveal the extent of the money deposited with them. Though they showed concern that there had only been withdrawals and no deposits in recent years.'

'So where does that leave us?' Bryn had slumped down on a chair and held the wooden cross between his knees. His hand was absently rubbing over the carved knot pattern as he had seen his father do often in his childhood. The wood was warm beneath his thumb and the gesture gave him small comfort. How was he supposed to restore his home and land when every lead to Carforth was obliterated either by death, tragedy or dead end?

'We keep hunting for Carforth,' Adam declared. 'From his work with the government, my friend Long Tom sent me a list of names of retired intelligence officers who can be hired. Some are already at work, but my last report informed me that your stepfather has not been seen in England for almost a year.'

There was a scuffling by the door, and Japhet opened it and marched in, propelling Josephina before him. 'I found her listening outside.'

'Of course I listen.' Josephina cast an imploring look at Bryn. 'Do I not worry for you? You are my dear lady's child. On her deathbed I promised to her that I would protect you.'

'Josephina is not the enemy,' Bryn protested.

Adam and Japhet regarded each other in a silence that was condemning.

The maid wrenched herself out of Japhet's hold and flung herself at Bryn's feet, weeping profusely. 'You know I would not harm you. Listening was wrong, but I have been so afeared for you, Master Alexander. I listen to hear that Carforth is no longer in control. Then I know you will be safe, and that I will not have to fear his return and punishment.'

'Yet you have not told us everything, have you, Josephina?' Japhet stood over her prone figure. 'Even if you were not here at the time that Carforth committed his worst atrocities, you knew his nature. I would hear more of the man.'

'He was evil.' She covered her face with her hands. 'You can see all around you what he could do.'

'That shows us his nature, but what of him? His background?

309

How he met Lady Bryant when she was widowed?' Japhet rapped out.

The maid's face crumpled in distress.

'A moment, Mr Loveday.' Bryn put the cross on the floor by his side and stood to raise the servant to her feet. He led her to a chair. 'Josephina, I was too young to know much of Carforth. Any information you have may help us to find him.'

She sniffed and wiped her eyes on her apron, taking several moments to regain her composure. 'What do you need to know?'

'How long did you work for Lady Bryant?' Japhet fired at the maid, showing none of his usual courtesy towards an upset woman.

'I was engaged shortly after her widowhood as her maid.'

'And how did that come about?' Japhet continued in a sharp tone. 'Were you recommended to her?'

'She was in Taunton interviewing women to attend upon her needs. She offered me a position at Willow Vale.' Josephina sighed heavily. 'I do so miss her. She could never abide cruelty.' The maid dabbed at her eyes before continuing. 'Lady Bryant was such a sweet and delightful woman. I was devoted to her.'

'And how did Lady Bryant meet Mr Carforth?' Japhet remained expressionless as he pursued his questioning.

Bryn returned to his seat, embarrassed that Japhet was taking such a stern tone with Josephina; he picked up the cross and kept his eyes on the engraving upon it as his fingers absently ran over its surface. Even as he listened to the interrogation, his mind was on honouring his intention of replacing the cross in the church.

Josephina's answer snapped back his attention. 'There was a local summer fair and Lady Bryant attended with friends. I remember the dear boys were so excited. There was to be a fire-eater, a strongman and a wild man in a cage.'

Bryn remembered that day. He and Howard had seen such wondrous sights that he had never forgotten them. They had fallen asleep exhausted during the carriage drive home. He had not realised that it had been the fateful day that Carforth had entered their lives.

His eyes narrowed as the maid added, 'I forget who Lady Bryant said had introduced them. Mr Carforth then became a regular caller at the house.'

'Arabella was his sister, and there was Spanish blood in the family.' Japhet surprised Bryn by changing the course of the interview. 'What do you know of this?'

'I was but a servant. Such matters were not discussed with me.' Josephina did not meet anyone's gaze and twisted her hands in her lap.

'Yet you are Spanish, are you not? Josephina is a Spanish name,' Japhet persisted.

'I am not Spanish.' The maid stared at him as though he had lost his wits. 'I was born in Exeter. My mother was a cook, my father a coachman. My mother heard the name in a play by travelling players and liked it.'

'Yet it is a grand name for the daughter of servants,' Captain Loveday observed with a frown.

'They called me Josie. My employer before Lady Bryant insisted I was called Joan. That she considered to be a proper servant's name. Lady Bryant was different. She called me Josephina.'

'That will be all, Josephina,' Captain Loveday announced abruptly.

'There is much work to be done in the kitchen,' Josephina said, hurrying to return to her work. Before she left the room, Japhet called after her.

'How long after you came to work for Lady Bryant was this summer fair?'

The maid recoiled as though he had shot her, but when she turned to face them her eyes were demurely lowered. 'It was so long ago I get confused over time, but I believe it was the same year.' She dipped a stiff curtsey. 'Will that be all, Mr Loveday?'

Japhet nodded. 'For now.'

When the woman had left the room, Bryn voiced his puzzlement. 'Why the inquisition? And why question Josephina's blood? She was a servant, nothing more.'

'I was curious, that was all,' Japhet replied. 'It seemed a strange coincidence.'

The strain of recent revelations had put Bryn's temper on a short fuse. There were few people he could trust and he had thought these two men were his staunchest allies. Why were they treating Josephina so shabbily?

He slammed the cross down on to the floor and flung out an

accusing arm. 'If it were not for Josephina helping me, I would never have escaped here. Likely I would be dead.'

Neither of the cousins paid him any heed. Both were staring at the floor. Bryn followed their gaze and pain twisted his heart. 'Now I have broken the cross. That was my father's.' Frustration almost choked him.

'I do not think it is broken,' Captain Loveday said, stretching forward to pick it up. He handed it to Bryn.

The base had come away from the cross, and a piece of paper was visible rolled up inside.

Chapter Forty-one

Josephina scrubbed furiously at the baked-on pastry crust on the copper dish she had used to cook last night's supper. Were the men appreciative that she had suddenly been turned into a slave to serve their every need? She doubted it. And the way that arrogant Loveday had put her to the question. Was she not the one who had saved Alexander? The gentry were all alike – if they saw servants at all it was as menials – or some asinine beast of burden with no wits but to follow commands.

She would not be treated in such a manner. The copper pan clattered against the side of the deep bowl as she battled to control her anger. The questioning had left her uneasy. These Loveday men were not like others that she had met. There was a predatory manner about them, an underlying strength of will and purpose, and a complete ruthlessness when it came to anyone who would dare to cross them. They were no fools. The older man had the eyes of one who had looked into the depths of hell and given the Devil a good kicking. They also had culture and charm and only a fool would underestimate them. These men now demanded justice.

A babble of excited words from Alexander carried through the open window. Although his speech was too soft for her to hear, she could sense the anticipation like the braying for blood during a hunt. She stopped her work and hurried to the door, and saw Master Alexander and the two Loveday men talking animatedly as they strode purposefully towards the meadows. She hoped that they would be occupied for some time. There was so much to be done, and so little time.

★

313

'What do you think this means?' Bryn whispered, his body bubbling with a thrilling expectation as they hurried across the field.

'It is a drawing of the church crypt and a niche over an altar.' Captain Loveday also had laughter in his voice. 'That may be all it is.'

'You do not think it could be a map to the treasure that Carforth sought?' Bryn could not help glancing over his shoulder, anxious that no one overheard him.

'You believed that there was no treasure,' Japhet reminded him.

'But there could be.' Bryn was too excited at this unexpected discovery for his enthusiasm to be easily dampened. He raised the cross to his lips and kissed it. 'That's for luck.'

Adam's laughter was rich and strong. 'It looks as though we may find that out in the next few minutes. But I have to warn you that if it is a map, it seems too convenient and easy.'

Japhet lengthened his stride. 'Stop raining on this young man's hopes. He will need a miracle to find the money to restore his home and land.'

The church was cooler than outside, the colder temperature raising goose bumps on Bryn's skin. Their boots resounded on the flagstones of the nave. As Bryn passed the tomb of his grandfather, he could not resist running his hand over the broken fingers of the effigy. The hand clasped the Celtic cross. Did that mean it was a hidden sign relating to the treasure? 'I was here praying for a miracle when you called out on your return. I had even thrown an offering into the pool that Mr Loveday said was a pagan well where offerings were made to ensure good fortune.'

'You have spent too long in my wife's company,' Adam jested. 'You have become as superstitious as her.'

They paused at the top of the steps to the crypt. Little light penetrated its sunken interior. Japhet drew his tinderbox and struck the flint repeatedly against the stone, the sparks illuminating the tension in his lean cheeks. When the tinder caught alight he held it aloft, casting eerie shadows over the fan-vaulted roof and crevices as they cautiously proceeded.

It was dank and chilling as a tomb.

'There is a candle stub on the altar.' Bryn grabbed it and held the wick to the flame. He placed the candle back on the stone altar, and as the flame steadied and flared higher he found that he was holding his breath. He exhaled with a rush. 'There is the niche above the altar the same shape as the cross.'

He pressed the cross into the aperture. He did not know what he expected to happen, but when nothing did, disappointment pummelled him like boulders in a landslide.

In his frustration he kicked out at a stone pillar. 'Nothing. Why draw a diagram of the niche with the cross positioned inside it? Was that some sick jest of Carforth's?'

Adam rubbed his chin as he stared at the wall and cross. 'That is how myths get started, I suppose.'

'There must be more to it.' Japhet pressed and prodded the cross. 'I've seen secret compartments revealed by similar devices.'

'But not this one.' Bryn whirled and ran up the steps and out into the fresh air. His chest was weighted with disillusion. His hopes had been high, only to be cruelly crushed. He marched to the house. He needed to be alone. The enormity of the task that would lie ahead of him if he was ever to restore the Bryant property seemed impossible. It would have been better if his memory had never returned than the brutal reality of all that he had lost.

He hurried through the house, his feet following old patterns as he headed to the north tower. The stone spiral staircase to the upper reaches of the turret was steep and he was breathing raggedly as he wrenched open the trap door at the top and stepped on to the roof. His eyes narrowed as he stared at the empty flagpole that had not raised the Bryant standard since his father's death. In a light breeze the rope lanyard clanged against the wooden pole and he fingered the frayed hemp. That would need replacing along with just about everything else. The flag must be stored somewhere, and he hoped that the moths had not eaten its silk.

His mood remained sombre as he stepped to the crenellated wall and gripped the stonework, and his stare misted as he regarded the devastation and neglect all around him. His back slid down the side of the masonry until he squatted on the lead roof and lowered his head into his hands. It was a lifetime ago that he and Howard had come here as children playing out piratical or crusader adventures. Then, as far as they could see, crops had ripened in the sun, livestock had idly grazed and fattened, and the drone of voices from the gardeners, grooms, maids and field workers had carried on the air.

Those had been the good days. The happy days. The loving and carefree days.

Later the tower had become a place of retreat to escape the beatings and punishment of his stepfather. Finding no peace on the roof of the tower and only more unanswered questions, Bryn returned despondently to the lower level. As he stepped out of the staircase turret, he saw Josephina unlocking the door of his stepfather's old bedchamber and going inside. Why had the door been locked, and what was she doing there? And why had she looked so furtive?

Still inside the crypt, Japhet and Adam continued to stare at the cross as though it could convey to them its secret meaning.

Japhet finally raised his hands in surrender. 'It is all some nonsensical ploy. Old estates always have their myths and legends. The tragedy is that this one has created more damage than most. It feasted on a man's greed and caused untold suffering and the death of innocents.'

'I am not so sure.' Adam rubbed his chin thoughtfully. 'It has been too easy and obvious. Perhaps we have missed something.'

'Now I know where that rapscallion Joel gets his crack-brained fancies from. His father.' Japhet shook his head in mock sadness. 'It would have been too miraculous to find a casket of gold hidden behind this wall.'

Adam kept his focus on the carved cross. The candle stub was flickering oddly, throwing the carving into higher relief. He spun on his heel, staring into the shadows of the crypt. The air was musty, and he could feel his chest tightening from lack of air.

'Are you having trouble breathing, cousin?' he asked.

'I have no love for confined spaces. I spent too long in them when I was arrested. The air is somewhat stale.'

'Then why is the candle flickering so energetically? If I was a fanciful man, I would say it is all but beckoning us to look closer.'

'And if I were still a gambling man, I would wager my last guinea that there is another source of air.'

Adam had stepped closer to the niche and snatched the cross from where it rested. 'There is more to this engraving than first appears. The middle section has three raised segments.' For a long moment he stared intently at the carved aperture and then ran a finger over its surface. With a grin he replaced the cross, but this time the carving was positioned against the wall, the undecorated side facing them. He gave it an extra tap. There was a faint click, but nothing else happened.

'Nice try,' Japhet taunted. 'Now let us go. I have spent too long down here.' He strode purposefully to the steps.

'Wait!' Adam called; he was scraping at the edge of a stone with his dagger. 'I could do with some extra leverage. Put your dagger here.' He had run his finger down a hairline crack in the aperture and pointed to a mark about a foot above the floor.

Japhet complied, and found to his surprise that the blade slipped into a deep crevice.

'Keep working at it,' Adam said, as he pushed his own dagger deeper into the wall and forced it further along the crack.

'There's something here, an obstruction like a lever,' panted Japhet from his uncomfortable crouching position. There was a louder click and the wall and altar moved a fraction forwards. 'By all that's holy!' he chuckled. His fingers prised the edge of the slot, and with Adam working above him, they managed to pull the altar forward a few more inches.

Adam held the candle to the crack and gave a low whistle. 'There is definitely a room or gap behind here.'

It took several more minutes of struggle before the two men were able to move the wall far enough open to peer inside. 'There are stone steps and what looks like a tunnel leading away,' Adam declared.

'We had better go and find your ward.' Japhet sounded as excited as Adam would have expected his young son Joel to be.

He put a hand on his cousin's arm to stop him. 'It could just be a tunnel used as an escape route in more troubled times, or a hiding place for contraband, for that is a trade that has existed for centuries. Bryn does not need to have his hopes raised and dashed again today. Let us investigate first.'

Japhet nodded. 'The way he took off, he did seem to need some time to himself. Time for him to explore later if it is just an old tunnel.' He bowed to Adam and handed him the candle. 'This was your discovery, so you have the privilege of leading the way.'

Chapter Forty-two

When Tristan halted by the Dower House, Rowena did not wait for him to assist her to dismount. She leapt to the ground and hurried to pay her respects to Aunt Elspeth with a grudging 'I am much obliged to you, Mr Loveday'.

The stairs creaked announcing her approach and brought Jenna Biddick running from the back of the house to call up to her, 'Oh, Miss Loveday, praise the Lord you be safe. But you cannot go into Miss Elspeth, Mrs Loveday be changing her dressings.'

'Bring me something hot to drink, Jenna,' Rowena ordered, disregarding the maid's announcement.

She burst through the open door of her aunt's bedchamber, her voice gruff with worry. 'How is she? I thought she had been killed.'

'Rowena, that is no way to conduct yourself in a sickroom.' Senara had been cleansing the wound on Elspeth's temple, and although her tone was sharp, her face relaxed with relief at discovering her niece apparently unharmed.

Elspeth had been lying with her eyes shut and they now snapped open. She twisted her head to regard Rowena, the poultice Senara had put in place sliding on to the pillow, the herb balm staining the lace border. 'Can I not have a moment's peace? If it is not one person making a great ado over me it is another. How are you, child? You do not look too much the worse for your ordeal. I trust those knaves are in custody.'

'Elspeth, do not vex yourself so. I will have to prepare another poultice now.' Senara scooped the mess from the pillow and glanced at Rowena. 'I will be finished here soon. Then I shall examine you. We have been witless with worry over you. You were limping and your face is scraped. Have you other injuries? Where were you taken? Are the men apprehended?' The outburst was so unlike Senara's usually cool composure and showed the depths of her fears. Her sharp stare was assessing Rowena's injuries and judging that they were not too serious. 'You do not look as though you are badly harmed. I am relieved that you are safe.'

'So many questions! They can wait until we reach Boscabel.' Rowena was flippant, determined to show a brave face. 'Is Aunt Elspeth out of danger?'

'They are making too much fuss,' Elspeth muttered. 'Where is my pince-nez that I may see you more clearly, child? Step closer.'

Senara straightened and put her hands on her hips as she stared down at her patient. 'As you can see, your aunt is not the easiest of patients. I will not be returning to Boscabel for another few days to ensure that she stays in bed and does no more damage to her hip, and that the fever does not return. Her leg is also in a splint and will take some weeks to heal. For now she must rest.'

'This woman is a shrew,' Elspeth snapped. 'My nephew's life must be a misery.'

'And for the first time in your life, our less than sweet-tempered aunt, you are not able to get your own way.' Senara wagged an admonishing finger at the woman few people dared to contradict.

'You sound in fine form, Aunt Elspeth,' Rowena chuckled.

'Even the young whippersnapper here shows no respect.' The old woman's glare was withering. 'Do not take advantage that we are all relieved to find you safe and apparently not too badly served from your ordeal. You have a great deal to be grateful to your cousin Tristan for, young miss.'

'He did not rescue me from those brutes.' Rowena flared. 'I escaped through a window last night and he found me on the moor this morning as I was walking home.'

'And you think that he has nothing more important with which to occupy his time than gadding about on the moor searching for an ungrateful minx? Senara tells me that he organised a search party taking men from their work at no loss of wages.' Elspeth scowled. 'Your prejudice is as ill-conceived as your ingratitude.'

'Perhaps you should wait downstairs, Rowena,' Senara said pointedly. 'Upsetting your aunt will not aid her recovery.'

The accusation stung. 'Did I not put my prejudices aside to come

319

here to ensure that Aunt Elspeth was recuperating? I had vowed never to set foot on this property.'

Despite her pain, Elspeth would not let the matter rest. 'After so many slights and recriminations from you, young lady, Tristan would be within his rights to ban you from the land where he is now master.'

'I have had the most horrendous ordeal and you defend him.' Rowena bit her lower lip to stop it trembling as her rage rekindled. 'I wasted my energy coming here. How am I to return to Boscabel?'

'You will go nowhere until I examine your injuries.' Senara regretted her outburst when she saw her niece's pain. 'We are all overset by your kidnapping and Elspeth's injury, and have had little sleep. We all need to take the time to calm ourselves.'

Tristan was about to enter the main house when the approach of riders drew his attention. His expression hardened at recognising his visitors. Lady Alys, who had been notified of Rowena's rescue, had stepped outside on her way to the Dower House. She gasped at encountering the intruders.

'Are they not the family of thieves and murders from the moor?' she whispered to her husband. 'And is that Rowena's mare they have with them?'

'Go inside, my dear. I will deal with this. There is no need for you to be subjected to coarseness.'

'I have encountered far worse when gaining information for our government,' she tartly reminded him. 'Pray do not patronise me.'

Tristan kept his narrow gaze upon the Jowetts and bit back a terse reply. Although he admired the courage of his wife, since their marriage he had found it difficult to accept the independence and fortitude that often put them at odds with each other. This last year their relationship had become more strained, their affection for each other coloured by resentment of a continual contest of wills.

'I hear there be a reward for this fine horse,' Gabriel Jowett declared. 'Five guineas, was it not?'

'You have keen hearing, for I was not aware of such a reward,' Tristan replied.

'She be a valuable mare. Thought an upstanding gentleman as yourself would compensate a man when he put himself to much inconvenience on your behalf.' There was a slyness to Gabriel's tone that Tristan did not trust. When the man pulled his forelock and nodded to Lady Alys, Tristan became uneasy. This was Jowett's way of seeking recompense for not taking retribution upon Davey Rabson for releasing the cattle hidden on his farm.

'A reward would be in order, would it not, Tristan?' Lady Alys suggested. 'Although such a high sum may not be appropriate when Mr Jowett is but performing a neighbourly duty to return the property of another. Horse stealing is a hanging offence.'

'A man can be hanged for many crimes,' Jowett sneered. 'I be as law-abiding a citizen as the next man.'

Tristan was done with Jowett's games and innuendoes. He replied dismissively, 'Take the mare and tether her to the hitching ring at the Dower House, Jowett. Then go to the estate office, where you will receive your reward.'

'I be obliged to you, Mr Loveday.' He trotted away.

When Gabriel returned to the estate office Tristan was waiting for him, and at encountering his expression Jowett no longer looked so cocky.

'Try something like that again and I will kill you,' Tristan promised.

'Five guineas is little enough for the price of the lives of the two men who died in the farmhouse fire.'

'Learning who they worked for and why my niece was kidnapped would have been a greater advantage. Did you discover that?'

'That mare be worth five guineas to you,' Jowett sullenly countered.

'And for the information I wanted I would have paid a great deal more. That is why you and your brothers are small-time crooks and always will be without me. By coming here you sought to embarrass or intimidate me. I would have rewarded anyone who returned the mare. Here, take your money – one silver crown – for your trouble.' He slammed the money on to the desk. 'Now get out of my sight.'

Rowena was dozing in a chair in Elspeth's parlour when Senara came to tend her injuries. She had eaten a thick slice of cherry cake and drunk several cups of tea and her ordeal had finally taken its toll on her stamina.

Senara wrinkled her nose at the smell of pigs that rose from her niece's clothing. The velvet was smeared with ingrained filth, the crushed nap of the material ruined beyond repair. A knife had been used to cut away Rowena's riding boot to release the swollen foot and her stocking had been removed, the bruised ankle resting on a footstool.

'Cool compresses will reduce the swelling. Fortunately the ankle is sprained and not broken,' Senara said after her examination. 'The cut to your head is not serious, but your riding habit has not survived its mistreatment. You will need a new one when Adam again permits you to ride.'

'It was not my fault,' Rowena protested. 'Why was I taken and Aunt Elspeth attacked? Was it connected to the attack upon Bryn?'

'I fear that may be so. Tristan is making enquiries. And before we go any further, you owe him an apology for your your rudeness.'

'Never.' Rowena remained mutinous.

'Perhaps when you look outside you will change your mind. Now are there any other injuries I have not seen? Bridie will prepare a tisane, which will help with the pain when you return to Boscabel. Fraddon has been summoned to collect you.'

'Will Elspeth recover with no ill effects? The damage to her leg and hip, will it allow her to ride? She will hate it if she loses her greatest passion.'

Senara shook her head sorrowfully. 'It will take some months, but if she is a good patient she will recover and be able to ride again.'

There was a scrunch of wheels and a shout from Fraddon outside. Rowena levered herself from the chair and put her foot tentatively on the floor. Without the pressure of the boot it was a great deal less painful. Then she heard a familiar whinny and hobbled to the window.

'It is Misty. They found her.' Uncaring that her injured foot was unshod, Rowena limped outside as fast as she was able to throw her arms around her mare's neck. 'I feared she had been harmed, or I had lost her.' Her words were muffled as she buried her face into the mare's mane.

'Tristan offered a reward for her return,' Senara said, having joined her niece. 'Five guineas I believe it was. Another reason why you should address him with more respect.'

Rowena hung her head, relief at her reunion with Misty

dispersing her anger and resentment. She drew a deep breath before replying. 'I will seek him now and ask his pardon.'

'You cannot walk on that foot, especially without a shoe.' Senara knew she was wasting her words. Rowena was already proceeding with slow precision to prevent the need to hobble at an ungainly gait.

Tristan appeared from the estate office on his return to the main house and frowned as he saw her approaching, but he did not halt his progress.

She lifted a hand to detain him, which he apparently did not notice. Then she called, 'Mr Loveday, one moment if you please.'

Again he did not halt. 'Mr Loveday.' She raised her voice. 'Mr Loveday!'

He paused reluctantly, his tone clipped. 'Should you be walking on that foot? I would not have my cousin accuse me of neglecting your welfare.'

'Mr Loveday, I would crave your pardon. I have been ungracious and ungrateful.'

'You have indeed, child, but it no more than I expect from you.'

Her chin titled in defiance. 'I ask your pardon, but if you do not choose to grant it, then so be it. But Aunt Elspeth is safe because of your consideration and diligence, and I had feared that I would not see Misty again. She is very precious to me. Uncle Adam will reimburse you for the reward you paid for her return.'

'Again you insult me.' He stood with legs braced and his hands gripped the lapels of his fashionable jacket. The sun glinted off the heavy chain of a hunter watch draped across his embroidered waistcoat and a large emerald ring also caught the rays of the light. 'The ties of kinship bind us, I expect the courtesy of the correct form of address.'

Her pride rebelled. He expected too much. Was her gratitude and humble supplication not enough? Her eyes flashed dangerously and she saw the corner of his full lips twitch, but could not discern whether from anger or mockery.

Controlling her ruffled temper, she dipped a curtsey, her voice taut. 'I am beholden to you for your generosity, sir.'

He raised a dark, sardonic brow, clearly not satisfied. He was intent upon making her squirm, the words of gratitude like crushed glass gagging her throat. 'I am beholden to you for your generosity

. . . Uncle Tristan.' The final words were a hoarse whisper.

He bowed, the mockery and challenge vibrant in his reply. 'Your servant, niece. You are welcome to visit Aunt Elspeth whenever you please during her convalescence.' He frowned at the sight of Rowena's bare foot protruding from the hem of her habit. 'I trust you do not sustain any lasting injury from your experience. Fraddon is waiting to convey you back to Boscabel.'

Dismissed like a recalcitrant schoolgirl, Rowena summoned all her dignity to wait for Fraddon to bring the carriage to her. Misty was already tethered behind. She muttered to herself, 'Do not think that this means I have forgiven you.'

Tristan's amused chuckle caused her hackles to rise, and her head to tilt more defiantly as she stepped into the waiting carriage.

Chapter Forty-three

Bryn moved slowly and silently to lift the latch of his stepfather's bedchamber. As the door inched open, he gagged on the stench from within. It was the smell of putrefying flesh and sickness. He put a kerchief to his nose and mouth and was about to open the door wider when he heard Josephina talking softly as she shuffled around the room.

'Not long now, my love. A slow death was what you deserved. I knew once you learned that the boy had been snooping around that you would come back. Even I could not have predicted how aptly fate would have played into my hands when you did.'

The words were chilling and halted Bryn from stepping inside. Who was Josephina addressing? There was no response. The thought of entering Carforth's room sent shivers along Bryn's spine. He could never walk past the closed door as a child without feeling absolutely terrified.

The continued speech within kept him frozen with horror.

'The pain must be beyond endurance,' Josephina chuckled. 'Is it bad enough to drive you insane? You always preferred to be the one to inflict great suffering on another. Like all bullies you are weak and craven when the tables are turned.'

A floorboard creaked and Bryn edged back from the door. When the voice continued on the far side of the room, he leaned closer, caution restraining him from bursting in and confronting the servant. Her words puzzled him and also aroused his curiosity.

'After all the pain and jealousy you put me through and all that we had planned and endured together, you were going to abandon me here. Did you think after so many years of me waiting for you to acknowledge our love that I would meekly allow that to happen?

But the young master changed your plans by his visit. You knew you needed me. You were too arrogant to understand in the past that none of this would have been possible without me by your side. You thought I was a foolish girl too besotted with you to see through your treachery.'

An inhuman, muffled sound iced Bryn's blood. Again Josephina laughed softly. 'Have you not learned by now that no one will hear your cries? A pity that our visitors returned so speedily, otherwise your suffering would have been more prolonged.'

There was another strangulated noise, and the sound of the maid's cruel chuckle enclosed Bryn's heart with ice. Her next words shook the foundations of all he believed.

'You played me for a fool, Eugene. You betrayed me. Flaunted your mistresses. In your conceit you thought yourself the master. You forgot that I had planned it all and made it happen. I did it for you. You were my love – my life. Yet in the end your greed destroyed our chance of happiness.'

Bryn reeled from the confession. If what he had heard was true, Josephina and not Carforth was the evil that had invaded his home and destroyed his family and the lives of countless others.

He pushed the door wide, and what he witnessed drained the blood from his face. His stomach churned with horror. Josephina was bending over the bed, a phial held to the contorted mouth of a man. The face looked disfigured, and it took some moments for Bryn to realise that it was because it was distorted by the iron bands of a scold's bridle. The torture device held the man's lips slightly open whilst allowing only muffled sounds to emerge from his mouth. Josephina was holding the phial over the opening and allowing a trickle of liquid to spill over his tongue. The man's eyes were bloodshot and stared in bulging terror. The stench within the room made Bryn gag, and he noticed that the lower part of the bedcovers was soaked in dried blood.

He could not control a shocked gasp.

Josephina emptied the phial into Carforth's mouth and turned to face Bryn. Her eyes were glazed and her malicious countenance was that of a hate-filled stranger. 'A pity that you witnessed that, Master Alexander. No doubt you also heard my words. Another misfortune. I had hoped to spare you and your new-found kin – at least until you had remembered where the treasure was hidden. We tore the place apart, but your home guarded its secret closely.'

Bryn could not drag his gaze from the bed. He had thought never to set eyes on Carforth again without disgust and loathing. Now he felt chilling horror. His stepfather's body was jerking and straining at its bonds, the muscles twitching in a macabre death dance. Spittle frothed at his mouth, his face locked into a silent scream of agony before the body sagged and went completely still.

While Bryn's attention had been upon his dying stepfather, Josephina had grabbed a curved dagger from a chest top behind her. 'Now you give me no choice, Master Alexander.' She moved with surprising speed for a woman of her weight and age. 'It is your turn now to die. This blade is dressed with the same poison as I used on the man who betrayed me. It is a lingering and painful death.'

Unaware of the danger facing his ward, Adam advanced slowly into the widening space behind the altar in the crypt. The fragile light from the candle revealed the darkness of a narrow tunnel stretching ahead of them. The roof was about four feet high and both men were forced to bend double. He moved cautiously, aware of the dangers of cave-ins and the lack of oxygen that could claim an unwary life. The continued flickering light confirmed that oxygen was present, but that could be coming from the opening behind them. There was no telling if this was an escape route dating back to the time of the nuns, or a hiding place for contraband. It looked too large for the latter, and he held the candle higher, examining the walls.

Deep grooves showed where picks had been hacked into the rock as the floor sloped steadily downwards. Adam stopped abruptly when a black cavern appeared at his feet.

'There's a ladder leading down to a deeper level,' he stated, trying to peer into the darkness.

'It will be old and rotten,' Japhet advised. 'It could be a death trap. We will have to return later with better equipment.'

'It looks sturdy to me.' He put a foot on the first rung to test it and examined the side rails of the wood more closely. 'There is no sign of rot. It is remarkably dry down here. The drop does not look more than ten feet. You stay there while I investigate in case I get into trouble.' He began to descend.

'This is madness, Adam. With more men and rope it will be

easier.' Japhet had lain on his stomach to follow his cousin's progress.

'I will take no undue risks,' Adam called back. 'I am beginning to suspect that this is some kind of a mine working. It may be heartening news for Bryn. He has suffered one disappointment on top of another since arriving here.'

'If it was a mine, it will have been worked out.' Japhet did not share the same enthusiasm. He was no expert on mines, although they provided Cornwall with its greatest income, and stone mine housings both current and in ruin were evident all over the county.

The faint ring of light disappeared as Adam advanced further and Japhet was pitched into complete darkness. He felt his throat close and the walls press in upon him. His abhorrence of confined spaces made an icy sweat break out on his body, and he forced himself to breathe slowly and evenly. He glanced behind him, but they had come too far for the entrance to the tunnel to be visible. Instead he kept his focus on the distant sound of his cousin's movements. The candle stub would not burn much longer and he did not relish having to claw their way back to the crypt in total darkness.

Each beat of his heart thudded loudly in his chest, and the feeling of oppression grew with every second. The need to get out of the tunnel was overwhelming. He urged, 'Adam, you will not discover anything with such a poor light. We should go back and get some lanterns at the very least.'

'Hell and damnation!' Adam's voice was sharp.

'What's happened? Are you hurt?' Japhet shouted.

'The candle has gone out. I am on my way back. It was a single tunnel but the air is not good.' His voice was slow and laboured.

'Do not waste it by talking.'

Japhet eased back from the top of the ladder, relieved when he felt the wood judder as Adam began his climb.

The sound of his cousin's ragged gasps for air made Japhet aware of the tightness to his own chest. When he felt the touch of his cousin's hand on his leg, he retraced their steps to the crypt. Twice he grimaced as his head thudded against the roof. Lack of air had turned his limbs leaden, and behind him Adam groaned and stumbled to the ground. Japhet halted to aid him.

'Go on,' Adam gasped. 'No air.' Too weak to walk, he heaved himself forward on his hands and knees.

Japhet fared little better. His head was floating and his legs had turned to aspic. 'Keep going,' he urged. 'The crypt is not far.'

He staggered on. The entrance to the crypt had swung back so that only a crack of air was squeezing through. On the point of collapse, Japhet threw all his weight against the stone, and as it swung further open, he fell to the floor of the crypt. He drew great gulps of air and was about to turn and haul Adam to safety when his cousin flopped sweating and panting on the ground beside him.

It was several moments before either had the strength to speak.

'That has got to be the most foolhardy escapade in years.' Japhet had rolled into a sitting position and drew his knees up, his head resting against the wall of the crypt.

Adam grunted with laughter. 'I would have given my boys a sound beating if they had been so reckless.'

'We are getting too old for such nonsense.' Japhet wiped the sweat from his face with his hand, his breathing becoming less painful and easier.

'But he who never ventures never gains.' Adam grinned widely. 'I believe it is an old mine. I am sure there is lead down there, and though I am no expert, possibly a small seam of silver.'

'Why was it never brought to the surface?'

'The cost could have been prohibitive and the amount too small, but there may be a way that it can be used to bring some sort of order to this estate.'

'Or it could all come to nothing and Bryn would have had another hope dashed,' Japhet warned. 'We could have discovered the answer to the riddle of a hidden treasure, which could have grown out of an earlier expectation of the mine yielding riches.'

Japhet stood up and held out his hand to assist Adam to his feet. The cousins slapped each other on the back and grinned.

Adam felt optimistic. 'Bryn deserves some luck. The lad has had so much taken from him. This estate has the taste of evil and destruction in the air, but those times are past. Come, let us tell Bryn the good news. His troubles could be over.'

Chapter Forty-four

Catapulated from his shock and horror, Bryn countered the maid's attack. Hatred had given her surprising strength, but the years of his fencing training had sharpened his reflexes. The blade was glinting close to his neck when he grabbed Josephina's wrist, forcing the dagger away from his flesh.

'Good God, woman, what has possessed you? Carforth was evil, but for you to cold-bloodedly murder him . . .' His disbelief that she could be so ruthless dried his speech.

'He did not deserve to live.'

'But to kill him makes you no better. How could you murder someone you profess to love?'

'My love for him was all-consuming. Love thrives on hope. When hope is constantly ground to dust and there is only pain, it festers into hatred. What is left is an abiding need for vengeance, to have him suffer as he inflicted wretchedness and misery upon me.'

Bryn stared at her whilst a new horror dawned upon him, her earlier speech now making greater sense. 'They say poison is a woman's weapon. Did you also murder Mama?'

'I did this to save you. He wanted you dead.' The wildness in her eyes increased as she struggled to break his hold.

Bryn twisted her hand and the blade was now within a finger's breadth of Josephina's neck. 'Why did you want Mama dead? What had she ever done to you but shown kindness?'

'I saved your life. And Arabella's.' Her eyes were rolling in desperation as she watched the dagger rest almost upon the skin of her neck.

'You got us out of the way. Why?' The puzzle that had for so long eluded him was clicking into place. 'What was Carforth to you? Did you introduce him to Mama? It was not long after you became her maid that he began to pay court to her.'

'You would not kill me, Master Alex. I adored your mama.'

'But Carforth was more to you. Why? As a child I remember you and he often whispering together. I saw you coming out of his room.'

'I was a servant. Nothing more,' she protested.

'I saw him kissing you once.' The memory smote him. Incensed by her treachery and lies, he pressed the dagger closer to her skin. 'Tell me everything, or you will die a long and painful death as did my mama.'

'You mistake the matter, Master Alex. He was a lecher. No maid was safe.' She craned her head back and sweat glistened on her face. 'I spit on his memory. He betrayed your mama. He betrayed everyone. He wanted the money. The treasure that could not be found.'

'That was not what I overheard when you were goading him. Did he betray you, Josephina?' Bryn accused. 'Was he your lover?'

'It was me he loved. Not her.' Hysteria slashed the last remnant of sanity from her reasoning. 'He was to marry your mother. We would live well on the money. I would still be his mistress and in time, when his rich wife died, we would marry. But that was not enough for him. He wanted everything for himself. It became an obsession. What he could not have, he destroyed.'

'Was that also your maxim, Josephina?'

'I saved you,' she pleaded. 'It was Carforth who murdered your poor brother and dear mama, not me. I was taunting him to add to his suffering. I was lying. Carforth is the one who is evil. I saved you from him.'

The need to know the answers to so many questions stopped him plunging the dagger into her treacherous heart. To get her to speak he must make her believe that he wanted her to die slowly.

'How long did it take Mama to die? Days? Weeks? Tell me the truth, Josephina, or that will be your end. What happened to the villagers? Why was the hamlet destroyed?'

'That was Carforth.' Her expression was wild, her terror building that he would carry out his threat. 'Rumours were being spread about the deaths of your family. He blamed the villagers. A few of the more loyal ones began to demand that you be shown to them.

They believed he had also killed you. A lawyer came and asked awkward questions. Also the lord lieutenant of the county questioned him. In his rage Carforth turned the villagers from their homes. It was winter and they had nowhere to go but the poorhouse. The men rebelled and that night set fire to the manor. In retribution Carforth razed their cottages, then he fled the district.'

'And you, how came you did not go with your lover?' he ground out in his fury.

'He had beaten me senseless and left me for dead. But I did not die. The need for revenge gave me the strength to survive.' She was whining and wheedling in her terror.

Bryn hardened his heart. It would have been easy to accept that she spoke the truth. Because he had trusted her and believed her lies, the pain of her betrayal was far worse than if it had been Carforth who had killed his family. 'So why would he have come back, if there was nothing left?'

'Because he was obsessed by the tales of treasure. He could not stay away. He feared the locals would kill him, so he hired henchman to keep them away and put mantraps in the grounds.' Her laugh was shrill and hysterical. 'He blundered into one when returning drunk one night from his whore.'

How much of that was true and how much was the maid's desperation to save her own hide? Bryn was stunned by her revelations. Had she been responsible for all the carnage and destruction to his home and family? If so she deserved to die. At the very least she had been a party to her lover's treachery.

She must have sensed the change in him; the disgust and anguish that smote him had to be carved into his eyes and expression.

'It was Carforth who destroyed your home and murdered your family,' she insisted. 'I stayed here to save you. I knew you would return and that Carforth would never allow the treasure to slip from his grasp. He would torture and kill you to reveal its secret. How could I allow my sweet lady's son to so suffer?' she babbled. 'Do not poison me. Not with that dagger. Plunge it into my heart, but not the poison, I beg you.'

'I would not stain my soul with murder,' Bryn snarled. 'But you will die. By the hand of the law. My guardian's men are out gathering evidence from any who will give witness to the persecution that went on here after my mother's death. Your crimes are many: not least murdering the kindest and sweetest of women, ordering my kidnap – which must have been you and not Carforth – the destruction of my home and embezzlement of my fortune. The punishment for such crimes is to be flogged at the cart tail whilst you are paraded through the town, spat upon and reviled, and then you will be hanged.'

'No, young master. I am innocent. I killed Carforth to save your life,' she pleaded.

Her lies and betrayal sickened him. 'On the morrow you will be taken to Taunton and charges laid against you.'

The loud, excited voices of the Loveday men shouted to Bryn from below. It caused him to momentarily look away from the maid. It was enough to allow her to break free and she ran from the death chamber.

'Up here!' Bryn yelled as he ran after her. He cursed his inexperience and stupidity in letting her escape.

Josephina was heading for the turret. He ran after her and could hear the Loveday cousins pursuing them. When he ran out on to the roof, Josephina was climbing on to the parapet. Adam and Japhet were seconds behind him.

'Do not jump, Josephina!' Bryn cried.

She teetered precariously. Bryn edged forward, holding out his hand. 'Do not do this, Josephina.'

'You think I could survive prison?' Her eyes remained wild. 'This way is better.'

'Noooooo!' His scream echoed around the nearby hills as she leapt over the side.

Adam grabbed his arm as he ran to peer over the edge. Her body was twisted and a slow stream of blood spread across the flagstones. Bryn could not stop shaking as the horror of the last hour gripped his body.

'She killed Carforth. He was in a room below us all the time we have been here and we did not know. She poisoned him. She poisoned my mother. She tried to kill me with a poisoned dagger. She was the one who introduced Carforth to my mother. She was his lover. All that happened here was her plan for them to get rich. She thought nothing of destroying my family. I never suspected her. She duped us all.'

Adam held him tight. 'Do not blame yourself for that. She is dead now. It is better this way.'

'But I have not avenged the wrongs to my family. I failed them.' Bryn beat his hands upon the parapet until his knuckles were bloody.

Adam gripped them and shook him hard. 'You did everything you could. You discovered the truth. You could not have stopped them before this. It took courage to face the demons from your past.'

'But it achieved nothing. I could not even bring her to justice.'

'Would you rather have had her blood on your hands?' Japhet said sternly. 'A trial would have taken months. It would have dragged your good name through the mire. This is justice. In prison she would never have lived to come to trial. Once her evil deeds were known, especially that out of greed she had thrown families with young children out of their homes to face the winter without an income or shelter, the other inmates would have inflicted every degradation and torture upon her. Would you have wanted that on your conscience?'

'Japhet is right,' Adam consoled. 'Their evil is no more. You have avenged your family by putting an end to their reign of terror. Now you have to think to the future.'

Chapter Forty-five

The cycle of the year moves inexorably on and man is but a part of nature's force. That was how Senara saw the passing of the months. If May Day marked the beginning and rebirth of life upon the land and a time of forward thinking and looking to the abundance of the future, then All Hallows Eve was the time of honouring the ancestors, of reflection within and of giving voice to gratitude for the blessings of the harvest.

It had certainly been a year of discoveries and mixed blessings for the Lovedays, and the time was right to pay tribute to their dead in a celebration by the living.

Old quarrels and antagonisms were put aside and a compromise united the Lovedays. They were gathered in the grounds of Trevowan, which was part of the agreed truce, as Adam and Rowena were both adamant that they would not enter the main house while Tristan was its master. At the same time they were beholden to him for his part in the rescue of Aunt Elspeth and Rowena.

The celebration on the last day of October was held a week after the men returned from Somerset. They had stayed until a mine engineer had given his report on the minerals within the tunnel and the cost of extracting them. As an outward mark of unity they had chosen as a moment of reconciliation the unveiling of the aviary designed by Adam for Lady Alys. Even the weather had smiled benignly upon them. The first of the autumn gales had yet to arrive, and although the trees were scattering showers of russet leaves on the sea breeze, the sun was shining and the day was unseasonably warm.

Tristan had no intention of not using this moment to the full. Not only was the aviary to be presented to his neighbours in its full glory, the occasion marked a turning point in his acceptance as

335

master of Trevowan and a member of the Loveday family. It was an opportunity to show to the community that he had the wealth to match any of his cousins, and to that end no expense had been spared to impress everyone present.

The bird flight was screened from the guests by a vast expanse of fabric stretched between two tall poles. Despite the lateness of the year, a garden luncheon was planned for the family and their friends. A silk pavilion had been erected on the lawn near to the orangery where food and drinks would be served, with chairs set out for the ladies should the weather turn cooler. Another large pavilion had been erected with a wooden floor laid within for dancing. A quartet of musicians had been engaged to play. The older children had returned to their boarding schools, but the younger ones were not forgotten. A troupe of tumblers had been hired and a puppeteer had set up his small theatre in the garden. Also games of battledore, hoop-la and lawn skittles had been provided for their amusement.

Elspeth, using crutches, had hobbled to the chaise longue set amongst a group of chairs and tables near the aviary. Rowena sat beside her. The younger woman visited her great-aunt every day at the Dower House, passing the time at cards, backgammon or chess to stop Elspeth fretting that she would be unable to hunt this season.

Since his return, Bryn had been the centre of attention, the family and neighbours intrigued by the drama of his experiences and his change of circumstances.

The men had drawn aside from the seated women and the noise of the children cheering the puppet show. The bluff figure of Sir Henry Traherne, his thinning red hair lifting in the breeze, was most interested in the mine. Of his own three tin mines, two of them were still productive. 'Will it be profitable to sink a shaft and mine the ore?'

'The engineer could give no guarantee how long the silver seam would last,' Bryn replied. 'They are not common in Somerset. Neither could he say how much it would yield. He was not optimistic that the yield would be high. Also he would need to make deeper cuttings to predict the durability of the lead to be mined.'

'It can be a costly business,' Sir Henry confirmed. 'Not just a tower and building for the mine workings, but keeping the mine drained at deeper levels and of course bringing the ore to the surface.'

'The silver seam is not far from the surface, neither is some of the lead ore,' Bryn explained. 'It could be open-mined, but that would destroy a lot of the farmland and may not be viable. If there is enough silver to allow me to rebuild, that would be sufficient for my present needs. There is also the position of the mine to consider. It will be closer to the house than would be desirable. Where we were advised to dig the shaft to increase the ventilation to the mine was in the centre of the hamlet. That could be a reason why, if the seam was small, with little profit, it would not have been practicable to excavate in the past.'

'If that is the case, Carforth did you a favour by razing the cottages,' Tristan observed. 'They could be rebuilt elsewhere. Miners will need accommodation, as well as the workers on your land. You may find quite a large community is created. And what of the cost of the renovations to the house? Would it be cheaper to rebuild further away from the mine?'

'It will cost a great deal,' Adam confessed. 'And take many years of work. Bryn is young, and that is to his benefit.'

'Unless he has a mind to take a wife before he is thirty,' Japhet jested. 'Expensive luxury, wives. Stay free and single as long as you are able.'

Bryn blushed. 'I am too young to consider that part of my future. Willow Vale will take all my energy and time for many years to come. Yet much relies on the bounty of the mine.' He refused to be downhearted. 'A less expensive option would be dig the shaft directly over the seam of silver and bring it up that way. That would take fewer miners and we could learn if the seam extends further. There should be profit enough to plough the land for crops, clear the meadows and fix the boundaries for livestock to be reared. With a good mine captain this can be done whilst I live simply in the undamaged rooms of the house. Within five years I hope to be in a position to rebuild the property. I would first spend some months working in other mines to learn something of the industry.'

'That is most commendable,' Sir Henry returned. 'There are papers at the hall detailing the work and expansion of my mines over the years, which you are welcome to study.'

'I would be most appreciative of that, Sir Henry.'

'It is important that you hire the right mine captain,' Sir Henry added. 'I shall make some enquiries if you wish. And of course you are welcome to visit my mines and speak to my captain whenever you like.'

'That is more than I had hoped, sir.' The lines of worry that had creased Bryn's brow in recent weeks became less prominent. At first the task ahead of him had seemed overwhelming. Living as far away as Somerset, he could not expect the support and help from his adoptive family that would have been his if Willow Vale was closer. His future path would not be easy, but it was looking as though in time he could achieve his goals of re-establishing the land and house.

Bryn turned to Davey who had been silent throughout the conversation. He was here alone, Hannah and his sisters having returned to Devon. 'My adventures this summer have been no less exulted than Davey's. He has established himself as master of the Rabsom farm, his encounter with the Jowetts no less courageous.'

Davey shook his head. There was an air of maturity and confidence that had not been apparent when he took up his inheritance in April. 'I did nothing that any Loveday would not have done to protect their land and loved ones.'

Adam grinned and respectfully put a hand on his nephew's back. 'Your father would have been proud of you. The Jowetts are dangerous men.'

Tristan studied the young farmer, his expression guarded. 'They tested the measure of you and if they are wise will not make the same mistake again. Your bravery was admirable.'

Bryn saw a clouding in Adam's eyes as his gaze flickered over Tristan. Was his guardian still suspicious of Tristan's motives? There was definitely a crackle of tension now in the air.

A gong sounded and Tristan raised his voice to carry to all their guests. 'The time for the unveiling has come. That honour falls to my dear wife.'

Lady Alys, elegant in a gown of jonquil-sprigged muslin with a deep blue pelisse and matching feathers in her coiled hair, smiled graciously at her audience. 'This is a proud moment for me, the more especially as it is shared with such supportive and wonderful friends and family. I ask that you do not applaud when I unveil the aviary, as that will unsettle the birds, which are still becoming acclimatised to their new home. Also I have to honour the architect who designed this beautiful bird flight, Captain Adam Loveday, and my dear husband Tristan for digging so deeply into his coffers to ensure that I would continue to enjoy the pleasure many of these birds have given to me since my childhood. May they also give you all great pleasure.'

She pulled the cord and the curtain slide aside. There was a fluttering of many wings, mingling with the sighs of delight as the bird flight and its colourful occupants were revealed.

The popinjays in their bright array of red and blue and yellow coats bobbed up and down on their perches like actors bowing at the end of a grand performance. Within smaller sections of the large construction finches twittered and the canaries and linnets competed to raise the loudest song.

'I have never seen anything so splendid,' Senara praised, whilst the children ran around the sides of the aviary pointing in excitement at birds they had never seen before.

There was a loud screech and two pairs of peacocks marched in front of the cage, the males shaking their long tails and twitching them ready to display the great fan of their feathers with their decorative eyes. There was regality to their parade, as though they refused to be upstaged in their splendour.

Japhet shielded his eyes from the sun to gaze up at the tall structure. 'Is building aviaries instead of ships to be a new venture of yours, cousin?' He grinned. 'They could become quite the vogue.'

'I believe I shall stay with ships. I have neglected my duties at the yard this summer. I thought as we became older that our lives would be less fraught with these escapades.' Adam kept his voice serious, but there was a mocking glint in his eyes.

'A man needs his challenges if his wits are not to go stale,' responded Japhet. He nodded towards Tristan. 'I doubt that one will keep his fingers out of any illicit pies for long. I heard rumours that he has been in league with the Jowetts on more than one occasion.'

'Then between ourselves we should keep an eye out that he does not bring any of the family down with him. He could destroy all the work you have achieved with your stud farm and the integrity I have built up with the shipyard if his actions bring our name into ill-repute.'

'Our cousin has too much to lose himself now, and he has the wits to stay several steps ahead of the law.' There was grudging admiration in Japhet's voice.

Elspeth lifted her hand to beckon Lady Alys to her side and then sucked in her lips when the younger woman began to fuss.

'Are you warm enough, Aunt? Shall I summon Jenna to fetch your shawl? Or would you prefer more mulled wine?'

'I have everything I need,' Elspeth sniffed. 'And voice enough to command servants to do my will.' Her expression brightened. 'We have come far this day to get those three fighting cocks together on Trevowan land.'

'Though not without you and Rowena suffering outlandishly.' Lady Alys patted the old woman's hand with affection.

'Adam will never forget that Tristan organised the search for Rowena. The minx has caused more than her share of upsets in recent years. She seems more settled at Boscabel.' Elspeth nodded her approval. 'She insisted that Thea and George be allowed to attend. It would have been a shame if they had missed the puppet show. I fear however that she herself is grudging in her presence here. She has not forgiven Tristan.'

'It means a great deal to me that the family are here today, and to Tristan.' Lady Alys sighed. 'Though Felicity still shuns us.'

'She rarely ventures from the cottage.' Elspeth's eyes flashed with disgust. 'Trevanion's conduct this spring humiliated her. She takes such gossip too much to heart.'

Lady Alys leaned forward and lowered her voice. 'There is news. I do not wish Felicity to hear this from any but one of the family. Trevanion married last month. It is said his bride is barely sixteen. She is the youngest of five daughters of a Member of Parliament very close to the Prince of Wales, all of whom are reputed to have been much in the company of the royal dukes.'

'There is no fool like an old lecher,' Elspeth tutted. 'I hope the young flibbertigibbet leads him a merry dance.'

There was an outburst of laughter and Lady Alys smiled when she saw Rowena and Bryn in animated conversation.

Bryn had been appalled when he had learned of Rowena's suffering at the hands of the kidnappers, and blamed himself that she had been in such danger. 'You have been spending a lot of time with Aunt Elspeth. I have not had a proper chance to express how sorry I am that you faced such a terrible ordeal because of me. Tristan said that the kidnappers were in the pay of Carforth. They had seen the closeness we shared and thought by kidnapping you they would be able to get to me. I would have willingly given myself up in your place.'

'It taught me how unwise it is for a young woman to ride alone.'

'You were incredibly brave to escape from them.'

Now that the ordeal was far behind her, Rowena basked in the glory of his praise. 'It never does to underestimate a Loveday. They thought as a woman I would be at their mercy. It was enterprising of me to remove the glass from the window and climb out, was it not?'

'More than enterprising; it was magnificent.' Bryn humoured her; she had astounded him by her courage.

'Though there was no fun in tramping across the moor at night. For that alone I believe you should pay some forfeit for my suffering.'

'And what forfeit would you have in mind? Do I become your whipping boy for the next few months, or your personal slave? I am indeed your devoted servant.'

'That I have not decided as yet. But with winter approaching the days can be misty and confine us to our home. I expect during that time to be suitably entertained.'

'Will I not have to stand in line with a long queue of eager beaux?' he teased. 'You received your first proposal of marriage this year; that must have been gratifying, despite the unfortunate circumstances.'

'Felicity should be grateful to me for Trevanion showing his true colours.' Her mouth formed a provocative smile. 'But he was not my only proposal this summer.'

The laughter faded from his eyes. 'Indeed? Did you accept?'

'I have no wish to be an officer's wife.'

'What kind of a wife do you aspire to be?'

'Above all one who is married to a man who loves me and does not spend years of his life trailing the globe in search of glory. It would be nice to be mistress of my own manor and have my villeins and servants adore me.'

She was adept at flirting and Bryn felt himself floundering out of his depth. 'And no doubt this man you would honour would have to be immensely rich, young, dashing and handsome, and will rescue you from your life of deprivation and squalor on a white charger.'

'A young woman can dream, can she not?' She laughed.

'And like many foolish maidens tonight on All Hallows Eve you will be gazing into a mirror before you retire to see if the image of your future husband appears over your shoulder.' He kept a tight rein on the inappropriate rush of jealousy.

'That is for the addle-pated and superstitious. When I meet the man I wish to marry he will be in no doubt of my intentions, and in such matters I shall ensure I win the heart of the man I have chosen.' Her eyes danced with mischief and a hint of a sultry, beguiling promise. When Bryn did not rise to her baiting, she spun on the ball of her foot and walked away with a seductive sway to her hips, her voice soft as she glanced back over her shoulder. 'But for now I shall enjoy the hunt and choose with care my prey. Is that not the advice my uncles would give to you?'

As ever the sun seemed to lose it brightness and the merriment its vibrancy when Rowena walked away. Bryn shook his head. Heaven help the man that minx set her heart and mind upon.

There was a series of shrieks from the younger children, who were standing around a barrel that had been cut in half whilst they bobbed for apples in the water. George had fallen in. He stood in the barrel, water running from his hair and clothes, as Bridie and Senara ran to rescue him. He was howling with laughter rather than tears as he splashed the gathered children, sending them screaming across the lawns. Bryn laughed as he saw Captain Loveday scoop up his young nephew, drenching his own clothes in the process as George squirmed in the excitement that his misbehaviour had caused. With many of the children and also the adults wet from his assault, the Lovedays bade their farewells to each other and headed for their homes.

Elspeth waved aside Tristan's help to assist her to the Dower House and continued to watch her family with a secretive glow of contentment spreading through her. A rare moment of peace and equilibrium had settled over the turbulent passions of her loved ones. She would savour it while it lasted, for she doubted it would be long before tradition roused their rivalry or a quest for new adventures, and the peace would again be shattered.